HYMN TO MURDER

HYMN TO MURDER

PAUL DOHERTY

HEADLINE

First published in 2020 by
HEADLINE PUBLISHING GROUP

1

Cataloguing in Publication Data is available from the British Library

ISBN 978 1 4722 5918 9

Typeset in Sabon LT Std 11.25/14.5 pt by
Palimpsest Book Production Limited, Falkirk, Stirlingshire

Printed and bound in Great Britain by Clays Ltd, Elcograf S.p.A.

Headline's policy is to use papers that are natural, renewable and
recyclable products and made from wood grown in sustainable forests.
The logging and manufacturing processes are expected to conform
to the environmental regulations of the country of origin.

HEADLINE PUBLISHING GROUP
An Hachette UK Company
Carmelite House
50 Victoria Embankment
London EC4Y 0DZ

www.headline.co.uk
www.hachette.co.uk

*To our wonderful children
Julianna and Alexander Zajda,
with love from their parents.*

CHARACTER LIST

Edward I	King of England
Edward II	King of England, son of the above
Eleanor of Castile	Wife of Edward I, Queen of England
Isabella	Wife of Edward II, Queen of England
Sir Hugh Corbett	Keeper of the Secret Seal, Edward II's personal envoy
Ranulf-atte-Newgate	Sir Hugh Corbett's henchman, principal clerk in the Chancery of the Green Wax
Lady Maeve	Wife of Sir Hugh Corbett and mother of their two children, Edward and Eleanor
Chanson	Clerk of the Stables in the retinue of Sir Hugh Corbett
Ap Ythel	Welshman, master bowman in the retinue of Sir Hugh Corbett
Brancepeth	Welsh master bowman, Ap Ythel's henchman
John Wodeford	Mailed clerk in the service of Sir Hugh Corbett
Merioneth	Former bestiarius in the service of Sir Hugh Corbett

Richard Puddlicot	Bankrupt merchant, leader of a gang of rifflers
Tooth-pull	
Rievaulx	Members of Puddlicot's gang
Adam Warfeld	Benedictine monk, sacristan at Westminster Abbey
Walter Brasenose	Warfeld's henchman
Glaston	City jeweller
Sir Ralph Hengham	Tax collector in the king's shires of Devon and Cornwall
Sir Miles Wendover	Sheriff of Devon
Lord Simon Malmaison	Lord of the manor of the same name, former mailed clerk
Wolfram	Mailed clerk also in Corbett's retinue, Malmaison's henchman
Lady Katerina	Wolfram's sister
Edmund Brockle	Steward of the manor of Malmaison
Chandos	Steward of the manor of Malmaison
Lady Beatrice Davenant	Malmaison's first wife
Lady Isabella	Malmaison's second wife
Henry Malach	Malmaison's henchman
Grease-hair	Spit-boy at the manor of Malmaison
Colum the cook	Servant at Malmaison
Master Dunston	Courier at Malmaison
Tallien	Travelling tinker
William Fitzwarren	Captain of the cog *The Angel of the Dawn*
Odo Beauchamp	Captain of the cog *The Galliard*
Fulbert	Tanner, leader of the guildsmen of Felstead
Richolda	Fulbert's wife, leader of the guildsmen's womenfolk
Parson Osbert	Parish priest of the church at Felstead

Baskerville	Minehost and taverner of the Palfrey in Felstead
Lord Moses	Leader of the moon people
Aaron and Joshua	Lord Moses's henchmen
Peter Gaveston	Gascon favourite of King Edward II
Philip IV	King of France
Charles of Valois	Philip's brother
Boniface VIII & Clement V	Popes

HISTORICAL NOTE

The last decade of the reign of Edward I of England (1272–1307) was not a successful one. Edward was forced to make a marriage alliance with France for his heir apparent Edward of Caernarvon. He had conquered Wales, but when he turned on Scotland, his assault proved to be one disaster after another. The Scots resisted fiercely under William Wallace and then under his brilliant field commander, Robert the Bruce. English troops and treasure poured into Scotland, but victory eluded Edward. The question of money and the lack of revenue for the Crown worsened when the most daring robbery in English history was staged. In 1303, the Crown Jewels and countless other treasures stored in the great crypt at Westminster Abbey were plundered by a gang made up of not only the denizens of London's underworld, but monks of the abbey, who acted hand in glove with the city's wolfsheads.

The old king died on his way to Scotland in July

1307; his heir abandoned the Scottish war and retreated south to recall his favourite, the Gascon Peter Gaveston. The new king lavished treasures on Gaveston and created him Earl of Cornwall. If London needed strong rule, so did Cornwall and the south-western shires of the kingdom. Lawlessness prevailed across the realm, and in the dark that descended, all sorts of malignants emerged to wreak damage and bring the Crown's rule deeper into disrepute.

Please note: the extracts before each chapter are from the confession of the master thief Richard Puddlicot, still extant in manuscript form in the National Archives (Kew): King's Remembrancer: E/101/332/8.

PROLOGUE

The confession of Richard Puddlicot: he claims he was an itinerant trader in wool, cheese and butter.

1303

'And darkness fell.' The chroniclers of London often quoted this phrase, taken from the story of Judas's betrayal of Jesus Christ, to describe the sinfulness of their own city. In particular the men and women who had made vows to Christ yet spent most of their time and energy in violating such oaths rather than honouring them. This was certainly true in the king's own chapel, the great abbey of Westminster. By the last week of April, the Year of Our Lord 1303, the Blackrobes of Westminster, Benedictine monks, had waxed strong and prosperous, lavishly patronised by the Crown as they had been since the abbey's first great founding centuries before. How things had changed! The king's own chapel was no longer a house of prayer but a den of thieves. The monks, who were meant to follow the rule of St Benedict, had turned their energies to matters of the dark. They were supposed to love the light and live in it. Now they lay firmly under the rule of a false shepherd, the powerful and resolute Adam Warfeld, chief sacristan of the abbey, the monk directly responsible for its security.

For some time Warfeld had lurked in the twilight. However, during those last few days of spring, he brought his wickedness to full ripeness. On Wednesday 24 April, his great conspiracy to commit treason and robbery at last bore fruit. Warfeld had seduced his community. He and the bankrupt merchant Richard Puddlicot had entertained the Blackrobes to nights of revelry where wine flowed like water, served to the good brothers by a whole cohort of delectable ladies of the night. On that particular evening, however, Warfeld struck.

Darkness fell. All the lights in the cemetery were doused, as well as those across the great wasteland that separated the abbey from the royal palace. Men, hooded and visored, carrying powerful war bows and arbalests, patrolled the nearby royal gardens, God's Acre and the broad stretch of common. Warfeld and his coven were committed. The frescoes and carvings that decorated the abbey walls, depicting Christ at the Final Judgement, were totally ignored. The statues of saints and angels, the gargoyles and babewynes that festooned the stonework of the main church, meant nothing to the men assembling deep in the shadows. They had planned well. Earlier in the year, hempen seed had been sown, a swiftgrowing weed that masked their handiwork around one of the windows of the crypt. A great treasure hoard was almost within their grasp: the jewels and royal regalia of England as well as coffers and caskets crammed with precious stones, silver and gold coins, goblets, jugs, chalices, cups, saucers and spoons, not to mention unique treasures such as the Cross of Neath and the Rod of Moses. Above all, the crypt housed what was judged to be the most precious and gorgeous ruby in the world, the so-called Lacrima Christi, nestling in its thick gold casket. The ruby was priceless, worth more than a hundred kings' ransoms, a stone envied and lusted after by all the princes of Christendom and beyond.

On that night, the chosen night, the eve of the feast of St Mark, the Lacrima Christi was about to begin a strange journey. Edward, King of England, together with his council and troops, was far away. The old king had journeyed north across the Scottish March to wage war with fire and sword against Bruce and other Scottish rebels. The palace of Westminster lay empty except for its steward, William, but he too had been suborned by Warfeld and was a close accomplice to the mischief being plotted.

Edward of England truly believed that his treasure was well housed in the gloomy, forbidding crypt deep beneath the abbey, a sacred, hallowed place. The crypt was an octagonal building, its walls eighteen feet thick, and the king regarded it as most safe and secure. Its sole entrance was a strongly fortified doorway in the west wall that led onto a staircase, broken halfway down by a three-yard gap that could only be spanned by a moveable wooden bridge. It did, however, have one weakness, and Warfeld had discovered this. Its six windows were at ground level; one of these, protected by the screed of hempen seed, had been chosen by the robbers. Its stone sill had been hacked and cut away by a master stonemason, John of St Alban's. He had worked at night, the glow of his lantern hidden by the tangle of weeds, destroying the sill, and wrenching out the iron bars to create an open space through which the robbers could enter before sliding down into the crypt itself.

Richard Puddlicot, leader of the rifflers drawn from London's underworld, watched the final preparations. Once satisfied, he stood aside to allow the tall, forbidding Adam Warfeld first passage into the crypt. Warfeld had repudiated his own rule and didn't give a whit. He had plotted and planned for this great moment, so he had to be the first to slide down into the treasure house. He was followed by Brasenose and other monks, at least fourteen in number, and their henchmen Rievaulx and Glaston. The latter was a city jeweller who had advised Warfeld on what the crypt might hold, especially the Lacrima Christi.

Once they reached the hard tiled floor, lanterns were lit, cresset torches fired and placed in their sconces, the light strengthening to reveal all the treasures heaped there. The cries and shouts of appreciation drew more of the gang down. Scrambling into the crypt, they did not even wait but started to fill their leather bags with fistfuls of jewels, silver figurines and miniature gold crosses. The sight of such precious items only fired their greed, but they paused at the sound of a bone-cracking blow followed by a hideous scream. The robbers stopped their plundering to gape at Adam Warfeld, the bland-faced Puddlicot standing beside him. The sacristan looked a truly sinister, threatening figure in his black robe, a dagger in one hand, a blood-soaked battle mace in the other.

'Listen!' Warfeld pointed at the man lying on the ground before him, his skull shattered, blood, brains and fragments of bone, seeping across the tiled floor. 'Listen and listen well.' His powerful voice echoed around the crypt and up to where others stood on guard in the cemetery. 'All treasure must be piled here.' He turned and, using the battle mace, pointed at a stretch of canvas Brasenose had rolled out across the floor. 'Fill your bags by all means, but only to carry the treasure here. Blacktongue' – he kicked the dead felon's corpse – 'thought he could hide a pendant down the front of his filthy jerkin. He paid the price and you must heed the warning.'

The gang, at least twenty strong, murmured their agreement. They moved the treasure, piling it up on the canvas cloth so it could be inspected by Glaston the goldsmith, who was almost beside himself with excitement. One of Warfeld's monks had brought over a bulging velvet pouch. Glaston loosened the cord, drew out the small but heavy gold casket and opened this to moan in pleasure at the sight of the world's most precious ruby, the Lacrima Christi.

'Keep it well.' Glaston spun around. Warfeld, still holding the battle mace, was staring down at him. 'Glaston, that's your portion. It will be very difficult to sell, so what you do with it is up to you.' Warfeld pointed to the open window. 'Goodbye, my friend, but rest assured, you will be watched . . .'

Six months later, on the eve of All Hallows, Glaston the jeweller had good cause to recall that night and his first glimpse of the Lacrima Christi, which was now hidden away in his house just off Thames Street. Earlier that winter day he had joined the crowds surging out of London to witness the execution of Richard Puddlicot. The great robber and crypt breaker had been seized and tried before a special commission in the Tower. Puddlicot could offer no defence and had been sentenced to hang on a specially erected gallows outside the main gate of Westminster Abbey, as close as they could to where he had committed his outrageous crimes.

Glaston made his way down a needle-thin runnel. At least the frost had frozen the dirt and ordure strewn across the broken cobbles. The jeweller pulled his patched cloak closer about him. The weather had turned savagely cold, yet he was soaked in a deep sweat. In truth, he was terrified. His heart beat like that of a hunted hare, his skin soaked by the terrors that never seemed to leave him. Glaston lived alone: his wife had left him a decade ago and his trade had suffered. He had been reduced to selling gewgaws, paltry items for a few pence. Six months ago, he had hoped to use the Lacrima Christi, his portion of the plunder, to escape abroad and build a new life.

He clutched at his belly and winced at a sudden spasm, so strong he almost threw himself into a corner tavern boasting the sign of 'The Morning Star'. He hurried across its sweet-smelling taproom into the cobbled yard that housed the latrines. Once he had finished, his points tied securely, his cloak firmly clasped, he re-entered the taproom, where he sat in an ill-lit corner and ordered a goblet of Bordeaux, staring around furtively at the other customers. In the main, these were journeymen who had been entertaining the crowds as they surged down to Westminster. The garishly garbed storyteller now sat with the relic-seller with his tray of so-called holy items on the floor beside him. Across the taproom, the fire-eater quenched his thirst, raising his tankard in toast to the two whores he had hired to tumble in an upstairs chamber.

Glaston supped at his wine, trying to quell the tremor in his hand. He was certain he was being watched, followed, kept under close scrutiny, a feeling he could not shake off even though he failed to define the shadows haunting him. He cradled the goblet and stared down at the floor, kicking at the filthy rushes as a rat, sudden and swift, scurried for shelter. Glaston felt as if he was the same. He was hiding from the light, fearful of everything and everyone. How things had changed. Fortune's fickle wheel had turned. At first the great robbery at Westminster had been a triumph. The rifflers of London had toasted the perpetrators, hailing them as great lords of the underworld. Puddlicot and his gang had promptly disappeared into the stinking slums of Whitechapel and elsewhere. They did not wish to glory in their plunder. Most of the leaders desperately tried to seek passage abroad; until then, they would remain hidden. Adam Warfeld and his monks, however, had simply retreated behind the walls of their abbey, ever ready to claim clerical privilege and benefit of clergy to any law officer stupid enough to try to force his way into the monastic enclosure.

Sandewic, Edward I's boon companion and constable at the Tower, had tried his best, as had the London sheriffs, all to no avail. The king was being openly ridiculed and taunted. The London mob, that ever-hungry beast, flexed its muscles. Proclamations mocking the king and glorying in the robbery had been posted on the Standard at Cheapside and the Great Cross in St Paul's churchyard – and then Sir Hugh Corbett had arrived. The Keeper of the Secret Seal brought a retinue of mailed clerks to assist him: Ranulf-atte-Newgate, Wolfram, Wodeford, Lord Simon Malmaison and others.

Corbett fulfilled one verse from scripture in resolving the challenges and problems facing him. He feared neither God nor man. He had taken Sandewic's troops from the Tower and forced himself into the abbey, totally ignoring its abbot's strictures. He and his cohort had carried out a ruthless ransacking. Some of the monks had been very stupid. Treasure was found beneath beds, behind aumbries, in herb plots, flower beds, even in a latrine. Corbett had swept Westminster like God's own storm. Both abbey and palace were turned upside down. He then moved across the city, empanelling juries in every ward, listening to reports about anything suspicious. Arrests were made.

The rifflers decided to break and flee; those caught red handed faced summary justice. Two thieves were beheaded at the Cross in Cheapside, eight more hanged just outside Newgate. The gang scattered, every man left to his own devices. Some – and Glaston ground his teeth – had turned king's evidence; they became approvers, Judas men, suing for a royal pardon in return for a full and frank confession, listing the names of accomplices and providing evidence against them. The most serious of these was the betrayal by the riffler Rievaulx, who wreaked hideous damage with his revelations. Corbett had then divided his mailed clerks like a huntsman would a pack of hounds. Wolfram pursued this felon, Wodeford that. Lord Simon Malmaison – wolf-faced Malmaison with his slanted eyes, narrow, pocked face and thin, bloodless lips – was assigned to search for the Lacrima Christi and other precious stones. Glaston moaned quietly to himself as he slurped at the wine. He had glimpsed Malmaison around the city with his bullyboy Wolfram. A man of blood, Lord Simon had acquired a most chilling reputation.

A bell began to toll, and the other customers shuffled to their feet, shouting excitedly that the execution was about to begin. Glaston drained his cup. In truth, he should avoid the gallows and scaffold in Tothill Street, close to the abbey, yet he felt compelled to witness Puddlicot's final moments. He pulled his hood over his head and joined the rest hurrying along the maze of alleys and runnels, which reeked to high heaven of dirt and filth. The tenements, the mumpers' castles of the lost of London that lined these spindle-thin paths, were propped up by makeshift struts and rotting planks, their windows sealed by bulging iron-bound shutters. Nevertheless, people lived here; the dark-dwellers, the midnight folk crammed in like lice on a slab of putrid meat. Puddlicot had drawn his gang, his supporters from these nightmare places where smoke and stench constantly circled and shifted. Now and again a voice cried, a woman screamed, a man shouted. Glaston kept his head down, then froze when he heard his name called. He paused at a corner and turned to confront the weasel-faced man behind him.

'Master Glaston.' Weasel-face grinned, his sore mouth gaping to reveal yellow stumps. 'I am Tooth-pull,' he declared, bleary eyes glittering. His voice dropped to a whisper. 'I was with you at the abbey. I stood guard.'

Glaston stared in horror at this filthy shadow-dweller, then shook his head and hurried on. He pushed his way through the crowds and reached the execution ground at the end of Tothill Lane under the magnificent brooding mass of Westminster Abbey, a sheer forest of stone with its sculptured cornices, ledges, sills, statues and gargoyles. The entire area heaved with a throng seldom seen; all of London seemed to have emptied to witness Puddlicot hang.

The soaring three-branched gallows had been well prepared, the black hanging tree rearing up starkly against the sky with a thin ladder leaning against one of the gallows' branches. On the platform beneath, the hangman and his henchmen stood waiting, fearsome figures in their scarlet masks and caps, black leather jerkins and leggings. It was now late morning, a sharp grey day; the showers had died away, though everything remained soaked and slippery. The weather had certainly not dampened the enthusiasm of respectable citizens, or that of the horde of dark-dwellers from the Kingdom of Chaos and the Mansions of the Moon, where Puddlicot had been hailed as a prince amongst thieves. Miscreants of every kind and hue were impatient to watch the hanging of one of their own lords.

The grotesquely painted whores in their blood-red wigs and white-plastered faces were eager for business. These ladies of the night were herded by their pimps, garbed in motley rags, knives pushed through their rope belts; each carried a small bucket ready to collect the coins of anyone desperate enough to hire a common whore. The conjurors also sought business, clacking their dice ready to predict the future for anyone stupid enough to believe them. Heralds of the dusk, tale-tellers living in the twilight of the city, now emerged to recount stories and legends about the man set to hang. Executions always whetted appetites, so itinerant cooks, water-carriers, ale-sellers and wine-servers hustled and bustled to sell their goods. Guilds and fraternities continued to chant psalms and hymns of mourning. The air was riven by singing, jeering and catcalling. Smoke curled up from the moveable stoves to mingle with the stench of human sweat and other odours. Roasting meat, well past its prime as it crackled in rancid fat, exuded a foulness that merged with the sweet fragrances gusting up from incense thuribles and herb pots.

A shout went up. The execution party was approaching! Standing on tiptoes, Glaston glimpsed the wheelbarrow in which Puddlicot had been placed, a small cart being pulled by horses and escorted by Tower archers. It was pushed forward and stopped before the steps leading up to the execution platform. The noise of the crowd was deafening. The Fraternity of the Hanged and the Brotherhood of the Noose tried to chant the Miserere. A group of Friars of the Sack recited the De Profundis – 'Out of the depths do I cry to you, O Lord' – but their words were swept away by the hideous din. The bellowing of the mob was now constant as it surged backwards and forwards. A coven of witches, wizards and warlocks fought to draw closer, desperate to crawl beneath the execution platform, daggers at the ready, because the flesh and clothing of a hanged man allegedly contained magical properties.

Puddlicot, a mass of bruises from head to toe, simply stood, hands hanging by his sides, head down, moving like a sleepwalker, pushed and shoved to where the hangman wanted him. The executioner now moved a second, thin ladder to rest beside the one already in place against the gallows' branch. The sheriff in charge clapped his hands. The heralds flourished their trumpets and blew one fanfare after another until a profound, brooding silence descended like a mist over Tothill. One of the sheriff's men then proclaimed how Richard Puddlicot had been judged guilty of heinous felonies and was worthy of death with no hope of pardon, so sentence should be carried out immediately.

The hangman moved with alacrity. Held by the archers, Puddlicot was pushed up one ladder whilst the executioner scaled the one alongside it. He reached the top rung and, balancing himself carefully, fitted the noose around Puddlicot's neck, positioning the knot directly behind the left ear. Then he hurriedly descended, leaving the condemned man, hands tightly bound before him, perched on the top rung. Tambours began to beat. The hangman seized the ladder Puddlicot was perched on and abruptly twisted it. Puddlicot fell like a stone and the crack of his breaking neck could be clearly heard. A great sigh echoed from the crowd, a prolonged gasp of breath. For a few moments there was silence, but then the crowd's interest quickened as Puddlicot's corpse was stripped naked and placed on the cutting table. Glaston recalled how the king had proclaimed that the corpse should be peeled. The skin would then be cured and dried before being nailed to the door of Westminster Abbey, a grim warning to its miscreant monks.

Glaston had seen enough. He turned, pushing his way through the crowd, desperate to reach his narrow two-storey house on Thames Street. A dilapidated, decaying building, it nevertheless stood in its own large plot and was comfortable enough, even though the great city cesspit just beyond its garden wall was a perpetual nuisance, deep, thick and reeking of every filth. He scurried down the street and unlocked the front door, creeping along the stone-flagged mildewed passageway to the small kitchen and buttery. As soon as he entered, he realised he was in danger. It was cold. He glanced at the windows; one of them had its shutters pushed back. He looked to his right and gasped at the dark, threatening figure sitting in his chair at the end of the kitchen table.

'Good morrow, Master Glaston.'

The intruder lifted the large lanternhorn from the floor beside him and pulled back its shutters so the dancing light bathed the sharp, wolf-like face of Lord Simon Malmaison, mailed clerk, man-hunter, Corbett's living scourge. He bent down again and picked up a small hand-held arbalest, its feathered bolt ready in the groove. This he carefully placed on the table together with a Welsh stabbing dirk, its razor-like blade winking in the light.

'Sit down, Master Glaston, please sit down.' He gestured to the stool at his right. 'Sit down,' he bellowed. Glaston hastened to obey. 'Very good.' Malmaison leant closer. 'I won't waste your time so you must not waste mine. Understood?' Glaston gulped and nodded vigorously. 'You see,' Lord Simon continued as if conversing with a close friend, 'I am so very, very busy. I have so many matters to attend to here in the city yet I must hasten back to Malmaison, a fine manor house, my friend, high on Doone Moor. Do you know it?'

Glaston just shook his head; this intruder truly terrified him.

'I am needed back there,' Malmaison continued quietly. 'I have heard stories about my dear, darling wife Beatrice. Then there is my steward Chandos, whom I must hold to account. I really should hasten back. I have also got my eye on two young leopards. They are kept in the royal menagerie in the Tower – have you seen them?' Again Glaston, soaked in sweat, just shook his head. 'Magnificent animals, skilled hunters. Gifts from a prince of Morocco. The royal cages in the Tower are becoming rather crowded; I wonder if the Crown, in return for my good service, will allow me to purchase the beasts.'

He paused, smiling to himself. 'I did raise this with His Grace the king when the royal council sat in the Tower recently. We were there to discuss the robbery at Westminster Abbey.' He laughed. 'But of course you know all about that, don't you? Anyway, I asked the king and he said he was agreeable to such a sale, but he was being sarcastic. Do you know what he said next? No, no, of course you wouldn't.' Lord Simon stared around. 'I'd like something to drink, but everything in this place is filthy. Anyway, to get back to the matter in hand . . .'

He picked up the dagger and drove its point into the tabletop, a sudden, darting movement. Glaston moaned in fear. 'The king said I should use the leopards to hunt down and kill those wrecking ships off Monkshood Bay and other places along the coast, all within riding distance of my manor house. Well, I don't give a shit about that. Anyway, as I was in the Tower, I decided to have words with your confederate Richard Puddlicot. As you know, he took refuge in St Michael's Church until Sir Hugh Corbett plucked him out to be tried by a special commission held in the White Tower. Now,' Lord Simon leant closer, lips pursed, finger wagging, 'I won't waste your time, Master Glaston, and you must not waste mine, understood?'

The jeweller gulped, nodding vigorously.

'The Lord be praised,' Malmaison purred. 'Now, I visited Puddlicot in the death house beneath the gateway. He realised he was going to hang and there was nothing he could do about it.' Lord Simon tittered with laughter, fingers fluttering before his mouth, and Glaston realised that this most sinister man was wicked and wilful. 'Richard and I, oh yes, we became good friends. We reached an agreement. He would give me the name of the thief who held the Lacrima Christi, and do you know what I offered him in return?' Glaston just shook his head. 'I would arrange that the noose that hanged him would be placed carefully so his neck would break. He would die quickly.' Malmaison snapped his fingers. 'As quick as that.' He smiled cruelly. 'For as you might find out, if the rope is wrongly placed, you could choke for an hour.'

He smacked his lips as if savouring a fine wine. 'Now, Master Glaston, I want that ruby and its case. I want it now. I know you have it. Puddlicot maintained that Warfeld gave it to you, and of course I had my own suspicions. Tooth-pull has kept you under strict watch – oh yes, he sued for a royal pardon. You certainly act furtively, a man with a great deal to hide. Now, if you refuse to cooperate, I will arrest you. I will personally ensure that you strangle to death for as long as the flame on an hour candle burns from one ring to another. Before that, of course, you will be in the rat-infested condemned hold at Newgate.' Again Malmaison smirked. 'In fact the gaolers there are worse than the rats.

'Anyway, as you can see, I want the Lacrima Christi more than anything else in the world.' He jabbed a finger in Glaston's face. 'I have told you my reasons and I am more than prepared to be reasonable.' He dug beneath his jerkin and drew out a money pouch, which he threw onto the table. 'Give me the Lacrima Christi and you can have this purse and my assurance that you will be free as a bird. You see, once I have the ruby, I will be gone. Not just from London, but from this kingdom. I think it's time for me to bask in the sun – perhaps a pleasant journey to Lucca. You know where that is, Glaston?'

The jeweller, sitting like a rabbit held by the death stare of a stoat, shook his head.

'Italy,' Malmaison breathed. 'Lucca houses a great relic, the imprint of Christ's sacred face. You see, on his way to the Cross, our Lord and Saviour had his face wiped on a veil by a woman called Veronica. The imprint was his response to such compassion. Now, my friend.' He pulled his chair closer. 'How say you?'

Glaston stared at his visitor's harsh face, glittering eyes and hooked nose over a slit mouth. He was growing wary of Malmaison's long, bony fingers not far from the arbalest. He took a deep breath and relaxed. There was no escape from the closing trap. He had to cooperate fully with this demon incarnate, who seemed as mad as a March hare. He pushed back the stool and rose to his feet.

'I will show you,' he muttered. 'It's best if you come with me.'

'I certainly shall,' Malmaison retorted. 'And you know I am a man of my word. Puddlicot died in a matter of heartbeats, didn't he? His skin is going to be dried, cured and pinned to a door. Interesting, mind you.' Malmaison now seemed lost in his own thoughts. 'I have heard a rumour that Warfeld and his miscreant monks are going to be exiled to some godforsaken corner of the kingdom.' He pushed back his chair and rose to his feet. 'And do you know where that is? No, of course you don't. Not far from my own manor there is a desolate derelict priory, St Benet's. Rumour has it that Warfeld and his coven have been banished there. I do wonder why that place was chosen.'

'So you can keep an eye on them?' Glaston stuttered nervously.

'I don't intend to be gaoler to criminous clerics who really should hang beside Puddlicot. God knows why St Benet's was chosen. The land is wild and desolate there, though Felstead, the nearby village, is comfortable enough. Our monks will certainly be lonely.'

'Are there other religious houses nearby?' Glaston offered, desperate to break the tension of this highly dangerous meeting.

'Not that I can think of. There is a village church where Parson Osbert is the parish priest, but he is just some country bumpkin; I wouldn't give him a second glance. Well?' Malmaison patted Glaston's shoulder. 'Let me see my heart's delight.'

They left the kitchen. Glaston fumbled with the keys on the hook of his belt. 'Will you leave for Malmaison immediately?' he asked.

'I certainly shall. I need to have words with my lovely Beatrice as well as my steward.' Again he patted Glaston on the shoulder. 'The days pass. I think it's time I returned home. Now . . .'

Glaston found the key and opened the narrow postern door. It led into a shabby, overgrown garden where the cold air still reeked of the stench from the nearby cesspit.

'Well, well.' Malmaison placed his lantern on a nearby wall. 'Come on, Glaston, give it to me, then you can go, free as a bird.'

Glaston hurried across to the battered, ruined water fountain. He crouched down, lifted one of the paving stones and drew out a thick leather pouch, which he immediately handed over to his nightmare visitor. Malmaison took it over to the lantern, undid it and drew out the brilliant gold casket. This he opened carefully, staring down at the magnificent ruby, which even in the poor light glowed like fire trapped behind the purest glass.

'By the face of Lucca,' he breathed. 'And so I have it. Oh yes, my friend, to hold this, even here in the cold darkness.' He paused. 'Look up at the stars, Master Glaston; surely the Lacrima Christi is more beautiful than any of them, wouldn't you agree? Look, look, look!'

Glaston did as he was told, and Malmaison lunged, fast as any viper, his dagger slicing Glaston's throat. Coughing and retching, the jeweller, glassy eyed, slumped to his knees. He drew one last gargling breath and then collapsed onto his side. Malmaison crouched down, turned the body and watched the life light fade in his victim's eyes. Once satisfied, he wiped his dagger blade on the dead man's cloak and picked up the precious casket. This he thrust back into its pouch, which disappeared into the deep pocket of his cloak.

Dragging Glaston's corpse by the collar of his jerkin, Malmaison pulled the dead man across the garden, through a side gate and onto a slight rise above the cesspit. He shoved the corpse with the toe of his boot and watched it tumble into the man-made quagmire. For a while, it lay sprawled on the surface, until the filth swirled in and the cadaver sank, disappearing deep into the slime.

'There you go,' he whispered. 'As I said, free as a bird.'

1305

'Continue to live as you have and the Lord Satan promises you a place in his kingdom.' The preacher, his face and arms burnt black by the sun of Outremer, thundered his warning. This prophet from the desert had suddenly appeared in Lyons and was now walking alongside the papal procession winding its way down to Gourguillon from the church of St Just, where, on 14 November in the Year of Our Lord 1305, Bertrand de Got, Archbishop of Bordeaux, had been crowned Pope Clement V.

'I bring a letter for you,' the preacher continued in a trumpet-like voice. 'The devil tells you to despise the life of poverty and the teaching of the apostles. Fight it! Hate it as Satan himself hates it. My Lord Pope, the devil says this: "Your mother Pride greets you. Your sisters Trickery, Avarice and Shamelessness do likewise, together with your brothers Incest, Robbery and

Murder." This is all contained in a letter drawn up in the depths of hell to the acclamation of a horde of demons who impatiently await your arrival.'

The preacher, hands extended, would have launched into another tirade, but retainers of the papal household seized him and dragged him away, beating him senseless with their clubs and leaving the shabbily dressed wanderer to sprawl in a widening pool of his own blood. Clement V hardly spared the miserable wretch a glance. Seated on his beautifully caparisoned pure-white palfrey, he basked in his own glory, his yellowing face creased in a fixed smile as he stared from under heavy-lidded eyes at the crowd that had flocked to witness the first crowning of a pope on French soil. Clement, however, just wanted to be away, out of the power of Philip of France, who walked alongside the papal palfrey holding its bridle, whilst on the other side, Philip's brother, Charles of Valois, also helped guide the mount. Both Capetian princes were determined to keep a firm hand on this pope who had decided to escape the ferocious factional fighting between the great families of Rome.

Clement had taken exile in Avignon, just beyond the borders of France yet near enough for sudden flight back into Italy, or even across the mountains into Spain. He was determined to transform the place into his own private paradise. He would plant pear and peach trees in gardens covered with flowers. In the branches of his orchards fledgling doves would try their wings above gurgling streams pouring across moss-strewn rocks to water his Eden. He would bring his entire household to live in finely constructed mansions: his troupes of buffoons, jesters and mummers, servants both male and female, secretaries, pages, squires and a host of equerries. These would supervise his goshawks, falcons, hunting dogs and Arab horses. However, that was for the future. For the moment, he was determined to revel in his new-found glory.

He clasped his white-gloved hands as if in prayer before touching the gorgeously decorated pearl-white tiara with its blood-red lappets. He had insisted that the tiara, the papal crown, be brought from Rome, for it was a symbol of his authority over both the visible and the invisible. It was fashioned out of pure white silk and lavishly decorated with a myriad of precious stones, which gleamed in a dazzling shimmer of colour. The crowning glory was a large wine-coloured ruby placed firmly between the two golden ribbons wound around the tiara.

Those who knew called this ruby the Lacrima Christi – the Tear of Christ, one of those shed during the Saviour's passion: a blood-filled tear that fell to the ground at the foot of the Cross and miraculously turned into the most beautiful jewel the world had ever seen. A precious stone that passed from one hand to another. It had been plundered a few years ago from the King of England's treasury when the felon Richard Puddlicot and his coven had broken into the crypt of Westminster Abbey and stolen the Crown Jewels, and had emerged

in Rome, the coveted possession of Clement V's predecessor, Pope Boniface VIII. The pope had refused to
hand it back, claiming that the English Crown could
not prove true ownership and pointing to some charter,
definitely the work of one of Rome's finest forgers.
According to this document, the Blessed Virgin Mary
had picked up the Lacrima Christi from the foot of the
Cross and entrusted it to the first pope, St Peter. No
one could gainsay that. The English Crown could fret
and protest to its heart's content, but the Lacrima Christi
was now firmly in the hands of the pope, and there it
would stay.

Clement's determination to keep this most precious
ruby was equalled by his desire to frustrate the bounding
ambitions of the princes of Europe, including the two
princely rifflers walking either side of his palfrey. He
realised that Philip lusted after the Lacrima Christi as
he did the wealth of others, such as the Order of the
Temple, which he was determined to crush. The pope
suppressed a shiver. He himself might be the Vicar of
Christ, yet Philip, with his white, icy face, his snow-
coloured hair and soulless, glassy blue eyes, truly
frightened him. Nevertheless, he was determined to
resist.

He glanced behind him at the English envoys, led
by Sir Hugh Corbett, Keeper of the Secret Chancery
at Westminster. Corbett, Edward of England's official
representative at the papal coronation, had already
demanded that the Lacrima Christi be handed over
so he could take it back to its true owner. Clement

had promptly refused. The Lacrima Christi was his, and he basked now in the glory of that exquisite ruby. He smiled to himself and lifted a hand as the roar of the crowd deepened. Philip and Edward might have their council of ministers, but Clement had the cardinals, who rode behind him in their sky-blue gowns, violet coats, spurred boots and plumed bonnets. These men would help him resist the ambition of the temporal princes. Clement would exercise his power as he should, both temporal and spiritual. He would not be checked by Philip of France or Edward of England; he would keep clear of them as he did the blood feuds of Rome or even the strident warnings of that preacher sprawled in the dust behind him. After all, he was—

His palfrey suddenly startled at a deafening rumble. The ground quaked beneath him and the soaring ancient curtain wall that lined the procession route abruptly bulged. In gusts of thick dust, the stones buckled, cracked and crashed to the ground with a thunderous roar. The ancient masonry simply disappeared into a swirling mist of dust, grit, pieces of rock and wood. Clement reined in. Philip of France had fallen to his knees. Charles of Valois, struck by a piece of rock, lay unconscious, covered in dirt. Clement's palfrey reared, and as he fought to remain in the saddle, the tiara fell from his head. Equerries, coughing and spluttering, came staggering to assist. The thick veil of dust thinned and cleared. More help arrived. A squire picked up the tiara, brushing it gently with his hand. He lifted it up and gaped at the deep hole in the centre of the crown. The Lacrima Christi, that magnificent, lustrous ruby, had simply disappeared.

1312

Grease-hair, spit-boy in the great kitchen of
Malmaison Manor, which stood at the heart
of the dark wilds of Dartmoor, reluctantly
prepared to climb the ladder. He wiped at the shining
lard that glistened on his round red face, the reason for
his name, even though he had been baptised Theodore
when he had been held over the baptismal font of the
nearby manor chapel of St Briavel. Now he stared across
at the dark, huddled mass of that little church. A solitary, forbidding building with its lofty bell tower and
grim, iron-studded front door. He just wished the chapel
bell would cease its mournful tolling, whilst the roar
of those two great cats, Death and the Demon,
completely unnerved him. True, the magnificent leopards
were caged deep in the caverns below the manor, yet
their roaring was unsettling.

Shadowy figures were hastening through the dark
towards the chapel. The door was unlocked. Curses and

moans carried on the cold night air, but at least the pealing bell fell silent. Colum the cook, assisted by two scullions, was busy positioning the ladder so it soared up to rest against the shuttered lancet window of the principal guest chamber on the first gallery of that spacious manor. The window, as Lady Isabella had reminded the spit boy, was behind the chancery chair; the other, larger window was horn-filled, its shutters clasped close.

Grease-hair sensed that something dreadful had happened in that chamber: those bells ringing the tocsin, the dogs howling, the horses whinnying in their stables, and above all, the deep, ominous growling of the leopards. He closed his eyes and whispered a prayer to the Virgin for her protection. He had visited the caverns and seen those ferocious beasts prowling around their lair. His constant nightmare was that the fierce cats would be let loose in the manor and hunt him down. He wiped his hands on his jerkin and shivered at the cold night wind, which blew like some mournful hymn across the courtyard.

'We are ready now, boy. Come on,' Colum urged. 'You will be safe.'

Grease-hair slowly approached the long siege ladder. It reminded him of those resting against the lofty gibbet at the bleak crossroads only a short distance from the manor. He glanced up at the sky, dark and lowering, the thick clouds hiding both moon and stars.

'Come on, lad.' Colum seized him by the scruff of his jerkin and pulled him closer to the bottom rung.

'God only knows what has happened.' The cook pushed his red, sweaty face closer. 'Lady Isabella awaits,' he hissed, 'and we must do our best. Lord Simon is closeted in that chamber with his special guest John Wodeford. Yet the chamber remains locked and bolted.' He scratched his face. 'No one knows what happened in there, eh? So, lad,' he tapped Grease-hair on the shoulder, 'up you go.'

The spit-boy began his precarious climb. At least the leopards had fallen silent now too. The cold wind buffeted him, and occasionally the ladder seemed to sway. A night bird glided past him like a ghost, perhaps one of those that haunted this manor. Grease-hair and the other servants often talked about a secret malevolence that seemed to spread like a mist across this magnificent house. He startled as another bird cawed raucously from a stunted copse of ancient trees just beyond the manor walls, then took a deep breath and continued his climb.

When he reached the lancet window, he saw that its shutters hung loose, so by pushing and lifting, he managed to prise one back and stare at the horrors within. Candles still glowed on their spigots, as did the lanternhorn on its hook next to the chamber door. Grease-hair noticed that immediately, because his mistress had demanded to know if the bolts at top and bottom were fully pulled across and the large key turned in its lock. They were, but more importantly, who was responsible for the gruesome murders that had taken place there?

From where he stood perched on the top of the ladder, Grease-hair could clearly see Lord Simon sprawled in his chancery chair, his head turned slightly sideways. The stark black feathers of a crossbow quarrel made it look as if a small, angry bird had smashed into his temple. The other victim, Malmaison's guest, John Wodeford, lay sprawled in a thick pool of his own blood from the crossbow bolt embedded deep in the left side of his chest, a killing blow direct to the heart. There was more. Grease-hair glimpsed another blood-stained crossbow bolt driven into the door, the insignia of that dreadful night wraith the Sagittarius.

He swallowed hard. The chamber was now a room of shifting, darting shadows. A place of sudden death, of brutal murder. So what else could he see? He noticed how the high four-poster bed had its curtains pulled back, the coverlets undisturbed – but of course, that was proper, wasn't it? Wodeford had not adjourned for the evening. Grease-hair had helped the guest when he first arrived, taking his panniers up to this guest chamber, so where were these? He glimpsed something out of the corner of his eye, but when he turned, there was nothing. He gripped the ladder more tightly and it moved slightly beneath him. He wanted to go down, yet he was fascinated. Two important men lay murdered. Did their ghosts still hover there? Was Parson Osbert correct, he wondered, when he had preached on the feast of All Souls last that the dead walked amongst the living in a mist of pure spirit?

Grease-hair blinked. He found it difficult to swallow,

his mouth was so dry. He couldn't even turn to glance down and reply to the cook's shouted litany of questions. He began to tremble, quivering like a leaf on a twig. He had to get away from these horrors. He must escape. Hands now sweaty, and sobbing uncontrollably, he clambered down, crying, 'Harrow! Harrow!' Halfway down, he paused as he heard a voice screaming from the darkness.

'Death and the Demon have escaped!'

The watcher on the wasteland, as Tallien, the travelling tinker, liked to describe himself, was truly mystified. On the night following Lord Simon's murder, he had glimpsed a strange sight here up on the moor. On his most recent journey to Exeter, the tinker had met Sir Miles Wendover, the fat-faced sheriff, at the Guildhall, and informed him what he'd seen on a previous occasion. How he had glimpsed a cog, he did not know its name, wrecked on Langthorne Rocks, the fat-bellied ship sharply impaled, its timbers shattered by the pounding of the sea. He was sure he had glimpsed lantern light and figures moving across the rocks. A sea mist had then rolled in, and when it had cleared, shifting like an icy curtain, there was nothing but the pathetic remains of that cog breaking up. Sheriff Wendover had politely heard him out in his chamber deep in the gloomy Guildhall, but apart from that, he did nothing else.

Nevertheless, on that evening following Lord Simon's murder, when the news of it was still being proclaimed abroad, Tallien had returned to his vantage point above

Monkshood Bay. He had heard strange sounds, the roaring of a beast, and shivered as he recalled stories whispered in the taproom of the Palfrey in Felstead. How Lord Simon had been murdered and his magnificent beasts, the leopards, released into the wild. But surely that could not be the case? Nevertheless, his curiosity had got the better of him. He was a travelling chapman, and he earned his food and drink by passing on news and stories to those who might host him with a tasty meal, a tankard of ale or a goblet of rich wine. He had been drawn to the cove by hideous screams, which had rent the night air. As he lay flat on his belly, peering through the gorse, he was sure he had glimpsed the two leopards sloping like ghosts through the night, yet they moved slowly, as if both were injured, their snuffling and deep coughing proof that they were injured or suffering some form of malady. Tallien dared not move. He'd heard the screams, seen the shapes, and he decided it was best to wait until at least full light. He'd wrapped his cloak about him and lain hidden, dozing, now and again taking a slurp from the small battered wine skin he carried.

He awoke just after dawn, the sky brightening, the wind biting and salt tinged, the strident screams of the gulls echoing above the dull roar of the sea. He decided he must move on. He rose awkwardly and staggered back to the path. He dared not go to Malmaison; even when he was alive, Lord Simon was viewed as a lonely, sinister man, best left to his own devices. He did not want to go back to Felstead either, so, knowing the paths across the moor as he did the back of his own hand, Tallien the tinker took the coffin track leading to the priory of St Benet. He was sure he would get good comfort there, the chance to warm himself before a roaring fire.

He strode briskly, his satchel swinging across his back, the sturdy staff he carried firmly clasped in his mittened fingers. In truth, though, he was still half asleep, and the horsemen were around him before he knew it, appearing out of the misty murk like the devil's own cavalcade. They ringed him, at least eight in number, cloaked and hooded, their faces masked by visors woven out of straw. Tallien closed his eyes and murmured a prayer. He knew these men. He had heard the tales. They were the Scarecrows, under their leader the Sagittarius, the wolfsheads blamed for the wrecking of ships, not to mention the death of Lord Simon and another clerk at Malmaison. He swallowed hard, his fingers edging towards the thin knife he carried in its sheath on his rope girdle.

'Keep your hands where we can see them.' The leader of the Scarecrows urged his horse forward, lifting his primed arbalest and pointing it directly at the tinker. 'So you must be Tallien, the self-styled watcher on the wasteland, the travelling chapman who likes to share his tales in return for food, ale and wine?'

Tallien just stared, even as he realised his dreadful mistake. He had chattered like a squirrel in taverns like the Palfrey. This meeting was not by chance; the Sagittarius and his minions had come looking for him.

'I never said anything,' he stammered. 'People blame you for the wrecks, for the death of Lord Simon and the other clerk at Malmaison.'

'Do they now?' mocked the Sagittarius. 'You see our power, Tallien; not even a manor lord is safe from us. And you talk about the leopards?'

'There is something wrong with them.' Tallien wiped sweat-soaked hands on his cloak. 'I have seen them. I believe they attacked someone.'

'Yes, yes, so I understand, as I do that you have been to Exeter to seek audience with our slumbering Sheriff Wendover.'

'I have.'

'So he would recognise you again?'

'Yes, yes, of course,' Tallien stuttered.

'And where are you off to now?'

'To St Benet's Priory, to seek food, shelter from the cold.'

'Ah, the good brothers at St Benet's,' the Sagittarius taunted. 'Very well.' He urged his horse forward; Tallien stepped back. 'You are really no use to us.' The Sagittarius leant down from his horse. 'You are well known, aren't you?'

But before Tallien could reply, the leader of the wolfsheads raised the arbalest and loosed the bolt, a killing blow to the tinker's head.

PART ONE

The same Richard says he took all of these out of
the treasury.

1312

Sir Hugh Corbett, Keeper of the Secret Seal, the king's own envoy on all matters in the shires of Devon and Cornwall, and a justiciar of oyer et terminer, quietly murmured a prayer. He then stared around the great hall of Malmaison Manor, which stood at the very heart of the great waste of Dartmoor, that huge stretch of lonely, windswept moorland across the king's shire of Devon. Corbett crossed himself and glanced quickly at the two men sitting either side of him. On his right, his henchman Ranulf-atte-Newgate, principal clerk in the Chancery of the Green Wax, certainly looked the way Corbett felt: tired, impatient and deeply uneasy at the world they had now entered.

Corbett and Ranulf had been with the court at the palace of Winchester. Both clerks had been admiring the great round table that according to popular legend had been used by King Arthur and his paladins. Their enjoyment had been sharply curtailed by the royal scurrier, who brought letters ordering the king's special envoy to the western parts to proceed with all haste to Malmaison. They were to investigate the brutal murders, treason and theft perpetrated there.

Corbett glanced at Ranulf and hid his smile. The clerk of the Green Wax was a true child of the city, a roaring boy who, if not for Corbett, would have joined one of the sinister riffler gangs of London's underworld. He would undoubtedly have risen to become a captain before being either betrayed to the hangman or slaughtered in one of the usual blood-lettings between rival gangs. Instead, however, he had proved himself to be the sharpest of clerks, as well as Corbett's dagger man.

Ranulf broke from his reverie, scratched his cropped fiery-red hair then narrowed his cat-like green eyes as he realised Corbett had been studying him.

'It's a long way from Leighton Manor, master.' He patted his dusty leather jerkin. 'It will be so good—'

He broke off at a loud sigh from Sir Miles Wendover, who was sitting on Corbett's other side. The plump, bewhiskered Sheriff of Devon had ridden with all speed from Exeter to join this commission of oyer et terminer – to listen and decide, but about what? He had confessed to being totally mystified by what had happened, and had been slouched in a high-backed chair, half asleep as he cradled a blackjack of manor ale. Now he pulled himself up, sighed again and grinned at Corbett.

'A fine place, Sir Hugh, for a court.'

'Opulent as any palace,' Ranulf retorted. The clerk of the Green Wax leant forward and stared hard at this small, plump sheriff. On their journey to Malmaison, his master had warned Ranulf not to judge a book by its cover or Wendover by his appearance. Corbett had glimpsed the sheriff some weeks ago at the royal palace of King's Langley, a busy, loyal official. Wendover was also sharp and honest and not to be taken lightly. 'Opulent indeed,' Ranulf repeated, turning away and tapping his booted feet against the floor tiles, ornamented with paintings of wyverns, dragons, griffins and other mythical beasts.

He gazed up at the gilt-edged beams and murmured his surprise at the wealth of this manor. The hall where Corbett was holding his court was long but well aired and lit: it stretched from the dais on which they sat to a choir loft at the other end. The high table was covered with a green baize cloth on which rested Corbett's sword, a book of the Gospels, a crucifix, a noose and Corbett's letter of authority sealed by the king himself. Usually the court sat in some bare, stark village church, but the main hall of Malmaison was lavishly decorated; its walls exquisitely covered with frescoes and paintings celebrating themes from scripture and the ancients, be it the Holy Face of Lucca or an armoured knight kneeling in adoration of a gorgeously painted Holy Grail. The gleaming oaken woodwork of the roof beams and the pillars stretching down either side of the hall was gilded in shimmering metals. Hosts of beeswax candles glowed gloriously, whilst a fire burnt merrily in the broad, high hearth carved in the shape of a griffin's mouth. Here and there across the floor stretched heavy perfumed rugs from the looms of Spain and elsewhere, lending colour as well as warmth to the hall.

'Despite all the wealth,' Corbett murmured, 'judgement will take place here.' He pointed to the stark black chair facing him directly below the dais. 'Here in this place we shall begin our investigation into treason, murder and robbery. God save us all!'

'So let us begin.' Wendover pulled himself up and pointed at the great hour candle on its ornamented stand to the left of the dais. 'The flame burns, the wax melts, the hour passes. So what is the indictment?'

'A moment,' Corbett murmured. He opened the chancery satchel resting against the leg of his chair and took out some sheets of vellum, which he laid out on the table before him. Ranulf did likewise; he would act as witness, clerk and scribe to the proceedings.

Corbett excused himself, rose and stared down the hall towards the far door, where Chanson, his sleepy-eyed clerk of the stables, would act as guard and court usher. Corbett was still not settled. He left the dais and walked over to study a wall painting that had caught his attention earlier. Its colours were as fresh as if painted yesterday: sapphire and ruby, frog-green and butter-yellow. These colours depicted the Virgin Mary sitting in the centre of a red-blue sky flanked by two beings garbed in embroidered robes. They were identical twins, mirror images of each other: stern, handsome young men with beards and long hair. Each steadied the Virgin's crown with one hand whilst the other was raised, palm forwards as if in prayer. The two were Father and Son, whilst between them, just below the crown, hovered the Holy Spirit, a majestic white dove with outstretched wings, the tip of each touching the lips of the young men, so joining their mouths together. The Virgin Mary, garbed in blue and gold, dominated the scene with her reddish hair, fair skin and lovely long slim hands. Beneath the painting, almost as an impish addition, stretched the netherworld of hell, where bat-winged, monkey-faced demons worked bellows to boost the flames that engulfed a horde of nightmare apparitions with goat-like horns and hairy pigs' snouts.

'Eerie,' whispered Ranulf, who had come to stand beside Corbett.

'What a contrast, eh, Ranulf? But that's our world with all its show and glory. Like Malmaison, a house of life and prayer, but in the cellars below . . .'

Corbett was about to move to study a group of other paintings – the dead Lord Simon had had a great devotion to the Holy Face of Lucca, and this was celebrated in various parts of the hall – but he paused, aware that the hour was passing. Wendover was drumming his fingers on the table and tapping his booted feet against the floor. Corbett clasped his henchman by the shoulder.

'Come, Ranulf, we have been to mass, and we have broken our fast. Sir Miles is correct: business awaits, and what murderous mischief it is!'

He returned to sit behind the table that would serve as his King's Bench and so reflect the power of the royal court at Westminster. He apologised to the sheriff for the delay and leafed through the parchment sheets on

the green baize cloth. He was satisfied that he had
faithfully recalled what he had written so carefully the
previous evening, when he and his escort had arrived
at Malmaison.

'So we have it,' Corbett began once his two companions had settled themselves. 'Primo. Today is the eve of
the Annunciation, the twenty-fourth of March, the Year
of Our Lord 1312, the fifth regnal year of His Grace
King Edward II of England. We are three justices
appointed by letters patent.' He tapped one of the manuscripts laid out on the table before him. 'This gives me
the power to appoint magistrates. You, Master Ranulf,
and you, Sir Miles, are so chosen. You are my fellow
justices. Ranulf,' Corbett pointed to the elegant chancery
tray containing the clerk's quill pens, inkpots, sander,
parchment knife and other items, 'take careful note of
what is said, as accurate and true as you can make it.
We are about to enter a maze of murder. One day soon
we will have to thread our way to the very centre, where
the assassins, the murderers, the sons and daughters of
Cain, will await us. The crimes here – treason and
robbery against the Crown and its officials – warrant
the most severe sentence. So write well. You, Chanson,'
Corbett raised his voice and grinned as the dozing clerk
of the stables sprang to his feet, 'you will be our usher.
Proceedings should be peaceful, but when I ask, you
will summon Captain Ap Ythel and his archers.'

'Good men all,' Sir Miles breathed. 'I have visited
them. Like all veterans, they have quickly secured
comfortable, warm quarters.'

'Captain Ap Ythel is my man in peace and war, body and soul,' Corbett murmured. 'As are his companions, who all hail from the same valley in Wales.'

'Except for the bestiarius,' Ranulf intervened, 'a Tower archer but different. Skilled in the ways of the great cats kept in the royal menagerie.'

'Merioneth,' Corbett declared, 'is a true veteran. He has served in Outremer and,' he shrugged, 'we might need his expertise.'

'You mean as regards the two leopards that escaped from here?'

'Precisely, Sir Miles. We shall come to those in due course. Secondo,' Corbett continued, 'we are now sitting on assize in Malmaison Manor, a majestic fortified mansion on the wastes of Dartmoor, over which this manor enjoys most of the rights and income, be it from crops, grazing, mining, hunting,' he waved a hand, 'and so on, and so on.

'The main house where we now reside was built some forty years ago. Since then, outhouses, stables, granges, smithies and the rest have been constructed. The manor is protected by a fortified curtain wall and an embattled gatehouse. There are at least two postern doors. There is no moat. The house is built on rock with cavernous caves beneath that serve as cellars and store chambers. They also provided a lair for the two leopards that have now escaped to pastures new, where they are probably causing bloody mayhem amongst flocks and any unfortunates they catch out in the open. However, to return to the question of a moat. Malmaison does not need one because it is virtually surrounded by deep, treacherous marshes cut through by a number of causeways leading to the gatehouse. The present lord, recently deceased, inherited the manor and its estates, but he also built his own fortune during his days as a mailed clerk in the royal chancery.'

'Very much like yourself, Sir Hugh.'

'Yes, Sir Miles, though Lord Simon was an adventurer. True, he was a colleague, a comrade of mine in the chancery as well as in the battle line. We stood shoulder to shoulder in the shield ring. However, he was also a merchant who dabbled in the sale of precious jewels and rare metals, ornamentation beloved by the ladies of both court and city. He apparently amassed a fortune, and won the support and patronage of the old king as well as that of his successor. Now, I admit there are other stories we will come to: that Lord Simon made his fortune in more nefarious ways, though this is a question of much suspected and nothing proved. However, we will return to that. Tertio. Lord Simon fought in Gascony, Scotland and Wales but won his spurs as a warrior in Outremer along the valleys of Palestine and the deserts of Egypt.' Corbett paused.

'Lord Simon, I understand,' Wendover murmured, 'liked the exotic and the mysterious, be it his wives or his pets.'

'What does that mean?'

'It means, Ranulf,' Corbett replied, 'that he was eccentric in all he did. He married a local lady, Beatrice Davenant. However, after his return from royal service almost ten years ago, Beatrice decided she no longer wanted her husband's loving embrace and fled Malmaison with the manor's steward, Chandos. Some people claim they went overseas, others that they tried to but suffered some mishap. Anyway,' he sifted the documents on the table before him, 'Lady Beatrice and Chandos were never seen or heard of again. Lord Simon then met the lovely Isabella, whom we shall be questioning in a very short time. Much smitten with her, he petitioned the Bishop of Exeter for the annulment of his marriage to his first wife, paying good money to the canon lawyers to pursue his claim. A decree of annulment was eventually issued, and Lord Simon and Isabella were married and settled down to conjugal bliss.'

'And their household?'

'Edmund Brockle, steward of the manor, and Henry Malach, Lord Simon's henchman. Both good men. I have met them before.'

'And the leopards?'

'Ah, Ranulf, so we come to Quarto, our fourth question, and the journey into the past, that far-distant country. As I've said, Lord Simon Malmaison was a man of many talents, a merchant, a clerk and a warrior. He served with me and John Wodeford in the Secret Chancery. Now, just under nine years ago, on the eve of the feast of St Mark in the Year of Our Lord 1303, Richard Puddlicot broke into the royal treasury stored in the crypt of Westminster Abbey. You will remember this.'

'Puddlicot led a coven of the greatest thieves in London.'

'Correct. He also formed a most unholy alliance with a coven of Blackrobes in the abbey, led by its felonious sacristan Adam Warfeld, who was supposed to be in charge of security. Well,' Corbett sipped from his blackjack of ale, 'what happened is now common knowledge. Puddlicot's gang plundered the treasury. I hunted their leaders. Lord Simon together with Wodeford were to search for stolen jewels, in particular a priceless, exquisitely beautiful ruby called the Lacrima Christi.'

'The Tear of Christ?'

'Yes, Ranulf, the Tear of Christ. Originally the ruby was kept close to the True Cross, but when that was lost at the Battle of Hattin, the jewel fell into the hands of the Turks.' Corbett drew a deep breath. 'It remained there until the present king's father followed the Cross to Outremer. Prince Edward, as he was then, was attacked by assassins and, thankfully, he survived, but the attack was regarded as deeply treacherous. The caliph in Egypt was particularly aggrieved, so he sent a remarkable present to Prince Edward: the Lacrima Christi in its most precious jewel-studded golden casket. This was stored with other items in the crypt of Westminster until Puddlicot broke in.'

'And the ruby was taken?'

'Oh yes. And, as I have said, Malmaison and Wodeford were commissioned to hunt for it.'

'Why them?'

'Because, my esteemed sheriff, both men were skilled diamond merchants in their own right. They had also seen the ruby and knew of its precise formation and individual characteristics.'

'But they never found it?'

'No, Sir Miles, they did not. However, a year later we discovered that it had been taken to Rome and sold to Pope Boniface for a truly great price. Of course, our king protested. He lodged an appeal, demanding that both the ruby and its casket be returned. The papacy, however, claimed that the jewel had been purchased from an anonymous buyer for an exorbitant sum, so it would stay with the pope and his successors. They also argued that such a holy relic, bequeathed by the Virgin Mary to St Peter, the first pope, should remain in the papal reliquary. The old king was outmanoeuvred and trapped. Moreover, he desperately needed papal support against Philip of France, so he could not demur. The papacy not only kept the ruby, but placed it in pride of place in the very centre of the pope's tiara, which, as you know, the Bishop of Rome wears on all formal occasions. And then, at the coronation of Boniface's successor, Bertrand de Got, Pope Clement V—'

'You were there,' Ranulf intervened. 'You had left the royal service but the old king asked you to go to Lyons as one of his representatives. I stayed to look after the Lady Maeve and your two children.'

'I certainly did, Ranulf, and Edward and Eleanor have never forgotten your visit. Ah yes,' Corbett continued cheerily, 'I was at Lyons accompanied by John Wodeford and Lord Simon. We were not only envoys but, of course, deeply curious about the Lacrima Christi . . .'

'It was there?'

'Yes, Ranulf. A veritable blaze of light in the centre of the papal tiara. A truly dazzling sight, though it did not last for long. After he was crowned, Clement solemnly processed out of St Justin's Church. On his way, he passed a soaring curtain wall raised by the ancients. Now, whether it was the crowd or a mild earth tremor, I cannot say, but the wall cracked and crashed to the ground in a furious cascade of bricks and mortar that threw up a thick cloud of dust. Several people were killed and many more injured. Pope Clement's palfrey reared and, in the fight to remain mounted, his tiara fell off. When it was recovered, the Lacrima Christi was missing.'

'Missing?'

'Yes, Sir Miles, missing. No one knows whether it was stolen or still lies in some crack or crevice in the ground. The pope's household conducted the most rigorous search, but nothing was found.' Corbett smiled to himself. 'A true mystery!'

'And now?'

'Now, Sir Miles, it would appear that the Lacrima Christi has once again emerged. A few weeks ago, towards the end of February, the Secret Chancery received information from Lord Simon that he had been approached by someone who might possibly have not only the ruby but the precious bejewelled casket that contained it. He insinuated that for a veritable treasure of freshly minted gold coin, the casket and possibly the jewel could be acquired by the English Crown.' Corbett tapped the green baize cloth. 'It so happened that the Secret Chancery also received an anonymous letter that insinuated the same. We do not know the origin of that letter – Lord Simon's work, or someone else?' Corbett shrugged.

Sir Miles leant forward. 'For heaven's sake, Sir Hugh, why didn't you just dispatch a comitatus of Tower archers to seize Lord Simon and force the issue?'

'No, we did not want to do that for a number of reasons, some of which I cannot reveal. Moreover, Lord Simon made it very clear that this mysterious person would probably disappear at the slightest hint of a threat by the Crown or its retainers.'

'And?'

'Well, Ranulf, Sir Miles, you have not asked the question I thought you might.'

'How did the papacy acquire the Lacrima Christi in the first place?'

'Oh, we know that through our spies at the papal court. The pope's bankers, the Frescobaldi, offered it to Boniface.'

'And who sold it to the Frescobaldi?'

'Ah, Ranulf, that's the question. We – that is, John Wodeford and I – believed that during the hunt after the Crown Jewels had been stolen, Lord Simon found that ruby.'

'What!' Ranulf and Wendover chorused.

'I think so.' Corbett lowered his voice. 'Wodeford believed that Lord Simon trapped a member of Puddlicot's gang, a jeweller called Glaston, who held the ruby. Glaston disappeared and has never been found. Lord Simon may have murdered him to silence him forever. He would have done that. A true man of blood, he was a killer to his very marrow.'

'So Lord Simon murdered the jeweller and seized the ruby?'

'Yes, Ranulf. Then he sold it to the easiest purchaser: Italian bankers who might not pay the ruby's true worth – that would be extraordinary – but would certainly offer enough to allow him to retire from service to the Crown, refurbish his manor and settle down to a most comfortable life.' Corbett paused. 'Now, when Lord Simon wrote to us, we were very curious. We saw the logic of what was happening. He would be a natural choice for this mysterious personage to approach. After all, he'd been appointed to hunt down and seize all the stolen jewels, the Lacrima Christi in particular. Moreover,' he smiled, 'Lord Simon was in that papal procession at Lyons when the Lacrima Christi disappeared yet again. Anyway, we decided to play the game, and Wodeford and his dagger man Rievaulx were dispatched to Malmaison Manor.

'And so we come to Quinto.' He leafed through the manuscripts before him and drew out a sheet of vellum. 'Two weeks ago, on the eve of the feast of St Briavel, patron saint of the manor chapel, John Wodeford and Rievaulx arrived at Malmaison. Wodeford met Lord Simon in the principal guest chamber, which was locked and bolted from within. Both men were murdered by a crossbow bolt, delivered so close the barbs dug deep into their flesh. Just as mysterious, the pannier of gold coins Wodeford allegedly brought with him had disappeared. A week later, Sir Ralph Hengham, a royal official, principal tax collector in the shires of Devon and Cornwall, arrived at Malmaison. As a servant of the Crown, Hengham had the right to investigate the murders. I believe that you, Sir Miles, escorted him here?'

The sheriff nodded in agreement. 'Yes, I did. I think he was coming here anyway. However—'

'Well, anyway, Hengham brought his money pouches with him. He was also lodged in the guest chamber, the same room where Lord Simon and Wodeford were murdered. The next morning, he could not be roused, and the door, recently refurbished, had to be forced. Hengham was found dead on the bed, a crossbow bolt driven deep into his chest and, as with Wodeford, the money was gone.'

'In heaven's name,' Wendover blustered, 'one mystery after another. You know I was present on both nights.' He scratched his balding head. 'I mean, on the first occasion, Lord Simon invited me here, whilst Hengham demanded my protection. I also needed to talk to Lady Isabella about those leopards. A real danger and a thorough ongoing nuisance . . .'

His voice trailed away. Corbett just sat, tapping one booted foot against the floor. Ranulf glanced quickly at Old Master Longface, as he secretly described his master. Corbett's olive-skinned face was relaxed, his deep-set hooded eyes half closed as if he was listening to one of those melodious hymns he loved to chant. He was unshaven, his raven-black hair, tipped with silver here and there, tied in a sharp queue behind his head. After a long, hard ride, they had not yet washed or changed, and Ranulf sensed his master was impatient, eager to proceed, to confront the murderous mystery and bloody mayhem that seemed to haunt this stately, eerie manor house. Moreover, the clerk was curious. There was something else, he could sense it. Corbett would certainly not lie, but at times he would not describe the full truth. Ranulf was certain this was happening here, over the search for the Lacrima Christi. Master Longface was keeping close counsel with himself.

Corbett's gaze shifted abruptly to Ranulf and he smiled impishly. 'What a tangle, eh, my friend?' His grin faded. 'And there's more. They say this manor is haunted, yes, Sir Miles?'

'Oh yes.' Wendover was slouched in his chair once more, and Ranulf could see he would dearly love to be elsewhere, impatient to return to the many onerous tasks assigned to him. 'They talk of some malignant presence,' whispered the sheriff, 'which prowls this manor. A deep, dark shadow of the unquiet dead that stalks the living. I understand,' he added, 'the servants believe the murders are the work of vengeful spirits and vindictive ghosts. But Sir Hugh, there's enough human villainy in and around Malmaison to fill our cup to overflowing.'

'Indeed there is. And so, Sexto, Sir Miles. The wreckers, the Scarecrows and their leader the Sagittarius.'

A mystified Ranulf turned in his chair. 'Sir Miles, what is this?'

'Wreckers!' the sheriff echoed bitterly. 'Wreckers, outlaws and wolfsheads who dress like scarecrows in rags and fearsome masks. They appear after dark to wreak their villainy. Devon and Cornwall are the far-most shires in this kingdom. A welcome landfall for the cogs and merchantmen sailing up from the wine ports of Bordeaux, La Rochelle and elsewhere. These Scarecrows allegedly light false beacon fires and lantern-horns to lure ships onto Langthorne Rocks in Monkshood Bay and elsewhere. Then they kill any survivors and plunder the cargo. Mostly their prey are the heavy-laden wine ships from the vineyards of Gascony, but they also harvest a rich crop from vessels out of Spain carrying leather, silks and other precious goods.' Wendover leant his elbows on the table and rubbed his face. 'As I have said, they gather at night along some lonely stretch of the coast. No one has actually seen them wreck a ship; these villains have chosen well. The shoreline twists and turns with hidden inlets, narrow bays and concealed coves. I do not have the men to patrol it. The wreckers are well organised. As I have said, they are rarely seen, but now and again, people encounter them. We issue warnings. The local priest, Parson Osbert, thunders his condemnation from the pulpit.'

'And?'

'And, Master Ranulf, he and others are threatened for their opposition. Nightmare shapes, garbed garishly, faces horribly masked, will be waiting in the twilight or deep in the shadows along an alleyway or country lane.'

'And their leader, why is he called the Sagittarius, the archer, the bowman?'

'It's a name,' Wendover sighed, 'taken by many outlaws and wolfsheads, but this malefactor is different. One of the ways he warns people is a crossbow bolt aimed above someone's head as they leave a tavern or walk down a path. Occasionally there is a more macabre warning: he takes a sparrow, or some other bird, cuts its heart out, daubs a bolt with blood and looses it at someone's door.'

'One of the rituals of black magic, a gutted bird nailed to a door . . .'

'Yes, Sir Hugh, and the Sagittarius exploits the fears of the people of these parts. Not so long ago, a local woman was accused of witchcraft. Matters got out of hand and they hanged the poor wretch on the common gibbet at the crossroads close to the Palfrey tavern. When they cut her down, they skinned her corpse and plucked at her flesh with burning pincers and red-hot pokers before collecting the chunks of flesh into a bag, which they threw into a marsh. Ah yes, our Sagittarius knows the local lore and customs. Of course,' Wendover continued wearily, 'people object to the wreckers, repelled by their greedy cruelty. However, a crossbow bolt, its barb all glistening with blood, driven into a door at the dead of night soon stills all protest.'

'And you have no idea who these wolfsheads truly are?'

'As God is my witness, Sir Hugh, no. They dress grotesquely and seem to come and go like will-o'-the-wisps across the marshes.' The sheriff paused to sip at his blackjack. 'Sir Hugh, Master Ranulf, the three murders committed here, only a week apart, might be the work of the Sagittarius. The victims should have been safe in this fortified manor, sheltering in a chamber locked and bolted from within. Nevertheless, they were slain. On each occasion a crossbow bolt, smeared in blood, was driven into the inside of the door.' He shook his head.

Corbett glanced around. The hall did not look so merry now, despite the fierce fire, the Turkey rugs on the floor, and the thick tapestries and delicately etched frescoes that decorated the walls. 'It might be the work of the Lapsi,' he murmured. 'The Fallen.'

'Oh, them.' Wendover scoffed. 'Fourteen Benedictine monks condemned to live in the desolate priory of St Benet. They pray. They work the land and do whatever disgraced monks do. I certainly don't view them as a threat.'

'I am not too sure,' Ranulf retorted. 'They are Adam Warfeld's coven.'

'I agree, Ranulf,' Corbett replied. 'Adam Warfeld, once the high-and-mighty sacristan in Westminster Abbey, close friend of this and that great nobleman, secret confederate of the robber Richard Puddlicot. He and his coven should have hanged, Sir Miles, but you must know what happened. Warfeld and his confederates were monks, clerics, so the Crown has no power to try or convict them. Holy Mother Church,' he added sardonically, 'was ordered to deal with her errant sons. The entire cohort was banished to the wilds of Dartmoor. A truly austere life in the disused priory high on Doone Moor. Now, Sir Miles, are you sure they are not involved in this mischief?'

'As far as I know, Sir Hugh: no reports, no rumours, no gossip.'

'Now that does make me suspicious.'

'True, true, Ranulf. But,' Corbett waved a hand, 'Warfeld and his coven have to be very careful. If they are trapped in further mischief, they would spend the rest of their lives in a prison cell, garbed in sackcloth and fed only on bread and water.' He rose and stretched, then walked down the hall and stood listening to the murmuring in the vestibule beyond. 'Those we've summoned,' he declared over his shoulder, 'are getting restless. What other matters demand our attention?'

Wendover also rose and crossed to refill his blackjack at the buttery table, where Lady Isabella's steward Brockle had laid out a light collation. 'There is the matter of the Guild of Fleshers and Tanners.'

Corbett walked back to the table. 'Yes, you made reference to this in your letter to the council.'

'The Guild of Fleshers and Tanners,' Wendover replied sonorously retaking his seat, 'are a cohort of very prosperous merchants selling skins, hides and furs both here and beyond.' He slurped noisily from his blackjack. 'A smelly, reeking trade, yet they enjoy a most comfortable life.'

'And?' Ranulf asked testily, aware of the growing hubbub beyond the hall.

'Oh, most mysterious. About two weeks ago, on a Sunday evening, the guild gathered for one of its usual joyful celebrations in the Palfrey tavern, which lies at the centre of Felstead village. They hired the long chamber there and feasted most royally on beef brisket, roast pork, lampreys and—'

'Quite, quite,' Corbett intervened. Wendover was a plump man with a generous belly, an official who loved the cup of life and drank deeply from it. 'And?' he demanded.

'And, Sir Hugh, the celebrations finished. The guildsmen, much the worse for drink, left the tavern, and since that hour, none of them – and I mean not one of the twelve – has been seen again.'

'Neither hide nor hair?' Ranulf declared. 'If you can excuse my joke.'

'All twelve guildsmen vanished off the face of the earth. I have deployed a comitatus, bribed the tinkers and chapmen, all those who use the coffin paths across the moors.' Wendover pulled a face. 'Nothing,' he murmured. 'Nothing at all. And now, quite understand-ably, their womenfolk, led by the redoubtable Richolda, have heard that the king's envoy is visiting the shire and is lodged at Malmaison.' Wendover pointed at the door. 'I strongly suspect they have arrived and are waiting to speak to you. One mystery amongst many.'

'And the leopards, the great cats?'

'I don't know much, Master Ranulf. They escaped

and have caused some damage. On my arrival here, Henry Malach, Lord Simon's henchman, wanted to speak to me most urgently on that matter. I told him to wait. Now . . .'

'Yes, it's time.' Corbett tapped the table. 'Let us prepare our court.' He rose and went over to inspect the great hour candle. 'It's almost the tenth hour,' he declared. 'Let us sit at least until noon, then we shall see.'

The sleepy-eyed Chanson was roused and helped to prepare the chamber, humming beneath his breath until Ranulf snapped at him to shut up. The assizes table was ready, and Chanson brought benches to stand either side of the chair facing the dais. Corbett inspected everything and pronounced himself satisfied, declaring that all who wished to do business before the king's justices of oyer et terminer should now be admitted to the judgement hall.

A veritable crowd surged into the chamber. Ranulf, standing at the edge of the dais, had to roar for silence, hand on the hilt of his dagger to emphasise the gravity of the situation. Corbett, seated in the centre throne-like chair, studied the arrivals. The wives of the missing guildsmen were led by a woman with flame-coloured hair, a rubicund face and a voice like a bell. This, Wendover whispered, was the formidable Richolda. She and the other women were deeply agitated, but they were ordered to stay with Chanson by the door and at last the clamour subsided. The rest took their seats on the benches either side of the witness chair. These were led by Lady Isabella, widow of the late Lord Simon.

Corbett continued his scrutiny of those milling about below the dais. Isabella was certainly very fair, despite her black widow's weeds. A starched wimple framed a beautiful face under a silver-laced black veil. A woman of considerable elegance, he concluded. She exuded a quiet confidence, her unpainted face smooth and clear, her slightly slanted eyes ever watchful. She glanced at Corbett, caught his gaze, smiled and nodded. Corbett acknowledged this, dispensing with the usual courtesies. He had met the Lady Isabella the previous evening to express his condolences as well as his regrets that she had twisted her ankle. She now hobbled slightly, resting on a silver-topped cane, and sighed with relief as she sat down, both hands resting on her elegant walking stick.

The others took their place on the bench either side. Brockle, her balding, cheery faced steward, was garbed in a buff-coloured jerkin, green hose and rather muddy boots. A nervous man, Corbett reckoned, a fusspot, though one who would be most conscientious in his duties. Grease-hair the spit-boy, who, Corbett had learnt, had first discovered the murders, slouched nervously beside the steward, glancing furtively at Colum the cook, who patted him reassuringly on the shoulder. Henry Malach, Lord Simon's henchman, sat to Lady Isabella's right. A sallow-faced young man with a thick crop of black hair, he looked much younger than his years. Corbett knew something about him: a former mailed clerk who had seen service in the king's array in Gascony around the Bastide of Saint-Sardos. Also in mourning, Malach was dressed completely in black, except for the white cambric shirt peeping over his quilted jerkin. He sat, hands on knees, staring unblinkingly up at the dais. He looked distressed, and Corbett remembered that he had been totally devoted to his dead master.

Keeping his face impassive, Corbett shifted his gaze to the man sitting next to Malach. Rievaulx! John Wodeford's henchman was slender bodied, with scrawny hair above a sharp face. He reminded Corbett of a hawk on its perch, with his slanted eyes, beaked nose and bloodless lips. He was garbed in a tawny jerkin and hose, and sat tapping his booted feet against the paving stones as if impatient for this matter to be over with so he could get on with his own business. Corbett, as he had confided to Ranulf, knew a great deal about Rievaulx, the defrocked priest and Judas man who had cheerfully betrayed Richard Puddlicot and his coven to the king's justices. He tried to catch Rievaulx's gaze, but Wodeford's henchman sat lost in his own dark thoughts.

Corbett rose and banged the pommel of his sword against the baize-topped table. Ranulf shouted for silence and Corbett immediately intoned the Veni Creator Spiritus, asking for divine guidance. He then invited anyone present, if they so wished, to inspect the signatures of the seals of his commission. Everyone remained silent, so he introduced his two fellow justices and ordered everyone to sit.

For a while, he remained silent, his elbows on the

table, hands clasped as if in prayer. 'We are here,' he began at last, 'because of what happened at Malmaison on that fateful night when Lord Simon and Wodeford were foully murdered. You must all speak the truth. I have not put any of you on oath and I will not do so unless I think it's necessary. Now, my lady,' he pointed at Lady Isabella, 'some simple questions addressed to you and all those sitting with you. Master Rievaulx,' he gestured at the stone-faced Judas man, 'I take it that you understand my questions, and that what you secretly know could be a matter for further questioning privately between ourselves?' He did not even bother to wait for a reply, but turned back to Lady Isabella. 'Mistress, and those sitting with you, does the phrase "Lacrima Christi" mean anything to you?'

Lady Isabella glanced to her right and left as those with her whispered heatedly to each other.

'Lady Isabella?'

'Of course we have heard about that beautiful ruby, the great robbery at Westminster and my late husband's pursuit of those involved. I understand, Sir Hugh, that you, Lord Simon, Master Wodeford and others played a great part in those hurling times?'

'Mistress, I thank you, but I ask the questions. So, did you or anyone here, apart from Master Rievaulx, know the true reason for Master Wodeford's journey here?' Corbett's question was greeted with silent shakes of the head. 'Do any of you,' he persisted, 'have any dealings with the community who now reside at St Benet's?'

'Very little,' Malach replied, his voice strong and carrying. 'True, on the great feasts Master Brockle and I send them meats and other foods. Occasionally one of the brothers comes here to beg for this or that.'

'So you provide sustenance?' Ranulf intervened.

'Yes.'

'As do others.' Wendover tapped the table. 'Sir Hugh, the good people of the shire have heard rumours, but little else. I, of course, as sheriff, know more of the truth, but that is my business.'

'And that of the king.'

'Yes, Master Ranulf,' Wendover snapped back. 'That of the king and his council, of which—'

'Quite, quite.' Corbett swiftly intervened. Ranulf had an ingrained dislike of sheriffs, a memory of more youthful days, when, as a riffler, he and his confederates were harried the length and breadth of the city. 'Let us concentrate,' he declared, 'on that fateful day, the eve of the feast of St Briavel. John Wodeford and Master Rievaulx arrived here. Did this London merchant bring anything with him?'

'You know the truth, Sir Hugh,' Rievaulx replied. 'Master Wodeford carried a veritable treasure of gold coin in sealed panniers, which never left him.'

'And these panniers have now disappeared?'

'Stolen, Sir Hugh. Stolen the night my master was murdered here at Malmaison.' Rievaulx leant forward and looked along at the others.

'Don't hint,' Brockle protested. 'Don't insinuate. Search the manor!'

'Yes,' Malach rasped. 'Search Malmaison from cellar to bedloft. You will discover nothing. We are not responsible.'

'So what did actually happen that day?' Corbett nodded at Lady Isabella, who sat so elegantly, one hand resting on her walking stick. 'Mistress, you tell us.'

'Wodeford and Rievaulx arrived here around the Angelus bell. It was raining, blustery; both men were soaked. Wodeford seemed pleased to see my husband; Lord Simon likewise. During the late afternoon our two visitors made themselves comfortable. Wodeford was given our principal guest chamber, overlooking the manor garden and stable yard. A spacious room, it has a shuttered window filled with oiled horn and beside it a narrow lancet that can also be shuttered.'

'As it was that night?'

'Yes, Sir Hugh, but the shutter over the lancet is a mere strip of wood. It hangs loose and can be prised open.'

'Which I did!' Grease-hair almost yelled.

'Of course, of course.' Corbett smiled at the spit-boy. 'We will come to you by and by. Lady Isabella?'

'We had dinner. The conversation was interesting enough. News from the court, the depredations of Bruce,' she waved a hand, 'the doings of the great barons. Nothing more.'

'And Wodeford kept his panniers close by?'

'He certainly did, Sir Hugh. When they adjourned to the guest chamber, he took them with him. He insisted on meeting my husband alone. And so they left.'

'I went with them to ensure all was well,' Brockle declared. 'Malach accompanied me.'

'And?'

'Sir Hugh,' Malach replied, 'the chamber was clean, warm and comfortable. Braziers had been fired. Candles lit. The floor was swept and polished, the bed well prepared with clean bolsters, drapes, linen sheets and coverlets.'

'As we left,' Brockle added, 'I am certain I heard the chamber door being locked and bolted behind us, but I could be wrong.'

'And then what?' Corbett demanded.

'We returned here to the hall,' Brockle replied.

'We stayed here,' Malach added. 'Though on two occasions I went down to the caverns. The leopards were strangely restless.' He made a face. 'Perhaps they sensed something was wrong, some mishap was about to happen.'

'And so, my lady, apart from Malach, none of you left the hall?'

'No, Sir Hugh. The hours passed. We whiled away the time telling ghost stories. Dartmoor is a lonely, haunted place. They say the devil and his hell-hounds ride the moor and the spirits of the long-departed gather around the tors and other ancient stones.'

'My lady, I would agree.' Ranulf intervened. 'After we left Exeter and journeyed south, I thought we had entered a nightmare land.' He paused, lost in his own thoughts and memories, and swiftly crossed himself as he recalled riding across the great waste, the sea of gorse, the streams, meres, marshes and concealed morasses. The sky had been grey and threatening, the eerie cries of birds unsettling. Dartmoor was an empty landscape, bereft of trees except for the occasional copse of ancient gnarled and twisted firs.

Corbett glanced at his clerk and kept his face impassive. Ranulf hated open countryside, especially the windswept moors. He was cowed by the sheer expanse, and pined for the busy, bustling streets of London.

'So who raised the alarm?' Wendover's voice was harsh and impatient.

'I did, Sir Miles. I became deeply concerned about my husband, so I sent Brockle up to the guest chamber. He knocked and pounded on the door. Deeply alarmed, he returned here and informed me. Believe me, Sir Hugh, the peace of this manor was truly shattered. I asked Brockle to summon Colum the cook with his scullions to break down the door. However, I first decided to dispatch Grease-hair to see what was happening.' She turned and smiled at the spit-boy. 'And so he did, up a ladder to the lancet window—'

Corbett raised a hand for silence, then nodded at the spit-boy, who immediately leapt to his feet, acting out what he described.

'Colum brought the ladder. I have climbed it before,' he added in a rush, 'when Lord Simon wanted tiles or house bricks examined. Anyway, up as swift and nimble as a squirrel I went. I was afeared, sir, greatly afeared. The wind was strong and the roar of the great cats frightened me.'

'Of course, of course,' Corbett soothed. 'Sit down, lad. Take your time and tell me exactly what you saw.'

'I reached the lancet window. I prised open the shutters. Sir, I was greatly—'

'Continue,' Ranulf snapped.

'Lord Simon was sitting in his chair.'

'How?'

'Turned.' Grease-hair gnawed his lip. 'Yes, turned, slightly to the right. A crossbow bolt smashed into the side of his head.'

'And?'

'Lord Simon's visitor lay sprawled near the door, arms and legs flung out. He too had been killed by a bolt, here.' The spit-boy patted the left side of his jerkin. 'It must have pierced his heart; the blood had spilled out of his mouth and nose as it had Lord Simon's.'

'What did you see or glimpse?' Corbett insisted.

'There was something wrong with that chamber.'

'What?'

'I don't know. You see, Sir, I often take up food to the guests who stay there and clear away the platters when they have left. I know that room well. Something . . .' He shook his head.

'The third crossbow bolt.' Lady Isabella intervened. 'You saw that?'

'Yes, yes, my lady. Driven deep into the inside of the door.'

'And you must have noticed if the door was locked and bolted?'

'Oh yes, sir. Lady Isabella had asked me to check on

that. The bolts were drawn both top and bottom. The key looked as if it had been turned. I could see all this clearly in the light of a lanternhorn hanging from its wall clasp close to the door.'

'And what else did you see?' Ranulf demanded. 'Come on, boy.'

'I don't know, sir. I have been in that guest chamber many times. There was something wrong, but I can't place or recall it.'

'What?' the clerk insisted.

'Sir, I don't know. I cannot remember. By then,' Grease-hair continued in a rush, 'the hubbub had deepened. People were shouting and running about. Then I heard someone yell that the leopards had escaped.'

'There was confusion.' Lady Isabella tapped her cane against the floor. 'I told everyone to stay in the hall and dispatched Malach down to the leopard den again.'

'And?' Corbett turned to the henchman.

'I was wary,' Malach declared. 'I went down to the caverns and, lifting a torch, I noticed that the cages had been opened.'

'How?'

'Sir Hugh, the cages have no locks; only bolts held securely in clasps on the outside. They had been drawn back, and of course the cats had escaped. People heard their roars. I had no choice but to raise the alarm.'

'How easy would that be?' Ranulf demanded. 'For someone to free the cats?'

'There's a narrow postern door close by, leading out to the moor. One of the weaknesses of this manor.

Anyone could have entered through that, opened the cage door from the outside then quickly left.' Malach drew a deep breath. 'You see, the cats are fed, well provisioned. When they were young, they were weak enough to be taken out on a chain. Now fully grown, they take care of themselves. They are creatures of the wild, and God knows, it's wild enough beyond this manor.'

'Where did they come from?' Ranulf cleared his throat. 'How did it happen that two such beasts were kept at Malmaison?'

'My husband,' Isabella replied, 'bought them from the beast-master of the king's menagerie at the Tower. They were cubs, gifts from a Moroccan prince. The royal menagerie was becoming greatly overcrowded, the cost of feeding the various creatures rising by the month. My late husband . . .' She paused as if to still the tremor in her voice, hands grasping the top of the walking cane more firmly. 'My late husband, as you know, served as a Tower clerk. He'd also been a member of the king's array in Outremer. To cut to the chase, Lord Simon was fascinated by the animals. On leaving the royal service, he petitioned to purchase the cubs and the king graciously consented to that.'

'Did you like them?'

Lady Isabella simply smiled and gave a pretty shrug.

'Strange,' Wendover murmured, 'that the two cats escaped on the very night Lord Simon was murdered . . .'

'And only heaven knows why.'

'Quite, my lady,' Wendover agreed.

'They are no longer a danger.' Malach bowed towards Corbett. 'My lord, we have just heard rumours from travelling tinkers who claim that the corpses of both cats lie out on the moors, close to a sheep's carcass. But,' he shook his head, 'I know of no further details.'

Corbett, surprised, sat back in his chair. The path he was following to resolve these mysteries was narrowing fast as it twisted and turned.

'We shall leave that,' he declared. 'Yes, we shall leave that for the moment.' He pointed at Malach. 'So you realised the leopards had escaped. Lady Isabella, what happened next?'

'I ordered Malach to secure the manor, ensure doors were locked. Master Brockle here organised for servants, mostly scullions from the kitchen, to join me outside the guest chamber.' She tapped her walking cane on the ground. 'We climbed the stairs and broke down the door. Dreadful,' she murmured, her voice tremulous. 'Truly dreadful. Grease-hair was correct. My husband was slumped in his chair, that ugly barb lodged in his head. Master Wodeford lay sprawled on the floor, a bolt embedded deep; another, smeared with blood, had been loosed into the inside of the door.'

'The mark of the Sagittarius,' Wendover declared. 'That felon and his coven of malignant will-o'-the-wisps . . .'

'Did any of you,' Corbett asked, 'notice anything untoward in that room?' He waved a hand to take them all in. 'Any of you,' he repeated, smiling at Grease-hair, 'apart from our noble spit-boy here?' The others just shook their heads, whispering amongst themselves. 'And then what?' he continued. 'You, mistress? Brockle the steward?'

'You did not want the room disturbed,' Brockle offered.

'True, true,' Lady Isabella whispered. 'It was all a mystery. I wanted nothing disturbed.' She rubbed the side of her face. 'Yes, I told you all to go below, taking the servants who'd broken down the door with you. Master Brockle was to organise makeshift stretchers so we could remove the corpses to the chapel.'

'Yes, yes. We did that,' Brockle declared. 'We came up and removed both bodies. Malach assisted the servants whilst I escorted my lady back to her chamber. She had difficulty walking because of her ankle. I summoned a woman who acts as manor leech. She prepared a goblet of wine laced with a light opiate, which Lady Isabella drank.'

'So,' Corbett declared, 'that chamber was forced. The door had been locked and bolted from within. The large window was undisturbed. There was no trace of any violence or resistance. Two men had been murdered and the only things missing were Wodeford's panniers, allegedly crammed with gold coin. Would you say that's an accurate account of what you saw that night?'

'And that blood-smeared bolt, loosed into the door,' Malach declared.

'And the bed?'

'Sir Hugh, completely undisturbed; the bolsters, its coverlets. But,' Lady Isabella shrugged, 'I remember the curtains were pulled back to show that Wodeford had neither sat nor lain there.'

'And nothing untoward was noticed around the rest of the manor that night?' Ranulf queried.

'You mean,' Rievaulx jibed, 'apart from two murders, the theft of a fortune and the escape of two ferocious beasts?'

'You know full well what I mean,' Ranulf retorted, half rising from his seat then sitting back as Corbett pressed his arm. 'Was there anything that could explain such dire events?'

'Until Grease-hair reported what he'd seen from the top of that ladder,' Lady Isabella replied, 'all was peaceful. My husband was in good heart, and seemed pleased to meet Master Wodeford. Their meal here, a good rich supper, was most amicable. Master Wodeford looked content enough, keeping his panniers close by him. When they were moved, we could hear the clink of coins.'

'And you had no inkling why he had brought such a treasure with him?'

'None, Sir Hugh.'

'Did you?' Corbett pointed at Rievaulx.

'No.' The king's approver half smiled, a knowing look hinting that his dead master's visit to Malmaison would remain confidential.

'My apologies for repeating myself,' Corbett declared, 'but when you entered that chamber, you found no trace of those panniers?' A chorus of agreement answered his question. 'Was anything else stolen?'

75

'No, no.' Brockle spoke up. 'Sir Hugh, it was most eerie. I mean, we have discussed this amongst ourselves. Wodeford and Lord Simon were mailed clerks, seasoned soldiers, veteran warriors who fought strenuously in the king's array. Yet both were slain, murdered with no trace of any resistance, defence or struggle. Just two corpses, and those panniers taken. Nothing disturbed. No sound of violence heard. Nothing glimpsed.'

Corbett nodded his agreement and stared down at the sheet of vellum containing the short, sharp notes he'd made for himself. 'So,' he began, 'you supped here in the hall. The evening was convivial. Lord Simon and Wodeford adjourned to the guest chamber. You all remained downstairs, though Malach left now and then because of the great cats. The hours passed. Neither Wodeford nor Lord Simon reappeared. Lady Isabella became concerned. Grease-hair was dispatched up a ladder because of the eerie silence from that chamber. He saw what he saw and reported this to you. The two leopards had now broken free. The alarm was raised. Malach again investigated. You, Lady Isabella, along with others, climbed the stairs to the guest chamber, where Brockle organised the servants to break down the door. You entered and saw the horrors awaiting you. Your beloved husband, Lord Simon, and John Wodeford, his guest, had both been slain by a crossbow. There was no sign, no trace of any struggle. The Angel of Death must have swept in swift and soft. A spirit indeed,' Corbett murmured, 'for despite the two murders and the theft of the panniers, the door pierced by a blood-daubed bolt, the chamber was found to be locked and bolted from within. Yes?'

'Sir Hugh,' Lady Isabella replied, 'you have succinctly described what happened.'

'And afterwards?'

'Well, as you can imagine, my household were in deep shock.' She drew a deep breath. 'We mourned, we cried, but life moves on. I dispatched messages to Sir Miles in Exeter. There was a funeral to arrange, requiems to be sung. Parson Osbert, the parish priest of St Peter in the Marsh, had to be summoned. Sir Hugh, death can make life very busy.'

'Yes, yes, I agree,' Corbett replied. 'Both corpses were laid out?'

'Coffined in the manor chapel,' Brockle declared, 'and buried in the small cemetery beyond.'

Corbett sat for a while, staring down the hall. He could hear the murmurs of conversation, despite the distance and the two closed doors that sealed the hall from the buttery, where Richolda and her ladies were now gathered. He glanced around. The hall was brightly decorated, luxurious. He briefly wondered where Lord Simon had obtained the means for such display although he entertained his own deep suspicions. After all, he knew that some of those who'd pursued Puddlicot's gang were not above helping themselves to what they'd found. Nevertheless, despite the exquisite finery of the wall tapestries, the best from the looms of Bruges, the gold and silver ornaments from Castile and elsewhere, the polished oak and elmwood furniture, there was a sombre, even malignant air about Malmaison, as if some evil crawled like a spider across its walls.

Corbett closed his eyes. He recalled a similar feeling from many years previous, when, as a witness, he had attended the most frightening exorcism, carried out in the nave of St Mary's Church near Carfax in Oxford. That same feeling of nameless dread he'd experienced there now gnawed at his soul and disturbed his peace of mind. A darkness permeated Malmaison. Sin, serious sin, squatted deep in the shadows. God's peace and that of the king had been shattered. Justice had to be—

'Sir Hugh?'

Corbett glanced up. Sir Miles was staring at him, his puzzled expression shared by the rest.

'Sir Hugh,' Ranulf repeated, 'shall we now move to the murder of the tax collector Sir Ralph Hengham?'

'Yes, yes, by all means. So,' Corbett continued, leaning forward, 'we come to the third hideous slaying. A royal tax collector, a knight of the shire, the king's official and the keeper of monies owing to the Crown that I understand amounted to at least two thousand pounds sterling. I believe every coin was taken?'

'True, true,' Wendover agreed, looking longingly across at the buttery table.

'In a short while,' Corbett whispered, 'you can break your fast, but the hours pass. This is pressing business. Now, our tax collector?'

'Sir Ralph was responsible for the levying of royal dues across the shires of Devon and Cornwall. He heard about Lord Simon's murder and hurried to Malmaison to assist. Hengham was also a justiciar, and so—'

'Nonsense!' Lady Isabella rasped. 'Come, Sir Miles, we all know the truth.'

'Which is, my lady?' Corbett asked.

'Hengham was a well-known lecher. Ask any woman across the shires. He hurried here in very vain hope of comforting the grieving widow.'

'Ah, I see.' Corbett made a face. 'I have heard the same. There have been complaints, petitions to the council. So, my lady, Sir Miles, what happened when Hengham arrived?'

'I accompanied him here,' Wendover replied. 'He needed an escort because of who he was and what he carried. And, of course, Dartmoor is lonely and haunted by the Sagittarius and his Scarecrows. However, we arrived safely enough before vespers, and supped merrily in this hall. I admit,' Wendover added wearily, 'Hengham drank deeply. He was lecherous towards Mistress Isabella, both in look and speech. My lady ignored him. We then adjourned to our chambers. I was lodged in the far wing of the manor; Hengham insisted in sleeping in what I now call the murder chamber.'

'That had been repaired?' Ranulf asked.

'Yes,' Brockle replied. 'The door had been rehung. Our manor smith fashioned a new lock, though the bolts and clasps still need repair.' He paused. 'Hengham definitely asked for this chamber. He also indicated that he was committed to coming to Malmaison before Lord Simon was murdered. Yes, some other business, but what, I don't know and now it doesn't really matter. Anyway,' he added briskly, 'he was pleased with his lodgings.'

'And the chamber was secure?'

'Oh yes. I escorted him up to it and closed the door. As I walked away, I heard him humming beneath his breath. He also turned the key.'

'He didn't stay there long,' Lady Isabella declared. 'Sir Hugh, my chamber is on the same gallery. I am sure he came and tapped at least twice on my door.'

'I heard the same,' Brockle agreed. 'After the second time, I went down to his room and pressed my ear against the door. He was still awake, still humming that ridiculous tune. I knocked and tried the handle. The door was locked. Hengham asked who it was, and I replied that I was simply ensuring he had everything he needed.' He shrugged. 'I was also quietly warning him that others were aware that he had been vexing my mistress. Anyway, Hengham said that all was well, so I returned to my own chamber.'

'And the next morning?'

'Malmaison awoke,' Lady Isabella declared. 'Nothing extraordinary. Parson Osbert prepared to celebrate mass. The manor folk assembled in the buttery to break their fast. Only then did Master Brockle notice that Hengham was absent. What followed was almost a close repetition of what had happened the week before. Brockle went up to the chamber and knocked, but there was no answer. The shutters over the lancet window had been repaired, so there was no other way forward but to force the door. A little easier this time, because there were no bolts, but the key was still in the lock, fully turned. By then I'd joined the group. I went into the chamber. Hengham lay across the bed, back against the wall, a crossbow bolt embedded deep in his chest. Apart from that, no other sign of a disturbance, resistance or defence, though his panniers were gone.' She spread her hands. 'No sign of them whatsoever.'

'Very well.' Corbett rose to his feet. 'My lady, I sympathise with your foot injury.'

'Painful enough, Sir Hugh, though I thank God it is healing.'

'Quite, quite.' Corbett pointed at Malach. 'The rest of you must stay here. Refresh yourselves at the buttery table. Ranulf, Sir Miles, Masters Malach and Brockle will show us the murder chamber.'

The two henchmen ushered Corbett and the other two justices out of the hall through a side door to a staircase built in the central atrium of the manor. It had wide, sweeping steps, its balustrades, newels and floorboards highly polished. The plaster on the walls was light pink and decorated with embroidered cloths, paintings and triptychs all celebrating a devotion to the Holy Face of Lucca. They climbed the staircase, turning to the right onto the gleaming, oaken galleries that bounded the manor on three sides. The passageways were clean and sweet smelling, the chamber doors on either side polished to a shine. Shuttered lanterns and capped candles provided light, whilst pots of crushed, sweetened herbs fragranced the air. They reached the guest chamber, the splintered door still hanging awry. Brockle pushed this to one side and ushered them in.

The murder chamber was spacious and well furnished, with a chancery table, chair and stool facing the door. On the wall behind the desk was a large shuttered window, and close to that, the lancet sealed by two narrow slats. A high four-poster bed, its curtains tied back, stood to the right. Beneath it, travelling chests, casks and coffers had been thrust. The floor was polished to a shine and warmed with Turkey rugs, the bare stretches of wall decorated with coloured cloths. Candle spigots stood on the chancery desk, whilst an elegant lanternhorn hung on a hook close to the door.

Corbett rigorously scrutinised the latter. He noticed how its bolts and clasps had been ripped away at both top and bottom, whilst the lock and key were badly buckled, testimony to the force used to break down the door. He walked into the centre of the chamber and turned to face the rest standing in the doorway.

'So,' he began, 'this is where Wodeford was found stretched out on the floor, Lord Simon in the chair slightly turned? And the bed curtains?'

'Pulled back,' Malach declared. 'The curtains were tied. The chests and coffers underneath undisturbed, as they were on the second occasion.'

'Ah yes, Master Hengham.' Corbett crossed to the bed. It had been stripped of its coverlets and bolsters, though he could still see the dried bloodstains dark on the palliasse.

'He was lying there,' Brockle declared. 'Sprawled

across the bed in his nightshirt, slumped back against the wall, flung there by the force of the bolt.'

'And on both occasions,' Corbett mused, 'no sign of a struggle. No one heard or saw anything amiss?'

'Sir Hugh, we – I – have said as much,' Brockle protested. 'It's all as much a mystery to us as it is to you.'

'A murderous one,' Ranulf declared.

'I will take this chamber.' Corbett walked over to the window and pulled back the shutters to reveal the unbroken oiled vellum covering. 'Yes, I will sleep here. Have the door rehung with fresh bolts and lock. It can be arranged swiftly?'

'Yes, Sir Hugh.'

'Good, good, Master Brockle. Then have it done before vespers, yes? Once completed, Ranulf and Chanson will bring up my sealed chancery coffers. I would like similar rooms to be offered to my two henchmen, though,' Corbett smiled, 'my clerk of the stables may wish to lodge with his beloved horses. Now,' he rubbed his hands together, 'let me visit the rest of this manor.'

'Sir Hugh, we have Richolda and her ladies waiting below.'

'I know, Ranulf,' he clasped his henchman on the shoulder, 'but I need to read all the verses of this hymn to murder. I want,' he lowered his voice, 'to feel the very essence of this place, which I suspect will not be pleasing. So . . .'

Corbett called to Brockle and Malach, telling the

former to go back to the hall and instruct Lady Isabella and the others to eat, drink and rest. Once he had finished his walk around the manor, Corbett would join them.

'Chanson?'

'Yes, Sir Hugh.' The clerk of the stables pushed himself away from the wall against which he had been resting.

'Go and sit with Richolda and her companions. Assure them I will speak to them before this day is finished.' Corbett spread his hands. 'So, let us wander.'

Led by Malach, with Brockle joining them later, Corbett swept around the manor. As he strode along galleries, passageways and corridors, he sensed the true wealth of the place with its gleaming polished furniture, wall hangings and decorations. Thick Turkey rugs lay strewn on polished floorboards or regularly swept paving stones scrubbed to whiteness. The manor boasted kitchens, butteries, storerooms, larders and pantries for various foodstuffs. Ovens, pans and large pots stood crammed with charcoal for grilling and frying. A well-ordered manor both within and without. It possessed dry, sweet-smelling stables, outhouses, a smithy, small granges and sturdy barns. The servants seemed content enough.

As he walked, he questioned Brockle and Malach on the revenues of the manor, which were plentiful: grazing rights, livestock, hunting and fishing levies, rents, as well as dues from the small ports along the coast and the income from the many fairs and markets that took place throughout the year. Malach also described how the manor could import fresh fish. Lord Simon had been the proud owner of two large, very stout herring boats moored in a nearby inlet.

Finally they visited the small, ancient chapel adjoining the manor. A simple, stark church, nothing more than a barn-like nave stretching up to a crudely carved rood screen that separated the black-stoned sanctuary from the rest of the church. Brockle paused to light a taper before a statue to St Briavel, after whom the chapel was named. Corbett joined him, lighting three tapers for his family before wandering over to examine the wall paintings, most of them celebrating the Holy Face. He also noticed a devotion to Christ's journey to Calvary, each incident being celebrated by a carved diptych or station. There were fourteen in number, and all freshly fashioned.

'That was Lord Simon,' Brockle whispered. 'He was devout, at least by his own lights. Sir Hugh, shouldn't we rejoin the Lady Isabella?'

'No, no,' Corbett replied. 'We must visit the cellars and the leopard pen.'

'But there is nothing there.'

'I will be the best judge of that.' Corbett gestured across the cobbled yard.

Brockle glanced fearfully at Malach.

'My master,' Ranulf stepped forward, 'wants to go there now.'

Brockle shrugged. Malach cursed beneath his breath, but the two men led Corbett and Ranulf back through the manor house to a square storeroom adjoining the main kitchen. They lifted a trapdoor in the corner and went down steep stone steps into a murky, ice-cold passageway that stretched into the blackness. Brockle lit two lanternhorns and gave one to Malach, then gestured at Corbett and Ranulf to follow him along the narrow paved gallery.

The walls either side were of sheer rock. The cellars themselves were naturally hewn caverns, across some of which doors had been positioned. Corbett maintained his composure, though he felt a deepening unease, that sense of dread he had experienced earlier. The darkness and the fetid, rank odours that swept this gloomy, narrow place only sharpened his wariness. At last they reached the end of the gallery. Brockle lit more lanterns and cresset torches to reveal a long line of narrow bars sealing off the cavern beyond: a cave with a high dome-like roof, which brooded over an open space stretching into dark recesses. He pulled back the bolts and clasps and opened a narrow door in the cage. Malach explained how, on the night of the murders, the cage had been mysteriously opened, allowing the great cats to escape through the postern door

Corbett, now tense, a chilling unease tingling the sweat on his face and back, stepped through the narrow door into the cage. The stench was so noisome, he immediately placed one hand across his mouth and nose, then glanced quickly at Ranulf. His henchman was in no better state than himself. The clerk of the Green Wax was agitated: green eyes constantly blinking, his breathing short and sharp as he scratched at the sweat lacing his pallid face.

'This is a fearsome place,' Ranulf rasped.

'Foul!' Malach declared. 'A stinking cave where those two leopards prowled, ate, pissed and shitted till the air became unbearable. I hate coming down here. I always have. Master Brockle is no different. The sooner we are gone, the better.'

Corbett was determined to maintain his poise. He suspected, despite what they'd said, that Malach and Brockle were quietly enjoying the discomfiture of the two royal clerks.

'How was the cage cleaned?' he asked.

Malach turned and pointed into the darkness. 'There is another enclave protected by bars. Lord Simon would drive the beasts into that and then open the shutters to clean the mess.'

'He was not frightened?'

'Apparently not, Sir Hugh. The cats sensed he was their master, though as they grew older, Lord Simon became more wary. He would don armour, hard-boiled leather jerkin and leggings, and use flaming torches to cower the cats, whilst two retainers would always accompany him with crossbows primed and ready.'

'Did they ever attack?' Ranulf's voice betrayed his agitation.

'They tried to. But nothing harmful.' Malach tapped his boot against the ground. 'I didn't like them. I did not like coming down here and I still don't.'

Corbett murmured a prayer and walked deeper into

the cave, struggling against the creeping dread. He recalled an image of the Virgin Mother of Walsingham and recited an Ave. Then he glanced to his left and pointed to a sturdy oaken door fixed into the rocky side of the cave; both it and the lintel had been painted a deep black to blend in with the rock around it. He walked across and scrutinised it carefully. Like other posterns and entrances in these sinister caves and caverns, there were no locks; simply heavy clasps and bolts on the outside, also painted black. He peered through a grille set high in the door, only to realise that the slat beyond had been pulled across. 'What is this?' he asked.

'See for yourself, Sir Hugh.' Malach pushed by, lifted the clasps and swung open the door.

The chamber beyond was a long rectangle hewn out of the rock, about two yards high and four in length and width. There was a vent in the ceiling, a fissure through the rock, which allowed in air and acted as a flue. The furniture was sparse: table, chair, stool, a battered coffer, pegs for clothes, a cracked lavarium and a truckle bed, now stripped of its palliasse, sheets, bolsters and coverlets.

Ranulf, whistling under his breath, followed Corbett into the chamber, though he stood on the threshold, so the door could not be suddenly closed. Ranulf only trusted three people: Sir Hugh, the Lady Maeve and Chanson. He certainly did not trust the two men who had brought them down into what he considered to be an antechamber of hell.

'How long have you served at Malmaison?' he demanded.

'We came together, about five years ago, around the time of the old king's death, after Lord Simon's marriage to the Lady Isabella.' Malach paused. 'Why?' he asked.

'So these cages, hidden chambers and dark enclaves were already here?'

'Of course.' Malach shrugged. 'And who were we to question Lord Simon? He was a good master as long as you did what he asked.'

Corbett, standing in the centre of the chamber, stared carefully around. We are spiritual beings, he reflected, his hand going to the silver crucifix hanging on a chain around his neck.

'We are spiritual beings.' He voiced his thoughts. 'We live in the spiritual, be it good or bad. This place possesses a malignancy, a malevolence all of its own. Why was this chamber hewn cunningly out of the rock, its lintel and door specially fashioned?'

'We don't know,' Malach retorted, going to sit on the stool. 'On one occasion Lord Simon did tell me that he used the chamber to safely view his cats. He would stay here with a goblet of wine and watch them. He had the bed moved in because he maintained the cats became more active at night. He would also bring them carcasses and watch them eat.'

'And before you signed indentures and joined his household, we know Chandos was his steward. What happened to him?'

'Oh, that's a great mystery. You see, Lord Simon's

first wife, Lady Beatrice, and Chandos disappeared, simply vanished.' Malach smiled coldly. 'And before you voice your suspicions, nothing happened to them here. They were seen in Plymouth on a cog bound for Boulogne. The Lady Beatrice was French, though her family hailed from the English-held enclave of Ponthieu. Later reports describe how she and Chandos were also seen in or around Bordeaux in Gascony.'

'And Lord Simon's former henchman?'

'You mean Wolfram? He left Lord Simon's household and now lives with his sister, the Lady Katerina, out on the marshes.'

Corbett nodded. Wolfram had also been a mailed clerk who had worked in the Secret Chancery. Corbett had met both him and his lovely faced sister, but he would keep that to himself. For the moment, he was more concerned with this place; he was determined to master his mood so as not to be so deeply affected by these ghostly caverns.

He left the chamber, drew his long Welsh dagger and moved deeper into the dark. The fetid smell grew even more pungent. He pressed on until he reached a tangle of bones. Reassured by Ranulf standing behind him, he crouched down and, using his dagger, sifted amongst them. He was almost about to give up when he glimpsed one shard, concave, smooth and polished. He pulled this closer and picked it up.

'Master?'

'Ranulf, I am sure this is the crown of a human skull.'

Corbett carefully concealed his macabre find beneath his jerkin and continued his search. 'Yes, yes,' he whispered, 'there are fragments here, thin and curving. I am sure they are the shattered shards of human ribs.' He rose to his feet. 'Evil always shows its hand,' he murmured, 'and so it has here.'

He returned to the hall, where the others were summoned back and the chamber was swiftly prepared for what Ranulf proclaimed to be the second session of the court. Corbett readied himself. He'd slipped what he'd found into his chancery satchel, then washed his hands and face before eating and drinking a little at the buttery table. Now he called the court to order, taking deep breaths to ease his agitation.

At Ranulf's command, Parson Osbert led Richolda and her companions up to the dais. The parson took the centre chair whilst the guildswomen sat on the benches either side. As they settled themselves, whispering to each other and making themselves comfortable, Corbett swiftly studied the new arrivals.

Parson Osbert was thin, angular, with a bony face, sharp eyed and thin lipped, both head and face closely shaved. He reminded Corbett of a bird with his jerky movements, constantly looking around as if wary of some lurking danger. He was dressed in a simple grey robe with a belt around the middle, thick, sturdy sandals on his feet. Corbett narrowed his eyes. He was certain he had met the man before – something about his face, but there again, he'd met so many in his work. He'd learnt from manor gossip that Osbert was an energetic priest, well respected, who'd served in both the royal array and other parishes in the diocese.

He glanced next at Richolda, sitting to the parson's right, a florid-faced, burly woman with flame-red hair, dressed in a tawny robe. She was all a-bustle and would have launched immediately into her appeal if the good parson had not restrained her, clutching her arm and raising a finger to his lips for silence.

Ranulf again called the court to order and Parson Osbert rose to his feet. 'Sir Hugh, we are here,' the priest declared in a carrying voice, 'because of a most mysterious and sinister event. These good ladies are the wives of the guildsmen of Felstead. Their husbands were prosperous, hard-working tanners who did a thriving trade preparing skins, pelts and hides for both here and beyond the Narrow Seas. Now, on the eve of the feast of St Cyprian, they assembled, as was their custom, in the banqueting chamber of their favoured tavern, the equally prosperous Palfrey in Felstead. Minehost Master Baskerville had prepared a most tasty repast and all should have been well.' Osbert paused for effect. Corbett kept his face straight, for the priest was speaking as if delivering a homily from his pulpit.

'And?' Ranulf banged the table. 'Parson Osbert, the hour passes.'

'We know what happened,' Corbett declared. 'Those guildsmen left that tavern and were never seen again.'

'They were on foot?' Wendover demanded.

'Yes,' Richolda almost shouted. 'The night was fog-bound.'

'Had they drunk deeply?'

'Of course, Sir Miles. You know that.' Richolda jabbed her fat hand at the sheriff. 'And don't say all twelve of them staggered onto the moors, fell into the same marsh and disappeared without a trace. Even if they had, you wouldn't have found them. You haven't done much.'

'Mistress,' Wendover retorted, 'what can I do? I have alerted the shire's comitatus. We have dispatched hunters and those who know the moors to search that sea of gorse. We found nothing.'

'And you, king's man?'

'Yes, I am the king's man,' Corbett declared, getting to his feet. 'And so, mistress, accept my assurances that I shall do everything under heaven to resolve these mysteries and clear the murderous mist that has created such mayhem in and around Malmaison.' He gestured at Richolda and her companions, then retook his seat. 'You have my word, the solemn word of a king's man. I will do what I have just said.'

Within an hour of the session ending, Corbett, booted, spurred and cloaked, joined his comitatus in the spacious manor courtyard. Six of Ap Ythel's archers, including their captain and the former bestiarius Merioneth, together with Ranulf and Sir Miles, prepared to leave. Cloaked and hooded, their faces muffled against the biting wind, the horsemen milled about whilst Corbett had hasty words with the sheriff. Wendover assured him in a heated whisper that on the morning after

Hengham's murder, he had viewed the tax collector's corpse sprawled on the bed, and what Corbett had been told in the hall was the truth as he saw it. The sheriff then moved away as Corbett, striving to keep his mount placid, beckoned the wizened Merioneth closer.

'*Pax et bonum*, my friend. Let's have words.' He swung himself out of the saddle and led his horse away from the rest, beckoning Merioneth to follow. Once they were out of earshot, he grasped the man's shoulder.

'Merioneth, you have some knowledge of the great cats that were kept here?'

'Not now needed,' Merioneth replied mournfully. 'Sir Hugh, I understand that both beasts are dead, or so rumour has it. Poisoned out on the moors.'

'Would that have been easy to achieve? I mean those great cats are skilled hunters.'

'No, Sir Hugh, no animal will hunt if it is offered food literally on a platter. Lord Simon's cats were raised and fed, that was their custom. Once free, yes, hunger would make them stalk, hunt, kill anything that caught their eye or their nose. But if a carcass was found, they'd devour that just as eagerly.'

'And if the carcass was poisoned?'

'They would still eat. After all, wolves and foxes are killed in the same way. A carcass, tainted though it may be, exudes a powerful stench. Once the cats smelt that, they'd seek it out as any true arrow would find its mark.'

'So they were poisoned?' Corbett murmured. 'And thus my next question: was it an accident or deliberate?'

'Deliberate,' Merioneth replied. 'Definitely so. To kill cats as powerful as those, a great deal of poison must have been used, be it hemlock, henbane or wolfsbane. The carcass would have been drenched in such a potion.' He stared at the sky. 'A lonely, bleak place this, Sir Hugh,' he whispered. 'Look at the clouds, grey, lowering and oppressive. Wild and dangerous, even more so when darkness descends. At night, the mist sweeps in and those mysterious blue flames appear like ghosts to flit above the treacherous bogs, quagmires, morasses and marshes.'

'What are you saying, Merioneth? What are you implying?'

'Well, master, there is enough danger here without great cats roaming, roaring and seeking prey. Those two leopards were hand raised, but out there, as time passed and their hunger deepened, they'd revert to being what they truly were: cunning, ferocious hunters. Nevertheless, they would have rivals. The wolfsheads who prowl this place, they'd see them as a real and ever-present danger. No wonder the cats were poisoned.'

Corbett nodded his agreement, thanked Merioneth and climbed back into the saddle. His comitatus was ready. Lifting his hand, he urged his horse forward and led his retinue through the now open gates, ordering the royal pennant to be unfurled before cantering along the rocky causeway that stretched out to the bleak moors, the windswept gorse dark and threatening as it moved backwards and forwards under sullen grey skies.

PART TWO

One sack was full of cups whole as well as broken.

Grease-hair, standing by the kitchen door, watched Corbett's cavalcade leave the manor. He stared admiringly at the three royal clerks and wondered if he too could enter the king's service. Sir Hugh and his henchman Ranulf were powerful men, yet quiet, confident in themselves, so unlike the late Lord Simon. The manor lord had been secretive and close, yet he lacked the real authority of these king's men.

The spit-boy wiped his hands on his apron and stared at the Tower archers riding behind Corbett with their quivers of arrows looped over their saddle horns, their powerful war bows slung across their backs, the precious twine protected by a layer of light leather. One of the archers carried a pennant displaying the royal arms, a gorgeous array of red, blue and gold. Grease-hair wished heartily that he was part of that entourage. He'd even offered to be Corbett's guide across the moors to the lonely priory of St Benet. Colum the cook, however, had simply mocked him, pointing out that Sheriff Wendover knew the coffin paths as well as anyone. Moreover, Grease-hair was needed at Malmaison to roast a whole side of hog in preparation for that evening's dinner.

The boy sighed and re-entered the manor. The hall was deserted, all signs of the recent court removed. He wandered over to the fire as Colum and his black-faced scullions brought in the meats. They positioned the hog on the great spit and placed two pots close to Grease-hair's stool in the inglenook. The one with the ladle contained a thick, creamy oil showered with precious salts and keen spices; the other held square sacks of herbs for Grease-hair to place on the logs cracking and spluttering in the fiery embrace of the darting flames.

The cook and his minions left. Grease-hair sat down on the stool, flinching at the intense heat from the now roaring fire, the flames spluttering vigorously on the fat dripping from the succulent meat. He began his labouring, pausing now and again to throw on a sachet of herbs and savour the now delicious smells seeping from the fire. Half dozing, he reflected on what was now happening at Malmaison. He would never forget that night, climbing the ladder, peering into the murder chamber. What had he glimpsed that was so untoward? He'd even tried to scrawl on a wall as well as a scrap of parchment, yet for the life of him, he could not remember. He turned the spit and tossed another sachet onto the fire, and in the space of a few heartbeats, the flames seemed to roar and jump out towards him, catching at his grease-drenched clothing. The spit-boy started to his feet, the fire now holding him from head to toe. Screaming and yelling, he ran down the hall beating vainly at the flames, which seemed to feed on him, holding him fast in their deadly embrace as they raced up, down and around his body . . .

Corbett reined in and stared at St Benet's Priory, which stood at the crossroads of the gorse-covered plateau of Doone Moor. The huddle of granite buildings bounded by a soaring curtain wall looked like one of the high tors he had passed on the journey here. Hills and ridges crammed with a collection of eerily fashioned boulders, craggy stones and rough-hewn slabs of rock, placed there perhaps as the playthings of the giant who reputedly lived on the moor in ancient times. Such outcrops only deepened the sheer loneliness of the landscape, the iron-grey skies and the constantly wailing wind tinged with salt from the nearby sea. A vast, empty place. Corbett knew that in high summer the gorse would burst into eye-catching colours, the winds would fall and the bracken become alive, animals scurrying here and there, wary of the hunting birds circling above them – but not now. Spring might have announced itself with shoots of light greenery, but the recent winter had been hard and still had the land in its grip. Little wonder Ranulf was nervous, crossing what he called 'the moors of hell and the terrain of purgatory'.

'Sir Hugh?'

'Yes, Sir Miles?' Corbett broke from his reverie.

'Our hosts undoubtedly await us.'

'I am sure they do. Tell me, Sheriff, do the local people know why these monks shelter here?'

'As I have said, rumours.' Wendover pulled his muffler fully down. 'The good brothers leave people alone. They portray themselves as poor, humble people of good repute, so the moor folk have considerable pity for them. They do no wrong, they inflict no hurt.' He steadied his horse. 'So why should they not be accepted?'

'Why indeed?' Corbett laughed abruptly. 'But I know these men, as I do their worth. Believe me, my Lord Sheriff, those buildings house a coven of truly wicked men.' He grasped his reins and dug his spurs in. 'Unless, of course, we are now living in a new age of miracles. So come, let us salute these so-called holy men.'

He urged his horse along the sheep track, no broader than a coffin path or a narrow city runnel. The rest of his entourage followed, riding slowly up to the main gate built into the lofty curtain wall. Corbett noticed how both wall and gate had recently been refurbished. As they approached, a bell began to toll, a deep, mournful sound that echoed across the moor. The archer carrying the royal pennant spurred his horse forward to clearly demonstrate that they were king's men here on the business of the Crown. The bell stopped its tolling and the huge gates swung open. Corbett urged his horse through into the cracked, cobbled yard. He reined in and smiled at the group of men, about fourteen in number, who had gathered to meet them. They were garbed in the black robes and white cinctures of the Benedictines, heads neatly tonsured, though their faces were almost hidden by thick, bushy moustaches and beards.

Their leader stepped forward, a tall, sharp-faced individual. He held a dagger in one hand and a battle mace in the other. He drew closer and, as Corbett quietened his horse, put his weapons down on the ground, then raised his hands, palms displayed in a sign of friendship.

'*Pax et bonum*, welcome.' The monk's voice was gruff and carrying. 'Oh yes, we welcome and greet Sir Hugh Corbett, Keeper of the King's Secret Seal, special emissary of the Crown, His Grace's most trusted servant in the shires of—'

'Enough of that, Master Warfeld. You are going to tell me how pleased you are to see me, and I truly doubt that.' Corbett held a hand up for silence as he gazed around the spacious friary enclosure, which held a narrow ancient church, outhouses, stables and other buildings, all dominated by a long, high two-storey building built like a huge barn. He recognised this as an ancient long hall, with refectory, kitchen, buttery and pantry on the ground floor and narrow bedchambers above. The hall, like all the buildings, was fashioned out of that grey granite so easily extracted from moorland quarries.

'Well,' Corbett pulled back his cowl and stared down at the Blackrobe, 'Adam Warfeld, former sacristan of the king's own chapel at Westminster Abbey, greetings. I will now meet you and all your brothers,' he nodded towards the long hall, 'in your refectory.'

'And your business here, Sir Hugh?'

'My business is for me to say, you to listen then truthfully reply. So let us begin.'

Corbett dismounted; Wendover and the others followed suit. Corbett than rapped out orders to the archers who'd accompanied them. Some were to look after the horses, whilst four of them would follow him into the hall, bows notched ready to loose on his command.

The refectory was a long, stark yet comfortable room dominated by a broad trestle table with benches along either side. Corbett took a stool and sat at the top of the table. He glimpsed a throne-like chair pushed deep into the shadows of the wall close to the large hearth. Undoubtedly that belonged to Warfeld, who, Corbett suspected, would preside like any prince over his followers. As the others took their seats and the archers deployed close to the royal clerks, Corbett quickly stared around. The refectory was clean and well swept, the wall plaster smooth and shiny, decorated here and there with a simple triptych celebrating the lives of St Benedict and his sister Scholastica. A fire burnt fiercely in the gaping hearth, cresset torches blazed on the walls and candle spigots along the table provided light, as the unshuttered windows were no more than lancets.

Ranulf made to open his chancery satchel, but Corbett touched him gently on the arm and shook his head. 'Just watch and listen,' he murmured, then forced a smile as Warfeld took his seat at the far end of the table, his brothers ranged either side.

Corbett studied them leisurely, shifting his gaze as if

he was recalling each and every face. It was difficult to believe that this cohort of Benedictine monks, lay brothers and consecrated priests who had sworn solemn vows of obedience, poverty and chastity had once been the most audacious gang of rifflers in the kingdom. Now they were banished to Dartmoor and this bleak, abandoned priory. He had never discovered who had chosen such a desolate place, but it was one he agreed with. Warfeld and the other wolfsheads should be kept well away from anyone else.

'Shall we begin.' He shifted his gaze and stared at the Blackrobe, who, hands folded on the table, beamed back at him.

'Now, master, there's a Judas smile,' Ranulf whispered.

Corbett just winked.

'Sir Hugh,' Warfeld again smiled like a benevolent pastor eager to listen to some penitent's confession, 'to what do we owe this pleasure?'

'I am carrying out a visit on the orders of His Grace the king and the royal council at Westminster. I believe you know that place well?' Warfeld's smile faded. 'I am here to ensure all is well. Captain Ap Ythel and Sheriff Wendover are now doing a tour of this priory.'

'What for, treasure?' Warfeld's henchman Walter Brasenose, his thickset face mottled in anger, glared down the table at Corbett.

'No, they are carrying out a census.' Corbett smiled. 'I must say, you all look peaceful and well fed.'

'We are Benedictines, Corbett—'

'Sir Hugh to you, monk.'

'We are Benedictines, Sir Hugh. We make the desert bloom and the wasteland prosper. We now possess cattle, a piggery, chickens, a small warren, herb plots and vegetable gardens. We also have the right to beg for alms as far as Plymouth. The local people, who recognise us as God's poor men, are most supportive. They are generous in their giving and we respond by helping Parson Osbert in his priestly duties.'

'And you know what is happening at Malmaison? The murders and the mayhem?'

'Yes, Sir Hugh, we do. But surely Lord Simon's death and that of Wodeford and Hengham do not concern—'

'Murders,' Ranulf interrupted. 'All three were foully murdered.'

'And we had no hand in that,' Brasenose retorted. 'None of us go anywhere near Malmaison.'

'Sir Hugh,' Warfeld spoke up, 'I realise Lord Simon and Wodeford were of your party when you hunted us down. We were trapped, caught and sentenced, but we have now closed the door on the past. We did not plot against the men who were murdered, because,' he shrugged, 'we did not care a whit about them and we still don't.' He held up a hand. 'We had no part in the dire events that seem to plague these parts; in the murders of Hengham, Wodeford and Lord Simon or in the escape of the great cats and the disappearance of the guildsmen. And before the finger of accusation is pointed, we know nothing of the wreckers, the coven who call themselves the Scarecrows under their master the Sagittarius.' He shook his head whilst his comrades rapped the table in support. 'Remember, Sir Hugh, these miscreants, the Scarecrows, were prospering long before we ever arrived here.'

Corbett nodded in agreement and stared towards the door, firmly closed with archers on guard outside, whilst Ap Ythel would keep Wendover busy searching this benighted place.

'The Lacrima Christi.' He stared down the table. 'All of you were involved in its theft, not to mention that of other treasures. What happened to that beautiful ruby?'

'We don't know.'

'I could have this priory surrounded by Ap Ythel's archers,' Corbett retorted. 'I could lay siege to it until I starve you into compliance, so don't act the innocent, any of you. I repeat, the Lacrima Christi.'

'Why not ask Master Rievaulx?' Warfeld grinned wolfishly, his lips curled back like those of a snarling dog, his thick black moustache and beard seeming to bristle with fury. 'We have,' his voice was almost a snarl, 'unfinished business with Master Rievaulx.'

'Are you threatening him?'

'Sir Hugh, we are what we are. We accept you and yours for who you are and what you do, but as for Rievaulx . . .' Warfeld would have turned and spat, but, hands tightly clasped, he restrained his anger. 'Rievaulx,' he grated, 'was Puddlicot's henchman. He took the blood oath to be loyal in life and in death, but as soon as he was trapped, he turned king's approver. He is a true Judas man, more fit for hell than any of us.'

'And he has informed us that the Lacrima Christi and its casket disappeared very quickly after the robbery,' Corbett replied calmly.

'Oh, let's cut to the chase,' Brasenose rasped. 'Brother Warfeld, this is of little concern to us.' His words were greeted with growls of approval.

'Tell the king's man what we know,' another of the monks declared.

'Very well.' Warfeld drew a deep breath. 'Once we had seized the treasure, we went our own ways, and that was the cause of our downfall. Turds like Rievaulx, as the hunt for us became more intense, turned king's approver, eager for a royal pardon in return for cooperation.'

'The Lacrima Christi!' Ranulf pounded the table. 'Answer my master's questions. You can do so here or in the dungeons beneath Exeter Guildhall.'

Corbett could see that Warfeld was struggling to control his ferocious temper. A number of his brethren now had their hands beneath the table, and he wondered how many of them carried daggers or stilettos concealed in the folds of their robes.

'The Lacrima Christi,' he repeated quietly.

'Our treasure hoard,' Warfeld replied, 'was unbelievable. At least a hundred royal ransoms. Now amongst our following was a former jeweller, Glaston, who seized your famous ruby as his part of the plunder.'

'And the casket?' Corbett questioned sharply.

'Yes, and the casket,' Warfeld agreed.

'Describe it.'

'Oh, it was precious and beautiful.' Warfeld rubbed his hands together. 'Exquisite. Small yet gorgeous in appearance, quite heavy, pure gold studded with diamonds.'

'And?'

'I confess,' Warfeld gave a lopsided grin, 'I was tempted to take it myself.'

'You examined it carefully? Tell me what you saw.'

'The lid of the casket was concave. It bore an inscription in Latin and Arabic saying, if I recall correctly, that it was a gift from the Caliph of Egypt to Prince Edward of England. That's right, a declaration that both the casket and the ruby it contained were free gifts to a prince about to be king.'

'And you definitely saw this?'

'Of course I did, Sir Hugh, and you must have seen the same.'

'I agree. Shortly before the robbery, I and other clerks of the Secret Chancery did a formal audit. I examined the ruby and its casket. As you say, Warfeld, items of exquisite beauty. So,' Corbett's tone turned sharper, 'what happened to these possessions of the king?'

'Only conjecture, Sir Hugh, stories that passed from mouth to mouth. Glaston took the ruby, only to be captured and murdered by Lord Simon Malmaison and his henchman Wolfram.'

'You have proof of that?'

'None, Sir Hugh, only conjecture, Newgate gossip. More importantly,' Warfeld laughed abruptly, 'Glaston, over the last eight years, has never been glimpsed by his former comrades.' He spread his hands. 'Nor have his relatives or family heard or seen anything of him. He has disappeared as if he never existed. No, no.' He briskly clapped his hands. 'Glaston was murdered, Malmaison and Wolfram the guilty parties. We tell you this, Corbett . . . Sir Hugh,' he corrected himself hastily, 'to demonstrate the true state of affairs in this vale of tears. We were guilty, caught and punished, but royal officials, men such as yourself, closed in like scavengers do on a battlefield to sift and filch any juicy morsel.'

'The Lacrima Christi and its casket are more than a juicy morsel.'

'So they are, so they are,' Warfeld retorted. 'But my contention is that others committed crimes that went unpunished. Servants to the king, royal clerks, they were as guilty as we were—'

'So,' Ranulf interrupted, 'Malmaison seized the ruby. And then what?'

'He sold it,' Warfeld retorted. 'He had to. Not for its true worth, but still a goodly sum, which, as you must have seen, helped him to refurbish and adorn his manor house.'

'And the buyers?'

'You know that, royal clerk. The only people who could afford to purchase such items with ready money were the Italian bankers in Lombard Street. The Frescobaldi or some other gaggle of licensed thieves.'

Corbett hid his amusement at Warfeld's burst of self-righteousness. From everything he'd learnt, he believed this tonsured thief was telling the truth, probably for the first time in his life.

'It's true, isn't it?' Warfeld insisted.

'It's true,' Corbett agreed. 'The ruby was bought by Italian bankers, who took it to Rome and sold it to the papacy. And in the papacy's hands it remained until it was lost during a dreadful accident following Pope Clement's coronation at Lyons.'

He paused, aware of how silent the priory had fallen: no birdsong, no sound of either prayer, work or study. Just this long, darkening hall and these monks, a coven of outlaws watching him intently. He realised that if Ranulf was not with him, or his archers ever vigilant with their war bows notched, Warfeld and his Blackrobes would happily slaughter him, a man they must regard as the true cause of their downfall. They were ruthless, without conscience or care for anyone else.

Corbett leant his elbows on the table, staring into a shadow-filled corner. He let the silence deepen.

'Why are you really here, Sir Hugh?'

'King's business, monk!'

'Which is?'

'King's business.' He stared intently at Warfeld. 'You helped me,' he declared, 'so I will tell you one of my reasons for being here. The Lacrima Christi lost in Lyons may have returned to England.' He paused at the exclamations and cries his announcement provoked and smiled in quiet satisfaction. He had established one truth: these Blackrobes had little if anything to do with the ruby.

'Can you tell us more, Sir Hugh?'

'Certainly. After receiving an anonymous letter intimating that the Lacrima Christi was up for sale, Lord Simon Malmaison wrote to the Secret Chancery claiming he had been approached by a mysterious personage offering to sell the ruby back to the English Crown.' Corbett shrugged. 'Well, that's the impression he gave. Naturally, His Grace the king was intrigued, as was I. Accordingly we dispatched John Wodeford, a royal clerk, together with Master Rievaulx.'

'We know both bastards!' Brasenose bellowed, but then hastily waved a hand as Ranulf half rose, restrained only by Corbett.

'Well, you must know what happened. Wodeford was murdered, his treasure stolen. Lord Simon was slain in the same chamber; whatever secrets he held, he carried to his grave. A week later, Sir Ralph Hengham, knight of the shire and tax collector, was murdered in the same room and his money panniers stolen. One treason after another. Men slaughtered. So,' Corbett clapped his hands, 'you had nothing to do with any of these murderous mysteries and you can shed no light on them?'

'Nothing at all,' Warfeld sang back. 'We are what you see, Blackrobes living in poverty, following our rule, praying for the souls of other poor sinners. We are innocents—'

'No you are not,' Ranulf snarled. 'You are certainly not that.'

'Restrain your dog, Corbett.'

Ranulf would have sprung to his feet, but Corbett

pulled him back, aware that the archers behind him had taken a step forward. '*Pax et bonum!*' he shouted. '*Pax et bonum!*' He sat back in his chair, waiting for the commotion to still and the silence deepen. 'We may be finished here,' he eventually declared. 'Well, at least for the moment. But rest assured, I shall return.' He rose to his feet. 'Brother Warfeld, if I can call you that, you must join me outside.'

Corbett and Ranulf, escorted by the bowmen, with Warfeld trailing behind, left the refectory, going down the dusty passageway leading into the courtyard. Corbett abruptly paused outside a chamber and tapped at the door.

'Brother Warfeld, what is in here?'

'Nothing but an empty chamber.'

'Good, that's what I want.'

He pushed open the door, ordering the archers to stay on guard outside, and beckoned Warfeld and Ranulf to join him, closing the door and leaning against it.

'So, monk, you had nothing to do with the murders at Malmaison?'

'No, and you know that's the truth.'

'I agree,' Corbett conceded wearily, 'there is not a shred of evidence that you were involved.'

'Lord Simon was a blood-drinker. He must have had enemies,' Warfeld retorted. 'He may have been a royal clerk, but he was also a dyed-in-the-wool riffler.'

'And these wreckers?' Corbett's voice was so hard it surprised Ranulf, though he knew that the destruction and plundering of ships along the coast had absorbed his master's attention both before and during their journey to Malmaison. 'The wreckers?' Corbett repeated.

Warfeld's arrogance seemed to have drained away, his voice sinking into a whine. 'As I have said, the wreckers were busy long before we arrived here.'

'So you know nothing about them?'

'Sir Hugh, you have seen St Benet's here on Doone Moor, a desolate, sombre place even in the height of summer. At night, especially during winter, it's like travelling through the valleys of hell.'

'So why did you choose it? How do you come to be living in such a forlorn place?'

'We didn't. Our superiors chose it.' Warfeld shrugged. 'It was either this or the wilds of some Irish glen.'

Corbett nodded even as he stared at this most cunning of men. In truth, he did not believe a word of what Warfeld was saying. He could almost smell the mischief brewing here. But what mischief? Warfeld was correct, there was nothing linking him to the slaughter at Malmaison, and although the wreckers had been busy, increasingly so, over the last few years, they had been active long before Warfeld and his coven ever arrived on Doone Moor.

'Sir Hugh?'

'Ah, yes.' Corbett pushed himself away from the door. 'I understand your community is fifteen in number, but I counted only fourteen.'

'You are most welcome to view our good brother Stephen whose corpse now lies in our death house, his soul gone to God, his body ready for the soil.'

'And the cause of death?'

'See for yourself, Sir Hugh. Brother Stephen's lips are still coated with the phlegm that filled his lungs and created the malignant humour that killed him.'

They left the chamber and crossed the priory yard, where a flock of chickens strutted and pecked in a noisy flurry of feathers. Ap Ythel and Wendover stood there deep in conversation.

'Anything?' Corbett asked as he approached them. 'Did you find anything untoward or suspicious?'

Ap Ythel glanced over Corbett's shoulder to where Warfeld, Brasenose and others clustered close. 'We carried out a thorough search,' he said in a low voice. 'This priory is well provisioned: it possesses granges and storerooms, vegetable garden and a herb plot rich in all forms of shrubs. But we found nothing amiss except a corpse. Let me show you.'

He led Corbett and Ranulf out of the yard to a stone shed behind the ancient church. Opening the door, he ushered them over to where the corpse lay stretched out in a simple wooden coffin no better than an arrow box. It had been dressed for burial in a tattered black robe, a small crucifix attached to its chest and a pair of scruffy buskins on its feet.

'As you can see . . .' Corbett turned. Warfeld stood in the doorway. 'As you can see, Sir Hugh, Brother Stephen is ready for his last journey.'

'As we too must journey on.' Corbett forced a smile. 'Brother Warfeld, we shall undoubtedly meet again.'

Corbett and his party left St Benet's, clattering out

onto Doone Moor. The day was drawing on, the light weakening. Gusts of mist billowed, broke, gathered and dispersed again. Hunting birds and gulls from the nearby coast circled above them, their chilling calls only deepening the brooding malevolence that seemed to settle like a cloud around them. They followed the well-worn sheep walks, coffin paths and tinker tracks. Occasionally a lonely farmstead offered a little relief from the harshness with the sweet smell of woodsmoke and the flash of light from some torch or lantern. For the rest, the moorland rolled every side of them, a forest of black gorse, whilst the sombre tors, dark and forbidding, only emphasised the sinister stillness of the landscape.

At last they breasted a hill onto a broad, sweeping thoroughfare, which cut down through the bracken into Felstead. A surprisingly prosperous-looking village with a large number of fine houses flanking the road, a sharp contrast to the grim stillness of the countryside. Corbett, riding slightly in front of his escort, was immediately impressed by the wealth of this small town. The houses were of stone and granite dug from the local quarries, cut and shaped by masons. Window frames, doors and lintels were of polished wood. Small fire stacks built against kitchen and hall of these dwellings exuded a welcoming perfumed smoke. Some of the windows even had glass. The roofs were deeply sloped to carry off the rainwater, the red and black tiles glistening in the light. Finely laid gardens stretched either side of paved paths leading up to gleaming, well-hung doorways.

Corbett's arrival provoked great interest, and as the

party processed along the high street, a crowd began to follow, a constant hum of talk with well-meaning shouts of 'Greetings, king's man'. They kept riding until they reached the centre of the village, its crossroads dominated by a life-sized statue of the Virgin holding the Divine Child. Houses stood on three of the corners, with shops on the ground floor. The entire fourth corner was occupied by a spacious, indeed quite majestic tavern, the Palfrey. Built completely of stone, it soared over a high curtain wall with an impressive gateway leading into the yard beyond.

Corbett decided to avoid the hostelry for the moment and pressed on to the furthest edge of the village. He reached the spacious tanning compound housing huts, storerooms, furnaces and cutting sheds. The guildsmen, or so Wendover informed him, had chosen this place because of its wells and underground streams. He tried not to flinch at the foul smell that still polluted the air despite the fact that the tanning sheds had lain silent since the disappearance of the guildsmen. He had a few words with the watchman, who lived in a small cottage just within the gateway. The man informed him what Corbett knew already about the abrupt disappearance of those who'd once worked there. He thanked the fellow and summoned Wendover and Ap Ythel over.

'We are here in Felstead,' he declared, gently quietening his horse, which was disturbed by the stench from the slaughter sheds. 'A prosperous place, yes?' He didn't wait for an answer. 'Its citizens have crops, grazing and plentiful water, their houses and gardens are most pleasing—'

'Even though,' Wendover interrupted, 'the soil is of poor quality. Heaven knows, but it's not the richest.'

'Nevertheless, my Lord Sheriff, Felstead must be very prosperous. It stands at the principal crossroads across the moors, a good resting place for those travelling from Exeter and beyond to the coast.'

'I agree.'

'However,' Corbett continued, 'the real source of wealth must be the worthy and noble Guild of Fleshers and Tanners. I understand stock is driven here to be slaughtered and skinned. The hides are then treated. Once ready, they are dispatched across the shire or down to the coast to be exported to Dover or some other port, then across the Narrow Seas. So,' he turned his horse, 'let us sup in the Palfrey, look and learn, discover more.'

'About what?' Wendover demanded testily.

'Why, my Lord Sheriff, anything we can about the heinous crime of wrecking.'

Master Rievaulx, thief, former clerk, Judas man and king's approver, was intent on crime. He had watched Corbett and his party leave. Lady Isabella, Malach and Brockle were busy elsewhere. Rievaulx tried to remain impassive, staying in the shadows, but in truth, he chafed at being imprisoned in this gloomy manor at the heart of these haunted moors. He dared not go out. The countryside was treacherous and dangerous, whilst Corbett had issued strict instructions that he remain at Malmaison until the investigation was finished. Only then, when he was satisfied, would the Keeper of the Secret Seal issue licences for him to travel.

Rievaulx, housed in a narrow garret at the top of this godforsaken manor, fretted and plotted. He recalled those hurling days when he had been Puddlicot's henchman, a captain of rifflers who had plotted to break into the crypt at Westminster and plunder the royal treasury. He would never forget that heady night of success, sitting with the rest, surrounded by treasure, eating, drinking and toasting their success. All for nothing. Corbett and his dogs had soon broken through, hunting Puddlicot and the rest to destruction. Rievaulx had been captured and swiftly turned king's approver. He was handed over to Wodeford to serve as the royal clerk's henchman in the pursuit of fellow rifflers and the recovery of royal treasure. The years had passed. Wodeford had been benevolent enough, whilst Rievaulx had proved his worth. Like the others, he had glimpsed that gorgeous ruby the Lacrima Christi in its exquisitely carved casket. He lusted after that ruby, as did his master. He knew the full story of the Lacrima Christi's disappearance from London, its emergence in Rome and then its vanishing during Pope Clement's coronation. Like the rest, he had been deeply intrigued by Lord Simon's offer, the hint that the ruby was once again in England.

He rubbed his bony face. He was tired of Malmaison. He had disliked it as soon as he arrived, with the unearthly howling of those large cats, though thankfully there were reports that both monsters were dead, poisoned out on the moor. Yet their deaths had not changed much. Malmaison was haunted by the constant hollow murmuring of the wind, as though it exulted over the hideous murders carried out within. Rievaulx recalled the logic he had studied in the schools of Oxford before he had been caught housebreaking and forced to flee for his life. He must think, marshal his thoughts, use his wits and so profit from his stay here.

First, Lord Simon had claimed that he had been approached by someone who might hold the Lacrima Christi. Was that logical? Rievaulx decided it was; after all, Lord Simon had been given the special task of recovering the ruby and other precious stones. However, secondly, the jewel had disappeared in Lyons some seven years ago. Why had the person who'd seized it waited so long before trying to sell it? Thirdly, whatever the truth, Lord Simon claimed or seemed to hint that the ruby was within his grasp. Now the dead manor lord was no fool; a former clerk in the Secret Chancery, he wouldn't dare mislead the Crown on such an important matter. Fourthly, according to all logic, Lord Simon must have had something to show Wodeford, but what? Rievaulx realised it would be virtually impossible to establish just what Lord Simon had intended. However, fifthly, if he did have the ruby, where was it?

Rievaulx recalled what he'd learnt from manor gossip. Corbett had enquired whether strangers had been seen around the manor during the time Wodeford and Rievaulx had visited Malmaison, but the answer had been no. More importantly, as soon as he arrived,

Corbett had seized the keys to Lord Simon's chancery chamber and demanded that all the documents kept there be stored in caskets sealed with his own personal signet. So did he believe Lord Simon's claim? Did this manor still house that great treasure? Rievaulx reflected on this chain of logic and its inevitable conclusion. If Lord Simon had been holding something valuable, where had he hidden it? Rievaulx knew the manor house possessed an arca, a fortified chest, but others, such as Malach or Lady Isabella, might have access to that. So where would Lord Simon secrete the precious jewel?

He sighed noisily. Of course! The great cats, the leopards: their cage or cavern lay deep beneath the manor and on reflection was a most suitable hiding place. After all, Lord Simon was the only man who dared go down there by himself. Malach occasionally ventured there, but he'd openly declared how he hated visiting what he described as 'the bowels of hell'. Rievaulx clapped his hands gently. He was sure that he was close to the truth. The leopards were now gone, slain. Was their escape a mere coincidence on the same night their master had been murdered? Were they deliberately released so someone could safely search those caves and caverns?

Pleased with himself, he got to his feet. He opened the door to his garret and listened keenly, but the manor lay quiet. He pulled on his boots, fastened his war belt, slipped out onto the gallery and hurried down the stairs. When he reached the buttery, he pretended to be looking for food before entering the great kitchen. There was no one there. He glanced over to the far corner and sighed with relief. The trapdoor to the cellars was pulled back to allow servants to visit the storerooms below.

He tiptoed cautiously down the steep steps into the blackness. The dancing light of a cresset gleamed in the row of brass lanternhorns arranged along a shelf. He took one of these down, lit it with a tinder from his pouch and crept quietly along the passageway. Pausing at a corner, he stood listening to muted cries and exclamations. He edged forward past one of the enclaves and grinned: the cause of the noise he'd heard was one of the servants tumbling a wench on a bed of straw. The woman softly moaned her pleasure, as she lay completely naked, her legs wrapped around her seducer.

Rievaulx passed on, hurrying along the tunnels, which twisted and turned. The air grew thicker, the stench from the leopard den still hanging heavy and rank. He reached the cage area, opened the narrow door and slipped through, lifting the lanternhorn as he moved forward. The foul odours, the tangled heap of bones and the brooding, watchful silence chilled his blood. He half expected to see those gold-dappled predators come sloping out of the darkness, and tried to calm himself as he began his search, scrutinising the ground and rock face for anything that might betray Lord Simon's hiding place.

Glimpsing a door built into the cavern wall, he warily opened this, then paused at a sound from the darkness behind, a fluttering, eerie noise like that of a bird's wings beating the air. His hands clammy with sweat, he touched the pommel of his dagger and entered the long, bleak chamber. He closed the door, placed the lantern on the table and stared around. Surely, he thought, this was the place, this strange chamber with its reinforced door and its battered sticks of furniture. He walked to the far end, then jumped as the door behind him crashed open, turning and staring in horror at the cowled, masked apparition standing so silent, so menacing, garbed in black from head to toe.

'What . . .?' Rievaulx spluttered.

'This,' the apparition rasped, raising a crossbow.

Rievaulx lurched forward, hoping to close with his opponent, but the barbed bolt thudded into his chest and sent him crashing back against the wall.

Corbett led his party onto the great cobbled expanse to the right of the majestic inn. The Palfrey boasted a spacious stable yard, with livery for at least thirty mounts, as well as outhouses, storage sheds, grain bins, fodder baskets and even its own smithy. A busy, prosperous place. The main building, constructed completely out of stone, had large windows, a few of them filled with painted glass. The tavern's sloping roof was of blood-red slate, its window frames and door lintels fashioned from sturdy gleaming oak.

Corbett and his retinue dismounted. Ranulf shouted that every help be given to the visiting king's men, an order the ostlers and grooms hastened to obey. Corbett handed the reins of his horse to Chanson and, accompanied by Ranulf and Wendover, entered the spacious, sweetly fragranced taproom; a large chamber, its floor of polished wood, strewn with crisp dried herbs. A roaring fire kept the cold at bay, its flames leaping merrily around the logs and kindling piled high in the cavernous hearth. To the right of the fireplace stretched the main buttery board, where Minehost Baskerville and his minions served ales, wines and a range of savoury dishes from the busy, steaming kitchens behind them.

The taverner was a tall, severe-looking individual with a hood pulled over his hair, his body covered from chin to toe in a thick blood-red apron. Nervously rubbing his hands, eyes narrowed and watchful, he welcomed Corbett to his house of cheer. He immediately began to list the dishes available, Ranulf cut him short, demanding a chamber where Sir Hugh Corbett, the king's special envoy to these parts, could discreetly dine, be refreshed and take close and secret council with my Lord Sheriff. The appearance of Corbett and his comitatus had already provoked deep interest amongst those who frequented the tavern. Ranulf's ringing proclamation caused many in the taproom to remember they had urgent business elsewhere, and the place quickly emptied. Corbett hid his smile: it was obvious that Baskerville's customers feared his tavern might be used in a commission of oyer et terminer, where anyone could lodge a complaint or petition for redress.

'Just a chamber,' Corbett declared quietly. 'Minehost, as yet, I have no business with you except a warm, clean room and platters of what smells so delicious. Rest assured,' he gestured at Ranulf, 'my colleague here will pay you well for your troubles. There will be no purveyance without payment.'

Baskerville relaxed and beamed at what he declared to be his most favoured guests. He led them out of the taproom to a chamber with a broad, glass-filled window overlooking the tavern gardens. As Corbett and his companions made themselves comfortable at the long table that ran down the centre of the room, Baskerville and a horde of minions fired the hearth logs, wheeled in capped braziers crammed with fiery coals and laid the table with platters of steaming meats, freshly baked bread, pots of butter and bowls of stewed vegetables peppered with herbs and spices. He also brought jugs of the tavern's most delicious Bordeaux. Corbett immediately tasted the wine and complimented the taverner on his choice. Baskerville seemed rather nervous at that, and Corbett, taking another sip, recalled how the council was deeply concerned that a great deal of the Bordeaux that entered the kingdom was smuggled in with no customs paid.

Ranulf went down to ensure that Ap Ythel and his company were comfortable. Once he returned, Corbett ordered the chamber to be cleared of everyone except himself, Wendover and Ranulf, with Chanson guarding the door. At his insistence, they all broke their fast. Now free of cowls, cloaks, boots, war belts and other harness, they could eat, drink and relax to their hearts' content. For a while, they dined in silence until Corbett tapped his horn spoon against his deep-bowled wine goblet.

'Sir Miles, my good friend Ranulf, we are deep in this shire on a range of business secret to the Crown, not just the matter of the Lacrima Christi.' He paused. 'We are now into the first days of spring, the year of our Lord 1312, almost five years since the old king's death and the accession of his son. As we all know, the war in Scotland goes from bad to worse, whilst closer to home, the great lords, led by the present king's cousin, Thomas, Earl of Lancaster, lay siege to the Crown. The barons issue warnings that unless our prince exiles forever his favourite, the Gascon Peter Gaveston, there will be war. Now what affects us here is not only all these rumours, but also the fact that Gaveston has been created Earl of Cornwall.'

'And God help us all,' Wendover whispered, 'who live in these shires. What I say may sound like treason, but it is not. Gaveston is hounded the length and breadth of this kingdom. He has neither the time nor the energy to govern Cornwall and the nearby shires, including this one. Law and order have been gravely weakened.'

'And so we come to the wreckers,' Corbett declared. 'Since time immemorial, pirates and outlaws have used false lights to lure cogs and other sea vessels onto coastline rocks. The law on this used to be very clear. Such a crime was a capital offence, and our shoreline is peppered with scaffolds, gibbets and gallows for those caught and convicted of wrecking. However, the capture of such felons is very difficult. Indeed, the law protects them. Wrecked ships are vulnerable; for want for a better phrase, it is simply a case of finders keepers.'

'Consequently,' Ranulf intervened, 'if a cog is wrecked on the Devon coast, both the ship and its cargo can be mine if I come across them.'

'Precisely, Ranulf. The law is very explicit on this. The cargo of a wrecked ship does not belong to its master, its crew or even the merchants who own the vessel, but to anyone who discovers that wreck.' Corbett forced a smile. 'And just because they found it doesn't mean they caused it. Just because I am caught with a piglet beneath my cloak doesn't mean I stole it. I could argue that I saw the poor creature wandering so I picked it up intending to unite it with its mother.' He paused at Wendover's sharp bark of laughter.

Ranulf grinned, watching his master intently. The clerk of the Green Wax recognised that the wrecking of ships along the coast only a short ride from Felstead and St Benet's had deeply disturbed Corbett. Indeed, whenever they discussed it, he became tense, even agitated. From the little he had learnt, Ranulf believed that the wreck of one cog in particular, *The Angel of the Dawn*, had grieved Sir Hugh. The Keeper of the Secret Seal had mentioned in passing how a close and dear friend had also been lost when that vessel was wrecked.

'So we have it.' Corbett sipped from his goblet. 'Ships are wrecked and plundered, but unless we catch the perpetrators red handed, it's extremely difficult to prove such a disaster was caused by man rather than the weather. Now the Crown has special interest in these matters. The law declares that the seas are the king's and their waves his pack horses.' He shook his head. 'Thirty-two years ago, in the First Statute of Westminster, the old king tried to define what is a legitimate wreck as opposed to what could be defined as deliberate destruction and murder. He declared that if any man or beast escaped from a wrecked ship, that vessel and all it contained was still the property of its crew and their master.'

'In other words,' Ranulf said slowly, 'if anyone, or indeed any animal, staggers ashore, the wrecked ship and its cargo cannot be touched. Oh Lord,' he murmured, 'I can see the terrors that unleashes. If some hapless survivor crawls from the sea, he will be swiftly dealt with, for dead men don't tell tales.'

'Perhaps they do, Ranulf.' Corbett sighed. 'The dead truly do talk to the living. They demand justice. Now,' he drank deeply from his goblet, 'over the years there have been serious and deadly assaults along the stretch of coastline not far from here, as well you know, Sir Miles. Wealthy, fat-bellied cogs, their holds crammed with precious goods, have been wrecked.'

'How many?'

'Oh.' Corbett narrowed his eyes. 'Over the last twelve years, Ranulf, at least eighteen in all. The most recent grievous loss was the cog *The Angel of the Dawn*, which left Bordeaux on or around the feast of the Purification, the beginning of last February. It took the usual route, making its final run past the Scilly Isles and so into the

Narrow Seas. Like all such ships, it would seek safe harbour in Plymouth, then Dover, before passing round into northern waters, hugging the coastline until it entered the Thames estuary.' He paused and put his face in his hands.

'*The Angel of the Dawn* definitely reached Plymouth.' Wendover took up the account. 'According to the harbourmaster, all was well. The captain . . .' He paused as Corbett took his hands away from his face, and Ranulf glimpsed the tears brimming in his master's eyes.

'Its captain,' Corbett declared softly, 'was William Fitzwarren, former clerk, graduate of the halls and schools of Oxford. At one time Fitzwarren was a member of the Secret Chancery, and on his father's sad death, he became the inheritor of a most profitable trade in Gascon wine as well as luxuries from Spain and Morocco. Now,' Corbett's face and tone became more sombre, '*The Angel of the Dawn* left Plymouth, following the coastline closely, only to come to a sudden and abrupt end on Langthorne Rocks, which stand in a narrow cove, an inlet called Monkshood Bay. Sir Miles, you know it well?'

'Of course. Monkshood is screened by a row of jagged rocks not far from a level pebbled beach. Indeed, an ideal place for any vessel to be wrecked. The cog becomes impaled on the rocks, which are not far from the shore.' The sheriff kept his head down as he swirled the wine dregs around his goblet. 'A number of cogs have come to grief there over the last few years.' He stretched across, grabbed the wine jug and, hands shaking, refilled his cup. '*The Angel of the Dawn* was the last of these. A fishing smack sailed into the inlet and found the cog splintered on the rocks like meat on the teeth of a dog – a wild dog. It had been plundered of wine, precious woods and costly cloths. As for survivors, well . . .' He made a face. 'Including its master and his two henchmen, a cog usually has a crew of about twelve in all. They are deployed at the master's orders: usually two rudder men; lookouts, one in the bowsprit, the other in the stern; a team of four for the sails, and the ship's boy up aloft in the falcon's nest.'

'And you found corpses?' Ranulf asked.

'Not many. The cog was wrecked days before it was ever discovered. The seas run fast and strong. Tides swirl in and out, so corpses are carried further down the Narrow Seas or even out into the great western ocean.'

'But you found a few?'

'Yes, Master Ranulf, we found a few, and before you ask, their wounds could have been caused by violence or by the ship wrecking itself on the rocks. They were nothing but blood-soaked, sea-drenched bloated corpses.'

'And no survivors?'

'No, and that makes it truly suspicious: not one soul escaped.'

'Of course,' Corbett murmured, 'it is murder. As for the rest, I am sure, once the news spreads along the coastline, the moor folk gather. They'll seize what's left of the cog for themselves: its timber, cordage, iron and canvas, indeed, anything they can load onto a cart.'

'And I can do little,' Wendover retorted. 'According to the law, the wrecked cog, to all intents and purposes, is a true wreck and can be legitimately scavenged and stripped. Believe me,' he breathed, 'within a day of a wreck being found, most of it is gone. I do what I can. I have any corpses collected and carried for burial to Parson Osbert's church in Felstead.'

Corbett, as if distracted by the growing murmur of conversation below, rose, nodded at Chanson, half asleep on his stool, and opened the door. He stood and listened to a wandering chanteuse in the taproom proclaiming a story about a kingdom full of tangled things. The walls of its palaces were hung with velvet, black and soft as sin, across which demon dwarfs crept to plague the living on behalf of a sorceress who held a magical crystal the colour of the moon. Spiritually, Corbett reflected, was he in such a place now? He'd noticed how Wendover had become increasingly nervous on the question of the wrecks, and he wondered what the sheriff had to hide.

'Sir Hugh?'

Corbett closed the door and suppressed a shiver. This place, this world he'd entered, certainly reeked of hideous sin, but who were its true perpetrators?

'William Fitzwarren,' he declared, retaking his seat at the table, 'was a close and dear friend. A born dancer, a merry soul who did no harm to anyone and a great deal of good to anyone who asked for his help. I understand, Sir Miles, from the letters you sent to the Secret Chancery, that you were unable to discover his corpse,

God rest him. He left a widow and three small children. Fitzwarren was a true innocent, barbarously slaughtered along with others of the same ilk: honest seafarers murdered for filthy profit. The souls of these men, so cruelly dispatched into the dark, demand justice, and we must answer their plea. So, my friends, let us list the problems as we would describe them in the schools, those questions that must be answered. First, how did these wreckers commit their crimes? The cogs impaled on Langthorne Rocks in Monkshood Bay all sailed from Plymouth on the early evening tide, yes?'

'Correct,' Wendover agreed. 'The cogs take advantage of the tides whilst their masters welcome the cloak of darkness against the plague of pirates from France, Hainault, Flanders, Brabant, not to mention our own ports. They slip out of harbour, then keep close to the shoreline—'

'Where they use their maps and charts whilst keeping sharp watch over the lights along the coast – beacon fires, lantern flames and the rest. The wreckers must use the same devices to lure vessels in and so wreck them on Langthorne Rocks.'

'No.' Wendover shook his head. 'No, Sir Hugh. We do not have conclusive evidence for that. One cog wrecked in Monkshood Bay some weeks ago . . .' He closed his eyes in thought, then snapped his fingers. 'That's it!' He opened his eyes, scratched his double chin and smiled at Corbett. '*Pentecost*, that was its name. Now here's a great mystery. A tinker was passing Monkshood Bay. He saw the ship shattered on

Langthorne Rocks. He even glimpsed survivors, certainly people coming off the ship onto the rocks, but these were never seen again.'

'Heavens above!' Ranulf declared. 'And he saw no false lights or wreckers prowling around the bay?'

'Yes, yes, that's true. Moreover, Monkshood Bay is a very desolate spot; the darkness falls like a curtain to shroud the land. However, neither from sea nor from land has anyone glimpsed the false fires of wreckers.'

'A mystery,' Ranulf murmured, pulling himself forward in his chair. 'Along the Thames river, pirates use false lights as a constant weapon to lure craft through the mist onto a riverbank or hidden rocks.'

'Not here,' Wendover retorted. 'Nothing like that has ever been seen.'

'So,' Corbett demanded, 'my friends, how are these vessels enticed to destruction? What do you think?' Silence greeted his question.

'I have never discovered a thing,' Wendover declared. 'When it comes to hunting them, the wreckers are night wraiths, yet when it comes to what they do, they are demons incarnate.'

'Very well, very well.' Corbett lifted his wine goblet. 'Our second question. Who could be responsible? Lord Simon could be a suspect; he was a manor lord with seigneurial rights and responsibilities. What was his role in all of this, Sir Miles?'

'More mystery, Sir Hugh. Oh, Lord Simon claimed his rights as a lord over the wrecks, or rather their pathetic remains. However, this nasty business apparently did not concern him. He expressed his regrets, pointedly mentioned that I could do more, but apart from that, he didn't seem to bother.'

'Why?' Ranulf demanded.

'There's more than one answer to that,' Corbett replied. 'Lord Simon may have been part of the problem – perhaps all of it – or he might have been frightened off by the wreckers. However, knowing him as I did, I truly doubt he would have been cowed or threatened. And so we come to the only logical explanation: that he was paid, bribed by the wreckers to look the other way.'

'And that,' Wendover added wryly, 'is the most likely conclusion. Lord Simon could be menacing, but in the main, he ploughed his own furrow, more concerned about his cats and his manor house.' He blew his lips out. 'Then, of course, there's his second wife, the Lady Isabella, fragrant in all aspects. The daughter of a good family, her father is a merchant chandler in Exeter, a leading guildsman.'

'And Lord Simon's first wife, Beatrice Davenant?'

'Sir Hugh, you know the story. Lady Beatrice fled Malmaison along with Lord Simon's steward at the time, a fellow called Chandos. They were last seen in England at Plymouth, boarding a ship to Boulogne.'

'By whom?'

'Members of the Worshipful Guild of Fleshers and Tanners who were in Plymouth that day to organise the export of a bundle of hides and skins.'

'So the Lady Beatrice fled for God knows what reason?'

'Yes, Sir Hugh. Lord Simon argued that she had deserted him; there were no children, so he petitioned for his marriage to be annulled, which the archdeacon's court, probably the beneficiary of his generosity, agreed to. Lord Simon was declared a free man.'

'And when did he marry Isabella?'

'Oh, he returned from London about eight years ago. Lady Beatrice and Chandos fled a year later. Lord Simon's second marriage was around the time of the present king's wedding to his French princess of the same name.'

Corbett placed his goblet on the table, rolling it between his hands. 'So, my friends, we come to the third question. The malefactor who calls himself the Sagittarius and his fellow demons, the Scarecrows, a cohort of wolfsheads who prowl the moorlands. According to your report, Lord Sheriff, these malefactors are the principal suspects for the murderous wrecks along the coast?'

'Yes, they have been glimpsed. A gang of garishly garbed riders, rags flapping, faces hidden behind grotesque masks. They have horses, carts—'

'You say glimpsed?' Ranulf interjected.

'By pedlars, chapmen, tinkers, not to mention the tribe of moon people, those wandering mummers and magicians with their banners, standards and trailing ribbons; their tented carts and makeshift carriages are now a constant sight on Doone Moor. Of course, the Scarecrows have been seen in and around Monkshood Bay, but no one would dare approach them.'

'Yet apparently they have murdered innocents.'

'Oh yes. Certain courageous moon people decided to keep Monkshood Bay under strict watch. All four were found dead, crossbow quarrels embedded deep in their foreheads, the corpses propped against the stones as a warning. Other wanderers across the moor have just disappeared, and believe me, Sir Hugh, you could hide a legion of corpses in the deep quagmires and marshes, where the dead sink like stones.' Wendover cleared his throat. Once again Corbett sensed the sheriff's nervousness. 'I have few men, Sir Hugh. Lord Gaveston is a fugitive. The king's peace is hard to maintain, whilst any troops I levy must be sent to join the king's array against the Scots.' He heaved a sigh. 'I placed a watch along that stretch of coastline. Three men under the command of a bailiff. All four disappeared. The Scarecrows will also attack lonely farmsteads as well as merchants, plundering their carts and pack ponies of any goods. One such attack was on our own Worshipful Guild of Fleshers and Tanners. The guildsmen were taking cartloads of hides and skins for a cog berthed in Plymouth. On their return, late in the afternoon, they were attacked and robbed of all profit.'

'Who might these outlaws be?' Ranulf demanded. 'Moor people, surely?'

'Perhaps.'

'What about our good brothers out at St Benet's?'

'Master Ranulf,' Wendover snorted, 'where in God's name would they get the weapons, horses and carts? How could these relative strangers to Dartmoor thread their way along the narrow, mist-hung coffin paths across the moors? We searched St Benet's; we found nothing. Where could they hide their plunder, never mind sell it?'

'I would agree,' Ranulf half smiled, 'but surely the loot from these ships could be traced, detected?'

'Master Ranulf, my apologies if I seem to contradict you at every turn, but take the wine we are now drinking. This could be stolen or smuggled, and the same could be said of the furnishings in this chamber. Here we are in a shire where fairs and markets are as many as bees on a honeypot. It is virtually impossible to prove that something has been stolen, and even if you could, that doesn't mean the person who owns it stole it.' Wendover leant across and gripped Corbett's arm. 'Sir Hugh, God save me, but until you arrived, I was alone in all this. I concede I made little progress. I will not seek reappointment as sheriff when the next shire court assembles; this place is beyond me. I have come to hate the moors, and above all, that lonely, treacherous, haunted coastline. The sea has never been kind to me.' He forced a smile. 'On my last expedition to Gascony, I was on board *The Firecrest*. You know what happened to that vessel?'

'Who doesn't!' Corbett laughed. 'Its master was so drunk he beached his own cog on the approaches to Calais. The old king was furious and compelled the captain to do public penance garbed in hair shirt and ashes.'

PART THREE

He found six hampers of silver in a cupboard behind the doors.

Corbett's conversation with Sheriff Wendover was suddenly interrupted by shouting from the marketplace beyond the tavern walls. Women were screaming, a heart-rending keening, that soulsodden wail and pain of someone who has suffered deep loss. He and his companions sprang to their feet. Boots were pulled on, war belts buckled. Corbett led them out of the chamber and down the stairs to the taproom below, Ranulf bellowing for customers to stand aside.

They went out into the tavern yard, now thronged with garishly decorated carts, carriages, sleds and wheelbarrows all painted in eye-catching colours and festooned with streaming coloured ribbons. The horses, donkeys and sumpter ponies were also decorated with bright, fluttering pennants. The owners of these carts and horses were a motley collection: men, women and children, their faces almost hidden by long, straggly hair and deep leather cowls, their clothes cut from skins and hides, feet encased in mud-caked leather boots.

As Corbett approached, the throng parted to allow a sled to be pushed to the front. On this was sprawled a dirt-encrusted corpse, its head, face and body clothed in a shroud of thick peat. Beside it knelt Richolda, the guildswoman, rocking herself backwards and forwards, pausing now and again to wipe the face of the corpse with a cloth soaked in the bucket beside her.

'It's Fulbert, her husband,' a voice whispered.

Corbett turned and stared at Baskerville, who was wiping his greasy hands on his apron. Beside the taverner stood Malach, anxious faced and eager to speak. Corbett nodded at him.

'I arrived,' Malach stepped forward, 'just as the moon people did. Sir Hugh,' Malach's voice dropped to a hiss, 'we need you at Malmaison. Dreadful murders, Grease-hair flamed to death. Rievaulx found . . .'

He paused as Richolda returned to her shrill keening. Corbett glanced quickly around. Ranulf, Wendover and Chanson were deep in conversation behind him. Ap Ythel had gathered his archers in the far corner of the stable yard; they stood in their usual manner, bows strung, yard shafts notched ready to loose at any danger. Corbett sensed the growing unease of the crowd pressing in. More people were pushing and shoving their way into the yard. He walked over to the sled and stared down at the mud-encrusted corpse. Its eyes had already been eaten away, the nose, lips and other soft flesh badly decomposed. Richolda was still moaning and rocking herself. Corbett murmured a line from the De Profundis as he studied the crossbow bolt dug deep into Fulbert's skull. He wondered about the deaths at Malmaison. He was not surprised. Sudden brutal death had swept into that manor and would encamp there until the tangle of mystery, subterfuge and violence was resolved—

'Sir Hugh!'

'Ranulf, I know what you are going to advise. So clear the crowd, empty both this yard and the taproom. We will set up court there.'

Ranulf, assisted by Wendover and Chanson, soon imposed order. Ap Ythel and his bowmen moved to stand in the centre of the tavern yard before joining Corbett in the taproom, which had been transformed into a court by the addition of a table and chairs. The leader of the moon people was summoned, a giant of a man with thick straggling hair, moustache and beard. Flanked by two acolytes dressed like friars in earth-brown robes, he swept into the taproom and stopped before the table, leaning on his war staff as he glared down at Corbett.

'My name is Moses and I am the leader appointed by God over my people.'

'I am sure you are,' Ranulf retorted, 'and this is Sir Hugh Corbett, also appointed by God to be the king's special emissary in these parts. Keeper of the Secret Seal—'

Ranulf fell silent as Corbett rapped the table.

'My Lord Moses, it is good to see you.' Sir Hugh sketched a bow and gestured to the acolytes. 'I greet you, my lord, as I do your henchmen Aaron and Joshua.'

'Sir Hugh, it is good to look upon your face.' The moon leader's voice was no longer strong and carrying but soft and mellow. 'I thank you for the licences you have issued so we can travel untroubled along the king's highways.'

'Yes, yes, quite.' Corbett pointed to the bench ranged in front of the table. Moses and his two henchmen sat down. 'What are you doing on Dartmoor?'

'What we do best, Sir Hugh, wandering.' Moses smiled apologetically as Ranulf half rose. 'Hush, Red-hair.' He waved his hand. 'We trade, we barter. We sell and buy at this market or that fair.'

'Have you been to Malmaison manor?'

'Never, Sir Hugh. It enjoys a most sinister reputation.'

'Why?'

'Oh, those ferocious cats.'

'They are dead now.'

'So I have heard. People also say the manor is haunted.'

'By whom?'

'Heaven knows, Sir Hugh, but I think Malmaison is a hostelry for restless spirits. I cannot say the true reason. I simply report what I have heard.'

'And the murders recently committed there?' Ranulf asked. 'The royal clerk Wodeford, the king's own tax collector Sir Ralph Hengham and, of course, Lord Simon?'

'Why not ask him?' Moses retorted, pointing across the taproom to where Malach sat in a window seat.

'True,' Ranulf replied. 'But everything in its due time. You have nothing to do with Malmaison?'

'That's the truth, Red-hair.'

'Or the wrecking of ships?'

Moses simply drew himself up, sighing in exasperation, whilst his two dark-faced acolytes glared fiercely at Ranulf.

'The wreckers.' Corbett spoke quietly. 'Lord Moses, you know that matter concerns the king, as it does his council. We hunt those guilty of the slaughter of innocents. A pack of wolfsheads who call themselves the Scarecrows and are led by that hell-hound the Sagittarius.'

'Oh, we have glimpsed them sure enough. They arrive like Satan's own messengers, but they leave us alone and we do the same to them. Sir Hugh, if we knew anything, we would tell you.'

'And so we come to the corpse, Fulbert's mortal remains,' Wendover declared, stirring in his chair. Corbett glanced sideways; the sheriff looked exhausted.

'Not yet, not yet,' Ranulf declared. 'Lord Moses, it is good to see you and your people.' He forced a smile, quietly conceding to himself that if Sir Hugh accepted these wanderers, then so must he.

'It is good to see you too, Ranulf-atte-Newgate,' Lord Moses replied. 'Sir Hugh's henchman, senior clerk in the Chancery of the Green Wax. Now,' he tapped his war staff against the ground, 'you must have more questions, I am sure.'

'The community at St Benet's under their self-styled prior, Adam Warfeld; you know of them? Their history, the reason they now shelter in a bleak priory up on Doone Moor?'

'Oh yes, oh yes.' Moses grinned. 'Naughty nuns, fornicating friars and mouldy monks have a special fascination for us. Yes, yes,' he added hurriedly at Ranulf's impatient rapping on the table, 'we know about their crimes in London, but,' he shrugged, 'we find no wrong in them.' He stared meaningfully at Corbett, shaggy head forward, hands grasping his staff. 'Sir Hugh, we visit St Benet's and the Blackrobes barter with what they have for what we can provide.'

'Mostly filched,' Wendover sneered.

'We sell and buy what is rightfully ours.' Moses did not deign to even glance at the sheriff. 'We are courteous and honest with the monks. In return, they celebrate mass for us, shrive our souls,' he ignored Wendover's harsh laugh, 'baptise our infants and bless those who need a blessing. They have fine herb plots, and at least two of the brothers are skilled leeches, so they treat our wounds and anything that upsets our humours. Sometimes we use their buildings and outhouses to dry our carts, whilst Brother Isadore helps our blacksmith.'

'You have many horses and ponies?' Ranulf demanded.

'Yes, quite a number, about thirty-six in all. But Master Red-hair, do not misjudge us. Do not think we use these mounts to hunt like the devils across the moors.' Moses smiled in a display of strong white teeth. 'Oh no, rest assured of that. As for the Blackrobes, I cannot even raise the faintest suspicion against them.'

'And the corpse sprawled outside?' Wendover demanded. 'How did you find it?'

Moses's smile faded. 'We found it on Grimdyke Moor.

It had been tossed into a quagmire. Now, Sir Hugh, these marshes are treacherous. They can hide a corpse forever but sometimes cast it back within the hour.' He belched loudly, murmured his apologies and loosened the great belt around his bulging belly. 'One of our urchins thought he glimpsed a rabbit. Some rabbit,' he snorted. 'Anyway, we pulled what the boy had found free of the marsh,' he clapped his mittened hands, 'and there you have it.' He got to his feet. 'Sir Hugh, may we leave?'

'With God and the king's blessing, but stay close to Felstead.' Corbett rose, waited till the moon people had left the taproom, then walked back into the stable yard. The crowd had thinned. Baskerville stood in the entrance to one of the outhouses. Corbett walked across. Minehost stepped smartly aside.

'Stay here.' Corbett tapped the taverner on the shoulder. 'I need urgent words with you.'

He entered the outhouse and crossed the mud-caked floor, where Fulbert's corpse, now clean after being doused with buckets of water, sprawled grotesquely. The tanner had certainly been a large man. Corbett noted the well-stretched hose, good leather boots, thick woollen fleece with its silver clasps, and broad war belt, the ornamented dagger still pushed into its brocaded sheath.

'Look, Ranulf,' Corbett whispered to his henchman, who had followed him in, 'Fulbert was murdered, but his costly boots, jerkin and war belt were left untouched. So he was certainly not killed for such possessions.' He crouched down and examined the clasps and hooks along the war belt. 'See, no purse.'

'Yes, yes, Sir Hugh. Fulbert was murdered, his purse emptied and probably thrown into a marsh, but other costly items were left. Surely the reason for that is that his killer did not wish to take anything that might be traced back to its rightful owner.'

'True, true, Ranulf. We must also reach the logical conclusion that if Fulbert has been murdered, so have his eleven comrades.' Corbett breathed out noisily. 'What can we do about that, eh?' He got to his feet. 'Sheriff Wendover is correct. He doesn't have the comitatus to sweep the vast, desolate moorland, and even if he did, what's the use? As our good sheriff has already remarked, you could hide an army of corpses in the many marshes, quagmires and bogs of Dartmoor. Moreover, Wendover has his own problems and they are legion, including a search for the royal taxes stolen from Hengham. Nevertheless despite such busyness, I sense all is not well with Sir Miles. I have growing concerns about his role in all this. Ah well.'

He turned and shouted for Chanson to bring in Baskerville, who was waiting in the yard. Minehost came bustling in, narrow face all puckered with concern. Corbett sensed a deep fear gripping this taverner.

'Master Baskerville, a sad day, surely?'

'Yes, Sir Hugh. I have Richolda weeping in the buttery with the other guildswomen. All are now afeared that if Fulbert has been murdered . . .'

'Then God have mercy on their poor husbands.'

'A time of deep mourning, Sir Hugh.'

'Look.' Corbett plucked Baskerville by the arm and the taverner reluctantly followed him over towards the corpse. 'Look,' Corbett repeated. The taverner, one hand across his mouth, his Adam's apple bobbing vigorously, stared down at the cadaver, then turned away. Corbett waited for him to compose himself. 'Master Taverner, I must ask you to recollect. Is that how Fulbert was dressed on the night he attended the festivities here in the Palfrey?

'Yes, yes, it was.'

'And when he and his comrades left, it was after midnight?'

'Yes.'

'By horse or by foot?'

'Foot, of course.'

'Master Baskerville,' Corbett stepped closer, staring into the taverner's fearful eyes, 'did anything significant happen that night or in the days before or, indeed, following that might explain the mysterious disappearance of twelve leading men of this village as well as the subsequent murder of at least the master of that guild?'

'No, no,' Baskerville whispered hoarsely. 'Nothing.'

'Nothing occurred during those celebrations?' Ranulf demanded. Again the taverner shook his head.

'You are certain?' Corbett paused at a rapping at the door. Wendover, cloaked and cowled, bustled in.

'Sir Hugh,' he extended a gauntleted hand, 'I must be gone. We will meet again.'

'We certainly shall.' Corbett grasped the sheriff's hand, as did Ranulf, then Wendover, muttering how he had done what he could, left the outhouse. Corbett stood listening to the noise in the yard as the sheriff and his comitatus departed in a jingle of harness and scraping hooves. He waited until they were gone, then returned to the taverner, noticing how Baskerville's agitation had deepened.

'Tell me, my friend,' he clapped the man gently on the shoulder, 'have you ever been threatened by the Sagittarius and his coven?'

'I once spoke out against the night-riders.' Baskerville stumbled in his speech. 'I did so when I was deep in my cups. A rare event,' he added hastily.

'I am sure it was. And?'

'The next morning, as I was leaving for Sunday mass, I found their mark, a blood-soaked crossbow bolt, embedded deep in my tavern door.'

'And you were here the night the guildsmen disappeared?'

'Yes, I have told you so.'

'And so was I.' Corbett and Ranulf turned. Parson Osbert had slipped through the half-open door and stood, staff in hand, against the fading light. 'Sir Hugh, we have all been threatened by the Sagittarius and his Scarecrows.' The priest walked over, a cold smile on his face. 'Such violence,' he continued, 'is part of living in Felstead.'

'But not part of the king's peace.'

'Certainly not.'

'Parson Osbert, you were here with minehost on that fateful night? Did you notice anything untoward?'

'No.' The parson thumped his staff against the ground. 'I have told you what I can.'

Corbett turned back to the taverner. 'Master Baskerville, I thank you. I need words alone with your priest.'

'What words?' the parson demanded once Baskerville had left.

Corbett stared at him, wondering once again where he had seen that face before, yet even as he did, he conceded ruefully that he had been in so many places at different times, be it hallowed churches, luxurious palaces or blood-strewn battlefields.

'What words, Sir Hugh?'

'Oh, I think you know.' Corbett stepped as close as he could, whilst Ranulf moved over to guard the door. 'You are the parish priest of St Peter in the Marsh. You celebrate mass there as well as in the manor chapel at Malmaison. You must be extremely knowledgeable. You were also at Malmaison on both occasions when the murders were perpetrated.'

'Yes, Sir Hugh, I was there as a guest, a hard-working, law-abiding parish priest protected and respected by Holy Mother Church. I was invited by Lord Simon and Lady Isabella to sup and talk with them, as I have been on many occasions.'

'Father, do you know anything about a ruby called the Lacrima Christi?'

Osbert blinked, glanced away and swallowed hard.

'I have heard stories about the ruby, as I have about our brethren out at St Benet's'

'Stories and nothing else?'

'Stories and nothing else, Sir Hugh.'

'Parson Osbert, I suspect you know much more. You hear confessions, you shrive sinners, you give them absolution for their hideous crimes against God, the king and their neighbour.'

'And if I do, Sir Hugh, I do so under the sacramental seal of Christ and his church. I cannot divulge anything a penitent has confessed in the sacrament.'

'But you know, don't you?' Corbett whispered. 'You know that malignant, murderous spirits prowl Malmaison and Felstead, as well as the bleak landscape that stretches like a desert around them?'

'Sir Hugh, I do, but take my sworn word: I have nothing to do with Malmaison, the murders committed there, the famous ruby or the wickedness being perpetrated in and around Felstead.'

'I hear you, priest, but I still believe murder has set its banners up over this place. Only God knows when this litany of slayings, this hymn to murder will cease.'

'I agree. Are we finished, clerk?'

'We are finished, priest.'

'You will leave soon?' The parson gestured at the corpse. 'Fulbert needs to be blessed with oil and water.'

'Oh yes, but only when we have gone.'

Parson Osbert made to leave. Ranulf opened the door and mockingly bowed, gesturing the priest across the threshold then slamming the door behind him.

'A suspect, Sir Hugh?'

'What do you think, Ranulf?'

'In my eyes, all priests are suspects. I should know; my father was one.'

Corbett nodded in agreement. Ranulf had neither forgiven nor forgotten the father who had sired him then abandoned both Ranulf and his mother to the stinking slums around Whitefriars. He glanced sharply at the door.

'Ranulf, I have seen that good parson before, but for the life of me I cannot recall where or when.'

'Never mind him, master, it's best we go. Soon it will be dark as pitch out on those moors.'

'Aye, Ranulf, time to be gone.'

They left the outhouse and were halfway across the yard when a hooded figure slipped out of the taproom and hastened across as if hurrying to the stables. As he passed Corbett, the man seemed to stumble on the horse dung that greased the cobbled yard. Corbett went to steady him, grasping him by the arm. The stranger broke free, but not before he had pushed a thick parchment scroll into Corbett's hand. Corbett stood and watched the man, head down, shoulders hunched, hasten through the tavern gate.

'Master?' Ranulf had seen what had happened and now stood, dagger half drawn. 'Shall we pursue him?'

'No, no.' Corbett slipped the scroll into his pouch. 'Just one further mystery, Ranulf.'

* * *

Corbett stood at the entrance to the stable yard of the Palfrey carefully watching the milling crowd disperse under the direction of Ap Ythel. The hour was drawing on. He chewed the corner of his lip. Once Moses and his company had left Felstead, banners and ribbons streaming in a strengthening wind, he'd had urgent words with Malach, who, in a sharp, clipped voice, informed him about the murders at Malmaison. Corbett had listened to him intently, reflecting that Malmaison truly was the haunt of murder, but as for the why, the who and the wherefore . . . He smiled grimly to himself. Was the cause of all this brutal death, this rapidly spreading murderous mist, the Lacrima Christi, that exquisitely beautiful ruby that everybody wanted whatever the cost to life and limb?

He wondered the same again as he squatted in the narrow closet chamber that served as the manor death house next to the chapel at Malmaison, staring down at the long arrow chests that had been placed across trestles to serve as coffins. Rievaulx lay, arms pinioned, eyes rolled back as if, even in death, he wanted to see the jagged bolt that had pierced his skull. A dire sight. The blood that had gushed out of his nose and mouth had now dried to form a macabre mask. Grease-hair, however, was virtually unrecognisable: nothing more than a hunk of flesh burnt black by the inferno that had engulfed him. The spit-boy's face had been obliterated. The rest of him was nothing more than a shrivelled mess, which still stank of burning oil. Corbett crossed himself, murmured a requiem and glanced over his shoulder at Lady Isabella and Malach, standing just within the doorway. Both were deathly pale. The lady of the manor had one hand resting on her walking stick, the other on Malach's arm.

'Let us return to the hall.' Corbett got to his feet. 'It's best if we talk there. Chanson,' he snapped his fingers at the clerk of the stables, who now stood with his back to the corpses, hands firmly clasped over his mouth and nose, 'see that all is ready.'

Chanson needed no second bidding, and fled from the death house. Isabella and Malach made to approach Corbett, but Ranulf gently intervened, whispering for them to follow Chanson to more comfortable quarters, where Sir Hugh would soon be joining them. They left, Ranulf closing the door firmly behind them before joining Corbett at the window, staring out into the gathering night.

'Two murders, Sir Hugh.'

'Undoubtedly, Ranulf.'

'Poor Grease-hair must have been sitting in the ingle-nook turning the heavy spit, basting the meats, throwing on pouches of herbs to fragrance the fire. Amongst these, the assassin must have mixed sachets of oil.'

'I agree.' Corbett pointed to the door. 'We will look at this in more detail when we leave. However, let's imagine what happened. Grease-hair, half asleep, lounging deep in the inglenook. He has a tub close by. He tosses in one pouch after another. Eventually he picks up a sachet of pure oil. This too he throws onto the flames. Now, as we know, Ranulf, for we have attended enough sieges, those who prepare the fire bundles for catapults must be careful not to have oil on their own clothes, for the flames jump, the fire assumes a life of its own. The catapult men wear heavy aprons drenched in water and smeared with sand. Even so, hideous accidents still happen.'

'And of course,' Ranulf murmured, 'Grease-hair's clothes would be deeply stained with oil. The same is true of the tub beside him. The fire leaps, one flame after another, and the poor creature becomes a living torch. Yes, yes, Sir Hugh, I have seen the same happen to engineers at sieges. Throwing water is no solution. Heavy sacking or thick horse blankets must be used to smother the flames.'

'And I suspect that did not happen here, though we will see.'

Corbett turned and pointed at the second makeshift coffin. 'Rievaulx was different. He was an assassin, a dagger man, a born street fighter. He was killed in the caverns below, actually the leopards' den. So what was he doing down there? He must have felt safe. The great cats have been freed and destroyed, so it was nothing to do with them. The caverns are sombre, a place of shadows. Why did he go down?'

'He was looking for something.'

'Of course, and it must be the Lacrima Christi. Rievaulx was a former clerk, a man of logic. He suspected that Lord Simon had, by God knows what means, secured the Lacrima Christi. In Rievaulx's eyes, the best place to hide such a treasure was the leopards' den. However, he was being watched; the assassin followed him down to the caverns and killed him, as he, she or they did Grease-hair.'

'But who?'

'Apparently,' Corbett replied, 'the Sagittarius's gruesome insignia was found close to both victims. A blood-encrusted crossbow bolt driven deep into a window shutter near the inglenook where Grease-hair sheltered; the same in the door to that sinister secret chamber in the leopards' den.' He paused to sniff at the perfumed pomander Brockle had given him.

'Now, I can see why Rievaulx was murdered: he was involved in the hunt for the Lacrima Christi, a former member of Puddlicot's gang, henchman to the now dead Wodeford. The good brothers out at St Benet's would have loved to have taken his head. A number of individuals will not weep at his death. But that poor lad, the hapless spit-boy . . .' Corbett walked over to the door and stood with his hand on the latch. He opened it and peered out into the cold, deepening darkness. Chanson, half asleep, came stumbling out of the gloaming.

'All quiet, master. Lady Isabella is waiting in the hall.'

'Thank you, Chanson, we will see her soon.' Corbett went back into the chamber, closed the door and leant against it. 'Grease-hair,' he declared, 'claimed he saw something amiss when he climbed that ladder and peered into the murder chamber. He glimpsed something that troubled him. He must have voiced his concerns, repeating them time and again, so he had to be silenced. Of course, we do not know what he glimpsed, what distracted him. He would relax, memories would flood back. He would visit that chamber, continue to chatter, and he eventually paid for that with his life. Now, Ranulf.' Corbett, still leaning against the door, opened his wallet and drew out the piece of parchment thrust into his hands at the Palfrey.

'What is it, master?'

'Wolfram, Lord Simon's former henchman, a mailed clerk and a man of blood, skilled, sly and subtle. According to what the Secret Chancery learnt, he left Lord Simon's service and returned to his birthplace, where he now lives with his sister, the fair Katerina, in some desolate farmhouse out on the moors.'

'How do you know Katerina shelters him?'

'Oh, I met her when her brother was in London; she is very protective.' Corbett grinned. 'Moreover, as you well know, I always keep a watchful eye on former clerks of the Secret Chancery, and that even includes you, Ranulf-atte-Newgate.'

'Life is never simple, Sir Hugh. So what does Wolfram want?'

'To meet me.' Corbett tapped the parchment. 'He seeks sanctuary, my protection. He is also ready to turn king's approver and plead for a royal pardon.'

'A royal pardon for what?'

'For all crimes and felonies he has committed.'

'Such as?'

'I don't know, Ranulf, but we are going to find out.

Wolfram has suggested that he and his sister meet us in the secret chamber built into the leopards' den. He must realise I have discovered it. Heaven knows how they will get here, but at least it proves one thing.'

'Sir Hugh?'

'We do not know all the entrances to this desolate, formidable mansion. Wolfram certainly does, and I suspect he can come and go like a shadow in the night. He says he will meet us when the great hour candle reaches the purple ring of midnight. So until then, Ranulf, let us busy ourselves. The lovely Lady Isabella and her grim-faced henchman Malach await us.'

Corbett settled into the cushioned chair before the roaring fire in the great hall. All around him a host of candles glowed, sending the shadows dancing. Ranulf sat on his right, the Lady Isabella and Malach to his left. A servant had placed a small table between the chairs and served hot posset, spiced sausage and sweet honey comfits. Corbett had listed his concerns and now stared at the ugly black stain against the inglenook that marked where Grease-hair had been turned into a living flame. The grey mantel-stone had been scorched so fiercely, it had begun to flake, as had the floor where the spit-boy had rolled, screaming in his death agony. Corbett then moved his gaze to the window shutter where the Sagittarius had driven his blood-soaked bolt as a memento mori.

'So,' he murmured, 'poor Grease-hair was sitting in the inglenook turning the spit, throwing the occasional sachet of herbs onto the fire. Then he tossed a bag, maybe more, of pure oil. He was warm, tired, half asleep, not really aware of what he was doing. And then what?'

'Servants heard him screaming and rushed in.' Malach pointed to a gap in the wall where an arras had once hung. 'They pulled that down and tried to smother the flames, but it was futile. Grease-hair died.' His voice choked with tension. 'Sir Hugh, so sudden, so unexpected.'

'And the crossbow bolt?' Ranulf demanded.

'Oh, that wasn't glimpsed until hours later.'

'So the assassin must be someone here in Malmaison?'

'Not necessarily so.' Lady Isabella's voice was soft, mellow. She smiled dazzlingly at Ranulf. 'We provide good shelter against the cold loneliness of the moors. People come and go: couriers, tinkers, traders, not to mention manor servants and their families. Gates and doors are left open. Even I,' she added wearily, 'do not know all the secret postern entrances. Master Ranulf, we are a shire manor, not a royal fortress.'

'So no one glimpsed anything suspicious before or after Grease-hair's murder?'

'No, Sir Hugh,' Malach replied. 'Nothing at all. Murder slipped in like a shadow.'

'And Rievaulx?'

'Sir Hugh,' Isabella's voice was now hard, 'Rievaulx, I understand, was well known to you, as he was to my late husband. He was a secretive man, a former wolfshead. Heaven knows what he was doing down in the cavern. One of our servants and his paramour had gone to inspect the leopard den. Servants still see it as a place of mystery. Anyway, they glimpsed the lanternhorn Rievaulx had used, and stumbled on his corpse and the blood-soaked crossbow bolt loosed into the door of that secret chamber. Again, Sir Hugh, nothing and no one suspicious was glimpsed before or after his murder.'

'And your husband's business here?'

'Sir Hugh, you knew Lord Simon, a former clerk in your chancery. He was most reticent about his affairs. He rarely referred to the flight of his first wife with his henchman Chandos, nor about his life and work at Westminster.' She shrugged prettily. 'Lord Simon said little and I dared not question him. He could become angry and sullen. He deeply resented being questioned about his past, so I let it be.'

'A good husband?'

'In many ways, yes. Are you, Sir Hugh?'

'And the great mysteries plaguing Malmaison?' Corbett continued, ignoring the woman's barbed question. 'The Sagittarius, the Scarecrows, the disappearance of the guildsmen? Do you know anything about these?'

Lady Isabella smiled thinly. 'Only what I have been told.'

'Was your husband concerned about the wreckers?'

'Of course he was, but he saw that as a matter for the Crown, the shire reeves, particularly Sir Miles. My husband busied himself about his own affairs. Sir Hugh, we pay taxes, we support Sir Miles. We work for the community. We do not have the resources to ride the shoreline searching for wolfsheads who lurk deep in the darkness.'

Corbett stared hard at Lady Isabella; she held his gaze coolly.

'And the Lacrima Christi?'

'Oh, my husband, deep in his cups, made reference to a most remarkable ruby, but as I have said, I know very little about his past. I am what you see, Sir Hugh, nothing more than the lady of the manor, busy with household chores and hoping to be so until,' her voice quavered, 'these present troubles recede. I was born in Felstead, the only child of a prosperous chandler. I met Lord Simon during the Twelfth Night celebrations. I was, I am, a simple manor lady. I know nothing of the demons that seem to prowl this house and the moors beyond.'

'And you, Master Malach?'

'I am a household retainer, Lord Simon's henchman. I have served in the royal array. I, too, was a mailed clerk.' He shook his head. 'But I know very little about what happened before I entered Malmaison.'

The meeting ended soon afterwards. Corbett sat dozing before the fire while Ranulf and Chanson went down to confer with Ap Ythel about their horses and harness and to ensure the archers were comfortable. Ranulf also prepared for Sir Hugh's midnight meeting before returning to join his master before the fire.

The flame on the hour candle burnt fiercely. When it was over halfway between the red and purple rings,

Corbett readied himself. Escorted by Ranulf, Ap Ythel and six of the archers, he made his way down to the cellars and caverns beneath the manor. A cold, dark journey. The leaping cresset torches of his escort shifted the shadows around them. In the secret chamber, lanternhorns glowed and small wheeled braziers, heaped with fiery charcoal, provided some warmth against the damp cold.

Corbett and Ranulf entered that sinister chamber. Ap Ythel deployed his archers outside. Corbett sat tense, his hand not far from the hilt of his dagger. Ranulf, quietly cursing the place, got up, walked to the door and peered through the grille.

'It's macabre,' he whispered. 'Like a tunnel into hell. Not just the stench and the silence, but—' He broke off at a scraping sound behind him, and whirled around, drawing his blade. Corbett leapt to his feet, snatching out his dagger. He yelled for Ap Ythel as a paving stone in the far corner, covered in dirt, was slightly raised then pushed forward. The captain of archers slipped through the door, war bow ready, arrow notched.

A voice sang out. '*Pax et bonum*, Sir Hugh. Do not be alarmed, it is your old comrade Wolfram.'

Corbett nodded at Ap Ythel, who lowered his bow, cursing softly in Welsh. The raised flagstone was pushed further forward. A man clambered out, then turned to help his companion, a woman garbed in a deep-cowled cloak. The man pulled back his hood and walked towards Corbett, hands extended. Ranulf made to move between them, but Corbett signalled at him to stand aside. He grasped Wolfram's hand and pulled him closer.

'Well, well, Wolfram, you have certainly changed! No crimped hair, no shaven cheeks; your beard, moustache and hair are thick as a wild bush on a full summer's day.'

Wolfram laughed and then turned to his companion, who now pushed back her cowl. Corbett smiled at the woman. Ranulf noisily caught his breath.

'As fair and fragrant as ever.' Corbett bowed. 'The years haven't changed you, nor has time staled your loveliness.'

'It certainly has not,' Ranulf murmured. 'Lady Katerina, such a pleasure to meet you.'

The woman smiled prettily and extended her ring hand for Corbett and Ranulf to kiss.

'My two favourite clerks,' she declared. 'As honey-tongued as ever.'

'Let's not tarry here.' Corbett rubbed his hands.

'I agree.' Wolfram pulled his cloak closer about him. 'Sir Hugh, this truly is a house of the red slayer, and this chamber has certainly seen the devil's own work. We should leave. But first . . .' He went back to the displaced slab, and, assisted by Ap Ythel, pushed this back into place, using his booted feet to kick out and spread dust and debris so the paving looked as if it had never been disturbed. Then they left the caverns, making their way up to Corbett's chamber.

Chanson and Ap Ythel stood guard outside whilst Ranulf made their visitors welcome. Stools and small tables were set out, hot crackling braziers brought closer. Chanson went down to the buttery for mulled wine and whatever meats and bread could be served. During these preparations, Corbett closely studied his two guests. Wolfram had certainly aged, his russet hair streaked with grey, his usually smooth, well-kept head and face almost covered in hair. He was dressed like a verderer in bottle-green jerkin and hose, with stout riding boots on his feet. He looked tired and, despite his apparent bonhomie, Corbett sensed his former comrade's weary agitation. Lady Katerina, however, garbed like a nun in veil, wimple and tawny riding gown, was as serene and lovely as ever. Her smooth oval face, lustrous grey eyes and full lips had not changed. Corbett knew Katerina to be a merry soul who, despite her circumstances, was only too willing to play the flirt with Ranulf.

They settled themselves down. At first, the conversation was about former friends, no mention being made of the late hour and why this midnight meeting had been arranged. Eventually Corbett drained his tankard and put it down noisily. Then he rose, locked and bolted the door and returned to his chair, gesturing at Wolfram.

'It is good to see you, my friend, and the Lady Katerina. So why did you want to meet? Where have you been and why all this subterfuge?'

'Sir Hugh,' Wolfram gulped from his cup of posset, 'as you know, I was born in these parts. My father was a shepherd, a farmer, a prosperous peasant who could send his son to the cathedral school in Exeter—'

'Wolfram,' Corbett intervened, 'the hour is very late and time passes.' He smiled at this nimble-witted clerk who loved nothing better than to declaim some hymn or poem in a tavern or alehouse.

'Brother,' Lady Katerina teased, 'what have I said about the sound of your own voice?'

'Peace be with you all.' Wolfram grinned.

'To the chase,' Corbett retorted. 'My friend, when Puddlicot robbed the Crown Jewels, the old king dispatched me and other mailed clerks to hunt his gang to extinction and, of course, recover the plundered treasure. Lord Simon, together with you, Wodeford and Rievaulx, was entrusted with the specific task of recovering the king's most precious jewels, in particular the Lacrima Christi. Now there's been a deep suspicion ever since that he discovered the whereabouts of this most beautiful ruby.'

'Oh, he had it,' Wolfram agreed. 'He seized it from the jeweller Glaston, whom he murdered to silence him forever. I know he did. Then he made a swift sale to the only people he could do business with.'

'The papal bankers, the Frescobaldi?'

'The same, Sir Hugh. He couldn't sell it for its true price, but he certainly made enough to allow him to resign from the royal service and enjoy the most comfortable retirement.'

'But we have always suspected that,' Corbett replied. 'It's nothing new. The old king and I had our suspicions, but it was case of conjecture with little proof. Anyway, it wasn't long before we learnt that the Lacrima Christi was firmly in the hands of Pope Boniface, and little could be done about that. So,' he leant forward, 'why are we here? Why do you ask to turn king's approver and receive a pardon for crimes you have committed?'

'True, true,' Wolfram murmured, as if talking to himself. 'Enough said. We are in the house of murder.'

'Wolfram!' Katerina warned. 'Confess, shrive yourself.'

'In a word,' Wolfram's reply came in a rush, 'I was party to the murder of Lady Beatrice Davenant, Malmaison's first wife, along with his steward Chandos. The killings still weigh heavily on me.'

'In God's name,' Corbett exclaimed, 'is this true?'

'Think.' Wolfram almost smiled. 'You worked with Malmaison, a mailed clerk who fought in both Wales and Scotland. He loved it. He was a true blood-drinker. Anyway, he left the royal household. We now suspect the reason why. He returned home, and asked that I stay with him. I accepted. In many ways, Malmaison was a good lord, a *bon seigneur*, generous, even lavish when the mood was on him. In addition, he truly loved his first wife, Beatrice. To cut to the chase, he discovered – and I know he was right in this – that she had been playing the two-backed beast with his steward. God pardon me,' he sighed, 'but I was party to proving that. I questioned retainers. I followed the pair on their secret assignations, and then the sword fell. At my master's instructions, I lured them both down to the caverns where Lord Simon had fashioned the leopard den for his great cats, now grown to maturity.' He rubbed his face. 'I did not believe what was going to happen.'

'Really?' Ranulf interjected. 'You knew Lord Simon wasn't building a pleasance, a grotto, a soothing herb garden. He was—'

'I know what he was, Ranulf, but at the time, the blood coursed hot. By then Lord Simon nursed an intense hatred for his errant wife and faithless steward. This ran deep like a wound that rots. The chamber below was already fashioned, the paving slabs laid by some previous lord.'

'And the secret entrance?'

'Known only to Lord Simon and myself. A small cave in the escarpment on which this manor is built, cleverly hidden behind gorse and rock. A narrow cleft leads into a tunnel stretching to steps up to that slab, which can only be removed from below. Move that and you enter a chamber almost hewn out by nature. Lord Simon's only task was to dress the stone, fashion a lintel and hang that heavy door with a spy grille at the top. No one was allowed to come down.' Wolfram laughed sourly. 'No one wanted to. Lord Simon gave out that he was constructing a viewing chamber from where he could study his beloved cats. So all was ready.

'On that fateful night, after a rich banquet in the hall, all four of us went down to the leopards' den. Lady Beatrice and Chandos had drunk deeply.' Wolfram's voice faltered. 'Malmaison penned in the cats and ushered us into that secret chamber, bolting the door behind him. I can remember it now, every detail. He picked up an arbalest, all primed and ready, and loosed the bolt. A killing blow direct to the heart. Chandos must have died within a few breaths. Lady Beatrice just slumped down in complete terror, but that was only the beginning of the nightmare.' He held up his hands. 'As God is my witness, I did not know what had been planned, what further horrors awaited us.' He paused.

'Tell him,' Katerina urged. 'Shrive yourself, brother.'

'Lady Beatrice was tied to the chair. Lord Simon was now like a man possessed. He dragged Chandos's corpse from the chamber and, with an axe he'd secretly hidden away, severed his steward's head. He placed the head on a platter and put that on the table. He then kept both Beatrice and the mouldering head of her dead lover locked in that chamber. I . . .' Wolfram gulped noisily. 'I felt as if I had lost my soul, my will. The horrors Lord Simon released trapped me in a vice-like snare. I had become his accomplice. I was terrified. I had to do what he told me.'

He drank greedily from his posset cup. Katerina whispered for him to continue. Wolfram just sat shaking his head. Corbett stared at Ranulf, who simply blinked and glanced away. Corbett gazed around. He took meagre comfort that he'd been proved correct. Some malevolence, a creeping, insidious evil, haunted this manor house, and one of its root causes was Lord Simon's brutal, horrendous treatment of his faithless wife and steward. A malignant seed had been sown and the harvest had been blood soaked. The fires and candles might provide light and warmth; the rooms could be richly furnished, but this could not stifle or conceal the heinous sins committed here. Corbett murmured the Miserere.

'Horror piled upon horror,' Wolfram continued, urged on by his pleading sister. 'Lord Simon kept that head, leaving it to rot on its wooden platter. He dragged the rest of Chandos's corpse into the open and gave it to the leopards.' He paused at Ranulf's exclamation. 'Yes, yes, he did. He just tossed it to them as if it was offal. The cavern stank of blood and guts. Then he left Beatrice and returned to the manor. I had no choice but to help him. He packed coffers and panniers to create the illusion that his wife and Chandos had fled Malmaison. He had planned and plotted so skilfully, he had no trouble convincing his household to accept the grotesque chronicle of lies he'd created.'

'And the Lady Beatrice?' Ranulf demanded.

'She remained imprisoned in that stinking chamber. Oh, she could scream, but no one would hear her, and no one dared go down to the caverns, not with those great cats prowling about. Indeed, after Chandos's murder, the leopards became even more aggressive. You could often hear their chilling roaring.'

'That poor woman,' Corbett whispered. 'Whatever her sins, she did not deserve that, locked in that gruesome chamber with her dead lover's decapitated head rotting in front of her, and ferocious leopards prowling outside. They had feasted on human flesh and they must have sensed she was there, fresh meat for them.'

'Oh, they did. Now and again, Lord Simon and I

– he forced me to accompany him – would enter that chamber the same way I did earlier. He would bring a little wine, some food, but he refused to listen to her pleas. After a week of this torture, he gave her a sack. It contained a dagger, a noose and a phial of poison – henbane or belladonna, something he'd prepared with roots from the herb garden. He was offering her a choice of death. A day later,' Wolfram breathed out noisily, 'a day later,' he repeated, 'she took the dagger.'

'And her corpse?'

'Thrown to the leopards. Lord Simon then cleaned the chamber and continued to live the lie that his wife and her lover had fled beyond the Narrow Seas.' He pulled a face. 'There was no one to gainsay him.'

'But there's the mystery,' Corbett declared. 'Didn't members of the fleshers and tanners guild, merchants of Felstead, claim to have seen Lady Beatrice and Chandos board a cog for Boulogne or some other port along the Norman coast?'

'Yes, yes, I have heard the same, Sir Hugh, but such witnesses were either greatly mistaken or lying. If the latter, I cannot say why. Anyway, the murderous masque continued. Here in the manor house "poor Lord Simon" ostensibly tried to cope with the betrayal and elopement of his wife and steward. Meanwhile, in the caverns below, the mortal remains of those two souls were hacked and hewn and fed like a tub of scraps to the leopards.'

'Both cats have been found dead, poisoned out on the moors. Was that your work?'

'No, no, but I wish to God it was.' Wolfram paused and glanced away. Corbett had caught the lack of conviction in his reply and wondered what this subtle, very cunning clerk was still concealing. Wolfram sighed and looked up sheepishly. 'Rest assured, Sir Hugh, there are many who would have rejoiced at silencing those two beasts. They had to be killed. Malmaison himself acknowledged that. Once they had tasted human flesh, they would regard any human, including himself, as prey.'

'So what happened afterwards?'

'Oh, I realised what I had done. I was guilty, deeply so. I had committed mortal sin. I wanted to be away. I also suspected that it was only a matter of time before Lord Simon turned on me, the only witness to the horrors he had committed. What we had done, what I had participated in, was truly sinful.' Wolfram crossed himself. 'I asked to leave his service, and swore by the Holy Face of Lucca, Lord Simon's one and only devotion, that I would remain silent. I also warned him that I had drawn up a true and honest confession of my sins, and that if anything happened to me or mine, copies of my confession would be dispatched to you, Sheriff Wendover and Parson Osbert. In turn, Lord Simon vowed that if I broke my word, he would hunt me down and kill my beloved sister.' He turned and grasped Katerina's hand. She stared hard at Corbett, nodding in agreement with her brother.

'Like pieces on a chessboard,' Wolfram gasped, 'Lord Simon and I checked and trapped each other. However, he continued to act the aggrieved spouse, ensuring enough proof was dispersed to demonstrate that Lady Beatrice and Chandos had fled. Matters settled down. My sister joined me, and one day we simply slipped out of Malmaison. Lord Simon let us go, but not without one final warning.' Wolfram stroked his sister's arm. 'Katerina is a wise woman, a leech and apothecary skilled in herbs. As I have said, we live out on a lonely farmstead. Lord Simon warned me that if I did not honour our silence on these matters, he would publicly accuse her of being a witch and have her burnt before the common gibbet at the crossroads leading into Felstead.'

'Tell me,' Corbett extended his hands towards one of the braziers, 'the Lacrima Christi. Did Lord Simon ever make any reference to it?'

Wolfram scratched his head and narrowed his eyes. 'I asked him once about its whereabouts,' he said, 'but he just gave that cold, knowing grin of his. He declared that what people searched for, he kept safe beneath the sixth veil, but no more than that.' He shrugged. 'Sir Hugh, I have made my confession.'

'You are certainly guilty of crimes,' Corbett retorted, 'though only as an unwitting accomplice. So look, assist us here. Both I and the Crown may well need your good services.' He paused. 'Do you wish to stay tonight?'

'No, no, we will go. We have left our horses tethered. Despite the dark, we know which tracks and pathways to follow.' Wolfram got to his feet. 'Sir Hugh, if that is all, and as far as I am concerned it is, we will leave through one of the postern doors.'

Corbett nodded, telling Ranulf to collect Ap Ythel and a few of his archers to accompany their guests out of the manor. Once they had made their farewells, he decided he was finished for the day. The hours had cost him. He was tired, his mind agitated by all that he'd seen and learnt.

'Sufficient for the day,' he murmured, 'is evil enough. Lord High God, have mercy on me.' He recited a litany and blessed himself, then took off his boots and belts, wrapped his thick military cloak about him and lay down on the bed. For a short while he thought fitfully about the mysterious murders perpetrated in this room, until his mind drifted to the horrors of that macabre chamber in the caverns below. He whispered a requiem, said a hurried Ave for his wife and family, and drifted into sleep.

He was roused the next morning by the clanging of the matins bell in its narrow steeple on the manor chapel. Ranulf and Chanson arrived from their chamber to say all was well. They had delivered Corbett's message to Lady Isabella and Malach, who were already in the buttery breaking their fast. Corbett stripped, washed and shaved in the bowl of hot water Chanson brought up. He donned fresh linen and finished dressing, then collected his war belt and cloak and went down to the small buttery, where a sleepy-eyed cook was serving creamy oatmeal laced with honey together with small, freshly baked bread buns soaked in a tangy meat sauce.

'Sir Hugh?' Lady Isabella waved to the seat on her

left, opposite a stern-faced Malach. 'You slept well?' Her smile faded. 'We understand you had a late-night visitor.'

'Come and gone like a watch in the night,' Corbett replied evasively. 'Lady Isabella, Master Malach, you know the moors. Once the Jesus mass is finished, I would like to ride out to Monkshood Bay to view Langthorne Rocks.'

'We received your message, Sir Hugh. Malach and myself will take you there together. You will bring an escort?'

'Of course.'

'Mist-bound,' Malach declared. 'A thick sea mist has swept in.'

'Yes, yes, so I understand.' Corbett got to his feet, brushing the crumbs from his jerkin. 'Sea mist or not,' he continued, 'let us put our trust in the Lord and the strengthening sun. Speaking of which,' he sketched a bow towards Lady Isabella, 'I shall now ask the Lord for his divine assistance.'

He walked away, then turned abruptly and went back to the table. He leant over, his face only a few inches from Lady Isabella's. 'Lord Simon's first wife, Beatrice – did you know anything about her? Did Lord Simon ever—'

'Never.'

'He was insistent on that,' Malach declared, getting to his feet. 'He said he'd vowed never to speak her name, and never to hear it.'

* * *

Corbett recalled Malach's words as he stood just inside the rood screen of the manor chapel, a simple, ancient building. He noticed how both its floor and walls had been freshly scrubbed, whilst an artist had begun to depict the wounded face of Christ on at least two of the pillars. Lord Simon, so Malach had confirmed, had also instituted the Via Crucis, the Way of the Cross, with its fourteen stations each commemorating an incident on Christ's painful journey to be crucified at Calvary. Such a rite was similar to the Creeping to the Cross, a devotion in which the faithful could commemorate Christ's death between the hours of twelve and three on a Friday afternoon.

As he watched Parson Osbert celebrate the mysteries over the small stone altar, Corbett wondered about the soul of a man like Lord Simon and the contradictions in his life. He was a manor lord who had slaughtered his wife and steward in the most disgusting and grotesque fashion. He had committed horrid murder with malice aforethought. He had destroyed two lives only to wipe his lips and proclaim his innocence in public. Did such a man view religion and his devotion to the Sacred Face of Jesus as a part of his life totally separate from the rest? Was that true of other men, including himself? He broke from his reverie as Parson Osbert began to intone the solemn words of consecration. Corbett crossed himself and quietly vowed that when all this murderous affray was resolved, he would sift amongst that heap of bones in the leopards' den. He would search for the pathetic remains of Lady

Beatrice and Chandos and give them consecrated burial here in Malmaison.

Once the mass was finished, Corbett, booted and spurred and cloaked against the cold, led his cavalcade out of the manor and up onto the desolate moorland. Malach's warning about the mist proved correct: a cloying, shifting curtain had swept in to create a world of silent, sombre greyness. Corbett ordered his party to ride close and watch the lanternhorns held on rods by two of Ap Ythel's bowmen. These followed Malach as he carefully led them along tracks and pathways known only to himself. The breeze was cold and salt tinged, biting at exposed flesh; conversation was virtually impossible with the riders pulling cloaks and mufflers close about them. The chilling stillness was broken only by the clatter of hooves and the constant clink of weapons, as well as the haunting sudden scream of some bird drifting far above them through the murky sky.

At last they reached the approaches to Monkshood Bay, and the mist began to thin. They had passed similar coves, bays and inlets where the sandhills steeped to run down to pebble-strewn beaches, and the sea, trapped by the cliffs on either side, rushed in furiously. Malach explained how a similar inlet, close to the manor, housed two great herring boats, which were used to bring in fresh fish for the slaughter sheds at Malmaison. Of all these inlets, however, Monkshood was the most spacious.

Gorse-covered cliffs reared in an arc around the bay.

Such terrain would have provided a perfect natural harbour if it wasn't for the rocks jutting up like sharp teeth close to the shore. Corbett followed his guide down to the water's edge. He reined in, wiped the sea spray from his face and stared out across the rocks; although sharp and slippery, these would provide excellent stepping stones from the sea onto the beach. He could see little evidence of any wreck having occurred there. Virtually everything from those ships, be it wood, cord or canvas, would be swiftly spirited away. Only occasionally a drifting piece of jagged timber provided some hint of the hideous crimes committed in this place. Stroking his horse's neck to quieten it, Corbett wondered how the wreckers lured vessels in to impale themselves on these rocks. Did they fire beacons above the cliffs or along the shoreline?

'Sir Hugh?' Ranulf pushed his horse alongside Corbett's.

'I was reflecting, Ranulf, how this stretch of coastline is a place of slaughter. Now most masters and captains are shrewd, cunning men. They are seasoned and know their trade, using charts and crude maps. Surely this place must now have the most sinister reputation amongst seagoing folk? Cogs must have been warned, captains and their crews alerted to the real dangers along this stretch of coastline.'

'And yet the wrecking continues.'

'Yes, Ranulf, it certainly does.'

'Sir Hugh?'

Corbett turned his horse. Lady Isabella, with Malach

beside her, had pulled down the muffler of her cloak and was staring beseechingly at him, her beautiful face soaked by the wind-borne spray. 'Sir Hugh? Have you seen what you want? Monkshood Bay,' she smiled, 'was my favourite playground when I was a child. I recall summer days hiding amongst the gorse or in the small caves and caverns in the cliff face, but now . . . now it's all different. Sir Hugh, I wish to be gone from here; can we journey home?'

They'd gone no more than a mile when the attack was launched. Crossbow bolts whipped out of the mist. One of the leading archers was struck in the arm. Another had his horse felled beneath him. Corbett, recalling his days fighting along mist-hung valleys, screamed at his escort to dismount and crouch. Another flight of bolts, at least three, whirred above their heads as Ap Ythel's archers hurried forward to form a kneeling line. War bows were notched and shafts loosed into the thick mist before them. Ap Ythel shouted an order; his line crept forward and loosed a second shower of arrows. They edged forward again, now no more than indistinct, shadowy shapes almost hidden in the wispy embrace of the swirling mist. Ap Ythel called a halt and sent two of his men to scout ahead. They returned swiftly, saying they could find nothing.

'Master,' Ranulf demanded, 'who knew we were here?'

'Most of Felstead,' Corbett replied caustically. 'And the same applies to Malmaison Manor. It would be easy to follow us down to the coast. So, Ranulf, what does this remind you of?'

'Wales, Sir Hugh. Fighting the War of the Mists, as we called it. Arrows out of the murk aimed at a certain height to catch horsemen.'

'Ah, so that's why we dismounted.' Lady Isabella, hobbling slightly, led her palfrey towards them.

'Yes, my lady, we dismount, we crouch and we return with a volley of our own. And so—' Corbett broke off as Ap Ythel called him over.

The wounded horse had now been put out of its agony with a swift slash across the throat, its saddle and harness heaped onto another mount. The injured archer was already being treated by Brancepeth, who also acted as leech and herbalist for this cohort of royal bowmen. Corbett ordered the wine skins carried by Chanson to be shared out. Once everyone had taken a drink and Ap Ythel's scouts had returned to declare that there was no mischief ahead, Corbett ordered his retinue to mount and follow Malach through the mist onto the trackway leading to Malmaison.

The entire company rode silently, still recovering from the shock of the recent assault. They'd hardly gone another furlong, however, when Ap Ythel's scouts raised the alarm. Again archers hurried forward, but the mist abruptly lifted like a veil being pulled back, and Corbett, standing high in his stirrups, glimpsed the garish banners, streamers and ribbons of the moon people. Shouting at the archers to fall back, he urged his horse forward, accompanied by Ranulf. Lord Moses, flanked by Aaron and Joshua, rode out to greet them. Corbett and the moon leader met and clasped hands.

'Where to?' Corbett demanded.

'We hope to camp near Malmaison,' Moses replied in a loud, carrying voice.

Corbett turned. Lady Isabella raised a hand in agreement.

'Have you seen anything untoward?' Ranulf asked. 'Here, out on the moor?'

'Everything.' Moses smiled. 'Everything is untoward in this wilderness.'

'No hunters, travellers, chapmen?'

'No, nothing under the face of the moon. Only you and these.' Moses turned and shouted in the lingua franca of his people.

A cart rumbled forward, and Corbett stared down at the corpses of the two leopards sprawled there. The cadavers of these magnificent beasts had begun to swell as putrefaction set in. Their glossy black-spotted hides were now faded and scuffed, their powerful jaws, stained with a thick, creamy paste, sagged open to display dagger-like teeth. The breeze shifted. Corbett caught the stench of corruption and hastily covered his mouth and nose with his muffler.

'Exactly.' Moses gestured that the cart be withdrawn. 'Found them out on Doone Moor. Definitely poisoned. Once we reach the deepest mere, in they go. So, Sir Hugh, let us accompany you. You are returning to Malmaison?'

'We certainly are.'

* * *

Corbett made himself comfortable in the chair behind the desk in his chamber. Ranulf, too, was relaxing in the cloying warmth, the braziers crackling furiously. The tapers of light from the beeswax candles fluttered in the draughts that seeped through any gap. They had both taken off their harness, washed, and broken their fast, and now, as Corbett had declared, they were intent on imposing order on the mysterious events swirling around them. The manor house lay silent. Lady Isabella, complaining that her foot was not fully healed, had retired to her chamber; the rest of her household were busy on various tasks.

'So,' Corbett stretched out his hands to cup the warmth from one of the braziers, 'we have our mysteries. So let us make a schedule of what confronts us. Item.' He paused as Ranulf's pen broke. The clerk cursed, picked up a fresh one, dipped it into the pot of blue-black ink and grinned at his master.

'Nothing lasts forever, Sir Hugh.'

'That's true in every sense, and that includes time. So, item. We have the most beautiful ruby, the Lacrima Christi, stolen from the crypt at Westminster by Puddlicot and his gang. Mailed royal clerks, ourselves included, hunt these down. Whilst we were busy with Puddlicot, Lord Simon, aided by Wolfram, searched for the stolen jewels, the Lacrima Christi in particular. These royal clerks were assisted by Wodeford and his henchman, the former felon Rievaulx, who turned king's approver.' Corbett sighed noisily. 'To cut to the chase, we strongly suspect that Lord Simon found the ruby in the possession of the jeweller Glaston, whom he undoubtedly murdered. Our manor lord then made a swift deal with the Frescobaldi, selling the ruby to them for a mere shadow of its worth. Nevertheless, this was a small fortune. He bought his leopards, and left the service of the Secret Chancery for a comfortable life here in his manor.'

'He also returned to wreak hideous mischief.'

'Yes, Ranulf. Lord Simon came back to his family home to discover that his wife and steward were deeply involved in an adulterous affair. In revenge, he imprisoned, tortured and killed them in those silent caverns below. He then hacked up their corpses and fed the remains to his leopards. Time passed. Lord Simon maintained a public face. Wolfram, an unwilling accomplice, left Malmaison for refuge out on his lonely farmstead, closeted with his adoring sister. Lord Simon took a new wife and a new henchman.

'More time passed, and, God knows for what reason, Lord Simon made his move. An anonymous letter, hinting that the Lacrima Christi was still available, was sent to him and a copy to the Secret Chancery. We do not know its true origin; it could be Lord Simon himself. He then wrote to the Secret Chancery implying that he had also been approached by a mysterious stranger offering information about the ruby. Remember that, Ranulf. I studied Lord Simon's letter; it's very clever the way it twists and turns. I doubt if there was any mysterious stranger, whilst Lord Simon is not at all clear about the truth of the matter. Both his letter and the anonymous one are hard to believe, as I shall later demonstrate, but the matter was still worth investigating.

'Wodeford and Rievaulx were dispatched to Malmaison. They arrived here. They were entertained. Lord Simon and Wodeford adjourned to this chamber. We do not know what they discussed, though I suspect it was verbal fencing, with Lord Simon repeating what the mysterious stranger, not to forget that anonymous letter, had said about the Lacrima Christi. Rievaulx stayed in the hall below with Lady Isabella, Brockle, Malach and Parson Osbert. They wined and dined, waiting for Lord Simon and Wodeford to return. What then?'

'At first,' Ranulf paused in his writing and lifted his head, 'nothing amiss except those leopards, more vocal than usual. Malach went down to quieten them.'

'Yes, yes, that's so, and the night was drawing on. Eventually Lady Isabella, now rather concerned, sent Brockle up to this chamber to make sure all was well. He received no reply, so Lady Isabella ordered her minions to investigate. Grease-hair the spit-boy climbed the ladder and saw Lord Simon slumped in his chair, Wodeford sprawled on the floor, both killed by a closely loosed crossbow bolt. Grease-hair also glimpsed the insignia of the mysterious Sagittarius, the leader of that evil coven the Scarecrows, a blood-drenched bolt driven into the chamber door.' Corbett gestured around. 'It all happened here, yet the door was locked and bolted from within, the window firmly shuttered, whilst there is certainly no other entrance to this murder chamber.

'Grease-hair also noticed something amiss, but he could not place it and he never did. The poor boy's absorption with the problem, which he probably repeated time and again, led to his own brutal murder. Half asleep in the inglenook, busy turning the spit and basting the roast, he threw herbal pouches onto the flames, but the assassin had also placed sachets of pure oil in that pot.' Corbett crossed himself. 'And so it was,' he murmured. 'Now, Ranulf, what can you recall? What did we record about what happened after Grease-hair announced what he had seen?'

Ranulf sifted amongst the parchments littering the desk. 'Ah yes,' he declared. 'The leopards continued to be restless. Isabella and her steward then went up to the chamber. The door was forced.' He pulled a face. 'The corpses were apparent, as was the fact that Wodeford's money pannier was missing.'

'Yes, yes,' Corbett agreed. 'According to the record, Wodeford had been furnished with silver and gold in case he needed to pay bribes; even the means to purchase back the Lacrima Christi. Ranulf, what else?'

'The chamber was undisturbed, another mystery. How could two mailed clerks, dagger men, veterans from the royal array, be slaughtered so easily, so quietly? Nothing was seen, no disturbance heard, be it the attack or the defence you would expect.'

'I agree,' Corbett said, 'and yet the crime committed here was very violent. Two men murdered followed by a crossbow bolt loosed into the door as a mocking farewell. The bulky panniers Wodeford so jealously guarded spirited away.'

'What else?' Ranulf murmured.

'On that night of murderous mystery,' Corbett replied, 'Lord Simon's two leopards escaped to prowl the moors. There they were poisoned, but by whom, and why, remains a mystery.' He sat back in his chair.

'Sir Hugh, the assassin must be someone inside Malmaison.'

'Really, my friend, do you think so? Yet we have seen Wolfram and his sister come and go from this manor like ghosts. God knows what other secret entrances exist and who uses them. Now, as regards the murders and the theft, we certainly know the movements of all the guests in the manor. Yet the mystery remains. How did the assassin—'

'Or assassins?'

'Precisely, Ranulf. How did the assassin, and any accomplice, enter a sealed chamber, kill two veterans so quietly, then leave with those panniers?'

'And the same is true of Hengham's murder, almost identical. An able-bodied man slain in a sealed chamber and his money bag stolen.'

Corbett rose to his feet and stretched. 'And then we come to those other mysteries. Who is the Sagittarius? Are his coven of Scarecrows the wreckers? They have certainly been seen out on the moor. However, for the life of me, I cannot see how or why they could be responsible for the three murders here, not to mention the slayings of Grease-hair and Rievaulx.' He sighed. 'As regards Rievaulx, Ranulf, I believe our conclusions are right. He was searching for some trace of the Lacrima Christi. He may also have had his own suspicions about the killings committed in this chamber. Rievaulx was nosy and he paid for this weakness with his life. Yet in the end, we still have no evidence, nothing to point the finger of suspicion at this person or that.'

'And the attack on us, out on the moors?'

'Oh, that could be the Sagittarius, or indeed, the assassin prowling Malmaison. It was certainly that well-known trick practised by the Welsh, who'd loose shafts aimed at the height of a mounted man. Yes, yes,' Corbett murmured to himself, 'that's how it was. It might only have been one person with two or three arbalests already primed. In truth, I would say our assailant was someone who knew the stratagems of war, not to mention how to find his way across a mist-hung moor. And what other mysteries, Ranulf?'

'The wreckers.'

'Yes, that could well be the Scarecrows, but how do they choose their victims? How do they know a vessel is on the seas approaching Monkshood Bay? How are such vessels lured in? Surely their masters would be well advised about the dangers of that particular stretch of coastline? Then there's the question of the lures. Lanterns? Bonfires? Flaring cressets? Yet no one has even seen any such light in the dead of night. In turn, that provokes another question. The wreckings always take place after dark, not during the day. I suppose that's logical enough, though at certain times of the year, a sea mist can be just as confusing as the dark. The wreckers are clever. God knows how we will trap them. And what else?'

'The disappearance of the twelve guildsmen.'

'Oh yes! Our twelve guildsmen, honest and true. They disappeared shortly after their revelry at the Palfrey. The corpse of their leader, Fulbert, has been found, dragged out of a mire with a crossbow bolt driven deep into his forehead. Definitely murdered, but by whom? For what reason? Was there a falling-out amongst the group, some quarrel that tipped into bloodshed? Fulbert is dead, and I strongly suspect that his comrades have been slain too. Now, Ranulf, that would be some undertaking. These were tanners, skinners, bold, burly men, strong in the arm and of sharp wit. I wager that at least half of them have seen service with the king. They would resist, they would fight back, yet there is not a jot of evidence for that. We know that it's not some accident out on the moors. Fulbert didn't just wander into a marsh. He was murdered and thrown there.'

Corbett sat down on his chair and closed his eyes, reflecting on what they had just discussed. Ranulf watched him intently. Old Master Long Face was a deep thinker and a shrewd one when it came to the pursuit of the sons and daughters of Cain. He was a true hunter, a veritable lurcher.

He opened his eyes and smiled. 'Ranulf, all this deception, my friend.'

'Master?'

'Deception, my learned clerk.' He straightened in his chair. 'So let us list these deceptions before I describe my own. First, the disappearance of Lady Beatrice and her lover Chandos. They were definitely murdered, yet members of the guild we have just mentioned claimed to have seen that lady and her lover boarding a ship to cross the Narrow Seas. A mistake? An error? No, I think it was a downright lie, but why?'

'Bribed, threatened by Lord Simon?'

'Possibly. Lord Simon was a true blood-drinker, not to be taken lightly. So did he know or suspect something about our not so honourable guildsmen? After all, he threatened and blackmailed Wolfram into silent compliance . . .'

'Could they be the wreckers?'

Corbett smiled at his henchman. 'I wondered the same. Is that why Lord Simon never intervened?' He leant forward. 'It might also explain the apparent wealth of the guildsmen and that tavern, which in turn leads us to another question. Who is their leader? Lord Simon, so recently deceased? Parson Osbert, our enigmatic priest? Or even Minehost Baskerville, master of a luxurious hostelry and the proud owner of a stable of good horses and carts that could be used for a night ride across the windswept moors?'

'Sir Hugh, how can that be? The guildsmen have disappeared, their leader killed, yet the Sagittarius and his Scarecrows, who we believe must be responsible for the wrecking, still ride the moors.'

'True, true, my friend,' Corbett replied wearily. 'Now that's a question I can't resolve.'

'Sir Hugh, you talked of other deceptions?'

'Yes, yes, I did.' Corbett walked to the door, opened it and stared out before patting the sleeping Chanson on the head. Then he returned to his chair, making sure the door was firmly closed. 'Ranulf, this is only for you. People believe I am here because of the Lacrima Christi. I am not, because I know where it is. I have it.'

'Master!'

Corbett grinned at his henchman's shocked face. 'I was given it *per manum Dei* – it's a deodandum, a gift from God.' He leant over and touched his companion gently on the back of his hand. 'Remember, Ranulf, I had left the royal service but the old king wanted to keep me close. He asked me, as a personal favour, to be one of his representatives at the coronation in Lyons of Bertrand de Got, our present Holy Father, Clement V. Wodeford and I journeyed there with other members of the royal household, including Lord Simon. Of course, by then we had learnt how the Lacrima Christi was held by the papacy, being given pride of place in the pope's treasury. Naturally, we made representations, but Clement and his lawyers pointed out that the successor of St Peter was the legitimate custodian of a such a precious ruby, such a unique relic. We could only watch and fume. Then a miracle occurred. Well,' Corbett pulled a face, 'what I called a miracle. We attended the coronation and were making our way down into the city when an ancient wall on which spectators were standing abruptly collapsed.'

'An accident?'

'Yes. I believe so. No malicious intent was discerned. The wall was weak, crumbling, and the weight of those standing along its broad parapet proved too much. The entire edifice cracked and crumbled. Chaos ensued. Pope Clement was nearly thrown from his palfrey; his tiara fell off and rolled away.' Corbett took a deep breath. 'And the Lacrima Christi virtually dropped into my grasp. Yes, yes, I know,' he smiled, 'was it mere coincidence or *per manum Dei*, through the hand of God? Anyway, I grasped it and hid it. In my mind, that ruby was the rightful property of the English Crown, whose representative I was.'

'And no one saw you?'

'No one, I am sure of it. I returned to England and showed it to the old king, who was truly delighted. The ruby was locked away in an iron-bound chest in the arca, the fortified treasure chamber of the Secret Chancery. It's still there.'

'So why all this? Lord Simon's message, Wodeford's dispatch?' Ranulf beat his fist against his thigh. 'And above all, our miserable journey to this wretched place?'

'Very simple, Ranulf. The Lacrima Christi belongs to England, but if the papacy learnt what truly happened in Lyons, you know what would happen. Letters of condemnation, bulls of excommunication, demands for the ruby's return with full compensation for injury caused. Pope Clement would be gleefully supported by Philip of France; that fox in human flesh would be only too willing to fish in very troubled waters.'

'So what do we do?'

'Ah, now we come to the heart of the matter.' Corbett leant against the desk, eyes closed for a while. At last he opened them and stared hard at Ranulf. 'The Lacrima Christi belongs to the English Crown. It was presented to the old king years ago, before he succeeded to the throne. The Caliph of Egypt sent it to him in an exquisitely beautiful bejewelled casket.'

'Yes, yes. So I gather.'

'Now on the inside of that casket is a very clear inscription in both Latin and Arabic declaring that the caliph gave the ruby as a personal gift to the English Prince Edward.'

'Ah.'

'Ah indeed, Ranulf. If we could have both casket and ruby, then the circle is complete, the chain unbroken. We have proof, evidence of ownership, and the papacy, or anyone else for that matter, could do little but keep quiet.'

'And you think Lord Simon had that casket?'

'Yes, I do. I am certain of it. I suspect that in the hunt for Puddlicot's gang, he seized both the ruby and the casket.'

'And the latter he could not sell?'

'No, of course not. That sort of evidence could have had him hanged. People would be very reluctant to buy it. Lord Simon kept it and, I believe, hid it away here. Rievaulx thought it must be in the leopards' den and was slain searching for it. However, according to Wolfram, Lord Simon made a reference to treasure concealed beneath the sixth veil.'

'Master, is that a reference to scripture?'

'It might be, but in the book of the Apocalypse, it is seven veils, not six, that hide God's secret plan. Anyway,' Corbett scratched his stubbled face and quietly promised himself a thorough wash and shave, 'Lord Simon had that casket. I don't believe, I never have, all that nonsense about someone approaching him, a mysterious stranger connected to the Lacrima Christi.' He chewed the corner of his lip. 'Ranulf, I'm still a little mystified about all this. You see, the Secret Chancery was first alerted by that anonymous letter copied to both Westminster and Malmaison.'

'What did it say?'

'In truth not much, except that Lord Simon could, if he so wished, be most helpful in the English Crown regaining the ruby. In his letter to the king, he certainly did not deny this. He created the impression that he did not have the ruby but he knew someone who did, and so on and so on. I admit I was intrigued, and so was Wodeford. He and Rievaulx, whom neither of us really trusted, were ordered to travel to Malmaison and discover what Lord Simon truly held.'

'Did Wodeford know you had recovered the ruby?'

'No, but he was highly suspicious about what Lord Simon intended, which is why the panniers he carried were crammed not with gold and silver but with metal scrapings, not worth a shilling.'

'So in truth nothing was lost?'

'Well, we lost a good clerk, and two strong leather panniers. Wodeford's death weighs heavily on me. We did not trust either Lord Simon or Rievaulx. The assassin, whoever it might be, must be furious. And so we pass to another deception.' Corbett paused. 'Lord Moses, leader of the moon people.'

'He is not what he appears to be?'

'Yes and no, Ranulf. Lord Moses is now in the pay and under the protection of the office of the Secret Seal. In a word, he is my spy. I issue him with licences and passes to cross the shires of this kingdom without opposition or interference by local officials. He is, as are others, my eyes and ears in the various shires. At the beginning of this business, before we left for Malmaison, I ordered him to Dartmoor, where he and his tribe were to wander but also watch and listen.'

'And he has discovered nothing?'

'So far, although he might be of use in a plan I am slowly forming.'

'One further mystery, Sir Hugh . . .'

'Ranulf?'

'Rievaulx. Master Chanson and I visited his chamber to search his effects for anything that might be of use.'

'And?'

'Sir Hugh, everything he owned – panniers, clothing, even harness for his horse – has disappeared. The closet chamber he lodged in has been cleared of every rag and stitch, and no one knows why or who did it.'

'How does that fit into what has happened?' Corbett

mused. 'Anyway, thank you, Ranulf. More grist for the mill.' He rose and patted his clerk on the shoulder. 'I should have informed you before about the ruby, but as you can appreciate, such information is highly dangerous. If the pope or any of his minions in this kingdom even suspected I had it, literally all the power of heaven would be thrown at me. So let us return to the hunt.'

PART FOUR

It included twelve jugs and in every jug he put
some jewels.

For the rest of the day Corbett busied himself about the chamber. He studied certain missives dispatched to him and also insisted that he sift through all Lord Simon's chancery records. Ranulf assisted him, but they found nothing significant. The records were banal and boring. Corbett did wonder if Lady Isabella and her henchman had inspected the manor muniments and removed anything contentious, but there was no proof of this, so he let the matter rest. He retired early that evening, only to be aroused before dawn by the tocsin pealing out across the manor. The chapel bell clanged ominously, its metallic sound drowning all others. Corbett quickly dressed. He ordered Chanson to stay and guard the chamber, and hurried down to the hall, where Ranulf was waiting, warming himself in front of the fire. The clerk greeted him and pointed to the tiled passageway leading to the kitchens, buttery and other cooking chambers.

'The larder for dried meats,' he whispered, then

paused at a crashing sound that echoed hollowly across the hall. 'Apparently,' he declared, 'it's locked and bolted—'

'Come,' Corbett interrupted.

They strode across into the passageway, where manor servants were being shooed away by Brockle, all anxious, his face sheened with a fine sweat. He gestured down the gloomy corridor.

'Lady Isabella, Parson Osbert and Malach are there.'

Corbett hurried on around the corner to where a group of servants were lifting a long bench, which they were using to batter down a strong reinforced door.

'Sir Hugh.' Lady Isabella beckoned him forward. She told the servants to pause and pointed down at the blood seeping like wine across the dirty white tiles. 'It's Colum the cook. Yes?' She turned to a morose, unshaven Malach.

'He went in there just before dawn,' the henchman declared. 'I was preparing to welcome Parson Osbert, who had kindly agreed to celebrate a memorial mass for Lord Simon.'

'Yes, that was my idea.' Isabella suppressed a shiver, her lovely face pallid and drawn. 'Colum was to prepare meats and pastries to break our fast.'

'And this passageway was deserted?'

'Of course. This is the larder of dried meats, nothing more than a storeroom. I suppose we never gave it a second thought. Anyway, Colum went in and never came out.'

'I went to see what was happening,' Malach declared.

'I tried the door, I knocked on it, and then I stared down. I saw the blood seeping out so I raised the alarm. I am sorry,' he added in a mutter. 'Perhaps I created more chaos, and yet what I saw . . .' The henchman stepped closer and stared fixedly at Corbett. 'You know,' he grated, 'you must do, what waits for us behind that door. A corpse! Another murder! Little wonder my mistress . . .' He turned and stared at Lady Isabella.

'Mistress, do you want to flee? Do you want to leave this place?'

'Sir Hugh, at this moment, yes, but shall we deal with this first?'

Corbett agreed, and the pounding on the door continued. During a brief respite when the servants paused for breath, Malach explained how the door was of thick oak. Its lock was ungainly but heavy enough, whilst the outside catches were mere hooked clasps at both top and bottom. At last the battering had its effect: the door buckled, the lock snapping as the thick leather hinges twisted. The servants pushed at it until it fell like a drawbridge into the larder.

A lanternhorn glowing brightly on a shelf illuminated the gruesome sight. Colum the cook, his white apron a mess of blood, squatted, a spit pole thrust straight into his stomach so he was pinned to one of the larder's stout oaken pillars. His eyes all glassy, he was caught in the shock of death by the crossbow bolt embedded deep in his forehead. Corbett, who had insisted on entering the chamber by himself, held up a hand to still the clamour behind him. He stared around the larder.

The strong light from the lanternhorn shimmered on the glistening slabs of meat hung to dry on hooks fastened into the rafter beams, pillars and walls. The air smelt slightly rancid. He glimpsed the sloping shape of a rat as it raced across to a hole in the far wall.

Beckoning Ranulf to join him, he walked towards the corpse. Colum had dressed for the day's work: battered boots on his feet, a thick apron tied around his chest and waist. Crossing himself, Corbett crouched down to study the corpse. Colum's arms were by his sides, hands turned up, fingers splayed. Corbett glimpsed the ink on the dead man's right hand, staining the index and thumb, as if Colum had recently held a pen. He peered closer.

'See, Ranulf, a cook with fresh ink on his fingers.'

'He could have been doing a tally of stores?'

'At this early hour? Look around, can you see a ledger?' Corbett edged closer and swiftly went through the blood-soaked apron and the jerkin beneath but could find nothing to explain the ink stains.

'Sir Hugh.'

Corbett turned. Malach was pointing to a pillar just to the right of the doorway. Corbett rose and inspected the blood-soaked crossbow bolt dug deep into the wood.

'The Sagittarius,' he whispered. 'Is he truly behind this murderous mischief?' He glanced at the others gathered in the doorway and returned to his scrutiny.

He could see that the larder was stoutly built. No other entrance through the plastered stone walls, not even a window; only vents, mere slits high in the outside wall to allow in a little light and air. A proper larder, where meats soaked in salt or brine could be stored during the winter months.

'So how could this have happened, eh?' He crossed to the fallen door. He had this turned over and crouched beside it. The clasps at top and bottom were two slivers of steel that slotted into deep clasps. He tapped the bent key in the smashed lock; both of these were sturdy devices, whilst the oaken door was at least two inches thick.

'This chamber.' Lady Isabella, escorted by Malach, came to stand beside him. He glanced up. 'This chamber,' she repeated, 'was locked by Colum from within. So how could this happen?'

'A true mystery, but listen.' Corbett rose and walked over to the corpse. 'Those ink stains have jogged a memory. Look.' He turned back to Lady Isabella and raised his voice so that others in the passageway could hear. 'Does anybody, and I repeat anybody, know anything about this, anything about Colum before he was slain? Anything that might explain this?' No one replied. 'Very well.' He snapped his fingers. 'Lady Isabella, have the corpse removed and prepared for decent burial. You will take him to the death house, yes?'

He didn't wait for an answer, but turned to Ranulf. 'Question the servants. Ask them the same as I have now. Oh, and go to where Colum and Grease-hair lodged. Brockle or Malach will show you.' His voice dropped to a whisper. 'Search their possessions. Look for ink or any scrap of parchment, anything two kitchen scullions really should not possess.'

'I will, and you, Sir Hugh?'

'There's another corpse I wish to view.'

Corbett left the hall, going out in the mist-hung half-light. He crossed the grease-stained cobbles towards the death house, which lay beyond the ancient chapel. Lights glowed in the sanctuary's lancet windows, a sign that Parson Osbert was preparing to celebrate the Jesus mass. Corbett pulled open the door to the death house and went into the dingy, reeking chamber, poorly lit by the light piercing its narrow windows. Grease-hair still lay in his arrow-chest coffin, his corpse drenched in pine-wood juice and other crushed herbs to lessen the stink. Apparently his requiem mass was to take place on the morrow. Corbett stared down at the sunken face, the empty eye sockets and frazzled lips. He felt a profound sadness at Grease-hair's pathetic remains, a ragged beggar boy who had seen what he shouldn't have, then made the deadly mistake of voicing this to the world. He had simply mentioned that something was amiss in that murder chamber, yet he never really said what. Corbett bent down and moved the dead boy's hand so he could scrutinise the fingers. These were scorched black as cinder. However, the skin on the fingers of his right hand had not fully burnt, and Corbett glimpsed the faded blue-black ink.

'Yes, yes, I saw that before,' he murmured. 'My friend, you tried to draw something, didn't you, but what, I wonder?' He recalled the great hearth in the hall where

Grease-hair had squatted turning the spit. 'Yes, I do really wonder who killed you, Grease-hair, and who then slaughtered your friend Colum the cook. What happened in that larder? Did the assassin strike first with that spit pole, or did he kill Colum with a crossbow bolt, then pierce his belly? But who and why?'

He closed his eyes, rocking backwards and forwards on the balls of his feet. Colum the cook, he reflected, had been writing something, and so had Grease-hair, and despite the fire that had consumed the poor spit-boy, Corbett truly felt that the dead were speaking to him. How was it that Grease-hair's right hand had not been fully burnt so as to hide the ink stain?

'Do you know something?' He opened his eyes and stared down at the pathetic corpse. 'Grease-hair, I believe you might be the key to resolving all these murderous mysteries.'

He started at a knock on the door. Still distracted by his own thoughts, he walked over. He had his hand on the latch when he abruptly paused. Why the knock? The only person who knew he was coming here was Ranulf. So who else had been watching and waiting for him? And again, why the knock? Why not just open the door? This was no private chamber. He took a deep breath and drew his dagger.

'Come in!' he shouted. There was no reply. He lifted the rusty latch and flung the door open, but then used it to shield himself from the crossbow bolt that whirled through the air to smash against the far wall. Another swiftly followed. Corbett crouched down. He realised the trap set for him. He must not move. He drew a deep breath, then shouted the usual plea for help, 'Harrow! Harrow!' He repeated the cry. He heard doors opening and voices calling. He remained crouching until Ranulf appeared in the doorway. Then he rose, sheathing his knife as he quickly described what had happened.

'I heard you call, master, as did others. I left the hall and crossed the yard but I saw no one.'

'A will-o'-the-wisp, Ranulf.' Corbett pointed to the far wall. 'But a very well-armed one. So let us thank God for our deliverance.'

They left the death house and crossed to the chapel, where Parson Osbert was about to begin his mass. Malach appeared to enquire what was happening. Corbett simply shook his head; as he whispered to Ranulf, their golden rule was now in place. Trust no one.

Once mass had finished, Corbett led Ranulf into the small sacristy, where Parson Osbert was divesting. He gave the priest an offering for requiems to be sung for the souls of all who had been slain at Malmaison. The priest deftly pocketed the coins. Corbett continued to stare at him, as he had during the mass.

'Sir Hugh,' Parson Osbert smiled wanly, 'you look at me as if I have done something wrong.'

'No, no, my apologies.' Corbett raised a hand. '*Pax et bonum*, Father. As I have mentioned to you already, I am sure we have met before I came to Malmaison, but as God is my witness, I cannot place it. Have you ever visited Westminster?'

'Yes, as I have other places, Sir Hugh.' The priest stepped closer. 'We have both served in the royal array; our paths may well have crossed.'

'Yes, yes, that could be true. Ah well. Adieu, Father.'

Corbett and Ranulf left the chapel and made their way back into the deserted hall, where a boisterous fire flared merrily in the great hearth. Corbett walked over to the inglenook and stared down at the spit-boy's fire-stained stool. He then examined the enclave built into the side of the great mantled hearth. He smiled as he glimpsed the drawing in charcoal against the dull white plaster.

'Look, Ranulf.' His henchman joined him. 'The charcoal drawing is still clear on the plaster. I wager that this was drawn by Grease-hair.'

'A box,' Ranulf peered closer, 'a box containing parallel lines, the one at the top being longer than the others. But what does it mean?'

'I am sure Grease-hair drew that,' Corbett murmured, 'but God knows what it signifies. So let us continue our hunt, but remember, Ranulf, as I found out at the death house, we too are being hunted. Oh,' he tapped the charcoal drawing, 'by the way, did you discover anything amongst the possessions of Colum and Grease-hair?'

'Nothing but trinkets, Sir Hugh. However, there is a small chancery table close to the kitchens that contains scraps of parchment, pens and an inkpot for those who want to make notes or write lists or messages. Colum and Grease-hair, if they could write, may have used that, but . . .' Ranulf made a face.

Corbett spent the next few days going up and down the stairs scrutinising the hall, the solar, buttery and other chambers. He also visited the caverns below the gloomy manor house, as well as the terrain outside, until he was completely satisfied that he had a proper survey of what he described as 'the meadows of murder'. Afterwards, he spent hours writing notes in his own secret cipher. He once again scrutinised the contents of Lord Simon's chancery chest, but discovered nothing significant. He had expected this. The murdered manor lord had once worked in the Secret Chancery and, like all such clerks, believed that the less that was written down, the better.

Outside, the weather improved. A strengthening sun warmed the moorland, transforming the gorse into a sea of different colours. Corbett kept Ranulf and Chanson close, mindful of the murderous attack on him at the death house. He dined with Lady Isabella and the others, but remained tight lipped and wary about what he planned, discussing it with no one, not even his clerk. Instead he went back to his own musings. As last he was satisfied, and moved to implement the scheme he had drawn up. A plot, albeit a dangerous one, to trap a cohort of killers.

He dispatched Chanson, accompanied by Malach and an escort of Ap Ythel's archers, with a letter for Lord Moses. He then waited a further day before leaving the manor with Ranulf to ride into Felstead. The two clerks, cowled and hooded, slipped into the courtyard of the Palfrey, having stabled their horses at a small alehouse on the far side of the village. Corbett immediately ordered Minehost Baskerville to keep their arrival secret and to furnish them with a chamber. The taverner hastily agreed and hurried away, whilst Corbett and Ranulf prepared to break their fast in a shadow-filled corner of the taproom. Baskerville, all anxious, promised he would personally ensure that Lord Hugh and Sir Ranulf should feast on the very best the tavern could offer: fresh lamb from a nearby farm, the meat soft, succulent and heavily basted in its own juices.

They had hardly finished eating when a man dressed like an itinerant chapman, his head and face hidden by a mud-encrusted capuchin, wandered into the taproom. The travelling tinker raised a hand as he glimpsed Corbett, adjusted the portable tray strapped around his neck, then proclaimed he had items for sale that he believed his chosen customers would need. Corbett beckoned the man over. The chapman sat on the proffered stool, pulling down the rim of his cloak.

'Master Wolfram,' Corbett murmured, 'good to see you. I wondered what guise you would adopt. Let us adjourn.'

They crossed the taproom and climbed the stairs to the chamber Baskerville had prepared, a comfortable room, a square table set in the centre with benches either side. Corbett and Ranulf sat down, with Wolfram opposite. Ranulf filled their tankards from the jug

Baskerville had left. Wolfram, pulling back his hood and loosening his cloak, drank lustily, smacking his lips as he extended his blackjack for a refill. Corbett studied him closely. He remembered Wolfram as a skilled clerk when he was at Westminster, his hair closely shorn, his face finely shaved. This truly was a different man.

'The Lady Katerina?'

'She is well, Sir Hugh, but why did you summon me here? Lord Moses's messenger simply gave me the day, the hour and the place.'

'Let me be blunt and truthful,' Corbett replied. 'You are a felon, Wolfram, an outlaw who was involved in the torture and horrific murder of two loyal servants of the king. Whatever they had done, neither had broken any law worthy of death. You, however, could be dragged on a hurdle to a gibbet and hanged out of hand.'

Wolfram visibly flinched and his hand fell beneath the table.

'*Pax et bonum*,' Ranulf whispered. 'Master Wolfram, don't even touch the hilt of that dagger.' Wolfram placed his mittened hands back on the table. 'Good,' Ranulf breathed. 'Now keep them there.'

'Yes, keep them there,' Corbett warned, 'and listen well. You are *utlegatum*, a wolfshead, but you have turned king's approver. Now, in return for services to the Crown, you could receive a full pardon for all crimes committed without fear of further indictment.'

Wolfram relaxed, almost sagging against the table as he gasped with relief. 'The price?'

'The price, my friend, is high. The dangers will be great and pressing. You will live, as the theologians say, in sudden peril of death. What I will ask of you could cost you everything.'

'I have lived in danger all my life, Sir Hugh, as have you. Danger on land, danger on sea. Believe me, at this moment on God's hour candle, Dartmoor, Malmaison and Felstead are places of deep peril for me.'

'You mean the Sagittarius and his Scarecrows?'

'Yes, those night riders, the wreckers, and there's more. Perhaps you haven't been told about the disappearances: not just the guildsmen, but solitary chapmen and, on occasion, some poor serving wench from an outlying farm or one of the women from the small mining communities deep on the moor.'

'Such disappearances are common in any shire.'

'Ah yes, Ranulf, but so many in such a small area?' Wolfram spread his hands. 'I merely mention that. You talk of danger, Sir Hugh, but I've always believed that in the midst of life we are in death.'

'True, true, my friend and you certainly shall be . . .'

Corbett paused at the sweet singing from below. A young boy, his sister and father intoning a three-voiced rendition of the Salve Regina. He had noticed them gather as he finished his meal in the taproom below, and now he felt deeply touched by the beautiful, haunting music. The wonderful words of praise to the Virgin seeping into this close, dark chamber where the most dangerous trap was being primed and a lure set: a subtle device that might cause sudden and violent death. As the singers reached the verse 'To thee do we cry, poor banished children of Eve, to thee do we send up our sighs, mourning and weeping . . .' Corbett rose. He walked to the window, pulled back the shutters and stood staring out. The window overlooked the rear yard of the tavern. Beyond this stretched a broad path leading to the crossroads and a three-branched gibbet. The bound corpses of hanged felons swayed in the breeze, long black bundles sinister against the lightening sky.

'. . . mourning and weeping in this vale of tears.' The words of the travelling chanteurs rang clear in their three-voiced arrangement. Corbett closed his eyes and listened as the singers swept on to the great invocation. 'Oh clement, oh loving, oh sweet Virgin Mary.' He wished he could leave his own vale of tears; go down and join the singers as he loved to in his own manor chapel.

'Sir Hugh?'

Corbett grimaced, closed the shutters and returned to face a man he was probably sending to his death. 'Master Wolfram, I want you to travel, garbed as you are, to Plymouth. You are to go to the quayside and search out the royal cog *The Galliard* under its master Odo Beauchamp.' He drew a square of vellum from his pouch and tapped the scarlet wax, which carried the insignia of the Secret Seal. 'Give Master Odo this and take a berth on his vessel, which will sail two days from now on the evening tide, its destination Dover.' He also passed across a small coin purse. 'You will need this.'

'Is that all?'

'I think you know that is all, Master Wolfram. You probably suspect what we intend.'

'Of course, of course. I see the trap you are priming. You are going to use *The Galliard* as a lure. Strange,' Wolfram shook his head, 'you have been very busy, Sir Hugh.'

'Why is that strange?'

'Lady Katerina often visits Felstead. She shops in its markets, she visits Parson Osbert, not to mention mine-host here, and she has heard rumours.'

'About what?'

'About *The Galliard*, Master Ranulf. Rumours that it has some precious cargo. Sir Hugh, do such whispers have anything to do with you? I know Lord Moses and his tribe have been busy in Felstead. If you create the spark, they can fan the flames.'

'Never mind.' Corbett rose to his feet and extended a hand, which Wolfram clasped. 'Remember, you must be aboard *The Galliard* within two days. God speed you, sir, and,' he leant over the table, 'God protect you, for this truly is the season of murder. My friend, I bid you adieu.'

Corbett and Ranulf left Felstead as swiftly and secretly as they had arrived. On their return to Malmaison, they found the manor a hotbed of frenetic preparation and excitement. A breathless groom informed Corbett that the cause of all the clamour was Lady Isabella, who had decided that Malmaison had lain under the shroud of mourning for too long. Parson Osbert, who'd arrived at the manor about the same time, and was busy with his sumpter pony, strode across to confirm the ostler's words.

'Grief and tears will now give way to rejoicing,' the parson declared, unbustling his snook. 'Lent is soon at its end, with its strict fast and abstinence. Lady Isabella wants some rejoicing to mark the great Spring renewal, and I certainly agree.' He fell silent as Malach came hurrying into the bailey to announce that Lady Isabella wished to see all three of her visitors in the solar for morning ales and buttered manchets.

They sat in chairs around the solar fire, sipping at blackjacks of ale and popping pieces of freshly baked honey bread into their mouths. Parson Osbert talked about the approach of Spring and how he would personally arrange the liturgy for the manor chapel.

'And this revelry,' Corbett declared. 'Mistress, do you want that?'

'Of course I do. I have decided,' Isabella laughed prettily, fingers fluttering before her lips, 'yes, I have decided to be the Queen of Misrule.' Her smile widened. 'And I have decreed that we shall have a magnificent banquet with the most succulent meats, the freshest bread, vegetables soaked in herbs and, of course, jugs brimming with the best from Bordeaux or the Rhine. Steward Brockle is busy preparing the occasion. The banquet will take place in three days' time, after dusk. Now,' she leant forward, clapping her hands softly, 'we shall all dress in special gowns of red, gold, green and silver or black, and wear leopard masks fashioned by myself and my servants.'

'Mistress,' Corbett toasted her with his tankard, 'revelry indeed, but won't that evoke memories of those great cats that once prowled here and held everyone in fear?'

'Oh, they were amusing enough. Anyway, they have gone now and we can rejoice in that.'

'You did not like them, mistress?'

'Sir Hugh, I did not like them, and nor did many in this manor and beyond.' All good humour drained from her face. 'They were ferocious and dangerous, and as you know, enough nightmares prowl our moors and bay at the moon.'

'You still mourn your husband?'

'A personal question, Sir Hugh. Of course I do.'

'And his first wife?' Corbett caught the sharp shift in Lady Isabella's eyes, whilst Malach sat back abruptly in his chair.

'Lord Simon truly was a strange man.' Parson Osbert tactfully intervened.

'In what way, Father?'

'Enigmatic, secretive, a man who watched everything around him but never really commented on what he saw or heard. At times,' the parson cleared his throat, 'I truly wondered if he believed in anything, yet he had a profound devotion to the Holy Face of Lucca. Mistress, I believe that Lord Simon owned a copy, a close replica of the relic.'

'May I see it?' Corbett made to rise, but Malach swiftly stood up.

'My lady, I will fetch it for your guests.'

'Yes, yes, of course.'

'Let Ranulf go with you.' Corbett gestured at his henchman. 'It's best if such a precious relic is kept safe, and it might be heavy.'

'The frame is of solid oak,' Lady Isabella agreed.

'Good, good. I look forward to seeing this. The old king . . .' Corbett proceeded to describe the relics kept in the crypt at Westminster, after which Parson Osbert listed those he hoped to purchase for his freshly furnished chantry chapel. Corbett let him talk, studying the parson's face, wondering again when and where he had seen this priest before. He prided himself on his good memory, his ability to recall a face and an occasion, but this was frustrating him and creating an unease he could not resolve.

Parson Osbert broke off from his account as Ranulf and Malach returned with the heavy frame covered by a thick purple cloth. Ranulf removed this and Malach handed the painting to Corbett, who carefully rested it on the table beside him. He turned it slightly to catch the light as he studied this very lifelike depiction of the tortured face of Christ. On his head, a crown of thorns, the blood dripping down the sacred face. Corbett crossed himself, kissed the painting and, murmuring his thanks, handed the picture back to Malach. He then glanced quickly at Ranulf, who simply shook his head, a sign that he'd glimpsed nothing untoward in Lady Isabella's chamber.

Earlier, Corbett had wondered about Lord Simon's widow and her relationship with Malach. Surely Lady

Isabella must entertain her own suspicions about her predecessor's abrupt disappearance, and yet she showed no sign of being troubled, nor did she act the grieving widow. Corbett nodded to himself. He had found no different at the king's court in Westminster. Men and women who had been obliged to accept an arranged marriage to enhance their status as well as increase their wealth.

'So,' he rose to his feet, 'we are going to celebrate. Lady Isabella, I look forward to it. In the meantime, other pressing business demands my attention.'

The two clerks adjourned to what Corbett thought of as the murder chamber, where they made themselves as comfortable as possible. Corbett, now free of his boots, cloak and war belt, sat down on the edge of his bed and grinned at his companion.

'So you saw nothing suspicious in my lady's chamber?'

'Nothing, master. A bed that only one person has slept in. Triptychs and crucifixes on the walls between a range of tapestries. I glimpsed no sealed coffer or casket. A lady's chamber in every sense of the word. Why, Sir Hugh? Do you suspect our noble lady?'

'I do, but I also have suspicions about everyone else. Everyone here, Ranulf, is a possible murderer, and there are those who live beyond the walls of this manor too who might well have innocent blood on their hands. We have clearly established that the likes of Wolfram can come and go as they please. We have no real knowledge about what other secret passages and tunnels exist.'

'Are these only suspicions, Sir Hugh, or do you have evidence, some sort of proof?'

'Not yet. I am trying to summon up the ghost of poor Grease-hair. I wonder, Ranulf, what that hapless spit-boy saw in this murder chamber. He glimpsed something that wasn't right, something that shouldn't have been here. Our assassin is like one of those conjurors who set up their stall in the marketplace. They attract the crowds and, by a charade of patter and clever finger tricks, create a reality that in truth is only a sham. On the night Lord Simon was murdered here, our assassin staged a macabre masque. He now knows, however, that Grease-hair noticed something amiss, a serious mistake, though what it was remains a mystery. Anyway,' Corbett rubbed his hands together, 'we continue our hunt.'

Corbett returned to his quiet reflection, sitting at the chamber chancery desk or walking the manor as if he wished to memorise every detail. He spent considerable time in the various larders, especially the one where Colum had been murdered. He managed to secure a set of keys, and he went up and down opening doors and slamming them shut. The servants looked surprised, but they were now growing accustomed to this eccentric yet powerful royal clerk, who walked their manor and would often pause to whisper to himself.

Malmaison was certainly busy enough, with the preparations for the great Spring renewal feast going ahead. Lady Isabella, through Malach and a very solemn and withdrawn Brockle, ordered a great purge to take place, a thorough spring-cleansing to prepare the manor for the great feast of Easter and the onset of summer. Chambers, including Corbett's, were cleaned, swept, scrubbed and polished. Rubbish of all sorts was loaded onto carts and, under the supervision of Malach, taken out to be burnt or dumped in one of the great mires high on the moor. Under the pretence of helping, Corbett sent Ap Ythel and three of his trusted bowmen into the caverns beneath the manor to clear the tangle of bones, the remains of what had been fed to the leopards. Secretly the archers were ordered to search carefully for human remains, which were to be kept separate, placed in an arrow chest and stored away.

On the morning before the great revelry, Corbett attended Parson Osbert's Jesus mass in the manor chapel. With Ranulf standing close by, he prayed for the souls of both Lady Beatrice and Chandos, begging an angel of light to assist Ap Ythel in his gruesome task. After the mass had finished, the chapel lay eerily silent. Corbett remained. He prayed for his wife, the Lady Maeve, and their two children before lighting six tapers in the narrow lady chapel and kneeling on the prie-dieu before the statue of the Theotokos, a replica of the famous statue at Walsingham.

Afterwards, slipping his Ave beads back into his belt pouch, he walked the chapel, stopping now and again to admire the crude, yet startlingly vivid wall paintings. Most of these depicted the eternal struggle between heaven and hell. The motif was repeated time and again:

golden-haired, silver-faced angels formed a shield ring against surging hordes of demons with scarlet skin, fiery hair and cat-like green eyes. He also studied the erected stations of the cross, fourteen in number, describing Christ's journey to the place of crucifixion. Eventually, blessing himself with holy water from the stoup, he genuflected towards the pyx hanging on its golden chain next to the glittering red sanctuary lamp and left.

For the rest of the day, he concentrated on writing down everything he had seen, heard or felt at Malmaison. The hour of festivity arrived. The manor folk prepared themselves. Malach and Brockle distributed the leopard masks and the tawny robes, which replicated the dark-spotted skin of the leopards. The revellers gathered in the great hall, its furniture polished to a glittering shine. A fire roared in the hearth, and greenery from the garden and orchards decorated sills and ledges.

The great table had been erected on the dais. Lady Isabella took the seat of honour, a majestic throne-like chair under a silver-edged canopy. Parson Osbert sat on her left, with Corbett given the seat of grace to her right. The table had been sumptuously prepared. Thick snow-white linen cloths covered the boards, and in the centre stood a massive silver nef, jewel encrusted, along with an array of goblets. All these precious items glittered in the dancing light from a cluster of beeswax candles on a many-branched candelabra. The great Catherine wheel above the table had been lowered, its rim crammed with small, fiery tapers.

Cresset torches blazed along the walls. The air turned sweet, the smoke from these perfumed lights mingling with the fragrance from the nearby kitchens and bakery. Here, lamb, pork, bacon, lampreys and various kinds of fish were roasted, grilled or toasted whilst being basted with lavish coatings of herb-rich oil and sweetened fruit.

Trumpeters, musicians, chanteurs and troubadours gathered to perform their tricks. Jesters and acrobats assembled in the shadows, heightening the expectancy. At last a horn brayed to mark the beginning of the feast. A grim-faced Brockle and two servants moved along the dais with a deep bowl of rose water for the principal guests to wash and perfume their hands. Course after course was served. The manor folk sat at tables stretching down either side of the hall. They toasted their mistress and each other as they drank and feasted long past the chimes of midnight. Now and again there was a respite from the constant banqueting to watch the acrobats or jugglers display their skills. Then the feasting would continue.

Ranulf ate and drank as merrily as any of them, matching Chanson goblet for goblet and platter for platter. Corbett, however, ate and drank sparingly, watching intently as the evening drew on. People swirled about, their cloaks flapping, faces hidden behind masks. It truly was a time of revelry and misrule, until a woman's piercing scream chilled the festivities and a slattern, hair all loose, burst into the hall through the narrow door under the choir loft. Screaming and yelling, she pushed revellers aside only to pause and point fearfully back. The noise died. The musicians in the loft put down their instruments; servants drifted away from the buttery table. The juggler and the fire-eater stood still, all watching the slattern hurry towards the dais, where Lady Isabella and Malach rose to greet her, Corbett and Ranulf likewise.

'Mistress!' the woman gasped. 'Mistress, it's Master Brockle.'

Corbett, escorted by Ranulf, went around the table and grasped the woman's ice-cold hand. She tried to speak, but he pressed a finger against her lips.

'Just show me,' he murmured. 'Just show me.' He turned back to the dais, his powerful voice ringing through the hall. 'Lady Isabella, I ask you and everyone else to stay here.'

Still grasping the slattern's hand, Corbett strode down the hall into the stone-flagged passageway leading to the narrow, dingy chambers of the principal household men. He paused and smiled down at her.

'Your name?'

'Matilda, sir.' The red-cheeked young woman attempted a curtsy.

'So, Matilda, what is the matter?'

Shaking her head, the slattern pulled Corbett towards one of the doors. She stopped and pointed at the narrow grille high in the wood, and Corbett peered through. The chamber was bleak and poorly furnished. However, a large lanternhorn standing on the table shed light on a truly grisly scene. Steward Brockle lay slumped against the far wall, head to one side, face coated with blood, which had erupted through mouth and nose as well as from the hole in his forehead caused by a feathered crossbow bolt. Corbett pushed against the door, but it held firm.

'Master,' the slattern whispered, 'look at his hands.'

Corbett did so, and glimpsed the ring of keys still clutched in the dead man's fingers. He peered in, trying to see every aspect of that place of murder. A dingy room, with shelves, battered aumbries, a shabby table, small, cracked coffers and caskets and two cushioned stools. Again he tried the door, but it held fast. By now, the rest of the company, ignoring Corbett's request, had begun to leave the hall and were thronging down the passageway. Torches were taken down from their sconces. A candelabra borrowed from the hall spluttered and flamed. Shouts and cries echoed. Corbett beckoned Ranulf forward.

'Impose order,' he hissed. 'Then break down that door. Once it's done, only you and I enter that chamber. Brockle is dead, slain like the others, but as for the who, the how and the why . . .' He shrugged. 'Do as I ask.'

Ranulf acted swiftly. The household, apart from a fearful Lady Isabella, were cleared away. The chatelaine stood clutching Malach's arm, whispering hoarsely into his ear. Malach simply shook his head and led his mistress to stand further down the passageway.

'Sir Hugh, can Lady Isabella return to her chamber? We realise there is more tragedy.'

'More tragedy,' Corbett confirmed. 'Brockle the steward lies slain like the rest.'

'You will force the door?' Malach shook his head. 'There was only one key to that chamber, and our worthy steward guarded it jealously.'

'In which case, take your mistress to her chamber.'

Corbett returned to where Ranulf was now organising six burly servants to lift a yew log taken from its store in the hall. He glanced over his shoulder; Lady Isabella and Malach still stood there.

'We must become busy, Master Malach, so go now. Take your mistress and everyone else with you.'

Malach led his mistress away and the passageway emptied. The battering began, a nerve-jarring crashing sound as the great yew log battered and broke the door, rupturing its lock, bolt and hinges. Dust and dirt swirled through the air. Corbett waited for this to clear before stepping over the fallen door and crouching before Brockle's blood-soaked corpse. The man was slumped on a low three-legged stool. He wore the same festive robe as the rest, with a tawdry leopard mask on the floor beside him. Beneath the robe, Corbett noticed that his jerkin and belt were undisturbed.

'Master,' Ranulf whispered from where he stood at the fallen door, 'to your right.'

Corbett followed his henchman's direction and glimpsed a second crossbow bolt smeared in blood driven deep into one of the wooden shelves.

'The Sagittarius,' he declared, returning to his scrutiny. 'So,' he whispered to himself, 'you came in here, Master

Steward; you were probably tired and deep in your cups. You locked the door.' He leant over, took the ring of keys from the dead man's hands and handed them to Ranulf. 'Find the one that fits. Now,' he returned to his soliloquy, 'you locked the door behind you and sat down on that stool, taking off your mask. Why did you come here? Was your assassin already waiting for you, or did you admit him? Either way, it's a mystery, for there is only one key to that lock, and you held that yourself.' He glanced over his shoulder at Ranulf, kneeling beside the fallen door. He'd thrust a key into the lock and was turning it.

'Master, it's damaged but this is the key. There are no bolts or bars on the inside; this sturdy lock held the door fast. So how the killer, the Sagittarius, entered and left is cloaked in deceit and deception.'

Corbett got to his feet, beckoning his henchman close. 'Mingle with the servants and the guests. Sheriff Wendover arrived during the feast, as did others. Where did they go, what were they doing? Did anyone see or hear anything untoward?'

'And you, Sir Hugh?'

'I will take Chanson back to my chamber. He can guard the door whilst I pray for poor Wolfram and Brockle. . .'

Poor Wolfram felt that he needed every prayer that anyone could offer on his behalf. Taking Corbett's instructions, the purse of coins and the letter for Odo, master of the king's cog *The Galliard*, he had slipped into Plymouth, lodged for a short while at the Golden Bagpipe, then made his way through the salt-encrusted alleyways down to the quayside, a hive of frenetic activity as various ships, cogs, fishing smacks and herring boats made ready to leave on the evening tide. He soon found *The Galliard* and met its captain, who stood guarding the gangplank with his two principal henchmen. Beauchamp was a veteran in the old king's wars and claimed to know Sir Hugh well. He carefully scrutinised Corbett's letter before gripping Wolfram by the shoulder, squeezing hard.

'I heard you were coming, and we can always do with an extra pair of hands. Seen service on the northern seas, have you?'

'Aye, and off Bordeaux.'

'Good, then up you go.' Beauchamp released his grip. 'You have a choice, a bag of straw in the hold or one beneath the mast. Anyway, quick as you can.'

Wolfram had scrambled up the gangplank onto the royal cog, its slippery deck moving sickeningly as it strained at the ropes holding it to the quayside. The patter of bare feet as the crew hurried around mingled with the screech of cordage and netting, the crack of timber and the constant creaking as the cog gently pitched up and down. It was a different world to the lonely farmstead high on Doone Moor. The air reeked of fish, salt, sweat and oil. Wolfram steadied himself, watching the crew crossing the deck or, nimble as spring squirrels, clambering down into the deep hold and up the mainmast. *The Galliard* was preparing for sea, and his sharp wits caught the usual tension, along with a fearful expectation of foul weather awaiting them beyond the port.

The Galliard's crew were about fifteen in all, including the master; however, when Wolfram went down into the hold, stinking of pitch and tar, he glimpsed other dark shapes huddling close for the night. He pulled his cowl close over his head, wrapped his heavy military cloak about him, grasped his pannier more firmly and climbed back up onto the swaying deck, settling down close to the taffrail on the starboard side. As the cog made ready to depart, shouts and yells carried and the sails flapped noisily in the strengthening wind. Then the vessel slipped its moorings and swiftly made its way out to the open seas.

Wolfram had served on war cogs and knew that the Narrow Seas could be nasty and highly dangerous. The voyage that night more than justified the fear shared by the crew before they left harbour. Turbulent storms were sweeping the sea, and *The Galliard* sailed straight into one of these. Heavy winds whistled through the rigging. Rain sleeted down to bounce off the deck as the cog staggered from side to side, battling the tempest. The crew were highly fearful, but about an hour out of port, the storm subsided, the men relaxed and the master left his post high on the stern. Wolfram watched as he dispatched a lookout up into the falcon's nest and ordered two more of the crew to watch from the taffrail along the cog's stern, with a third high on the jutting poop. He heard the shouts and cries of confirmation that the sailors were in post and all was well. Beauchamp shouted at the rudder men to keep to the course, whilst the sail riggers must let the ship make use of the wind.

With the storm fast abating, *The Galliard* was now able to control its own movements. Beauchamp brought the vessel in as close as possible to the coastline. The lookouts were warned to watch for any lights from the shore. Wolfram decided to mount his own vigil. Leaning against the taffrail on the port side, he peered through the constant spray. He could make out very faintly the dark line of cliffs. Now and again, the mist parted to provide a clearer view of the shoreline, though he could glimpse nothing untoward.

For a while, he reflected on recent events and how the murders at Malmaison had frustrated and brought to nothing the well-laid plans of both himself and Sheriff Wendover, so much so that he had had to accept this highly dangerous task. He heard a shout and turned. One of the sailors had fallen to the deck, followed by a scream from high on the stern. Wolfram grasped the taffrail as the cog abruptly turned. For a moment the ship thrust upwards to ride the soaring crested wave, then it lurched sickeningly as the returning tide forced it forward. He realised something was very wrong, and edged forward, hands slipping off the rail. Hearing a sound, he half turned, and the shadows closed in. He took a blow to the head, then he was falling, hurtling down into the cold, surging angry sea.

* * *

Corbett spent two days following Brockle's murder studying Malmaison both within and without. He listened intently to what Ranulf reported on the conversations he'd had with the manor folk, yet the clerk had discovered nothing to explain the steward's brutal slaying. They were discussing this in Corbett's chamber when Ap Ythel came hurrying up, rapping at the door. Once he had caught his breath, the captain of archers pointed to the window.

'Sir Hugh,' he gasped in his sing-song voice, 'the watch we placed above Monkshood Bay . . . They are back.'

'And?' Corbett rose to his feet.

'Nothing there, Sir Hugh, though there are reports of *The Galliard* being wrecked further up the coast at a place called Cormorant Cove. Corpses lie floating in the water. The ship is shattered, as if it's been pulled up and thrust down on the rocks . . .'

Corbett and his henchman, escorted by Ap Ythel and his entire comitatus, left Malmaison within the hour. The day was bright enough, though the sunlight was beginning to fade as they thundered along the coffin paths and bridleways, a disgruntled Malach acting as their guide. They rode towards the coast, then turned to follow the mist-hung cliff edge; a hard ride. The dull crashing of the sea against the rocks below mingled with the strident screeches of gulls circling above them. When they reached Monkshood Bay, they reined in. Brancepeth, Ap Ythel's henchman, explained how he and three others had, as Corbett had instructed, set up silent camp here on the lea of the hill stretching down to the beach. They had erected a bothy and made themselves as comfortable as possible.

'Nothing.' Brancepeth's lilting voice rang out. 'Sir Hugh, we saw or heard nothing amiss until early today. A chapman who passed Cormorant Cove glimpsed the wreck. He was hurrying to Malmaison when we met him.'

'You are sure he was not one of the wreckers?'

'No, Sir Hugh, I would swear on my mother's soul. He was what he claimed to be.'

They rode on. Now and again the sea mist thickened, only to part now and again like a curtain. At last they reached the rise above Cormorant Cove. Corbett, calming his horse, stared down at the scene of devastation and breathed a prayer for help. The inlet was very similar to Monkshood, a deep gap in the coastline fringed by hills and cliffs, where the waves surged in to create what could be a natural harbour. However, rocks thrusting up from the seabed stretched across the cove, a real danger to any vessel. The waves battered against this stone barrier, though once they flowed past it, the sea became calmer. He also noticed how the rocks stretched almost to the beach, stepping stones, a makeshift bridge for anyone to use.

Ignoring the exclamations and curses of his escort, Corbett stared pityingly at the royal cog impaled on the rocks close to the beach. The vessel had been truly shattered; its mainmast, sail and cordage lay all tangled. Already the sheer power of the surging tide was making itself felt. The wreck turned and twisted, and even from where he sat soothing his horse, Corbett could hear the sharp crack of timbers. Bundles floated in the eddying water; flotsam and jetsam littered the beach, along with four water-drenched corpses.

Brancepeth spoke up. 'Sir Hugh, no one survived. We made sure of that before we hastened back to Malmaison.'

'Let us see.'

Corbett urged his mount down the rise and onto the pebble-hardened beach. He dismounted and handed the reins to Chanson before moving from corpse to corpse, turning the bodies over. Already the faces of the dead were soaked and bloated. Three of the archers waded into the water to bring in two more cadavers and lay them side by side. Corbett and Ranulf carefully scrutinised each of the corpses. They detected savage blows to the head and face of each. However, apart from one, a mere youth who, Corbett suspected, had probably been placed high in the cog's falcon's nest, the injuries could have been the result of the wreck rather than some murderous assault. He examined the blow to the look-out's head and wondered what had truly happened. These men were innocents. He felt a surge of utter bleakness, a sense of deepening despair, and fought back the tears.

Ranulf watched anxiously. It was rare indeed for Master Long Face to show any deep emotion, even though he felt it. But here on this godforsaken beach, with the thundering growl of the sea and the hiss of the wind, it seemed as if the evil that prowled the world of the invisible was about to break through. He stared around. A soul-chilling desolation hung over this place of sudden, brutal death. Sir Hugh was now kneeling beside a corpse, his hands joined in prayer, eyes closed as he rocked himself backwards and forwards. Ranulf went and placed a hand on his shoulder, aware that Ap Ythel and his archers were also becoming concerned.

'Master,' he whispered, 'they are all dead. We cannot find any trace of the cog's cargo or any true cause for this mishap.'

'Murder!' Corbett rasped, getting to his feet. 'Murder!' he screamed up at the sky, and the gulls answered with their own shrieking hymn.

He strode across to where Chanson guarded the horses and swiftly mounted, gesturing at Ranulf to do likewise. Standing up in the stirrups, he called Ap Ythel and his archers to gather around.

'See to the dead,' he ordered. 'Get carts. Take the corpses into Felstead. Tell Parson Osbert to observe the rituals and give these men the most honourable burial.' He gathered his reins as he stared out at *The Galliard*, nothing more than a broken shell, a ghost of its former grandeur. In his survey of the corpses he had not found anyone he recognised, be it the captain or, more significantly, Wolfram.

'Sir Hugh, what now?'

'Back to Malmaison,' Corbett snapped, 'where I will make my full confession.'

* * *

Once settled in Corbett's chamber, with a vigorous wind rattling the shutters poor Grease-hair had peered through, Corbett, his boots, cloak and sword belt piled on the floor beside him, stretched out one hand to the brazier whilst the other grasped the goblet of mulled wine Ranulf had poured for him. Corbett's henchman now sat on a stool beside his master, revelling in the warmth, pleased to be away from that macabre, chilly inlet and those terrifying moors where, he was certain, hellish creatures prowled.

'I prepared a trap,' Corbett began. 'I set a lure like a fowler would. I tied a noose but our quarry escaped. I have sent good men and a royal cog to utter destruction.'

'You are the king's captain, the Crown's henchman,' Ranulf replied quietly. 'Sir Hugh, you have the full power of fire and sword; your will in these matters is that of the king.' He leant over and tapped Corbett's war belt. 'Master, this place is as much a battlefield as one of those steep, ice-covered valleys in Wales or the deep wet glens along the Scottish March. True, there is a difference: our adversaries are well hidden, but we commit our forces and,' he shrugged, 'as on any battle-field, men fall. Some are wounded, others mortally. And I recognise,' he added in a half-whisper, 'that one day it will be my turn. I won't move fast enough. I will not duck in time. I will go through the wrong door at the wrong time in the wrong place and the only thing left will be a priest to sing my requiem.'

'Job's comforters we are,' Corbett forced a smile, 'but you are correct, Ranulf, so let me confess to what I plotted. I ordered Lord Moses to spread the story that *The Galliard*, berthed in Plymouth, carried a great treasure. I even hinted that I had discovered the Lacrima Christi at Malmaison and it was now on board that royal cog waiting to be transported back to Westminster. Lord Moses gleefully disseminated the seed, the lure to my trap. I reckoned that those who led the wrecking would not be able to resist.'

'Who?'

'I don't know, Ranulf. Anyone who wields authority over others could be involved: Sheriff Wendover, Parson Osbert, Lady Isabella, even Adam Warfeld, prior of that order of reprobates out at St Benet's. Of course, there are others, such as those guildsmen, some of whom might still survive; then there's Minehost Baskerville and his wealthy tavern.' Corbett paused at a shiver that tingled the nape of his neck. The list of possible culprits had sparked a thought. 'Horses!' he breathed. 'Oh Ranulf, sometimes I cannot see what's in front of me. The Sagittarius and his coven have horses, but where do they stable them? Not,' he laughed drily, 'at St Benet's, but at the Palfrey.'

'Or, Sir Hugh, out on the moors, with all those secret, lonely places. Sheriff Wendover is correct. You could hide an army out there; it might take weeks to find them. Think of the isolated farms, the derelict outhouses, the abandoned dwellings we've passed. Any of those could be used to house horses, carts and whatever plunder they seized. Anyway, what was *The Galliard* really carrying?'

'Nothing, Ranulf.'

'Sir Hugh?'

'Nothing at all except poor Wolfram. He was sent on board to watch and wait, spy out any false lights and see what actually happened.'

'What actually happened was that the cog was wrecked like the rest.'

'No, this time it was different. Ap Ythel and I set up a close watch over Monkshood Bay. His archers were to light a beacon if anything untoward occurred, but nothing did. This means that the Sagittarius and the Scarecrows suspected we might set a trap, so they moved their attack further up the coast to Cormorant Cove. They gained nothing from their hideous crimes, yet how did they wreck that ship?'

'Ap Ythel's archers saw nothing?'

'Nothing.' Corbett closed his eyes, then abruptly opened them. 'And Wolfram,' he murmured, 'what happened to that criminous clerk?'

Lady Katerina, Wolfram's sister, wondered the same as she sat before the peat fire flaming in the hearth of her stone-flagged kitchen. Her parents' farm was a lonely, forsaken place, yet Katerina was not perturbed. She felt safe and secure enough. The doors and shutters were firmly locked and bolted; a primed arbalest lay next to an Italian stabbing blade on the small table beside her. Outside prowled two of her battle dogs, Arthur and Modred, whilst two others, Lancelot and Guinevere, lay slumped on the floor beside her, dozing in the warmth after their hours of roaming outside.

Katerina listened to the rising wind rattling outside like some demon desperate to break out of the cold darkness. She sipped at her mulled wine as she wondered about the tales of a passing chapman. How a cog had been wrecked in Cormorant Cove. She wondered if Wolfram knew about that. She clasped the goblet more firmly. She was glad her brother had turned king's approver, sued for a royal pardon for crimes he might not have committed but certainly knew of. The scarlet sins of Lord Simon had continued to haunt him day and night, so intensely that Katerina had worried his wits would be turned and he would sink into his own dark pit of madness.

Now he was free, yet he did not act honestly with her. He had refused to share his suspicions about Parson Osbert, nor had he informed Corbett how he had discovered the mortal remains of two of the missing guildsmen. Fulbert's remains had already been dragged from a mire. Wolfram had then confessed to her how, on a recent hunting trip, his war hounds had unearthed two more corpses concealed by a thick fringe of gorse and grass. Despite the onset of corruption, he had immediately recognised them as men he had met in the Palfrey and elsewhere. To her horror, he had simply shoved the corpses back into the marsh and passed on. Katerina had grown deeply anxious. Wolfram had referred to a secret meeting with Corbett, and then, as he could so easily, he had vanished like one of those mysterious flames that sparked up from the heathland and disappeared into the night.

'Wolfram, Wolfram!' she murmured. She recognised that her brother was a born intriguer. She knew he'd had clandestine meetings with Sheriff Wendover. Apparently the pair were set on some great design, which, according to her brother's muttered curses, had completely collapsed after the murders at Malmaison. She rubbed her face. She should be more honest about herself. If her brother kept his secrets, she certainly did the same about both Lord Simon and Parson Osbert. She had, unknown to Wolfram, enjoyed secret relationships with both men, until each had grown abusive . . .

She tensed. The battle hounds outside were growling as they scurried about. Lancelot and Guinevere lumbered to their feet. Katerina grasped the arbalest and rose. Outside, the two hounds were howling, but this was cut to a whimpering whine. Lancelot and Guinevere flung themselves at the door, and Katerina hastened to unbolt it. Even as she did so, she realised it was a mistake, but it was too late.

The two war hounds sped out, clear targets in the light from the cresset torch flung on the cobbles, its dancing flame shedding a pool of light. Crossbow bolts whirred through the dark to smash into their skulls. The dogs floundered and skittered, then toppled onto their sides, legs moving frenetically as they choked on their own blood. Katerina lifted the arbalest, but her sweat-laced fingers were unable to grip the clasp, and she fumbled. A sinister figure emerged from the blackness, garbed like the night with a fearsome straw mask over its face. The arbalest was knocked from her hand, a hood pulled over her head. Katerina struggled, but it was futile: arms pinioned, she was hoisted up onto a horse, its rider roughly embracing her.

An order was shouted and the cavalcade broke into a canter, leaving the farm along a path stretching up onto the moors. They rode for a while, then reined in. Katerina heard a door being opened, and they clattered across a cobbled yard. Shouts and cries rent the air. She was dragged off the horse, and pulled stumbling and faltering into a building and down some narrow steps. When she reached the bottom, the mask was removed, and she blinked in the blazing light of the lanternhorn standing on a nearby table. She was forced to sit on a stool. The nightmare who had first confronted her pulled up another stool and squatted opposite, his face and voice disguised by the heavy, grotesque mask.

'Right, woman. Katerina, isn't it?' He slapped her face. 'I asked a question, you must reply.'

'Yes,' Katerina retorted, tears welling at the cruel blow.

'Beloved sister of that reprobate—'

'He is no reprobate.'

Another slap. 'Answer my questions, woman. We know Wolfram has been to Malmaison, and that he met that snooper, that prier into other men's souls, Corbett, yes?'

'I don't know.'

Again the harsh slap. 'Does Corbett hold the Lacrima Christi?'

'I don't know what that is.' Katerina screamed at the blow to her face that caused her nose to start bleeding.

'Why did Wolfram board *The Galliard*?'

'I don't know.' Katerina winced, waiting for the next blow.

'You know nothing of his doings?'

'I do not.'

'Did they find anything at the farm?' the grotesque called over his shoulder.

'No, master, nothing at all,' a voice replied.

'Have you seen Wolfram since he left for Plymouth?'

'No.'

The grotesque pushed his masked face closer. 'Did your brother ever tell you anything about the Lacrima Christi or the casket that contained it?'

'No.'

'Or anything about the Sagittarius and the Scarecrows he leads?'

'No. I just love my brother. I know nothing. He was troubled. He slept badly. He did not eat well.' Katerina fell silent as the grotesque pressed a gloved finger against her mouth, the eyes glittering behind the mask studying her carefully.

'I believe you,' he whispered. 'I believe you. Look up, Katerina, lift your head.' She did so, and swift as a striking viper, the grotesque lunged, slashing her throat in one swift cut with the dagger he'd concealed in his hand.

Corbett and Ranulf were breaking their fast in the manor buttery. They'd risen early to hear mass in the chapel, but Parson Osbert had sent his apologies that he was indisposed. Corbett was wondering what to do next when a servant burst through the buttery door.

'Sir Hugh, we have a visitor, cloaked and cowled. He carries your seal and insists on meeting you immediately.'

'In which case, bring him in.'

Corbett and Ranulf rose to their feet as their unexpected visitor came into the buttery. Closing the door behind him, the stranger pushed back his hood and lowered the muffler of his cloak.

'Wolfram!' Ranulf exclaimed. 'By all that is holy . . .'

'Come, come.' Corbett beckoned the man to a stool in front of the brazier. 'Take some warmth. Ranulf, a cup of mulled wine for our guest. Do you want food?'

'No, no.' Wolfram shook his head. 'Sir Hugh, I am wearied and worried. I returned to our farm. My mastiffs have been slaughtered, the house ransacked. Katerina is missing. I . . . I . . .'

His voice trailed off, and Corbett studied him. Wolfram had now doffed both cloak and hood; the clothes beneath were crumpled and ragged. His moustache, hair and beard were still thick as a bush: his eyes were red rimmed with exhaustion, whilst the hand holding the posset cup was in a constant tremble.

'Be at peace, Wolfram,' Corbett whispered. 'Tell us what happened. Swiftly now, because the malignants cluster like ghosts in the dark.' He crossed himself. 'A terrible vengeance is coming, but for the moment, Wolfram?'

'I did as you asked. I boarded *The Galliard*, and it slipped its moorings peaceably enough and made its way into the Narrow Seas, hugging the coast. The vessel mustered a crew of about fifteen. I thought there were more, but you see, I was only a mere passenger. Master Odo was cordial enough, though blunt; I was to choose a place to berth and keep out of the way. Once we left harbour, we encountered a sudden fierce storm, but that passed. I reckoned we were approaching Monkshood Bay and all those other inlets that pepper the coastline. And then it happened, so sudden, so silent. I heard a commotion from the stern, where the master stood with the rudder men. Murk, Sir Hugh, murky as hell. Then the ship abruptly lurched and turned, as if determined on reaching the shoreline.'

'You are sure?'

'As I am sitting here. I am certain of it, aiming like an arrow through the dark.'

'But the master, the crew?'

'I don't know, Sir Hugh, but *The Galliard* had certainly turned, the waves pushing it forward on the incoming tide. Believe me, it was stronger than any wind. Anyway, I was making my way towards the stern when I took a blow to the back of the head and was pitched over the side. I cannot swim and I was barely conscious. I thought my body was for the grave and my soul for judgement, so I mumbled the Miserere as I flailed out, turning and twisting in the racing water. Then my hand struck a piece of wood, the side of some box, and I grabbed that and clung onto it. Thankfully, the tide moved me further along, then in a sudden twist thrust me towards the beach. I staggered ashore. I was so relieved, so determined to escape from danger. Once up on the heathland, I realised where I was, so I made my way as swiftly and secretly as I could to our farm.' He paused, catching his breath. 'The house had been attacked and ransacked. Our four war dogs sprawled dead. Katerina gone. I changed, took money from a hidden cache and whatever weapons I could find, then hurried here.'

'Hell's teeth,' Corbett whispered. 'It is true what they say in logic: it is often the most obvious thing we fail to see or understand.'

'Master?'

'Ranulf, we have worked on the premise that all these cogs are lured onto the rocks by malignants lurking along the shore who entice vessels in with false fires and lights. This is not the situation here, yet it was so obvious. Wolfram, Ranulf, you are mailed clerks. How many times have you been involved in, or at least heard of, expeditions into an enemy harbour to take a cog by stealth and trickery?'

'Many times,' Ranulf replied. 'The same is true of river pirates, those who prowl the Thames. They hide in a culvert or hidden inlet and board a merchant cog when it berths mid-river or slows to avoid the mudbanks.'

'Yes, yes, I've heard the same,' Wolfram declared. 'Sometimes a vessel can be attacked from within.'

'So easy,' Corbett agreed. 'A cog berthed in Plymouth is set to sail on the evening tide. The wreckers choose their victim knowing they can hide their evil beneath the cloak of darkness. I noticed that, which is why I ordered poor Odo to sail at that hour.'

'But would a ship's master allow strangers aboard?'

'Of course, Ranulf, why not? Captains are constantly looking for crew members and, more importantly, paying passengers eager to avoid the roads and wanting safe, swift passage to all those ports and harbours along our south coast or across the Narrow Seas. What does the captain suspect? The cog sails. Night settles and the miscreants strike at a certain time in a certain place. Nobody expects it. Moreover, the crew are dispersed and either busy about tasks or fast asleep. They could be easily taken care of, as you were, Wolfram. No different from stealing into an enemy camp and killing sleeping men.'

'But if there were survivors,' Wolfram demanded, 'they would talk of these passengers.'

'Would they? Who met these attackers before they boarded, dark, shadowy figures, cloaked and cowled against the evening light? They'd use false names and other details. Moreover, how would any survivor know that it was these passengers? Perhaps members of the crew had turned on their master, or the ship had been boarded by pirates.'

'I agree, I agree,' Ranulf murmured. 'Master, we have sailed on war cogs and it is as you say. You never really know who your companions are, and at night, all people want to do is sleep and keep dry.'

'Oh yes,' Corbett murmured. 'Remember, the attack

was very swift, the cog turned and sent racing onto those rocks. So we are agreed,' he murmured, 'we have an enemy on board, emerging at the dead of night. Such predators are cunning. They would only strike if assured of success. They'd be careful, prudent. There may well have been ships that could not be taken over, as circumstances or fortune dictated, but this one certainly could. There were no false lights or beacon fires. Perhaps, at the very most, a shuttered lantern flashing from the shore that would indicate the ship was now off Monkshood Bay.'

'But the dangers?'

'What dangers?' Corbett retorted. 'Wolfram, Ranulf, you have served in the king's array. You have seen soldiers confront far greater dangers to secure a mere portion of plunder. Think of a cog forced into Monkshood Bay, wedged on those sharp rocks, which the perpetrators could use as stepping stones. Waiting for them would be the rest of their coven. They clamber onto the wrecked cog and pillage it. Any survivors are ruthlessly dealt with, their corpses swept out to sea, and then . . .'

Corbett sat staring into the brazier; the silence deepened. Ranulf coughed and shuffled his feet. Wolfram rose to fill his tankard. Corbett kept staring, lips moving soundlessly.

'Sir Hugh?'

'No, no, Ranulf,' Corbett whispered. 'Let us think. Open the chancery chest. I want the maps, the charts describing this part of Dartmoor. I also need the roll of evidence from when we shattered Puddlicot's coven, a schedule listing those monks arrested at Westminster and sent to the Tower . . .'

He paused at a knock at the door. Chanson, on guard, demanded to know who it was.

'Malach, Sir Hugh. Lady Isabella would like to meet you in the solar. She . . . we have information to share with you. It is urgent.'

'I will be there,' Corbett called back, 'with Ranulf and my unexpected guest Master Wolfram.'

'She may object,' Wolfram hissed.

'No, no,' Corbett replied. 'You, sir, are now firmly in the king's peace, so let us go.'

He rose, strapped on his war belt and grabbed his cloak. Ranulf and Wolfram did likewise. Malach was waiting near the stairwell. He glanced in surprise at Wolfram, but Corbett just patted the former clerk on the shoulder as a mark of approval. Lady Isabella was waiting in the luxurious solar, its grey-stone hearth crammed with burning logs, the herb pouches shredding in the heat exuding the most fragrant perfume. Chairs and a wine table had been arranged; jugs of Alsace and freshly made confits, if they wished to eat. Corbett and his companions made themselves comfortable.

'Lady Isabella, you wish to speak to me?'

'Yes, yes, I do. But first,' she turned to Wolfram, 'Parson Osbert, is he a friend of yours, Master Wolfram?'

'More of an acquaintance; my parish priest, no more than that. Why?' Wolfram stumbled over his words.

'My sister Katerina is closer to him. You know that for a while she acted as his housekeeper. She cooked, washed and supervised other parish servants.' He pulled a face. 'Then she left his service as she was needed at the farm, and I . . .'

'Peace, peace, my friend.' Corbett glanced at Lady Isabella. 'Katerina has disappeared.' He turned in his chair and gestured at Ap Ythel, who stood next to Chanson by the solar door. 'Captain, dispatch some of your men onto the moors between here and Felstead. Discover what you can about the Lady Katerina.' Ap Ythel nodded in reply and left, calling for Brancepeth and others gathered in the hall. 'Master Wolfram,' Corbett reassured his visitor, 'Ap Ythel's men are as skilled as any hunting dog. So, my lady, you have something to share with me?'

'Parson Osbert,' she replied, 'he attended the night of revelry here at Malmaison. He ate and drank garbed like us all. Remember he left the festivities on a number of occasions?'

Corbett just shrugged in reply. 'Neither me nor mine, my lady, kept a muster on who was here or who went where. So?'

'Sir Hugh, Malach and a servant removed poor Brockle's corpse to the death house. The servant found a ring close to the door. I recognise it as Parson Osbert's. Here.' Lady Isabella opened her belt purse and shook out a thick brass finger ring with a faded inscription across the top. She handed this to Corbett, who studied it curiously.

'It is Parson Osbert's,' Wolfram agreed. 'I have glimpsed it many a time when he gave a mass or a blessing.'

'I will keep it,' Corbett murmured. 'So,' he continued, 'we have the local priest's finger ring in the murder chamber, a room Parson Osbert had nothing to do with. How did it get there? I must question our good parson at a time and place of my own choosing.'

'What else do we know about this priest?' Ranulf asked. 'I mean, now that we have been brought here to discuss him. How long has he served here?'

'Oh,' Malach shrugged, his dark face twisted into a grimace, 'about twelve years. My lady?'

'Yes, about twelve years,' she echoed.

'And his reputation?'

'Oh, good enough, Sir Hugh. My husband and the parson were on the most cordial terms. I believe Lord Simon showed him all the secret entrances, doors and passageways to this manor. The good parson was also a keen observer of the leopards. I would say,' Lady Isabella added archly, pointing at Wolfram, 'that Parson Osbert knows as much about the secrets of Malmaison as you do, sir.'

'But there's more to it than that,' retorted Wolfram, clearly annoyed. He paused and drew a deep breath. 'As I have informed you, my sister Katerina served as the parson's housekeeper. She never told me much except that he was not as poor as he appeared to be. He was generous to her. Anyway, sometimes she wondered why his bed was not slept in, though she did say that on occasion, after nightfall, he would move into his parish church. He would fire the cressets, candles and tapers, then bolt the door. She could only conclude that he was practising penance during a night of prayer. Though there again . . .'

'There again what?' Ranulf demanded.

'I've seen our good parson, long after dark, riding across the heathlands, but there's no crime in that, is there? I mean, he could be visiting the sick and the dying . . .'

'Sir Hugh,' Lady Isabella smoothed down the front of her gown, 'how long will this matter continue? We have plans,' she forced a smile, 'plans to leave Malmaison, cross the Narrow Seas and visit the papal court at Avignon.' She stretched out her hands to the flames. 'It would be so good to bask in the sun and wander the wine-drenched valleys of Provence. I am tired of this bleak moorland, this wilderness that never really changes. So how long?'

'Madam,' Corbett got to his feet, Ranulf and Wolfram likewise, 'we will be finished when your husband's assassins, the people responsible for his murder and those of John Wodeford and Sir Ralph Hengham, not to forget Grease-hair, Colum, Rievaulx and Brockle, hang on the gallows next to those who caused so much devastation and destruction at sea. Now, I thank you for what you told me about Parson Osbert. I must return to what I do best.'

'Which is, Sir Hugh?' Lady Isabella now looked flustered.

'Hunting murderers, trapping them and sending them to God.'

Corbett returned to his own chamber. Ranulf recognised his master's mood: taciturn, withdrawn, totally involved with the challenge he had set himself. Sir Hugh could be charming and a source of many stories about his hunt for this assassin or that, but once he was absorbed in a task, he could not be moved or diverted to anything else. He was resolute on that, like a hunting dog who had picked up a scent and would not leave it until he had his quarry. Ranulf resigned himself to what he called 'the great silence', and did his best to help.

The Secret Chancery coffers were open, the seals on pouches broken, and Corbett went back down the years. He studied everything he had collected, sifted and reflected on during those hurling days when he had hunted Puddlicot and his gang the length and breadth of London's nightmare underworld. Dangerous times. He had arrested the criminal Blackrobes, the Benedictines of Westminster, led by their leader Warfeld, ignoring the protests of priests and prelates. He had seized the guilty monks, loaded them with chains and lodged them in the dungeons in the Tower. They were put on a fast of bread and water and refused any visitors or, indeed, any contact beyond the walls of the fortress. Instead, a cohort of clerks, led by the likes of Lord Simon and Wodeford, Wolfram and Rievaulx, had interrogated them day and night, drawing up a schedule on each and every one of them. Corbett now scrutinised these memoranda and felt a deep glow of pleasure as he noted the profession of three of these deviant monks, Brothers Peter, James and John.

'Fishermen from Galilee,' he murmured to himself. 'Of course.'

He then asked Ranulf to lay out maps of the area, especially the moorland that stretched from Monkshood Bay to the once derelict priory of St Benet, and then on to the village of Felstead. He recalled all he had learnt about the area; the inlets along the coast, the sheer desolation of the heathland, which contrasted so sharply with the prosperity of Felstead and the Palfrey in particular. Now and again he would break from his studies to meet with Ranulf and Wolfram. The latter had, at Corbett's request, been given a narrow chamber along the top gallery of the manor. Ap Ythel's scouts had returned to report they could find no trace of the Lady Katerina. Wolfram, beside himself with worry, secured Corbett's permission to carry out his own searches, but these proved futile.

'I visited Parson Osbert,' he informed Corbett, 'locked away in his priest's house. He seemed agitated and withdrawn. I noticed his ring was missing and I inno-cently asked him where it was. He replied that he'd taken it off during the revels here at Malmaison just before the banquet began, and that after that, he couldn't say. Sir Hugh, what do you think?'

'Possible,' Corbett declared. 'The rose water used to fragrance the fingers turns the skin slippery. The ring could have fallen off or been seized. Let us see, let us see.'

Corbett acted distracted, but once Wolfram had left, he opened his belt purse and plucked out the parson's ring. He then took a piece of thickened, riveted glass that he used to decipher faded script. In the pool of light from a spigot of beeswax candles, he studied the ring, turning it to get the best of the light. His heart skipped a beat as he deciphered the faded inscription, which, battered though it was, could clearly be seen to be the coat of arms of the abbey of Westminster: three strutting martlets above a mitre. There was more, but this had been erased by the passage of time.

'Sweet heaven, help me,' he whispered. He leant back in his chair, eyes closed, the ring tightly clasped in his right hand. He recalled Adam Warfeld as he had confronted him over seven years ago, then thought of the clean-shaven Parson Osbert. 'Very clever,' he murmured. 'They are kin, close kin.'

'Sir Hugh?' Ranulf, busy on the other side of the chamber, walked across.

'They are kin,' Corbett repeated. 'Warfeld and Parson Osbert, they are related.' He laughed sharply. 'Warfeld is now much older, his lying, deceitful face almost hidden behind a bushy moustache and beard, but think, Ranulf! Think of him when we confronted him in the sacristy at Westminster Abbey. Then think of Parson Osbert when we met him after mass.'

Ranulf closed his eyes, lips silently moving. He opened his eyes and his face creased into a grin. 'Sir Hugh, you are correct, there is more than a family likeness. A brother, a half-brother?'

'I was sure that I had met Parson Osbert before I ever arrived here. I was both right and wrong, and the confusion puzzled me. I am sure they are close kin, and if we conduct further searches, we would probably discover that the derelict priory of St Benet's, high on Doone Moor, was chosen by Warfeld because of its close proximity to his kinsman's church.'

'Wouldn't Lord Simon and Wolfram have discovered the same?'

'No. Neither of them had much to do with the monks at Westminster. They were embroiled in hunting down Warfeld's allies in the city: rifflers, wolfsheads and others, who, as you may recall, included a number of leading London merchants.'

'So,' Ranulf clapped his hands softly, 'so we have it. Master, I always regarded Parson Osbert as tense, nervous, watchful. I now know the reason why. He didn't inform us about such a tie with Warfeld.'

'If there really is one,' Corbett cautioned. 'At this moment it is only conjecture.'

'Sir Hugh, with all due respect, I think you are correct. So,' Ranulf shrugged, 'why didn't he tell us? Shame, or a conspiracy? Whatever, you are correct. If they are related, Parson Osbert may have been the principal reason why Warfeld chose St Benet's as his place of exile.'

'Even if I am right,' Corbett replied, 'we must not infer anything illogical, illicit or immoral about such a situation. Though in my heart,' he added grimly, 'I believe the worst. I am drawing up a bill of indictment and I believe it to be a true bill. Ranulf, I want you to dispatch Chanson to Exeter, to deliver a verbal message to the sheriff, because I do not want to put it in writing. He is also to seek out Lord Moses and his people with a similar message.' He rose to his feet, crossed to the far wall and took down the small crucifix hanging there. 'I swear,' he intoned, 'by the power given to me by the king, that I will impose the royal ban on this land and on those responsible for a litany of heinous crimes committed against our king and his loyal subjects. Punishment will be carried out by fire and sword.' He kissed the crucifix and placed it on the table beside him. 'And so it begins,' he murmured. 'Ranulf, busy yourself whilst I stay here to work on my indictment.'

After three days of utter seclusion, Corbett was ready. He rose very early, and shaved and washed in the manor bath house, which stood next to the laundry sheds. Afterwards, he donned clean linen and fresh robes. Dressed in a cotehardie, with his war belt looped over his shoulder, he broke his fast in the buttery, then adjourned to his chamber, inviting Ranulf and Wolfram to join him. Chanson was still absent on his errand to Exeter, so the door to the chamber was closely guarded by Ap Ythel and his henchmen. Corbett gestured at Wolfram and Ranulf to sit whilst he paced up and down the room.

'For the moment,' he began, 'let us put aside the murders and mayhem of Malmaison. First, I want to resolve a number of mysteries that may have some connection with the horrors committed here. So,' he paused in his pacing and lifted a hand, 'listen carefully to me. Correct me if I am wrong, question me if in doubt.' He smiled at his companions. 'However, I do believe we have trapped these demons. Let me explain. Here we are in the wilds of Dartmoor. A grim, forbidding, unrelenting place for some, though it could be ideal for others, a place to hide, plot and carry out the most hateful crimes. We have a prosperous village and an even more prosperous guild of fleshers and tanners who sell their produce both within and without the kingdom. They are very close and extremely well organised. Under their apparent leader Fulbert, our guildsmen waxed wealthy and strong.'

'Apparent?'

'Yes, Ranulf, because I suspect their real leader is Parson Osbert. Indeed, I believe our not so good priest is the Sagittarius, and that he disguised the guildsmen as the Scarecrows. Garbed in their ridiculous dress, these wolfsheads terrorised the people of Dartmoor and made Monkshood Bay their own private property. A number of these guildsmen often visit Plymouth. They have every right to do so. It's one of the places where they can do business and from where they can export their produce. Now let us, for the sake of an argument, say that six of the guildsmen visit the port and select a merchant cog, its deep-bellied hold crammed with all sorts of luxurious items – wine, cloths, furniture and the like. The cog is about to continue its journey through the Narrow Seas, hugging the coastline as such vessels do. The guildsmen discover the exact hour of sailing, and can soon reckon, all things being equal, when that cog will stand off Monkshood Bay.'

'But that can be difficult,' Wolfram countered. 'Tides, winds, seas and currents are fickle, the plaything of the weather. Cogs can be delayed.'

'Of course they can,' Corbett agreed. 'But our band of robbers are no different from any other that lurks along the highways of this kingdom. I agree, they may well have to wait, change their plans, even conclude that the cog in question is not easy prey. Let us say they plot to take a few but only choose one. They are still deep in profit. If their intended prey looks as if it is not ripe for the plucking, they can leave it be, or, if already on board, continue to act the good, honest passengers, then disembark at the next landfall so that they can make their way back to Felstead to join the rest of their pack. Yes, that's what they are, a wolf pack that gathers to seek out its prey, then strike. Sometimes they are fortunate, other times not, but of course that could be said for all doings under heaven.'

'So they choose their prey, some hapless cog, and then identify themselves?'

'No, no, Ranulf. They would present themselves under a number of guises: passengers, pilgrims, travelling chapmen, or even members of the crew. As I mentioned before, masters are keen to earn extra revenue from passengers, whilst many are desperate to recruit able-bodied crew. I am sure that our worthy – or rather unworthy – guildsmen numbered former seamen amongst their company.'

Corbett paused, chewing the corner of his lip. 'So imagine the cog with five to six assassins on board setting sail from Plymouth. Night falls. A relatively small number of crew are dispersed around the vessel. Most of the sailors are fast asleep, the remainder half so. We have established how a few determined men, intent on evil, can take care of the crew. They do so probably close to Monkshood Bay. If there is a good full moon, they can be seen from the shore. If not, a shuttered lanternhorn can send a brief signal. The crew are overcome; the vessel is seized and deliberately turned so it runs onto Langthorne Rocks, where it is impaled like a piece of meat on a skewer. By then, I suspect, the crew have ceased to exist, killed and thrown overboard. True, their corpses might be washed ashore, but where? The coastline is long, stretching east to the straits of Dover. Buffeted by the waves, hurled against rocks, many corpses would be unrecognisable, whilst the actual cause of death is most difficult to establish.'

'Yet still dangerous for the wolfsheads?'

'As it is for all outlaws, Ranulf, be it an attack on a party of merchants, a manor house or a castle. There's always a risk of being killed or captured. But for the life of me I cannot see how that could happen here. The local manor lord didn't give a whit, whilst our good sheriff is overwhelmed. Don't forget, my friend, the lure of wealth is greater than the fear of death. Our wreckers took risks but they also became very wealthy.

I am sure they all have money salted away with the goldsmiths in Exeter. Such wealth is very difficult to assess.'

'But how did they get rid of the plunder?'

'I must concede,' Corbett shrugged, 'I do have difficulty in defining just what the wreckers did when they came ashore, where their accomplices lurked and how they transported their contraband, but to answer your question, Wolfram, our wreckers were guildsmen. They would know all about the markets and fairs held across this shire and others. Wine, cloths and a thousand other items pour like a river through this kingdom. No one has the time, the energy or the inclination to find out what comes from where.' He pointed at his henchman. 'Ranulf, what did you last purchase at a stall, booth or shop?'

'A dagger sheath and a war belt. I bought them in Colchester market.'

'And did you ask where they came from?' Ranulf just grinned. 'Precisely. Wolfram?'

'The same, Sir Hugh. I never ask, I only want good value for money. But look,' Wolfram joined his hands together as if in prayer, 'I have other pressing business. The hours burn away, day slips into day, yet I can find no trace of Katerina.'

'I am sorry, my friend, but I can only pray that what I have planned might also lead to where she might be. Bear with me, please, but at this moment, I can do no different. God bless you, Wolfram, and . . .' Corbett paused just before he added 'your poor sister'. He bit back his words. He strongly suspected that the worst had happened to the hapless woman, and that she had been caught up in the murderous whirl of this benighted place.

'And who could oppose these guildsmen?' He returned to his indictment. 'Sheriff Wendover is not above suspicion, yet even if he was, what could he do? This kingdom is riven by tensions between the king and his leading barons. The Crown's commissioners have summoned up soldiers for the royal array. This shire like others is depleted of good fighting men.'

'And Lord Simon, Sir Hugh?'

'Oh yes, Ranulf, Lord Simon.' Corbett paused in his pacing. 'I am certain that our dark, sinister lord entertained his own suspicions about the wreckers, but what did he care? He had other matters to deal with. Lord Simon and the guildsmen probably reached an unholy agreement, though where, when and how, I cannot say. I have very little proof, virtually nothing, except,' he raised a hand, 'we now know that Lord Simon murdered his first wife and her lover, their remains strewn deep in those caverns beneath the manor. He needed to create the illusion that the pair had fled abroad, first to prevent any accusation being laid against him, and second so that he could plead, laced with a generous gift, for an annulment of his first marriage. He did this and was successful. The archdeacon's court handed down the ruling he wanted so he could marry the lovely Isabella.'

'And Parson Osbert, what proof, what evidence?'

'Ah Wolfram, again I must concede that what I say

is pure conjecture, with very little evidence, if any at all. However, the wreckers, the guildsmen, must have a leader, yes? They must also have a receiver for their ill-gotten gains. Now, I strongly suspect that the latter is Minehost Baskerville, whose tavern the Palfrey exudes a prosperity not totally founded on its own revenues. Baskerville's hostelry boasts, I am sure, cavernous cellars where goods can be stored. He also owns carts and a well-populated livery stable, which the Sagittarius and his Scarecrows use. However, let us leave Master Baskerville for the moment. We shall return to him in due course, because he is the weakest of our opponents. Once I mount my challenge, Parson Osbert, Warfeld and all his coven will scream they are clerics and plead benefit of clergy. Moreover, we must not forget that our disgraced Benedictines are hard-nosed villains steeped in mischief. These are the criminals who dared to commit treason, sacrilege and robbery at Westminster Abbey, this kingdom's greatest shrine, England's principal cathedral and the king's own house for his jewels and treasure. They have all the arrogance and insolence of the Lord Satan. Being exiled to the wilds of Dartmoor would pose little obstacle to Warfeld and his ilk, who, I am sure, are intent on collecting as much treasure as they can before they escape abroad.'

'Sir Hugh,' Wolfram shook his head, 'the guildsmen might be the wreckers, the disgraced monks could be their allies and Parson Osbert their leader. However, the wrecking continues even though the guildsmen have disappeared and, I agree, probably lie slaughtered out on the moor.'

'Too true, Master Wolfram. And so we reach the next chapter in this murderous masque. I have, as I have said, little evidence to indict Parson Osbert, though a thorough search of the cellars beneath his house and the crypt below his church might be interesting. No, these outlaws, as I have said, are like wolf packs, and wolf packs can and do turn on each other. This certainly happened here.'

Corbett sat down on a stool, hands clasped. 'I suspect the guildsmen were indeed the wreckers, the Scarecrows. Their leader, the Sagittarius, is Parson Osbert, a man who has seen military service in the royal array, a capable, cunning man, though God knows how a priest can be drawn into such murderous, malicious mischief. Yet the solution is clear enough. He is, of course, from the same stock as Warfeld. Perhaps wickedness can be passed on, as scripture says, to the third generation.' He paused to marshal his thoughts. 'Warfeld and those other miscreants were caught and indicted for the plundering of the king's jewels. The Crown could not touch them, so Holy Mother Church dispatched them into exile. Few people really bothered about where they went as long it was far from Westminster, in some godforsaken corner of this kingdom.'

'And this place truly is godforsaken!'

'Precisely, Ranulf, especially in a parish far away from the eye of both Crown and church, where Warfeld's purported kinsman could provide them with every help and assistance. Parson Osbert and Warfeld could have not have chosen a better location. I have studied both our chancery charts and those of Lord Simon. You can draw a straight line from Monkshood Bay to St Benet's, an ideal place for the wreckers and, indeed, for any survivors.'

'Survivors?'

'Yes, Ranulf. It's clear enough. What better place, or so any poor innocent might think, for refuge and sustenance after their vessel has been cast onto the rocks and them into the sea?' Corbett drew a deep breath. 'Of course they would receive no such assistance. They would be murdered in a matter of heartbeats. As for our wreckers, St Benet's, so close to the coast, is ideal for storing plunder unloaded from carts and sumpter ponies hidden away in or around that desolate priory. Afterwards, the carts and horses can be taken away and returned under cover of dark to the Palfrey.'

'But Sir Hugh . . .'

Corbett didn't reply; he just stared hard at this former clerk. Wolfram was a fighter, a man of war, and Corbett wondered how much he knew about the wickedness that swirled like a mist above Doone Moor. He and his sister lived out on a desolate farm, yet surely they must have seen and heard things that would provoke their curiosity? Corbett's suspicions, his unease over Wolfram, had not dissipated. Why, until recently, had Wolfram remained so hidden? One further matter troubled him. Wolfram was a former mailed clerk. He would have monies, but these must have been spent over the years.

Farmers were hardly prosperous, but he and his sister were well garbed. Perhaps this was insignificant, but Corbett wondered if the pair received other revenue, yet from whom?

'Sir Hugh, you are staring at me.'

'Yes, Master Wolfram, I am. Just speculating on the mystery and the fate of those guildsmen, all of them slaughtered, murdered. Do you know something? Their assassin could be anybody, even you. However, I believe their deaths can rightly be laid at the door of Warfeld and his coven.'

'What?' Wolfram demanded.

'Oh yes, I believe our black-souled, black-robed monks arrived in St Benet's and were soon drawn into the murderous mischief of Parson Osbert and his followers. Time passed, and Warfeld and our perjured parson reached a most cordial yet bloody understanding. They no longer needed the guildsmen. They had St Benet's, and Baskerville's well-stocked hostelry, and God knows whatever else they might need. Warfeld and his ilk have licence to beg as far as Plymouth, where they could don whatever guise they wanted. Three of their number were veteran seamen before they entered the Blackrobes, assuming the names of Brothers Peter, James and John.'

'Three of Christ's apostles, seamen who fished the waters of Galilee.'

'Precisely, Ranulf. Such men would present themselves to any ship's master and be welcomed with open arms. Remember, this would be at the close of day; the light would be fading. Moreover, heaven knows what disguise they assumed just in case a member of the crew they joined escaped the murderous assault planned on them.'

'Yet still so dangerous.'

'Of course. All those who plot villainy risk being trapped and confronted by their hideous sins. Warfeld is sly and cunning. He must know, deep in his heart, that all this mischief will have its day of reckoning. The Day of Judgement will arrive, as it did at Westminster. I believe,' Corbett rose to his feet, 'that after the destruction of *The Galliard* and the discovery of its empty hold, our malevolent monk must realise that the hour of dissolution is close at hand, so we must act. Let us begin by visiting the weakest link in this chain of wickedness. Let us bring this hymn to murder to a close.'

PART FIVE

He also took with him dishes, plates and saucers
for spices, a crown cut up . . .

Minehost Baskerville sensed changes emerging from the deep darkness that had cloaked his life ever since he and Parson Osbert had entered into their unholy pact. The taverner stood in the shadows, close to the cellar trap door, and wondered what he should do. Corbett had arrived at Malmaison, and the view of everyone involved was that the interfering royal clerk would stay until he had finished his task to his satisfaction and no one else's. Warfeld had compared Corbett to the keenest falcon, and Baskerville realised that the unholy brotherhood at St Benet's, together with Parson Osbert, were preparing to flee beyond the Narrow Seas.

So what should he do? He had a wife, but, thank God, no children. He felt a clammy, creeping fear as he gazed down the narrow path that cut through the cavernous cellars beneath his tavern; murky, shadow-filled caves that still contained plunder from various wrecks. Corbett's abrupt arrival, his sharp, darting ways, had caught them all by surprise. Baskerville had pleaded that all the plunder be removed, carted away, even flung into some marshy morass or mire high on Doone Moor. The Sagittarius, however, had ruled different. Carts of plunder must not be caught out on the open heathland whilst Corbett and his henchmen were constantly on the move. Ap Ythel and his mounted archers were now a common sight, and Lord Moses and his moon people were, according to rumour, in Corbett's pay.

Baskerville felt his throat grow dry as he sipped from the blackjack of ale he had brought down with him. He stood listening to the sounds of the tavern, but these did little to curb his mounting panic. What would happen, he wondered, if Corbett burst into the Palfrey with search warrants? What then? The reign of the Sagittarius and his Scarecrows was drawing to an end. Baskerville accepted that. Corbett would never give up. Parson Osbert had attempted to silence him through a sudden, swift ambush out on the moors, but that had proved futile. They could not repeat it. Next time they might not be fortunate enough to escape. Moreover, even if they were successful, Warfeld, who was furious that the attack had taken place without his knowledge, had warned how the powerful Secret Chancery at Westminster would never let the matter rest. The killing of its most senior clerk would provoke the full wrath of the Crown.

Baskerville crossed himself. At first it had gone so well. Parson Osbert had been appointed to this desolate, lonely parish, the Bishop of Exeter only too pleased to appoint a veteran priest who had served parishes in London as well as in the royal array. A capable, skilled, sly soul, Osbert had entered Felstead and suborned Baskerville and the powerful Guild of Fleshers and Tanners. Oh, it had been so easy, so swift, the lure of riches beckoning them on. The taverner closed his eyes. He had done no real wrong. True, he had provided horses and carts and stored the plunder, but he had taken no part in the killing. The worthy guildsmen, however, did not give a whit; they were used to slaughter, be it of man or beast, either here or when they served in the royal armies as purveyors of meat. All had been to the good.

Then Warfeld and his coterie had arrived at St Benet's. Parson Osbert had drawn them in. At first, as Fulbert had once remarked, they were a band of merry men in every sense of the word. Robin Hood might have had the greenery of Sherwood, but they had the black heathland of Dartmoor. Eventually, however, Baskerville had noticed the changes, slight though they had been at first. Warfeld had begun to flex his muscles as Osbert's leading henchman, and then that night . . .

The taverner broke from his daydreaming, tensing at the two raps on the trapdoor above him. He climbed the steps and pulled back the bolts so that Parson Osbert, as he had done so many times, could climb down to join minehost in his cellar. The parson was apparently ready to depart, garbed in a leather mailed harness. Baskerville also glimpsed the war belt strapped around his waist, with sword, dagger and a small hand-held arbalest hanging from a hook.

'Parson Osbert?' The taverner tried to keep the tremor from his voice. 'Father, you want to see me? You look as if you are preparing for a journey.'

'I am indeed, my friend. So come. I understand that we still have a number of items stored here from certain wrecks?'

'Yes, yes.' Baskerville led the parson down the stone-paved gallery, a narrow runnel stretching past the caverns and caves used as storerooms.

'The oil?' Parson Osbert demanded. 'We have some?'

'Yes, yes, here it is.' Baskerville led the way into a yawning black cave. He lifted his lanternhorn so that Osbert could clearly see the casks and oilskins piled there.

'All is well?' the parson whispered.

'All is well,' Baskerville replied over his shoulder, but then he froze and slowly turned. Parson Osbert had his crossbow levelled, its lever now winched back.

'Parson . . .'

'No, no, Baskerville. You know this is ending. It's just a matter of time before you reach the conclusion that the only way forward for you is to turn king's approver, sue for a royal pardon and confess everything. Now we can't have that, can we? Moreover,' the parson stepped forward, 'God knows what this tavern still holds: bills of sale, plunder from various wrecks, the remains of whatever we seized. No, no, Master Baskerville, it's time for you and your tavern to disappear. Me and mine reckon that within the day, Corbett and all the power he can muster will visit both this tavern and St Benet's. So farewell.'

He released the clasp, and a bolt flew to smash into Baskerville's forehead. The taverner staggered forward, coughing on his own lifeblood before collapsing to the ground.

'Oh, let us hurry, let us hurry,' the parson intoned mockingly. 'The flame burns. The candle flares. The hours are passing. Time to be gone.'

He picked up the lanternhorn and flung it hard to smash against the heaped barrels and oilskins. The flames erupted, tongues of fire leaping up as if desperate to reach and consume the dry wooden timbers above. Parson Osbert did not tarry, but hurried back to the trapdoor and up into the stable yard where his horse stood hobbled.

Corbett and his retinue thundered into Felstead as the fire at the Palfrey erupted, driving residents as well as petrified horses and donkeys into the street. It was a fierce conflagration: a blazing glow at every window, with flames piercing the black-slated roof. The entire village seemed to be hastening to stare and wonder. Some enterprising soul had attempted to organise a line of water buckets from a nearby well, but this proved futile. The fire would have to burn itself out. Horses and other livestock were now being herded, calmed and led away. Corbett learnt from the parish beadles that the only person missing was Minehost

Baskerville. No one had glimpsed the taverner even before the fire had erupted, and a group of village women were now clustered around Baskerville's wife trying to console her.

Corbett reined in at a safe distance from the main gate of the blazing tavern and ordered his retinue not to get involved. He half suspected what had happened. The fire was no accident. He questioned a beadle about the possible whereabouts of Parson Osbert, adding that the priest should be here to assist his parishioners, as this was time the flock desperately needed its shepherd. The beadle simply spat to one side and peered up at him.

'Strange priest that, sir! Got stranger still over the last few days, even more so today.'

'How is that?' Ranulf demanded.

'Well, there's this fire, but Parson Osbert is not here. He was glimpsed all harnessed, riding out towards Doone Moor.'

Corbett nodded. He had his answer. He turned his horse.

'Where to now?'

'Why, Ranulf, to that haven of iniquity, St Benet's priory. Please God, we will find our quarry there and not fled deeper into the darkness that is gathering to a storm around this benighted place.' He glanced back towards the fire. 'So judgement is given,' he murmured. 'Punishment must follow, which only proves the old saying: "The mills of God grind exceedingly slow but they do grind exceeding small." Ranulf, I want you to commandeer the stoutest cart, high sided, with a strong tailgate, together with four dray horses. We will ride ahead. You and four of Ap Ythel's archers must follow as swiftly as possible.'

Corbett led the rest of his comitatus out of the village. On the outskirts, he stopped to meet Wolfram, who had been busy searching for his sister.

'No one,' Wolfram declared mournfully, 'no one has even seen Katerina.'

'I am sure we will find her.' Corbett tried to sound as confident as possible. 'Heaven knows, she might even be at St Benet's.'

Wolfram seemed to take little comfort from that. Corbett glanced away. In truth, he feared the worst for Lady Katerina, but that would have to wait.

They continued on their way, Wolfram and two of the archers guiding them. They galloped like the devil's own horsemen along the winding lanes and coffin paths until they reached St Benet's, its roof and spire jutting up ominously like dark fingers against the sky. The gate in the formidable curtain wall was closed, and Corbett glimpsed shapes moving along the parapet. He reined in, holding his hand up whilst his comitatus deployed either side of him. Then he slowly urged his horse forward, stopping as a crossbow bolt thudded into the ground before him.

'Sir Hugh!' Warfeld's powerful voice cut across the open space. 'Sir Hugh!' The Blackrobe's voice trilled with anger and Corbett quietly rejoiced; he was correct! This gang of wolfsheads now realised their heinous crimes had been discovered and they were probably preparing to flee, but in truth, they were trapped.

'*Pax et bonum!*' Warfeld shouted, sheltering behind the crenellations.

'*Pax et bonum!*' Corbett retorted, raising his hand again. He then turned to grasp the crucifix Ap Ythel had taken from his saddlebag. 'Come with me,' he whispered to Wolfram, who had already dismounted and was staring fixedly up at the priory. 'Ap Ythel,' Corbett winked at his captain of archers, 'keep your eyes keen and your bow ready to loose a shaft at anything or anyone that threatens.'

Ap Ythel scratched his grizzled face, blue eyes twinkling. 'I will watch like a falcon does its prey,' he murmured, 'but for the love of St David, be careful, Sir Hugh. God knows who shelters there, God knows what weapons they carry and God knows what mischief they plot—'

The captain of archers broke off as the narrow re-inforced door built into the main gate swung open. Warfeld and another monk stepped through, then stopped, leaving the postern open behind them. Warfeld beckoned Corbett closer. The clerk simply stroked his horse's neck and stared back at this felon who had returned to mischief as a dog to its vomit. The silence deepened, broken only by the whinny of a horse and the scrape of leather and iron. Warfeld gave a deep sigh, then gestured at his companion to follow him a little way forward. Both men were cloaked from head to toe, and Corbett suspected they were mailed and armed for war.

Corbett coaxed his mount on, Wolfram, who had remounted his horse, riding slightly behind him.

'Well, Warfeld,' he reined in, 'I am the king's justiciar in these parts. I need to question you and your brethren over certain matters pertaining to the Crown.'

'Which matters?'

'Matters that will be raised in court.'

'I am a cleric. I plead benefit of clergy for myself and my brothers. We are not subject to the king's justice. We will plead to be heard by Holy Mother Church. You have no right to enter this priory without the permission of that same Holy Mother Church.'

Corbett just glared at this devious monk who had dared to lead a conspiracy to violate the sanctuary of Westminster. A man with no soul, no conscience, no scruples; truly a wolf in sheep's clothing who would plunder and kill to satisfy his own appetites.

'I believe,' Wolfram called out, 'that we have been down this same path some years ago, when you committed treason, robbery and sacrilege. You forfeit all rights.'

'We know your crimes,' Corbett declared. 'And those of your partner in sin, your kinsman, perhaps your brother, Parson Osbert.' He smiled as Warfeld started in surprise. 'Oh yes,' he smoothed the neck of his horse even as he strained to hear the approach of Ranulf and his war cart, 'we know all the verses of your hymn to murder, Master Warfeld. Some questions remain. Did you have a hand in the mayhem at Malmaison, the destruction of Lord Simon, Wodeford and the others?

Did you and yours slip into that manor as you were accustomed to, to have words with Lord Simon so that he would look away from your crimes as you would his?'

'What are you talking about?' Warfeld protested. 'Malmaison was not our concern.'

'Yes, it was. Those two leopards found poisoned up on the moor. That was your doing, wasn't it? You were out on the heathland, you and your coven intent on mischief, and those great cats attacked one of your retinue.' Corbett pointed directly at his opponent. 'The corpse you showed us in your death house was not that of one of your company, but some innocent traveller who stumbled into St Benet's. Poor soul! He expected to receive a warm welcome, the solace you Blackrobes are supposed to provide. But not you. He found himself in a wolf pack. You killed him, then dressed his corpse so that it would appear that a member of your coven had died of natural causes. The traveller was then laid out in a grave over the ravaged remains of the brother mauled by those leopards. You wanted to give your comrade a decent burial, unlike the others . . .'

'Who?'

'You know full well! The guildsmen you were in league with when it came to wrecking cogs as well as the murder of innocent men and women who crossed your path. You were party to all such killings, as was Parson Osbert, your leader. The kinsman who invited you to take exile here on Doone Moor.'

'Where is my sister?' Wolfram yelled. He would have urged his horse forward but Corbett restrained him. 'Where is Katerina?' he repeated.

'Heaven knows,' Warfeld mocked, and turned to gaze back at the priory. Corbett glimpsed a figure almost hidden by the crenellations whom he suspected to be Parson Osbert.

'Where is she?' Wolfram screamed. 'I have searched everywhere but here!'

'Corbett,' Warfeld yelled back, 'you talk of mischief and mayhem at Malmaison. Why don't you question Master Wolfram? He slipped in and out of that place like a rat down a sewer. His sister was no better. Lord Simon loved to tumble the wenches and, according to Parson Osbert, Katerina was a merry bundle in bed, always ready to play the two-backed beast, for which she received good coin.'

'You bastard root of a rotten tree!' Wolfram would have urged his mount into a wild charge, but Ap Ythel's archers closed in to seize the reins even as two crossbow bolts whirred through the air to smash into the stretch of ground in front of Corbett's line of horsemen.

'You dare to loose at a royal clerk,' Corbett shouted, 'and one who displays the Crown's own arms?' He turned in the saddle and pointed dramatically back to the stiffened pennant with its gorgeous colours of red, blue and gold carried by Brancepeth.

'We are clerics.' Warfeld's taunting voice carried. 'We plead benefit of clergy under the protection of Holy Mother Church . . .' His voice was drowned out by the rumbling crash of wheels as Ranulf arrived with the great war cart to stand behind Corbett. 'Any attack,' the Blackrobe spread his arms as if to encompass all his opponents, 'will mean instant excommunication and eternal damnation for each and every one of you. We will resist with all our power.' The strong breeze rippled his thick cloak. A threatening, sinister figure determined to break his opponents.

Corbett sensed that the monk's words found an echo in some of the archers, who stirred restlessly. They confronted a truly pernicious danger: possible death in any attack on the priory and the damnation of their souls to hell for all eternity. He turned in the saddle and ordered Ap Ythel to notch and loose. The master bowman swiftly replied and dispatched two-yard shafts to thud into the ground before the monks.

'You have our answer,' Corbett declared. 'We will force an entry.'

Warfeld had already turned, he and his henchman hurrying back, almost throwing themselves through the narrow postern door.

Corbett withdrew to set up camp. Makeshift bothies were erected, latrines dug and horse lines arranged, and a close watch was kept on the priory and its two entrances. Just before dawn the next morning, he ordered the attack to begin, heralded by a flight of fire arrows that kept their opponents hidden behind the walls. The massive war cart, its heavy, jutting tailgate as threatening as any battering ram, was prepared. It would also screen Corbett's party as they pushed it closer to the main gate.

The weather had improved, with patches of clear, ice-blue sky; the ground underfoot was firm and hard. The wolfsheads in St Benet's were truly trapped, yet Corbett remained uneasy. Warfeld and his coven seemed to be more assured and confident than they should be. He called a pause in the attack and dispatched scouts, but they could see nothing; no sign of Sheriff Wendover or any other force coming to their assistance. Only the occasional innocent traveller who informed them of rumours that Lord Moses and his moon people were fast approaching St Benet's. Corbett, hoping that Moses might provide some assistance, called off any further assault and waited.

The moon people and their line of colourfully decorated carriages arrived just as dusk crept across the moor. Corbett made them welcome and met their leader in the shelter of the great war cart, where Ranulf and Ap Ythel had built a makeshift bothy. He and his guest shared a wine skin, Lord Moses describing the chaos that had descended on Felstead with the utter destruction of the Palfrey.

'And now you believe, Sir Hugh,' he pointed dramatically at the clerk, 'that you have dug free the root and cause of all the wickedness that prowls this place?'

'One of the roots,' Corbett countered, watching his visitor's cunning face, which was made even more so in the light of the dancing flames.

'I did wonder,' Moses mused. 'Those leopards

poisoned out on the moor; that must have been the work of our noble brothers.'

'Yes, I am sure of it,' Corbett retorted. 'I noticed how the priory had its own herb plots. I am sure those house deadly plants such as henbane, belladonna,' he waved a hand, 'and whatever else can be found in the devil's litany of poisons.'

'Yes, they'd certainly clear the moor of any threat to them; indeed, anyone who might pose a danger if they glimpsed their wickedness. You know the rumours are spreading?'

'What about?'

'Oh, you must have heard them. Chapmen, tinkers, the occasional pedlar disappearing, not to mention women from the little mining villages that pepper this godforsaken landscape.' Lord Moses shrugged. 'There's no law here, no royal writ. Poor Wendover is busy in Exeter trying to raise levies for a king who doesn't seem to care a farthing about what happens in this remote corner of his kingdom.'

'Yes, he does,' Corbett retorted. 'That's why I am here. What I wonder about, as must my comrades,' he gestured at Ranulf and Wolfram, 'is why you have arrived here now. Lord Moses, soon we will attack. Do you wish to assist? You have helped me in other ways.'

'Ah, but we are not soldiers.'

'So,' Wolfram rasped, 'why have you come? To watch the tournament, to see men fight and fall?'

'To help you.' Lord Moses shuffled closer to the fire. 'We moon people wander the face of God's earth. We see things, we hear things, but we do not speak. Babbling can be dangerous.'

'The hour is passing . . .'

'Yes, it is, Master Ranulf. Have you wondered why those miscreant monks have fortified themselves so confidently? I doubt very much if they intend to fight to the death. Oh no, I am sure they have other plans.'

'What plans?' Ranulf declared testily.

'Oh, St Benet's is an ancient place; it was well chosen. It is like one of those peel towers you find in Ireland or along the Scottish March, easy to defend, difficult to take. But those monks are not waiting to fight you, to defend themselves to the death. No, they are preparing to leave.'

'What?'

'Sir Hugh, an ancient tunnel lies beneath St Benet's, a narrow corridor about two yards high and the same across that runs from the chapel to the mouth of a cave that opens up on Monkshood Bay, a cave well hidden by a screed of the thickest gorse.'

'Of course,' Corbett breathed, 'an ideal place for our wreckers. No wonder so little was seen in and around the bay where so many were slaughtered. They could come and go like ghosts.'

'Yet they were glimpsed?'

'Of course, Ranulf. Sometimes the very nature of the plunder would demand that; barrels, heavy chests and coffers had to be carted away. Many other items could be swept up and carried along that tunnel.'

'How do you know this?' Wolfram challenged. 'I don't, and I was born and raised in these parts.'

'You can look and look again, Master Wolfram, and still see nothing. Before the arrival of the Blackrobes, St Benet's lay derelict for decades. My people, other tribes, often used it as a haven, a shelter against the driving wind and rain. We moon folk search for the unexpected. We found what Warfeld and his coven also did and used for their own murderous ends.'

'And so?'

'Sir Hugh, they will leave by that tunnel and make their way to the beach, where two herring boats, pinnaces taken from the Malmaison inlet, will be waiting to ferry them across the Narrow Seas.'

'How do you know this?'

'Because we have just visited Monkshood Bay, and lo and behold, the two pinnaces are already there, moored close to Langthorne Rocks. They are probably awaiting nightfall.'

'Why haven't the monks fled already?'

'Think, Master Ranulf, of that needle-thin tunnel. How long it is! How difficult it will be to transport their precious plunder, anything valuable that can be sold in foreign parts. They haven't fled for the simple reason that they are not yet ready. It would have taken time to collect those boats from Malmaison.'

'Would Lady Isabella know about this?'

'Ask her yourself, Sir Hugh, but now you know,' Lord Moses waved in the direction of the priory, 'that all this is a sham, a pretence. The only reason for the delay is because they are still preparing to flee.'

'And once they do,' Corbett declared, 'it will be nigh impossible to trap and capture them. It could be days before royal cogs are dispatched to hunt them. No, no, once they are at sea, they are gone and I doubt if we will ever see them again.' He got to his feet, Ranulf and Wolfram likewise. Corbett grasped the former clerk by the shoulder and took him away from the rest. 'Master Wolfram,' he whispered, 'Warfeld has the mind and mouth of a sewer. But those insults to your sister?'

'No insult, Sir Hugh,' Wolfram replied wearily. 'My sister lived out on a desolate farm. She became lonely, very lonely, and I was little help. I showed her the secret ways into Malmaison. I strongly suspect she flirted with Lord Simon as she did Parson Osbert. She always had more money than I thought she should. Now I suspect why. She was easy prey for such men. Can you imagine, Sir Hugh, weeks, months, years in this lonely, haunted place? However, for the moment, all I care about is her safety.'

Corbett made no reply. He just patted Wolfram on the shoulder and walked back to Ranulf and Lord Moses. 'Fetch Captain Ap Ythel,' he ordered Ranulf. 'We must immediately dispatch Brancepeth and two of his master bowmen to Monkshood Bay. They are to search for that cave mouth, the entrance to the tunnel. Wolfram will help guide them. When they find it, they must keep strict watch.'

Once Ap Ythel joined them, Corbett repeated what

he'd said. 'Remember, Captain, make sure your men know they must loose at anyone they do not recognise. More importantly, they must keep a close watch on those herring boats and make sure they do not leave. Go now.' Corbett pointed at Lord Moses. 'You stay here, but safely so. I have a secret task for you and your people. First thing tomorrow morning, I shall share my good news with Brother Warfeld.'

Once dawn broke, Corbett, accompanied by Ranulf carrying the royal pennant, approached the priory gate, pausing at a safe distance. He held up the crucifix he carried and demanded to speak to Warfeld. He glimpsed figures moving along the parapet above the fortified gate.

'What is it now, Corbett? What news? Why are you bothering us? What do you bring?'

'Your deaths!' Ranulf shouted back. 'We know all about the tunnel to Monkshood Bay. We know about the herring boats. All of this is now in our power. Accordingly, I demand that you surrender yourselves to officers of the Crown and submit yourself to the king's justice.'

Even from where he stood, Corbett sensed the deep consternation caused by Ranulf's proclamation. There was a flurry of movement between the crenellations; lanterns moved in flashes of light, shouts and cries echoed indistinctly. Corbett raised his hand and let it drop. Immediately Ap Ythel's bowmen loosed a veritable rain of yard-long shafts, which rose to clatter against the priory wall, though one hit its mark and the morning air was riven by a tortured scream. A few of the archers remained to shower the walls. Another kept up a circuit of the priory to ensure that none dared escape or sally out to close with their attackers.

Corbett and Ranulf, both garbed in mailed jerkins, were helped by the remaining archers to harness the war cart, urging the great dray horses to pull it closer and closer to the main gate. The defenders could do little to stop or impede them; any attempt to lean over or between the battlements provoked a well-aimed arrow shaft. At last Corbett's party were close to the massive fortified gateway. Chanson, with his usual skill in managing horses, ensured the drays turned so that the heavy tailgate rested close to the gate. The animals were swiftly unhitched. Ap Ythel gathered his archers, leaving two to watch the walls. Then the battering began, a remorseless and constant pounding, a hideous crashing that soon had its effect. Wood splintered, cracked or tore loose, gaps and rents appeared. Ap Ythel's bowmen used these openings to loose a rain of shafts into the courtyard beyond.

At last a full breach was achieved. Corbett, war helmet on, forced his way through into the priory; others followed to deploy on either side of him. The defenders had withdrawn. One corpse lay sprawled in a spreading splash of blood. Some of Warfeld's coven had not retreated far, taking refuge in the outhouses; the rest had fled into the chapel, but its door, ancient and cracked, provided little protection. Corbett led his men into the cold, dark nave and the struggle swiftly began. The monks, however, were no match for their opponents: those not cut down fled nursing their wounds into the gloomy sanctuary, where they put their weapons down and slumped to the floor. Warfeld was only slightly injured. He sat scowling, surrounded by five of his brethren, all of them garbed in jerkins and woollen hose as if, as Ranulf remarked, preparing for a journey. Ap Ythel came to report that they had found the entrance to the tunnel, a cunningly contrived passageway hidden close to the baptismal font. Corbett instructed the captain to make a thorough search of the priory both within and without before returning to squat before the prisoners, their hands and feet now tightly bound by cord.

'So the wheel turns,' he murmured, staring at Warfeld. 'Many years have passed since I confronted you at Westminster. Souls like you never change, do they, Brother?'

He paused as Ap Ythel hurried back to say that he'd found Parson Osbert's corpse just outside the chapel, an arrow shaft through his throat.

'Lay it with the rest. I need to inspect it carefully. So now,' he turned back to a crestfallen Warfeld, 'you are going to answer my questions.'

'I will answer to nothing, Corbett. We are clerics. We appeal to the local ordinary, in this case, the Bishop of Exeter.'

Corbett glanced away. He'd suspected that Warfeld would do this. Now he gave silent thanks to God for the secret task he'd assigned to Chanson and Lord Moses.

'Well, well.' The Blackrobe's voice became taunting. 'What are you going to do, Corbett? What *can* you do, because I know what you should do and will have to do.' He apparently enjoyed this play on words, turning to grin at his companions.

'For the moment, I will do nothing.' Corbett rose, telling Ranulf to set close guard on the prisoners, and left for the narrow, filthy chamber adjoining the chapel that served as the death house.

The corpses of those slain were laid out on the floor, Parson Osbert's at the far end, the arrow that had killed him still piercing his throat. Corbett whispered a prayer and, averting his eyes from the stricken parson's face, crouched down. He opened the wallet on his belt and took out the battered ring, then inspected the dead man's right hand. There was an indentation on the little finger. He slipped the ring along the ice-cold finger; the knuckle created an obstacle that could only be overcome by pushing the ring as hard as he could, and he had to do the same when he pulled it off. He continued to kneel by the corpse, staring down at the ring in the palm of his hand. 'Even from beyond the grave, O Lord, an angel of light is busy,' he murmured.

'Sir Hugh?' Ranulf stood in the doorway. 'Sir Hugh, let me interrogate Warfeld. I will string him up from a hook, roast his feet over a fire.'

'No, no. A man such as Warfeld will not crumble. He also knows that torture is not accepted by English law, another device he would use against us. He wants all the bishops jumping up and down on his behalf, and some of them are stupid enough to comply. As I said, he will not crumble.' Corbett got to his feet. 'Not yet, not now. He will remain obdurate until I prove that he is well and truly trapped like the fox he is.'

'So?'

'Gather your men, Ranulf—' Corbett broke off as Ap Ythel strode into the death house.

'Sir Hugh, my apologies, but you must see this.'

Corbett and Ranulf followed the captain of archers out into the cemetery field behind the chapel, a derelict stretch of hard earth, wild grass, gorse and bramble. They crossed to where a group of archers, faces muffled, leant on their mattocks and spades around a narrow but deeply cut grave. The stench was noisome and sickening, the heavy smell of putrefaction seeping from the line of corpses laid out on the ground beneath filthy ragged linen sheets. Ap Ythel led Corbett and Ranulf around the pit, all three men now muffled. He didn't speak, but pulled back the sheets, pointing at one corpse in particular. Corbett stared down in horror. Corruption had set in, yet he still recognised the once beautiful face of Lady Katerina. The woman's eyes were now sunk deep in their sockets, her lips grotesquely parted as if still protesting at the deep slash across her throat, a broad, ugly black wound.

'God assoil her,' he whispered. He then inspected the other corpses. Despite the putrefaction, he recognised the cadaver Warfeld had claimed to be Brother Stephen, though he now knew that it was a substitute for the ravaged corpse lying next to it, balding and skeletal-faced, the rotting flesh still displaying the gruesome wounds of the leopards' savage attack. The other four remains he did not recognise. One was a chapman apparently, from the tray slung into the grave beside him. The other three were youngish women, stripped of all clothing so the death wounds to their neck, chest and belly could be clearly seen.

Ap Ythel tapped Corbett on the shoulder and led both clerks away from the gruesome scene and horrid stench. Only then did he remove the muffler across his mouth and nose.

'A dire sight, Sir Hugh.' The captain's musical voice conveyed a deep pity. 'Dire,' he repeated, 'on a day like this in a place so forsaken.'

Corbett nodded his agreement, pulling down the rim of his cloak. He glanced up at the greying sky, then stared around this most desolate God's Acre, where the tangle of bramble moved in a slow dance beneath the buffeting breeze.

'What made you dig?' Ranulf asked.

'Well, we searched the cellars and part of the secret tunnel. We found plunder in the passageway yet we discovered no corpses. I thought it was suspicious. These Blackrobes are killers. People like the Lady Katerina have disappeared on the moor. We know that; we have sent out scouts searching for her. Anyway, I came out here. Now it's some time since the first corpse was buried, but I noticed the soil was freshly turned, so I thought it was best . . .' Ap Ythel's voice trailed off. Corbett clasped him on the shoulder.

'Cunning,' Ranulf observed. 'They dug one deep grave, reopening it for every fresh victim and placing one on top of the other.'

'Bury them honourably,' Corbett murmured. 'Fashion a cross over each. We will deal with the requiems later. It's the living I am concerned with.'

Corbett and his comitatus returned to Malmaison. The prisoners were lodged in the cellars and closely guarded. Later in the day, Corbett received a message from Wendover: the sheriff apologised for his tardiness, but claimed that he had been heavily involved in raising troops for the king, who, with his beloved Gaveston, had fled from London. The kingdom now teetered on the verge of civil war. Corbett was not surprised. He deliberately did not become involved in court politics, although he was a sharp and keen observer of what went on. Gaveston was marked down for death and the earls would never give up the chase. All of the great offices at Westminster would be disrupted and Corbett grimly acknowledged he could expect little help from his masters in London. Instead he concentrated on the task in hand. Warfeld and his confederates were given food and sustenance, their wounds treated. Corbett then informed a taciturn Lady Isabella and her equally morose henchman Malach that he would set up a court of oyer et terminer in the great hall, where judgement would be carried out. In the meantime, he declared, he must prepare himself.

Once again he walked the manor, opening and shutting doors, closely examining the chambers where Colum the cook and the steward Brockle had been murdered. His constant slamming of certain doors irritated the household, but he remained lost in his own sharp study of this mansion of murder. Once satisfied, he returned to his own chamber and immersed himself in the manuscripts, documents and folios from Lord Simon's chancery, as well as a costly and exquisitely illuminated Book of Hours, a psalter for private devotions. As he leafed through this, he noticed how the cult of the Holy Face of Lucca was celebrated time and time again.

Turning one page, he caught his breath. He lifted the psalter up and scrutinised the exquisite miniature depicting the sixth station of the cross: Christ meeting Veronica on the way to Calvary. According to tradition, Veronica wiped the face of the Saviour, who left an imprint on her veil, the source and root of the devotion to the Holy Face of Lucca, where the original cloth was reputedly kept. The more he studied the painting, the more certain Corbett became. He closed his eyes and thought of the manor chapel and what he had seen along its walls.

He hastily summoned Ranulf, and they slipped quietly down to the chapel. Corbett bolted the door behind him and used his tinder to flare the cressets on the left-hand side. Along its wall hung seven stations of the cross; the other seven hung on the opposite side. Corbett stopped before the sixth station. Unsheathing his dagger, he prised the diptych free from the hooks and clasps driven into the wall. He kissed the holy scene, then turned it over and over again, carefully scrutinising it.

'Master?'

'Ranulf, Lord Simon truly was a strange soul, undoubtedly a man of blood, yet he had this unique devotion to the Sacred Face. The Lacrima Christi is part of this devotion, a tear flowing down the cheek of the crucified Christ. Now I have that beautiful ruby, but the casket?' Corbett turned the diptych again and scratched at its polished wooden backing. 'It's logical, as Rievaulx decided. He believed that if Lord Simon wished to hide anything to do with the ruby, he would secrete it away in the caverns below. However, those pits are rank and fetid, places of deep darkness. I do wonder if he chose a more sacred and fitting place, namely here, the sixth station of the cross.' He pulled a face. 'This would certainly explain his riddle about the treasure being hidden away behind the sixth veil, a reference not to any verse from the Apocalypse, but to this sixth station of the cross depicting Veronica and her veil. Yet I cannot see anything amiss . . .'

'Master, look.' Ranulf stretched up and tapped that part of the plaster against which the diptych had hung. He took a cresset torch and lifted it close so Corbett could clearly distinguish the fine lines running like veins through the freshly painted plaster.

'Good and faithful servant, Ranulf,' Corbett whispered. He grasped his dagger tighter and hacked at that portion of the plaster. It immediately gave way, nothing more than a cleverly prepared skein of stiffened parchment, smoothed, painted and fitted so it blended with its surroundings. He put his hand through the gap he had created and sighed in relief as he touched a leather pouch. He withdrew this, undid the cord and shook out the intricately carved casket, no more than six inches in both length and breadth. He handed this to Ranulf, who held it up so the sheer, heavy gold caught the light and shimmered as bright as the glow from a pure beeswax candle. The brilliant miniature gems that decorated the outside exuded their own delicate light.

'Beautiful,' Ranulf whispered. 'Truly beautiful.'

He passed the casket back to Corbett, who undid the clasp and lifted back the lid. The inside was undecorated, a glowing sheen except for the inscription etched in both Arabic and Latin, proclaiming how both the casket and the ruby were gifts freely given by the Caliph of Egypt to Edward, Prince of England.

'So I have it,' Corbett murmured. 'Ranulf, help me clean up here. Put the diptych back so it looks, as far as you can, as though it's never been disturbed. My net is closing fast; soon we shall move to judgement.'

Later that same day, Chanson returned to inform Corbett that both Sheriff Wendover and Lord Moses were approaching Malmaison. Corbett took some comfort from this as he prepared his carefully itemised indictments. Two days later, the sheriff and the moon people arrived together. The latter entered Malmaison with their carts all festooned with fluttering ribbons and streaming, garish banners. Wendover, on the other hand, was accompanied by a small comitatus, a cohort of well-armed hobelars. He and Moses met Corbett in his chamber, and the clerk was delighted with their news.

'Very well, very well,' he declared, rubbing his hands. 'A court of oyer et terminer will be arraigned in the great hall immediately after dawn tomorrow.'

The court duly sat, Corbett and Wendover acting as justiciars, Ranulf as both clerk and scribe. Chanson and the archers were ordered to guard the hall both within and without. The great chamber had been prepared. Benches stood to the right and left of the justiciars' table. On one side sat Warfeld, Brasenose and their four companions, who were constantly moving in a rattle of heavy chains. On the other were Lady Isabella, Malach and a deeply distressed Wolfram, whom Lord Moses, sitting next to him, tried to console. During these preparations, Corbett stared at the six monks garbed in brown sackcloth. They slouched sullenly on the bench. Warfeld, however, exuded an arrogant assurance, half smiling to himself as if he nursed some secret that would negate what would happen here. Corbett was determined that would not happen: he had what he wanted, but he would only reveal this at the appointed time.

Ranulf rose, rapped the table and called the court to order. He specifically demanded silence from Lord Moses's escort, who clustered with the manor retainers further down the hall. Corbett then brusquely began the proceedings, pointing directly at Warfeld and his confederates.

'The indictment against you I have already touched upon, but now I will do so in greater detail. You are outlaws, miscreants—'

'We are clerics!' Warfeld bawled back. 'We must be handed over to Holy Mother Church sooner rather than later—'

'Shut up!' Ranulf roared. 'Captain Ap Ythel, if the accused interrupts Sir Hugh again, deliver a sharp blow to his mouth, then gag him.'

'Here on Dartmoor,' Corbett continued, 'a heinous conspiracy was formed. Members of the Guild of Fleshers and Tanners, under the leadership of Parson Osbert, organised the wrecking of cogs and other vessels in Monkshood Bay. They were outlaws, pirates and killers. They did this for filthy profit, with no one to interfere, oppose or bring them to book. They chose a desolate stretch of a very lonely shoreline: no castles, no watchtowers, no soldiers or harbourmasters. They could run unchecked.' He ignored the gasps and exclamations from Lady Isabella and the others.

'These miscreants,' he declared, 'found and used a secret tunnel running from the chapel of St Benet's to Monkshood Bay to move their ill-gotten gains. Other times, they transported their plunder by cart or sumpter pony. Of course, they rode disguised. Osbert assumed the mask and title of the Sagittarius, his hellish retinue the Scarecrows. They terrorised the moorland and anyone rash enough to pose a threat to them. God knows how that priest brought them under his influence, but the lure of gold, the prospect of riches and their repeated success became motive enough. Parson Osbert and his close accomplice Minehost Baskerville deepened the pretence by claiming they too had been menaced by the Sagittarius and his outlaws. Of course that was nonsense, an arrant lie to protect themselves and so divert suspicion elsewhere.'

'And Lord Simon's role in all of this?' Lady Isabella demanded, her face pale and drawn. She sat rigidly on the bench, playing with the rings on her long white fingers.

'Oh my lady,' Corbett replied, 'you must know the answer to that! Lord Simon couldn't give a fig about the wreckers. Our so-called noble manor lord was more involved in his own affairs, be it the administration of this manor, the care of his great cats or, for a while, his murderous campaign against his first wife. You will all remain silent.' He lifted a hand to still the rising protest. 'Indeed,' he continued remorselessly, 'Lord Simon and the fleshers reached a mutual understanding. In return for him leaving them alone, members of that unworthy guild, whose oath would be taken seriously, would swear and swear again that they had seen Lord Simon's first wife Lady Beatrice and her lover Chandos board a ship for foreign parts. Only the angels know when and how such a perjured pact was reached, but it certainly was.' He let his words hang in the air before continuing. 'Because how could the fleshers swear to witness such a thing when we now know that Lady Beatrice and her lover were slaughtered and then dismembered in the caverns below this manor.'

'In God's name!' Wendover exclaimed.

'It's true.' Wolfram broke from his mourning. 'It's God's own truth, I know it is.'

'The guildsmen were organised and led by Parson Osbert. He was the Sagittarius, the leader who had discovered the secret hidden passageway from the desolate chapel at St Benet's down to Monkshood Bay. A born assassin, your kinsman, Warfeld. He and his followers garbed so grotesquely could harvest their plunder and, with the assistance of Baskerville's horses, carts and storage rooms, hoard their ill-gotten gains before proceeding to sell them.' Corbett paused. 'They would have little difficulty in doing this. Baskerville the taverner would supervise and distribute them to the fairs and markets of this shire and beyond.'

'The guildsmen too.' Wendover spoke up rapping the table. 'They had carts and horses. They also had every excuse to move their hides and skins as well as whatever else they wished to conceal beneath them.'

'I agree,' Corbett replied. 'Once the ships were wrecked and looted, the plunder was relatively easy to collect. Naturally, at times, the Sagittarius's cavalcade was glimpsed, but any real danger would be confronted. I understand a watch was set up over Monkshood Bay, but those involved were slaughtered, as was anyone brave enough to confront these miscreants . . .' He picked up a sheet of vellum. 'Of course the guildsmen indulged in the sham, a masquerade, mere mummers' play to protect themselves. For example, they maintained they were attacked whilst travelling to Plymouth. Baskerville and Parson Osbert also declared that they were threatened, all an illusion, a mockery of the truth.'

'Treason, murder and robbery,' Wendover declared, 'but for those guildsmen a very lucrative business enterprise, in a desolate part of this kingdom where,' he added bitterly, 'it is difficult enough to proclaim the law, never mind enforce it. The guildsmen are dead,' the sheriff's voice rose, 'but I tell you this, Sir Hugh. If I come across any of their corpses, I will have them gibbeted like the assassins they were.' He closed his eyes, lips moving as if he was talking to himself. 'And so we come to the arrival of the Blackrobes.' He opened his eyes and glowered at Warfeld.

'Oh yes, the arrival of the Blackrobes,' Corbett echoed, picking up another sheet of vellum. He glanced quickly at Lady Isabella and Malach, who sat tense and watchful. Warfeld, Brasenose and their companions still looked confident, even aggressive, moving in a clink and rattle of chains. 'Exiled, disgraced, the criminous clerics, for that is what they are, had to choose some desolate place, and where better than St Benet's, deep in the wilds of Dartmoor, hidden away in a sea of gorse high on Doone Moor. Of course,' he spread his hands, 'what was cleverly hidden is that the priory was offered by Parson Osbert, a close kinsman of Warfeld, who prepared the place for the arrival of a fresh cohort of demons.'

'That's true, that's true,' Wolfram interjected. 'I

remember it well. Parson Osbert made an appeal to his parishioners for help. My beloved sister Katerina provided assistance. She often talked about how busy Parson Osbert was on behalf of these poor Blackrobes, an act of charity, of compassion for disgraced yet penitent clerics. God have mercy on Katerina. She was fooled so easily, whilst I never realised the truth of her relationship with that hellhound.' He slumped, head down, still lost in his own twisted grief.

'And so Warfeld and his coven arrived at St Benet's. Strange,' Corbett rubbed the side of his face, 'Benedictine monks are clean shaven, yet you and your coterie have let your hair, moustaches and beards grow as thick as the gorse outside. A sign of penitence, or a disguise lest someone recognise your close affinity to Parson Osbert? I could have you shaved, but for what purpose? I recognised your kinship and you have not denied it.'

Warfeld simply rattled his chains and leant over to whisper into Brasenose's ear. Corbett would have loved to upset their obvious smugness, but that would have to wait.

'Parson Osbert,' he continued, 'was a truly ruthless man. He silenced all opposition, dealt out dire warnings and sometimes death. I believe he was responsible for that attack on us on Doone Moor, a solitary horseman but skilled in such an ambuscade. After all, he had fought as a king's chaplain in the royal array. Our good parson feared neither God nor man. He believed in nothing but his own advancement and pleasures. Heaven knows what she saw in him, but the Lady

Katerina had a relationship with that priest. A man who would absent himself from his bed and, most mysteriously, lock himself away in his church during the dead of night.' Corbett laughed sharply. 'Not to pray, but to plot more murderous mischief. An assassin to his very marrow, Parson Osbert viewed me as a real danger, a true obstacle, and why not?'

'True.' Wendover nodded. 'Your reputation goes before you, Sir Hugh. Warfeld must have advised his kinsman how you had destroyed the conspiracy at Westminster and brought those responsible to judgement.'

'Oh yes,' Corbett agreed. 'I was Osbert's nemesis. He tried to kill me on Doone Moor. Then I was attacked here in that narrow death house whilst inspecting poor Grease-hair's corpse. Parson Osbert was busying himself in the church, preparing for mass, but on that morning he was also plotting blood-red sacrilege. Ranulf and others were milling about in the hall. Anyone armed with a crossbow, slipping along a passageway or gallery, would have been noticed. Not so our apostate parson, who crept out of his church to commit murder before scuttling back into the shadows.'

'Parson Osbert,' Warfeld taunted, 'is not here to answer or defend himself.'

'And even if he was,' Brasenose bellowed, 'he too was a cleric.'

'I will gag you!' Ranulf bellowed. 'I will gag you until we hang—'

Ranulf fell silent as Corbett clutched his arm. In

truth, the clerk of the Green Wax had done exactly what Corbett had ordered him to, hinting that these proceedings might end not in the prisoners being handed over to the church but on the public gibbet close by the manor.

PART SIX

He also took with him rings, clasps, precious stones, crowns, belts and other jewels.

'To return to the indictment,' Corbett blithely continued. 'Into this murderous masque slipped the Blackrobes, exiled for life from Westminster. Unbeknown to the authorities, their place of exile had been suggested and prepared by Warfeld's criminous kinsman. Of course, they were soon drawn into the wickedness perpetrated in and around St Benet's. You, Warfeld, are attracted to murderous mayhem as a cat to cream. You soon controlled St Benet's, with its passageways and storerooms and, most importantly, that secret tunnel. Parson Osbert made it very clear to the fleshers that they accept the Blackrobes into their conspiracy or face being excluded from the wrecking, a loss of lucrative profit that would chill the hearts of those greedy merchants. So, an unholy alliance was formed.

'However, you had your own plans. You had no intention of staying in lonely exile, whilst Parson Osbert must have been sick of being a simple village priest.

Oh no! All of you were intent on acquiring wealth and fleeing to foreign parts; that was your vision, your dream. You would plunder, commit treason and mock the king, then escape to enjoy a life of luxury and relish your revenge. You knew the dangers, for no fox hunts unscathed. There were risks, but you and Parson Osbert would accumulate enough wealth to cushion you all your days.'

'What proof do you offer for all this?' Brasenose blustered. 'And I ask,' he added hurriedly, 'as a lawful question in court.'

'The proving is self-evident,' Wendover declared.

'It certainly is.' Corbett glanced at Brasenose and realised that the monk was probably simple minded, completely under Warfeld's influence. 'Master Brasenose, what about those corpses in St Benet's cemetery? The dead do talk. They do bear witness. Poor wanderers who stumbled into your hellish community, young women from the lonely mining communities taken for your pleasure.' He pointed to Warfeld. 'You are a killer to the very marrow of your soul, and you sit with assassins just as fit for hell as you are.'

'That is no way to talk about my loyal and trusted companions,' Warfeld jibed.

'I wasn't talking about them.'

Corbett let his words hang in the air. He did not glance at Lady Isabella and the others sitting on the bench to his right, but stared down at the manuscript on the table before him. At last he cleared his throat and glanced up.

'You and your coven settled quickly into St Benet's, even as you plotted to break out. The cellars and secret passageway beneath the priory were used. In addition, you, like the fleshers, had every right to be in Plymouth, having been granted a licence to beg there. You too became wreckers, Scarecrows under your kinsman Osbert, who rode the lonely moors as the Sagittarius.' Corbett paused, allowing the silence to deepen. Those involved realised that this indictment was both lengthy and powerful, and they would all be wondering what was coming next.

'Now, what was deeply puzzling,' he continued, 'was how the wrecks were caused. True, lights were sometimes seen, but no one ever glimpsed a wreck taking place. Now we know why. Monkshood Bay was a natural choice, a lonely inlet with Langthorne Rocks providing a path, precarious though it might be, back to the shore. However, it also had a cave mouth leading into a secret tunnel, and that was where the wreckers would assemble. Cogs and other vessels were not lured onto the rocks but driven into the bay. They were seized at sea and taken over. Their tired crew, dispersed about the ship, would be easily taken care of by a coven of determined assassins. Many vessels are seized by stealth even along the Thames or in enemy ports. You did the same with *The Galliard*. You wrecked that cog and sent good men to their deaths.'

'And poor Beauchamp,' Lord Moses interjected. 'Why didn't you tell him, Sir Hugh? Why didn't you warn him about what might happen?'

'As in war, a commander can only be told what he needs to know. How could Beauchamp have taken precautions without alerting the enemy? They would soon have sensed it and either left the vessel under some pretext or continued to act the innocent passenger.'

'But at least you would know who had attempted it.'

'And what would that prove? Attempted what?' Corbett retorted. 'These criminals would simply argue that they sought safe passage. We could not indict them for boarding a ship. I agree my campaign was as ferocious as any sea battle. We had to establish once and for all how these wrecks occurred. We sacrificed one to save many others, as well as bring the criminals responsible for previous wrecks to justice and judgement. We have done this. We now seek retribution for those murdered at sea. I mourn Beauchamp and the others as I do my good friend Fitzwarren. Just reflect, my Lord Moses, what would have happened if I had never come here, or if I had done nothing once I arrived. However, my presence on Dartmoor and the measures I have taken have brought these matters to a head.'

'And the guildsmen? Some of them were murdered; their corpses have been—'

'Oh my Lord Moses,' Corbett retorted, 'they were all murdered, for the very simple reason that they were no longer needed. The distribution of profits amongst so many could not be sustained. Parson Osbert and Warfeld would also have recognised the danger, the rivalry and the resentment that would soon occur. The guildsmen were as tight and close as any shield ring. The arrival of Warfeld and his Blackrobes would loosen allegiances and might even lead to clacking tongues. Osbert and Warfeld decided it was time to remove them, and we now know the full story.

'The fleshers celebrated in the Palfrey until long after the chimes of midnight. Much the worse for drink, they left that tavern and, lured on by Parson Osbert, made the short journey across the moors to St Benet's. Warfeld and his murderous community would welcome them with open arms. More wine was served, probably tainted with some potion, and the guildsmen fell into an eternal sleep. They were murdered, their corpses hurled into various bogs and morasses.' Corbett crossed himself.

'Every evil has its own dire candle flame. Time was passing. I arrived. You, Warfeld, Parson Osbert and the rest realised you could not indulge in your murderous mischief forever. The fleshers had been silenced. Minehost Baskerville was a likely candidate for a royal pardon, so he suffered the same fate. A weak man who would eventually turn king's approver and indict the lives of his confederates in return for saving his own. Little wonder he was marked down for death. Oh yes,' Corbett added quietly, staring across at Lady Isabella and Malach. 'Evil runs its course and those responsible, be it at St Benet's or Malmaison, have to face a reckoning. Sooner or later the axe falls . . .'

'What do you mean?' Malach's strident voice betrayed his fear.

'Why, Master Malach, the end of things. As I have

said, my presence here forced a conclusion. Parson Osbert, the killer, decided to remove any threat, anything to help and assist his good brothers at St Benet's. He poisoned those two leopards, silenced Lady Katerina, murdered Baskerville and set fire to the Palfrey so that whatever that tavern held was reduced to ash. He was as ruthless as any son of Cain bound for hell.'

'And of course he murdered others,' Wendover added. 'That bailiff and those three good men whom I instructed to watch the coast near Monkshood Bay. May Osbert rot in the deepest hell,' he added grimly. 'As for the rest, it all makes sense now. No one seeing any lights, or any sign of the plunder being taken away.' He paused. 'It also explains that tinker who saw one wreck. He claimed he glimpsed survivors moving across Langthorne Rocks. In fact, those were the wreckers searching their handiwork before disappearing into that secret tunnel. True, Sir Hugh?'

Corbett just stared at the sheriff, the unease he felt deepening. Wendover's reference to the watchers at Monkshood Bay provoked other questions, but, for the moment, they would have to wait.

'Parson Osbert,' he continued, 'also played a most sinister role in the murderous mystery surrounding Malmaison. In a way it was due to him that the edifice of lies built to protect another coven of assassins collapsed like a house built on sand. The storm of truth and justice swept in and caused its fall, and what a fall it was.'

'Meaning what, meaning what?' Malach could hardly

keep still, the mounting tension forcing him to half rise, fists clenched. 'What is it, clerk? What are you implying?'

'I am implying nothing,' Corbett retorted. 'I am just part of that storm of truth and justice for both God and the king. Let me explain. Parson Osbert sowed the seeds of his own destruction when he presented the woman Richolda to me shortly after my arrival here. In his speech, he claimed that the guildsmen,' he glanced down at the sheet of vellum before him, 'and I quote directly, "were prosperous, hard-working tanners". Were? Was this a slip of the tongue, or indeed the truth? Parson Osbert, beneath his mask of cant hypocrisy, knew full well the true fate of those guildsmen.'

He paused. 'And then you, Lady Isabella, and your henchman in sin. Your henchman in sin,' he repeated as both the accused leant forward, shouting their objections. He waited until order had been reimposed before he spoke again. 'You made a most dreadful and costly mistake. You believed Parson Osbert was what he pretended to be, a simple village priest. You decided to use him in your own wicked plots concocted here at Malmaison. The parson was a frequent visitor to this manor with its many entrances, gateways, doors and posterns. He was here when Wodeford, Lord Simon and Ralph Hengham were murdered. Accordingly, he could be depicted as their murderer, their assassin. A useful distraction in my hunt for the true killer.'

He opened his purse on the table before him and drew out Osbert's ring. 'Oh yes,' he murmured, 'our parson proved to be a source of unwitting assistance.

This ring happened to be forged and stamped at Westminster.' He waved a hand at Warfeld. 'This eventually led me to you, because it showed a connection between our village priest and the great abbey of Westminster. I then reflected on the physical likeness between you and Parson Osbert as well as the true reason for why and how St Benet's was chosen for your exile. Oh, I agree, it's not solid evidence, but it certainly signposts the truth.'

'Oh shut up!' Warfeld leant forward in a rattle of chains. 'This farrago of nonsense will soon end when the—'

'When the Archdeacon of Exeter, sent by the bishop, arrives?' Corbett queried. He was pleased at Warfeld's reaction. The Blackrobe could only stare, mouth gaping, shaking his head as Brasenose whispered heatedly in his ear. 'Never mind, never mind,' Corbett soothed. 'We will also come to that by and by.

'So, to return to this.' He held up the ring. 'On the night of revelry here, as was customary, a bowl of warm rose water was carried round for those feasting on the dais to wash their hands. Lady Isabella, I sat on your right, Parson Osbert to your left, Malach next to him. The bowl of water arrived. Parson Osbert took off his ring, a common occurrence because the water was very soapy and precious rings can be lost. He took off his ring and either you or Malach seized it. You planned to use it to incriminate your parish priest as the assassin prowling Malmaison.'

'Never, never!' both Lady Isabella and Malach

protested noisily. Ap Ythel, who'd returned to the hall after being dispatched on an errand by Corbett, put a hand on each of their shoulders, whispering that they should sit still or be bound. Once he had settled them, he raised a hand and nodded. Corbett smiled his thanks. Ap Ythel was a true searcher, a most skilled one. He had found what Corbett wanted.

'What is this?' Lady Isabella stammered.

'Yes, yes, what?' Malach echoed, his face white with fear as he slumped on the bench, eyes half closed.

'Lady Isabella Malmaison, Henry Malach,' Corbett intoned, touching the crucifix on the table before him, 'I do indict you of horrid treason, murder and robbery, many heinous crimes all worthy of death. Brother Adam Warfeld, self-proclaimed Blackrobe, I do indict you and your confederates of the same horrid crimes.' He held up a hand. 'And before you prattle on about benefit of clergy and other such nonsense, Master Chanson,' he raised his voice, 'bring in that messenger, the one the moon people stopped and held in the name of Sheriff Wendover, to whose comitatus Lord Moses and his henchmen have been sworn. Such oaths still hold good in this court.'

At Ranulf's request, Lord Moses, together with Aaron and Joshua, hurried across the hall to face down the still-protesting Warfeld and his coven. Once they were quiet, Corbett beckoned forward the travel-stained courier Chanson had brought in. The man was sworn to the truth in a few pithy sentences. He described how he had been given a message from Lady Isabella on behalf of Parson Osbert, who had visited Malmaison then left. The courier, who introduced himself as Master Dunston, a member of the Malmaison household, said the letter was to be delivered in all haste to the Bishop of Exeter at his palace close to the city gate, and only be handed over to the bishop's archdeacon.

'So,' Corbett stretched out a hand, 'Master Dunston, the letter?'

The courier dug into his broad leather wallet and drew out a thin scroll.

'As you instructed us.' Lord Moses, rubbing his hands together in pleasure at his new-found status, came in front of Corbett. 'It was easy enough,' he declared, full of self-importance, 'I dispatched my own couriers into Exeter. At the same time, I set up close guard over where the moorland tracks stretch down to meet at the great crossroads and the highway into the city. We knew what we were looking for. And so we met Master Dunston, who soon stopped protesting when I informed that I was on the king's own business.'

'Which you were,' Corbett agreed as he broke the seal fixed by the now dead Parson Osbert. He quickly scrutinised the short, sharp message warning the bishop and his archdeacon of Corbett's determination to arrest, imprison, try and punish clerics, priests and monks, in direct contravention of those privileges won by the martyrdom of St Thomas of Becket, a hideous violation of the rights of Holy Mother Church.

'And so on and so on,' he murmured. He lifted his head. 'Master Dunston, who told you to deliver this?'

'The Lady Isabella.'

'Why?' Corbett turned to the chatelaine, but she just sat, head down. 'In which case, I will tell you, Lady Isabella, that you totally underestimated Parson Osbert. On the night of revelry, you or Malach took that priest's ring and planted it in the chamber where poor Brockle was murdered. You thought you were dealing with a simple village parson, not too sharp or keen of wit. You thought he would be accused of murdering the steward and, perhaps, the others slain here. Of course, if accused, he could always plead benefit of clergy.'

'How would the parson know about his ring being discovered?' Lord Moses demanded, then smiled as he realised the obvious. 'Of course, of course,' he murmured. 'I understood that door was broken down by manor servants, whilst it was a manor servant who found the ring. All this would become common knowledge.'

'And Parson Osbert would hear about it and pounce like a cat,' Corbett declared. 'He came here, didn't he, Mistress Isabella? And you realised your horrific mistake. He knew that his ring had been stolen by either you or Malach, who were sitting close to him at table, and why should you do that? The only logical explanation is that you yourselves had murdered Brockle as well as those others slain at Malmaison, and were trying to cast the blame elsewhere. Did he blackmail you? Did he threaten you and state his price for your silence? That you hand over to him those two stout herring boats for his use and that of his coven at St Benet's? You agreed, you had to, on one condition. You and

Malach would flee with them across the Narrow Seas, taking whatever treasure you had collected, including the money stolen from Hengham. Again, another matter we shall come to by and by. Now, you may well have hidden that treasure, but I wager some of it would have to be shared with your fellow criminals now arraigned with you.' He glanced across to where Warfeld and his companions slouched silent and dejected.

'You Blackrobes are finished,' Ranulf taunted. 'You had three defences: the walls of St Benet's, and we took those; the secret tunnel to Monkshood Bay, and we now control that; and the two herring boats, but we have seized them too.'

'Four actually,' Corbett declared. 'Your benefit of clergy, and that will be set aside. I hold a royal commission. I will hang you on a special gibbet above Monkshood Bay, and you, Isabella, together with your minion Malach, will hang beside them. Justice will be swift.'

'I don't know, I don't know!' Isabella's voice rose to a scream.

'This is a court,' Malach protested, lunging forward, only to be forced back by two of the archers. 'This is a court,' he repeated. 'What proof do you have, what evidence?' His voice trailed away.

'Very good, very good.' Corbett rose, and at his bidding, Chanson moved a stool so his master could sit directly in front of the two accused. Malach was leaning forward, breathing heavily. Lady Isabella sobbed, taking her hands to and from her face.

'Mistress,' Corbett's voice was strong and carrying so all the hall could hear, 'you married Lord Simon, a dark soul if there ever was one, a man who cruelly slaughtered his first wife and her lover. Oh, he cleverly concealed his crime, but not from you. You would have had your suspicions. Did he threaten you? Did he hint that you too could be murdered? The very mention of that would keep you under control. Did you also learn about the secret visits by Lady Katerina, Wolfram's sister, to Malmaison? To be blunt, Lord Simon alienated you, as he did his first wife. He was menacing, frightening. You, my lady, decided to strike first. God knows . . .' He paused as Lady Isabella sobbed, hands fluttering before her. 'I cannot imagine what truly happened in your marriage. Lord Simon was certainly sinister enough, yet that does not concern this court. What does concern it is your plot, and that of your henchman, undoubtedly your lover, to escape Malmaison.

'I wager you knew the true reason for the arrival of Wodeford and Rievaulx here. You must have heard about the Lacrima Christi and Lord Simon's involvement in hunting down the thieves. You'd certainly know about Wodeford's panniers, clinking like the bells of hell, crammed, as you supposed, with silver and gold coins. On the day he arrived, Lord Simon asked you to entertain the others whilst he adjourned for his secret meeting, and that's when you decided to act. In a sense, it was so easy. The rest of the household milled in or around the great hall; Malach was involved in calming the leopards.' Corbett pointed at the henchman. 'You deliberately agitated those beasts. What with? Did they miss their evening feed?'

'No, no,' Malach protested. 'The leopards were restless. They did escape, but I had nothing to do with that.'

Corbett stared at him. The man was a killer, a liar and a traitor, yet there was something in his face and voice that seemed like the truth.

'But nobody else wanted anything to do with the beasts, only you.'

'I agree, but on that night, I swear, I did not agitate them nor did I allow them to escape.'

'Leopards or not, my accusation against you stands.'

'You have no proof, no evidence,' Malach rasped. 'It's all conjecture. On that evening, I was busy. True, I went down to see what was upsetting the beasts. I later discovered that they'd gone.'

'You were busy?' Corbett retorted. 'You had every right to be hurrying around Malmaison, but you also slipped up the darkened staircase to the guest chamber. Nearby, you had hidden two arbalests, primed and ready. Another crossbow bolt soaked in blood was in your wallet. You knocked on that chamber door and, of course, you were admitted.' He shrugged. 'Perhaps it wasn't even locked or bolted but was merely on the latch. Even if it was sealed, Lord Simon would open it for you, his trusted henchman.

'Now, both Wodeford and Lord Simon had feasted with the rest, eating heartily and drinking deep. They would be slow and totally unprepared. They would not have the wit or the time to respond or defend themselves. You loosed one arbalest at Lord Simon, and even as he died in his chair, you turned on Wodeford. He had staggered to his feet only to receive a barb direct to the heart. He collapsed to the floor, and you drove that blood-encrusted bolt into the door to nourish the suspicion that both murders were the work of the Sagittarius.'

'But Malach was seen in and around the manor,' Wendover declared. 'I distinctly recall people saying that.'

Corbett glanced at the sheriff. Wendover was acting as a justiciar, but he seemed preoccupied, and Corbett had noticed him exchanging glances with Wolfram, as if they knew something he didn't. He closed his eyes and quietly prayed for patience. He wanted words with Wendover, but first this business must be finished. He opened his eyes and resumed.

'Of course, once the murders were committed, once it had been established that something was dreadfully wrong in the guest chamber, Malach returned to that place of mortal sin. He entered the murder chamber, locking and bolting the door. Once it was secure, he went into hiding.'

'Where?' Malach yelled. 'Where in heaven's name could I hide in that room?'

'Oh, you know full well. The bed in that chamber is high and broad. Beneath it are packing cases and coffers. You simply moved those cases and slipped beneath the bed, pulling the cases and coffers back into position.'

'Is that true?' Wendover queried.

'Think,' Corbett replied, 'think carefully. Examine that chamber as I have. Malach certainly did so before he carried out his crime. Recall the events of that night. True, he was seen in and around the manor. People were waiting in the hall. Lord Simon couldn't be roused. The leopards were agitated. Malach used all this mummery to murder his master and Wodeford and then return. He lay hidden beneath that bed and waited for his accomplice. You.' He pointed at Lady Isabella, still sobbing into her hands, and wondered how long it would be before she broke. 'You entertained guests here in the hall. Malach kept coming and going, so much so that people would forget the actual times, the specific occasions and places.'

Corbett coughed and cleared his throat. 'Before Malach left the hall to return to the murder chamber and hide, he did the same as I've done just now: a cough, a gesture, some secret sign. You, Lady Isabella, bided your time, and then, pretending that your ankle was hurting, you sent Brockle to rouse your husband, who, of course, was well past human caring. On his return, you instructed Colum the cook to dispatch Grease-hair up that ladder, and you were most specific. The spit-boy was closely instructed on what to look for. Why? On reflection, Grease-hair, Colum and Brockle may have also wondered the same. I mean,' Corbett spread his hands, 'Grease-hair reported on the corpses, the way they lay, the lantern, the bolt and lock on the door, the blood-soaked barb. He did this at your bidding.

Again, I ask you why?' He did not wait for an answer. 'You know the reason. You were desperate to demonstrate how deep a mystery surrounded the murders of your husband and Wodeford. Certainly too baffling for any officer of the law.

'Now, my lady.' He rose and returned to sit behind the table, pulling a piece of parchment closer. 'You knew full well that Malach was hiding in the chamber. Of course there was the danger that he might be discovered, but that was a risk you had to take. You moved slowly up the stairs and ordered that the door be broken down. Inside, the murder victims were clear to see. But you are lady of the manor; you had the power to order people not to go into that room, and to do your bidding. You insisted that everyone went downstairs, demanding that Brockle return with makeshift stretchers to remove the corpses.'

'But that in itself was dangerous,' Wendover declared. 'I mean, if Malach was hiding behind those coffers under the bed.'

'He does not deny it,' Ranulf retorted.

'What is the use?' Malach yelled, breaking from his stupor of fear. 'We are already condemned, are we not?'

'You surely are,' Corbett retorted. 'And as for your question, Lord Sheriff, as I said: Lord Simon had been murdered and all authority and power now shifted to the grieving widow. Lady Isabella insisted that those who had accompanied her upstairs hurry away on certain errands. No one dared object. No one wanted to gainsay the lady of the manor during a time of such deep distress. Moreover, her orders were reasonable and logical. She wanted to stay close to her husband's corpse, and of course, she could plead a weak ankle. Once everyone had gone, Malach emerged in a matter of heartbeats so it would appear that he had hurried up the stairs to assist his mistress after running here and there about the manor.' Corbett sifted amongst the documents before him.

'The money panniers?' Wendover demanded. 'The monies Wodeford brought, they were taken?'

'Ah yes.' Corbett smiled at Malach. 'What a treasure, eh? You hid the panniers away, didn't you, either in that room or in some darkened recess, so that you could collect them later.' He gently clapped his hands. 'And when the pair of you opened them, you must have been furious. Nothing more than a hoard of rusty shavings, not even worth a farthing. Your murderous plot had produced nothing but rubbish. I can only imagine your anger. You had plotted to kill Lord Simon, seize the treasure and use that, as well as anything else you could lay your greedy hands on, to leave Malmaison for pastures new. For all your cunning, you had been mocked and frustrated, so you pounced on your next victim.'

'Sir Ralph Hengham!' Wolfram exclaimed. The former clerk had been sitting morose and taciturn, lost in his own thoughts.

'The king's tax collector,' Wendover declared, 'whom I brought here.'

'You knew that Hengham carried treasure. You were

furious at Wodeford's bags of rubbish, so what you plotted was revenge on the Crown through murder and theft. What puzzles me,' Corbett shook his head, 'is a reference Brockle made to Hengham being expected here long before Lord Simon's murder occurred. Ah well.' He shrugged. 'Hengham was a lecher with a keen appetite for you, Lady Isabella. This made him vulnerable. His murder was swift and easy. He occupied, probably at your insistence, the murder chamber, which is on the same gallery as your room. Of course, that was part of the plot you meant to weave. Now the bolts and clasps of that chamber had not been repaired, perhaps deliberately so, but the lock had, and I suspect there were two keys. On that night, Hengham adjourned to his bed hoping the grieving widow might visit him.'

He paused. Lady Isabella now sat more composed, hands clasped on her lap. Corbett suspected she was wondering what path she should follow to escape the closing trap.

'Despite your protests,' he continued, 'who knows what honeyed words you secretly whispered into his ear. Our tax collector, all lecherous, waited in his chamber. He became impatient. He even visited your room, then hastened back to sit on the bed, all keen and expectant. Eventually either you or your accomplice Malach, possibly both, stepped into the chamber, and Hengham was slain, his treasure taken and hidden away.'

Corbett fell silent as if listening to the distant sounds of the manor. This was, he reflected, a house of Cain, a place of murder that reeked of unresolved and un-absolved sin. The spirit of Satan the assassin brooded over this manor, and only judgement would dispel the gathering dark. He glanced around. Lady Isabella and Malach now sat apart. Wolfram had distanced himself from both, edging closer to Lord Moses. The moon leader just sat, face all expectant, astonished at what was happening. Warfeld and his confederates remained subdued; now and then a clatter of chains when they whispered heatedly to their leader as if proposing something he was reluctant to accept.

Good, Corbett reflected, he would secure full confessions, then what? There was so much evil here, a cloud that also cloaked Felstead, the haunt and home of Baskerville, Fulbert, Parson Osbert and the rest who had lured true innocents to a dreadful death. He recalled Fitzwarren's widow and young children, and all the crew of the *The Angel of the Dawn*, good seafarers, honest merchants. The list of victims was long: not only those drowned at sea, but anyone unfortunate enough to fall into the power of the wicked parson and his confederates. So what should he do, what judgement, what punishment? He had been given full power by king and council to wield royal justice and enforce the king's peace. If necessary, by fire and sword.

'By fire!' he exclaimed.

'Sir Hugh?'

'My apologies, Lord Sheriff.' Corbett shuffled the sheets of vellum on the table before him, then drew one out. 'You, my lady, along with your demonic familiar Malach, had what you wanted: the removal of Lord

Simon and the seizure of Hengham's treasure bags. You would also search for the Lacrima Christi. You needed to wander Malmaison turning this and that upside down, as well as to get rid of certain items. That is why you organised the great spring renewal, a common enough occasion in great manor houses as the seasons change. In truth, this was a pretext so you could search for the ruby as well as remove any trace of your murderous handiwork: the panniers of Wodeford and Hengham and, of course, the possessions of another of your victims, Rievaulx the Judas man.'

'Sir Hugh?' Wolfram exclaimed.

'Ah, our precious pair here worked hard to cast the blame for their crimes elsewhere. Parson Osbert is proof enough of that, but they also tried to do the same to Rievaulx. Our former felon posed a real danger to them. Sharp and inquisitive, he might not be so easily fooled by the murderous masques staged here. He was also eager to search for the Lacrima Christi and other treasures such as Hengham's money panniers. They watched him closely. Malach, silent as a shadow, followed our Judas man down to those caverns and killed him, then hurried to Rievaulx's chamber and removed all traces of him there and in the stables. You wanted to create the impression that he had fled, that he was the assassin, the thief, the fugitive, and why not? With his chequered past, he could be described as a logical explanation for all that had happened.'

'And yet,' Wendover spoke up, 'that didn't occur.'

'No, Rievaulx was murdered, but what was plotted

came to nothing. Remember, the caverns below were now empty of the leopards. Manor servants went down there, be it on some secret assignation or out of sheer curiosity. It became far too dangerous to remove Rievaulx's corpse and hide it deep in a marsh, so it was left there, even though his possessions had been removed and thrown into a quagmire never to be seen again. And by the way,' Corbett tapped the table, 'lest you wonder. Whatever secrets Lord Simon held about the Lacrima Christi, they are now securely in my grasp. The Lacrima Christi and its casket will be returned to their rightful owner.' He fell silent as Warfeld quietly cursed, damning all interfering clerks to hell.

'Rest assured, Blackrobe,' Ranulf retorted, 'your place in hell is already reserved and I look forward to sending you there. I shall tie the knot around your throat myself and twist the noose . . .' He fell silent as his master touched his arm.

'My friend,' Corbett whispered, yet loudly enough for the others to hear, 'I know what will happen.' He raised his voice. 'So now we come to the murder of three other innocents: Grease-hair, Colum the cook and Brockle the steward. Lady Isabella and Malach, you used all three in your murderous devices. Like all assassins, madam, you are deeply arrogant. You and your henchman dismissed Grease-hair and the others as being of little wit and dull of mind, hapless individuals to be used at your whim. The spit-boy was ordered to climb that ladder so he could view the great mystery through that window: two able-bodied men killed silently in a chamber locked and bolted from within. He was to be your witness to the impenetrable problems posed by that murder chamber.' He pulled a face. 'But Grease-hair and his companions were not as stupid as you thought.'

He paused at Lady Isabella's loud sob, then pressed on. 'First,' he declared, 'and I know this from his own mouth, the boy saw something in that chamber that was sorely amiss. What was it?' He shrugged. 'We truly don't know. I admit we never shall for certain, but afterwards Grease-hair drew a crude diagram of parallel lines, like the top and base of a box, with other lines between. He was trying to recall something. I believe his scribblings were to do with the coffers and caskets pushed beneath the bed.

'Malach, you had dragged those coffers and travelling chests away before crawling under the bed, then pulled them back so as to conceal yourself. Grease-hair, I understand, was accustomed to taking visitors' baggage up to that chamber, so he would know the room well. Did he notice the coffers out of line, disturbed, or did he perhaps see one of them move slightly whilst you lurked there waiting for your accomplice to appear? In a word, I believe he began to suspect that there was someone else in that room apart from the two corpses. He saw something that at the time he might dismiss as a trick of the light or his own nervous disposition, perched on the top of a shaky ladder with the wind buffeting him, the tocsin sounding and people shouting, spreading the news that the two fearsome cats had escaped.'

'Yes, yes. Most logical,' Wendover whispered, then smiled as Ranulf glared at him. 'Peace, my friend,' the sheriff declared. 'I am neither mimicking you nor imitating you, but what Sir Hugh describes is indeed logical. How often do we see things and then reflect on them afterwards?'

'Grease-hair certainly did,' Corbett retorted, 'and he shared his anxieties with Colum the cook and Steward Brockle. As I have said, he probably sensed there was someone hiding in that murder chamber, and so it became a guessing game of who that could be. All three would reflect on who was where and when. How you, Lady Isabella, were for some considerable time alone in that chamber before Malach appeared.' He drank from his goblet. 'Grease-hair tried to recreate what he thought he'd seen, a drawing of the bed with the cases beneath. He scrawled this on the wall close to the inglenook where he squatted, and grabbed a scrap of parchment to help him further. He shared his deepening unease with Colum and Brockle. Oh, they would not dare to make allegations, but their questioning about what happened that night and the evening Hengham was murdered was a constant irritation.

'Grease-hair and Colum were mere scullions and could be dismissed as such. Brockle was a different matter. Our noble steward, certainly in the days before his death, looked morose and withdrawn – little wonder after what had happened and the suspicions generated. Oh yes,' Corbett tapped the manuscript before him, 'these suspicions deepened. Grease-hair, Colum and

Brockle voiced their concerns, so all three were marked down for death. Grease-hair was turned into a living torch. Colum was in the larder. You, Malach, followed him in. Hapless Colum! He turned and your crossbow bolt tore the life out of him. You made his murder even more gruesome by pinning him with that spit pole as you would lance a fly with a pin.'

'I understand,' Wendover queried, 'that the door to the pantry was locked and bolted from within.'

'True, my Lord Sheriff. Locked from within with the inside clasps at top and bottom firmly in place.' Corbett shook his head. 'I agree, it looked as if the door was totally secure, but I doubt that was the correct key left hanging in the lock, or perhaps the lock was not fully turned.'

'And the clasps within?'

'My Lord Sheriff, I have walked this manor time and again. Servants have heard me slamming doors. I did so to the pantries. Those chambers have doors that can be secured from both within and without.'

Wendover scratched his head. 'Such trickery. I don't understand.'

'Quite simple,' Corbett retorted. 'You slam the pantry door shut and the inside clasps fall into place. If you want it open, you turn the key, push the door and create a narrow gap. You then use a thin blade to lift the clasps at top and bottom. Such a method provides protection against those who would like to slip in and seize whatever foodstuff is available. It is not just a matter of unlocking a door or turning a key; you have to stand there for some time, fiddling with those clasps.' Corbett cleared his throat. 'Colum the cook was slain in that pantry, the key left to dangle in the inside lock. The door was slammed shut, the clasps fell down and the entrance was sealed. Our efforts to break down the door damaged both lock and key, so it would be difficult to establish the truth of the matter.'

'And finally Brockle?'

'Ah yes, Ranulf, poor Brockle, who entertained his own suspicions. Now because of his status and office, he was a much more dangerous witness to the truth. Our steward was slowly reaching his own conclusions. He made the mistake of betraying his unease in both manner and mien. He had to be silenced. Malach followed him into that room, killed him with a crossbow bolt, left one key in the dead man's fingers and inserted another into the lock. And so it is, and so it was.'

Corbett rose, stretched and walked over to the buttery table. He poured a fresh tankard of ale and sipped at this as he stared at the accused. He had presided over similar commissions to deal with riot and disturbance of the king's peace. During such procedures, there was a moment, a time, when the accused, if truly guilty, would demonstrate that in their withdrawn posture, haunted look and lack of speech. So it was here. The disgraced Blackrobes sat leaning forward, heads bowed, Lady Isabella and Malach likewise. They could muster no defence nor provide any proof to demonstrate that Corbett was wrong. The others in the hall realised the same and were watchful, waiting for the inevitable judgement and sentence. Corbett was now ready to strike. He drained the tankard and rejoined his fellow justices.

'I have one last chapter of my indictment,' he declared. 'Lady Isabella and Malach, like Warfeld and his malignants, realised the hour glass had emptied, the candle had burnt itself away. They knew they were emerging as suspects for a veritable hymn, a litany of heinous, devilish killings. They intended to flee in one of those herring boats. Now I have mentioned earlier how they tried to trap Parson Osbert, and how he in turn trapped them. The resolution to this paradox was that the two covens would cooperate and escape on those herring boats brought round into Monkshood Bay. In other words, they are felons desperate to flee the kingdom. I have said enough. My fellow justices, what do you say?'

'Guilty,' Ranulf declared, 'and worthy of death.'

'Guilty,' Wendover rasped, 'and worthy of death on all counts.'

'And sentence?'

'To be hanged without respite or appeal,' Wendover declared. 'Sir Hugh, I will set up a special gallows high on Doone Moor with a clear view of both the sea and the heathland stretching from Malmaison to St Benet's and on to Felstead.'

'Very well.'

Corbett ignored the exclamations and cries from the accused. Lady Isabella shrieked her protests as Ap Ythel and his archers fastened both her and Malach in heavy chains and manacles. He let the noise and clamour deepen. Lord Moses and the other spectators milled about, staring at the accused or whispering amongst themselves. Corbett made a sign to Ranulf, who eventually imposed silence and order.

'The accused,' Corbett's voice was strong and carrying, 'will reflect on what I have said and the judgement they can expect. However,' he tapped his foot against the floor, 'if they may make full and free confession to my fellow justices here, I shall commute sentence to banishment. They will be allowed to board a vessel and trust their cause to heaven and the sea.'

'Sir Hugh, will you really do that?' Wendover demanded after the prisoners had been pushed, pulled and dragged out of the hall.

'Oh yes, my friend.' Corbett clasped the sheriff on the shoulder and squeezed hard. 'They will confess; that is the only door open to them. They have two days, and on the third, the sentence, whatever that is, shall be carried out. Now we must leave. I need urgent words with Ranulf and Ap Ythel. They carry my commission. I need to collect as much oil as possible.' He smiled at the sheriff's puzzled look. 'Rest assured, Sir Miles, you will see the light in more ways than one.'

Three days later, Corbett and his comitatus, together with the sheriff and the condemned, gathered close to the specially erected gallows high on Doone Moor with a clear view of the sea, the spire and roof of St Benet's and the pinpricks of light from Felstead village. The shadow of the scaffold brooded over them, soaring like some leaping monster frozen black against the bleak landscape, made more hideous by the naked corpses gibbeted there. All those slain during Corbett's attack on St Benet's had been stripped naked. Ap Ythel's archers had then strung them up, Parson Osbert included, like a farmer would an array of dead pests. They were left to dangle against the sky, heads askew, necks twisted. The dirty-white corpses, still stained with their death wounds, were a stark warning to outlaws, a sign for all to see.

The macabre gibbet was a horrid contrast to the day, for in truth the weather had improved, and it was a clear, sunny morning, as if heaven was giving its blessing to the justice being carried out below. Corbett quietened his horse. He stared at the prisoners huddled beneath the outstretched arms of the gallows. He had insisted that they stand below the bare feet of the corpses twisting above them, and they shuffled and shifted in a rattle of chains, terrified by what they saw. Wendover had received all their confessions, which in the main corroborated the indictments Corbett had levelled against them. Lady Isabella had tried to protest her innocence. Malach, angry and fearful, had claimed that she was in fact the instigator and his close accomplice in the murders at Malmaison. The manor house had been ransacked, as well as the hidden cavern at Monkshood Bay. Hengham's panniers had been seized and were now safely stored away.

Corbett quietly conceded to himself that there were still unanswered questions. Lord Simon had said that he had been approached by a stranger with information about the Lacrima Christi. Was this true? Secondly, Malach stoutly denied poisoning the leopards. Then who had, and why? Had Wodeford come to Malmaison just because of the Lacrima Christi, or was there something else? And Hengham? Was his visit motivated solely by lechery? Such questions deeply intrigued Corbett; it was like glimpsing something out of the corner of his eye, indistinct, shadowy, but still there. He crossed himself. These matters would have to wait.

He stared up at the lightening sky. It was judgement time. He gave Ap Ythel the signal to begin. The master bowman, accompanied by his lieutenant, Brancepeth, carrying a blazing cresset, stepped forward, war bow strung with an arrow, its tip laced in tar. The shaft was lit. Ap Ythel swung his bow up and loosed the fiery arrow, which scored the sky, followed by two more. The comitatus and the prisoners stirred restlessly, staring up at the sky. Then suddenly one of the archers shouted, 'Look, look!' and pointed to a fiery glow rising above Felstead.

'And there!' another yelled, pointing in the direction of Malmaison.

'And again!' a third voice bellowed. 'St Benet's is ablaze!'

Corbett, satisfied, turned to stare at each of the three fiery glows now clear against the morning sky.

'Sir Hugh,' Wendover demanded, 'why this?'

'By fire and sword, my Lord Sheriff. Malmaison and St Benet's have been crammed with oil, tar and kindling.

They will burn until they are crumbling ash. Ap Ythel's archers, assisted by Lord Moses, will ensure both places blaze like hell's fire.'

'And Felstead?'

'The compound of the unholy and unworthy Guild of Fleshers and Tanners will also be levelled by a cleansing fire.'

'But Sir Hugh—'

'But Sir nothing, my Lord Sheriff. All three places prospered through greed, violence, robbery and murder. Let them burn. As for the rest . . .'

Corbett urged his horse forward, grimly pleased at what he, Ranulf and Ap Ythel had planned for the prisoners. He led his comitatus down to Monkshood Bay, then issued a spate of orders to the bowmen, who had recruited local fishermen to steady both herring boats close to Langthorne Rocks. The prisoners were pushed down onto the beach, then onto the rocks, slipping and screaming as the surging tide circled them. The fishermen and the archers showed no mercy. The condemned were thrown aboard one of the herring boats and shackled to its side or the benches on which they sat. Once their task was finished, the fishermen hurriedly clambered onto the second herring boat moored alongside. Only then did the prisoners fully realise what was going to happen, and they screamed and howled in protest.

Corbett urged his horse down onto the beach, close to the water's edge, watching the final preparations for this voyage of the damned. The oars of the prisoners' boat had been removed, and it was firmly lashed to the stern of the second pinnace, manned by the fishermen. These were hard and resolute men, their faces scarred and weathered by the constant salt-biting sea, men who fought these turbulent waters so they could feed their families. They had been informed of the crimes the condemned had committed, and had no compassion for those who wrecked cogs and sent honest crewmen to a freezing, lonely death out on the dark waters of the Narrow Seas.

'A terrible punishment, Sir Hugh,' Wendover declared, urging his mount alongside Corbett's.

'A fitting one, my Lord Sheriff.' Corbett narrowed his eyes. The herring boats were now crossing the waters of the cove, about to enter a bank of rolling sea mist. The wails of the prisoners could still be heard. 'The punishment fits the crime, my lord. I promised them passage out of the kingdom, and so they have it. Once the boats are out at sea, the fishermen will leave the prisoners to the wind, the waters and God almighty. They can try to make their peace in the short time left to them. Don't weep for them, Master Sheriff. Weep rather for the likes of my dear comrade and his crew on *The Angel of the Dawn*. Weep for their widows. Weep for their children. Weep for poor Brockle and Hengham. I have no tears for these.'

'They are gone,' Ranulf murmured.

Corbett watched the last faint outline of the vessels disappear in the encroaching mist. Then he turned his horse and rode back to the high point above the cove, close to the gallows. He stared at the three fierce glows against the morning sky. Malmaison, St Benet's and the guild buildings at Felstead were being devoured by fire. He watched for a while, then turned his horse and rode down the rise away from the beach.

Ap Ythel had erected a bothy in the middle of a circle of ancient stones. A fire had been lit; scraps of meat on thin-needle skillets were roasting above the flames. Corbett, Ranulf and Wendover made themselves comfortable on makeshift seats. Ap Ythel served the meat on wooden platters along with deep-bowled cups of Bordeaux from the supplies on Chanson's sumpter pony. Corbett and Ranulf ate and drank quietly. Wendover tried to fill the silence with comments about proceedings. Corbett had prepared Ranulf for the coming confrontation, and the clerk of the Green Wax was in full agreement with his master's strategy. It was just a matter of waiting for Corbett to pounce.

'So it is all over, Sir Hugh?'

'Not quite, my Lord Sheriff. Not quite. During these proceedings, you have acted as a colleague and fellow justiciar. You have faithfully discharged your duty.'

'Thank you.'

'Don't thank me, Wendover.' Corbett's sharp tone alerted the sheriff. 'What concerns me about you, Wendover, I admit, is mere straws in the wind, yet it is deeply worrying.' Corbett leant forward. 'You see, my Lord Sheriff, before I arrived, you had done nothing wrong, but for the life of me I cannot say you did anything right.'

'I set a watch over Monkshood Bay.'

'Did you now? A bailiff and three men, I understand. Where were these from? Exeter? What were their names? Where are their kin? Have you petitioned the council for respite for their relatives?'

'I have my own exchequer, monies available to me.'

'Have you now, and so you have a record of these men?'

Wendover just glanced away.

'I cannot understand,' Corbett pressed on, 'why you did not at least concentrate on Monkshood Bay and Langthorne Rocks. You could have searched thoroughly and perhaps discovered that cave mouth leading into the secret tunnel.'

Wendover shook his head and gulped nervously at his goblet, hand trembling as he gripped the cup.

'Did you ever visit Plymouth? Do diligent searches along its quaysides? Weren't you a little suspicious about the criminous Blackrobes, those wolves in monkish dress out at St Benet's? Did you really believe Lord Simon's fardel of lies about his first wife? Didn't you press him to assist you in hunting down the Sagittarius and his Scarecrows? I couldn't depend on you; that is one of the reasons I brought in Lord Moses and the moon people. My litany of questions is long. For example, why were you at Malmaison on the two evenings the murders took place? Who paid you off, my Lord Sheriff?' He paused at Wendover's muttered curses. 'What is it?' he demanded.

The sheriff lifted his head. 'Sir Hugh, it's time you

learnt what was planned.' He gestured at Ranulf. 'Fetch Wolfram, he is the proof.'

'Very well, my friend.' Corbett turned to his henchman. 'Go with our sheriff, find Wolfram. He was on the beach, watching the herring boats leave. I wager he is still there. Say that I need urgent words with him.'

The two men left Corbett to his meditations. He wondered what Wolfram would say. Would his answers resolve the still unanswered questions? Within the hour, a mournful, dirty-faced Wolfram arrived, escorted by Wendover and Ranulf. Corbett murmured that they were to make themselves comfortable, filling cups and offering scraps of food. Both Wolfram and the sheriff ignored the latter but greedily drank the wine.

'Tell him,' Wendover grated, pointing his cup at Corbett. 'Tell Sir Hugh exactly what we planned. Everything,' he declared. 'The truth, on the future of our immortal souls.'

Wolfram wiped his mouth on the back of his sleeve and edged a little closer.

'Sir Hugh, you know who I am and what I did. I was a hunted and haunted man. Wendover here was no different. Sheriff of an isolated shire where wolfs-heads prowled without a care in the world. Matters went from bad to worse, even more so when the old king died. The realm was swept by one tempest after another: famine, pestilence, defeats in Scotland and the worsening relationship between our king and his leading barons. We all know the reason.'

'His Grace,' Corbett agreed, 'is besotted with his

Gascon favourite Peter Gaveston, whom he created Earl of Cornwall, a situation that has certainly not helped this shire.'

'I realised I was failing,' Wendover confessed, 'failing deeply. One night I rode out to Wolfram's farm. I used to go there now and again. I chose an evening when the Lady Katerina was elsewhere, probably with Lord Simon. Anyway,' he went on hastily, 'Wolfram and I met. To cut to the chase, we were visited by the Sagittarius and his minions. The confrontation was brutally brief. We were given a choice: a purse of gold on the table before us, or swift, sudden death for my wife and three children and the same for the Lady Katerina. Sir Hugh, we took the gold. I promised – no, God help me, I swore not to interfere.'

'We felt like cowards,' Wolfram declared. 'Both Sir Miles and I were furious, so we concocted a plot with many strands. First, Lord Gaveston is lord of this shire. Secondly, we know that he wishes to hide, flee from his enemies. Thirdly, no one will help him. The great lords have clearly proclaimed that to all sheriffs and Crown officials the length and breadth of this kingdom.'

'You would?'

'Yes, Sir Hugh, we would.'

'And what better place than here, out on Doone Moor?'

'Correct, and so we began. Wendover here,' Wolfram declared, 'travelled post-haste to King's Langley.'

'Ah yes, I glimpsed you there earlier in the year.'

'I sought private audience with the king and Lord

Gaveston. I pointed out how the caverns beneath Malmaison would be a perfect hiding place. We would provide provender and Gaveston could safely shelter there.'

'Close to Monkshood Bay,' Wolfram declared. 'Those two pinnaces could soon be ready for a swift journey across the Narrow Seas to Boulogne.'

'My Lord Gaveston was in favour and so was His Grace. Except for one thing.'

'The leopards?'

'The leopards, Sir Hugh. Gaveston has a peculiar fear of such beasts, no different from many other people. I,' Wolfram pulled a face, 'I am used to them. Through Wendover, I gave my solemn oath that the leopards would be removed. I kept my word.'

'And Lord Simon's part in this?' Ranulf asked. 'Was he brought into these matters?'

'No one trusted Lord Simon, His Grace in particular. What happened there was my doing,' Wolfram declared. 'I was the author of that anonymous letter to the Secret Chancery, a copy of which was sent to Lord Simon. He later elaborated it, claiming he had been approached on the matter of the Lacrima Christi by a mysterious stranger.'

'When I received the letter in the Secret Chancery,' Corbett half smiled, 'I did wonder who the author could be. I even suspected Lord Simon might be playing some subtle game. After all, he was involved in the hunt for the Lacrima Christi, and we always suspected what he might have done. More importantly, there was the question of the missing casket.' He shrugged. 'Only then was I brought into the game. At the king's instructions, I dispatched Wodeford and Rievaulx to Malmaison. They were to negotiate with Lord Simon and, whatever the outcome, serve him with a royal summons to join festivities at the royal court, along with his wife and household. Wodeford and Rievaulx were to escort them there. I wondered at the time about the invitation, but there again, the depredations of the wreckers did concern the royal council. Lord Simon needed to be questioned. I just wondered what my role in this was going to be; why I wasn't informed from the start.'

'No, Sir Hugh,' Wolfram pleaded. 'Rest assured your presence here was what both I and my Lord Sheriff demanded. You see, by the time Lord Simon and his household left for court, the leopards would have escaped and been permanently removed. Malmaison would be deserted. You would move here and set up camp to hunt down the wreckers, as well as shelter, protect and provide for Lord Gaveston. Sheriff Wendover and I were to give you every assistance as well as inform you of exactly what had happened.'

'Our revenge!' Wendover slurred. 'We would hunt the wreckers down, and I would regain my self-respect. I knew you would protect us, Sir Hugh. We would not be alone. Wolfram here hoped for a royal pardon as well as readmission to the service of the king. In addition, Lord Simon would learn that the Crown had not forgotten his involvement in the disappearance of the

Lacrima Christi, and would be held to account for other matters, such as the wrecking.'

'And Sir Ralph Hengham's part in all of this? I heard tittle-tattle that he did not just come to comfort the so-called grieving widow.'

'Of course. He was to stay at your disposal, Sir Hugh.'

'What do you mean?'

'The taxes Hengham collected would be kept by him so you could provide for Lord Gaveston. His Grace maintained you were too busy to be involved with all these preparations.' Wolfram paused and scratched his head. 'However, when all was ready, you would sweep into Malmaison like God's judgement incarnate. You would protect the innocent and hunt down the wicked.'

'And so I did. But tell me, Wolfram, did you ever suspect the Blackrobes out at St Benet's?'

'Of course I did, but there again, the wrecking did not begin with their arrival here.'

'And the Guild of Fleshers and Tanners?'

'No, in truth I never suspected them. I did sometimes wonder about Lord Simon's part in all the mischief, but . . .' Wolfram shrugged. 'At first I thought all was going well. Wodeford arrived. God knows what he discussed with Lord Simon, but I chose that night to free the leopards.'

'That explains the disturbance.'

'Yes, Sir Hugh, it certainly does. I slipped into Malmaison. I arranged their release through a narrow postern so that they could prowl the moors until I killed them: their escape and death would become common knowledge. Of course, our well-laid plans and subtle plots came to nothing. Unwittingly, the escape of the leopards helped Lord Simon's assassins. It gave Malach an obvious excuse to flit like a deadly sprite around Malmaison, though he was more concerned about murder than about any wild beast.' Wolfram sighed. 'After the slayings of Lord Simon, Wodeford and Hengham, the edifice we had built collapsed like a house of straw. Malmaison became far too unsafe to provide any refuge for Gaveston, and what use would it be to inform you of what had been plotted? That made no sense.'

'Our only consolation, Sir Hugh,' Wendover declared, 'was that you arrived to resolve the murders and help me, a hapless sheriff, bring the wreckers to justice. It is true that I lied, I prevaricated to hide my cowardice, but once you were here, I vowed I would help bring the nightmare to an end.'

'I too welcomed your arrival,' Wolfram declared. 'I talked to Lady Katerina and decided to make a full confession and seek a royal pardon.' He cleared his throat. 'I admit I was frightened, indeed terrified at developments, especially the disappearance of the guildsmen around the same time as the slayings at Malmaison. I confess I found two of the corpses spat back by the quagmire they'd been thrown in. It was obvious they had been murdered. I did not want to be accused or caught up in that bloody massacre. I needed a royal pardon!'

'Which you have.' Corbett smiled. 'To be honest, I

knew something of this. Before I left the court, the king plucked at my sleeve and led me away into a small garden arbour. He asked me whether, during the present troubles Lord Gaveston found himself in, I would at the opportune time do all I could to help. I replied that I would. The king seemed satisfied. I left the court, but nothing came of that remark, and now I know why. So, my friends, let us survey what we have done.'

Corbett and his companions collected their horses and rode back to the brow of the cliff overlooking the bay. The three red glows against the sky were now beginning to fade, whilst the herring boat carrying the fishermen was returning alone.

'We are finished, master.'

'Yes, Ranulf, for the moment we are finished, but murder is never done.'

AUTHOR'S NOTE

Hymn to Murder is, of course, a work of fiction. Nevertheless, it is firmly grounded in historical themes and events from the Middle Ages. The robbery of the Crown Jewels from the crypt at Westminster Abbey was carried out in April 1303. It was the work of an audacious gang led by Richard Puddlicot, a bankrupt merchant who drew in not just the rifflers of London's underworld, but law officials, prosperous merchants and men who really should have known better! Puddlicot wanted to recoup his losses as well as punish the Crown. However, the real moving spirit in this criminal enterprise was Adam Warfeld, sacristan of Westminster Abbey and therefore directly responsible for its security. It was certainly a case of the fox being allowed to manage the hen coop! Warfeld drew in other monks and the seed was literally sown. Hempen weed was planted to screen off the great windows that stood on ground level leading down to the crypt. Warfeld hired a professional stonemason,

John of St Alban's, to remove the sill of one window as well as the iron bars embedded there. Then they could just slide in and help themselves.

The monks of Westminster Abbey, during the preparations for the great robbery, were diverted by lavish parties at which food, drink and ladies of the night were supplied for their pleasure. The robbery was carried out after dark. It ended in a free-for-all, with treasure littering the abbey grounds. Some of it was never retrieved. Puddlicot and what I would describe as the secular arm of the robbery went into hiding. Warfeld and his monks retreated behind the privileges of the abbey and the benefit of clergy.

Edward I, his court, officials and troops were busy in Scotland fighting the Bruce. When news of the robbery reached the king, he was beside himself with fury, not only at the theft but at the failure of officials to recover his regalia and punish those responsible. He dispatched a leading royal clerk, John Drokensford, to deal with the crisis. (Drokensford, of course, inspired my creation Sir Hugh Corbett, though I must add that he was a celibate cleric who later became Bishop of Bath and Wells.) Drokensford swept through London and Westminster like God's own battle storm. He and the Constable of the Tower deployed troops and officials across the city and beyond. They moved from ward to ward, empanelling people and asking them for any information about the robbery. Of course, such people were on oath: if they lied, they would suffer the punishment for perjury and conspiracy, which was death. The confessions and admissions are still extant. In places they make hilarious reading, such as how one of the monks of Westminster gave a precious necklace to a leading courtesan so that they could become 'very dear friends'.

Drokensford took no nonsense from the Blackrobes, and, for a while, at least a hundred of these miscreants were lodged in the Tower. The great conspiracy began to break up, men and women turning king's evidence and divulging other names and information. Of course, they were desperate to avoid the noose. One leading robber, the apostate priest John Rippinghale, confessed to a litany of nonsense in a vain attempt to avoid hanging. His confession in manuscript form still exists.

Puddlicot was high on Drokensford's list. The riffler leader was trapped in London and took refuge in St Michael's church, claiming sanctuary. Again Drokensford would have none of it, but paid a cohort of burly bailiffs to violate sanctuary and drag Puddlicot out. He was imprisoned in the Tower, tried there before a special commission and sentenced to hang. He was taken to the scaffold at Tothill Lane in a wheelbarrow, hanged, gibbeted and his corpse skinned.

You can still visit the crypt of Westminster Abbey, with its reinforced door and steps deliberately broken in the middle, the gap now being filled by a wooden bridge. The crypt lies empty, but if you walk around the outside, look for the window without a sill, for it was through there that the great robbery took place.

* * *

Edward II's accession to the throne ushered in a period of great instability for both Crown and country. The war in Scotland went from bad to worse. Matters were not helped by the king's utter reliance on his Gascon favourite Peter Gaveston, whom he did create Earl of Cornwall. Edward and Gaveston may well have thought Dartmoor might be a good hiding place for the royal favourite. Legend persists that he sheltered there, and his name is still attached to certain places where he lurked free from the fury of the great earls and barons of the kingdom.

The Tower of London did house a magnificent zoo/menagerie, which included leopards, wolves and even more exotic animals. Edward II in particular seemed to be fascinated by the gifts he received from the princes of North Africa and elsewhere. He kept at King's Langley, a royal palace, both a camel and an elephant.

The collapse of law and order, due to Edward II's involvement with Gaveston, did have an effect on preserving and maintaining the king's peace in London and the shires. The plotted destruction of ships did occur. However, more dangerous than the wreckers was the possibility of ships being seized by 'the enemy within'. Indeed, a survey of naval history delineates the incredible number of occasions where vessels were seized thus by stealth. One consequence of this was that captains were virtually given the power of life and death over their crew. By Nelson's time, at the beginning of the nineteenth century, a sailor could be hanged for mutiny simply for grumbling about his captain and officers! Of course, this led to fine drama exemplified in such literary works as *Moby Dick* and *Billy Budd*.

Finally, the Lacrima Christi is a fictional jewel, but it is based on a most curious incident mentioned in the novel. Clement V was crowned as described and the triumphal procession was marred by the collapse of an ancient stone wall. The pope was thrown from his horse, his tiara rolled away and a particularly precious ruby in the centre of the tiara was prised loose. The tiara was retrieved, but despite the pope's best efforts, the ruby disappeared forever.